Debbie Johnson is an award-winning author who lives and works in Liverpool, ... een writing, caring for a s............................... and not doing the housew............................... onal women's fiction, and .... ooks worldwide. She is p............................... two books optioned for film and TV.

 facebook.com/debbiejohnsonauthor
 x.com/debbiemjohnson

Also by Debbie Johnson

The Comfort Food Café series

Summer at the Comfort Food Café

Christmas at the Comfort Food Café

Coming Home to the Comfort Food Café

Sunshine at the Comfort Food Café

A Gift from the Comfort Food Café

A Wedding at the Comfort Food Café

The Comfort Food Café

Standalones

Cold Feet at Christmas

Pippa's Cornish Dram

Never Kiss a Man in a Christmas Jumper

The Birthday That Changed Everything

The A-Z of Everything

A TOUCH OF MAGIC AT THE COMFORT FOOD CAFÉ

DEBBIE JOHNSON

ONE MORE CHAPTER

One More Chapter
a division of HarperCollins*Publishers* Ltd
1 London Bridge Street
London SE1 9GF
www.harpercollins.co.uk
HarperCollins*Publishers*
Macken House, 39/40 Mayor Street Upper,
Dublin 1, D01 C9W8

This paperback edition 2025
2
First published in Great Britain in ebook format
by HarperCollins*Publishers* 2025
Copyright © Debbie Johnson 2025
Debbie Johnson asserts the moral right to be identified
as the author of this work

A catalogue record of this book is available from the British Library
ISBN: 978-0-00-878577-2

To my lovely Auntie Christine, one of the kindest people I know

Chapter One

Budbury, Dorset

My moving van is blocking the street, and I feel a familiar sense of anxiety creeping over me at the sight. This village consists of one long, winding road that ends in the sea. It is a road that comes complete with a pub, a florist, a pharmacy, and a small scattering of independent shops. It is a pretty road, lined with whitewashed terraced houses that used to be fishermen's cottages. It is a road that is now completely gridlocked because of me, and my stupidly wide moving van. Day one, and I have wrecked the place.

I cringe as I park my much smaller car behind it and sink back into my seat for a few moments. I can tell without looking that the normally pale skin of my neck and chest is blotchy and red, because that's one of the things that happens when I get stressed. That and my face looking like a tomato. I suck in a few deep breaths, letting them out slowly through my mouth. It is okay to feel stressed – I am moving house, and that is right up there with divorce and bereavement on the 'crap things to deal with in life' list.

I close my eyes, squeezing them shut and shaking my head as I get a grip of my emotions. Freaking out will not help – getting this sorted will help. I jump out of the car, and root my keys from my bag. The moving men clamber out of the cab of the lorry, big and burly and apparently completely unconcerned by the fact that they are causing chaos. I suppose they're used to it. They don't shrink and shrivel under the spotlight.

Vehicles are backing up in both directions, as there is barely room for one lane of traffic to get past, never mind two. I brace myself for a barrage of beeping horns, screamed abuse, and physical threats. I have lived in London for over a decade, where this kind of thing could result in a machete attack or a full-on riot. For the time being, though, nobody seems too angry – cars take it in turns to drive on around us, with much polite flashing of lights and waving through windscreens. Huh. Weird. Still, it's only a matter of time, I'm sure. Some massive farmer type will come down on a tractor and get so frustrated that he whips out his shotgun and yells 'get off my land!' before blasting us all to smithereens.

'Shall we get started, love?' the van man says, gesturing at the door of the house. 'Quicker you let us in, quicker we're out of your hair.'

I nod, glad to have someone telling me what to do. It's been a weirdly warm day even though it's October, and I'm overdressed in a big cable-knit jumper. The hair he's keen to get out of is flying all over the place, escaping its bun and sticking to the sides of my face. I feel a mess, and I'm sure I look it. I hate standing out, hate being the centre of attention, and this is difficult because now I'm the Woman Who Blocked The Road, and we're attracting significant interest from both drivers and passers-by. This is my first day here in my new home, and it's not going well.

I fumble the keys into the lock of the red wooden door, dropping them twice before I find the right one. Even when I do, I just can't get it to turn. Why are keys so hard? Surely there's a simpler way? I'm getting increasingly hot and bothered, doing all of this under the watchful eye of the moving men, feeling like a complete idiot. I've never even been in this house, never mind unlocked the door.

'Here, let me help,' says a quiet voice from behind me. 'There's a knack to it.'

I turn around to see a petite blonde woman somewhere in her thirties, with kind blue eyes and a softly spoken manner. 'I'm Katie,' she says simply. 'I used to live here, and this door is evil.'

An evil door. Possessed by demons. I totally believe that is possible. I puff out a tense breath, and nod gratefully. She takes the key from my shaking hands, and inserts it. 'It needs a little push to the left before you turn it to the right,' she explains. 'It's just old. You'll get the hang of it.'

'Or,' I reply, as the door opens, 'I could get the lock replaced with one that works.'

'Only if you get it approved by the Historic Buildings and Heritage Keyhole Society first,' she says seriously. Shit. Is this going to be one of *those* places?

Her face breaks out into a smile. 'That doesn't exist by the way, don't worry. Anyway. I work at the pharmacy across the road. Pop in if you need anything.'

'Do you have Valium?'

'We only crack that open on very special occasions. Anyway – do you need any more help?'

The older moving man is shouldering past us with a huge box in his arms, and he nods. 'We never say no,' he says before I can respond, 'to an extra set of hands.' I would definitely have said no.

Katie says she'll sort it, and disappears across the road. I realise belatedly that I didn't even tell her my name. The traffic is constant because of the blockage, but someone stops to let her cross, giving her a friendly wave as she goes. It's so relaxed it's surreal, and I'm a bit worried I've landed in some kind of rural Stepford.

I wanted this, I remind myself as the men bustle around me. I wanted a fresh start. I wanted to escape my problems, and not feel like a failure every day. The subtle and not-so-subtle fears that were swirling around me in London, the real and the imagined peril. I needed to get away from the big city, and find my little bolthole by the sea. I always loved the sea, and find nothing more soothing than walking by water. It's even better than Valium for me.

I'm an author, and I've been on a deadline for what feels like years. There is never enough time to do everything I need to do. I love writing my stories, but I don't enjoy the other demands – the events, the media, the meetings. All of the stuff that my sister Sally would love, I hate. I have always craved solitude, and life in London was too overwhelming for me. I tolerated it for years, for the sake of my marriage, my career, to be near to Sally and her family – but I'm going to be fifty in January, and this is my gift to myself. A landmark move for a landmark birthday. A place to finally feel safe after everything that has happened.

I've kept my flat in London too, but I'm hoping that here, in this tiny seaside village, I will be able to concentrate on my work, and live the quiet, self-contained life I've always wanted. I bought this house without ever even visiting, which in hindsight seems reckless. I'm not normally reckless, about anything at all, but something about this place called to me. One minute I'm browsing on Rightmove, the next I'm putting in an offer.

I couldn't resist it, simple as that. The pictures of the cute little cottage were complemented by pictures of the horseshoe-shaped bay at the bottom of the sloping road, surrounded by red-gold cliffs and views into infinity. It wasn't a bustling metropolis, but that was one of the things I liked best about it – a bustling metropolis is wasted on me. I needed somewhere with the basics, in a beautiful location, and nothing more.

Now, as I stand gazing into the hallway, I wonder what kind of madness had infected me. How could I have bought a property without even visiting it? The younger moving man excuses his way past me, and takes another big box up the steps. I'd marked the boxes 'upstairs' or 'downstairs', and had been pleased with my level of organisation. Now I just feel like a bit of an idiot for doing this at all. Sally was so shocked when I told her, especially when I revealed that I hadn't even been to visit.

'But why there, and why somewhere so small?' she'd said, when I showed her the pictures. 'It's very nice, but it's tiny. You could afford somewhere much more spacious.'

'That's part of the appeal,' I'd replied. 'I like small homes; I like cosy more than I like grand. And let's face it, I'm a weirdo. I couldn't stand living anywhere too secluded or out in the countryside, because my brain would go into full meltdown. I'd be freaking out every night about killer goblins or ghost sheep.'

'Your brain is a very strange place, you know that, don't you?'

'I do. It always has been, and I'm okay with that. I've spent years of my life trying to be normal, and it's never going to happen. This is *my* normal, and I'm content enough in my own way. My happy doesn't have to look the same as your happy, Sally – we've had this conversation so many times! Can't you just wish me well?'

Of course, she doesn't know all of my reasons. She'd overreact, which is probably exactly what I'm doing. She'd sighed, then laughed resignedly, and then done exactly that – wished me well, and made me promise to come back for Lucy and Libby's eighteenth birthday party. I'm kind of dreading that, and had hoped to skip it – I love my nieces dearly, and I'm especially close to Libby, who is sadly for her very similar to me at that age. I'd planned to take them out somewhere special, just the three of us. A big shindig at a fancy hotel with my parents present isn't my idea of fun, but I felt obliged to agree.

After that, she promised to visit me in Dorset as soon as I was settled. Now, as I stand here watching the place fill up around me, I wonder when that might be. I never loved my London flat – I bought it after Will and I got divorced – but it was familiar at least. This is new, and I know it will take me some time to get used to it.

I wander through into the living room. The front window looks out onto the pretty high street, and the back looks out onto the courtyard garden that was so appealing to me online. It's October now, so it looks different – but still gorgeous. I see a little wrought-iron table and chair set covered in windblown leaves, deep autumnal red ivy climbing up the whitewashed walls, a small herb garden currently in retreat. A scattering of terracotta plant holders, and a gorgeous potted tree, which is now evergreen but I know is gloriously lilac in summer. Big enough for me to sit out and work, or do a little yoga when the weather is good, but small enough to make me feel safe behind its walls.

I put my hand to the glass and smile as I look outside. It's a clear, bright day, and a tiny black and white wagtail is hopping around out there, pecking at the ground. A robin is perched in the branches of the California lilac, and suddenly all feels well with the world. Even in London, we had these familiar feathered friends, and I used to love sitting in my little roof garden watching them come and go. I will buy some feeders and a bath, and there will be some continuity from the new to the old at least.

'Hi! Where do you want the sofa?' someone asks me from behind. I whirl around, and see two strange men carrying my couch. I blink in confusion – these are definitely not the guys from the moving lorry. Has there been some kind of weird rupture in the space-time continuum?

I gesture to the space where I think I'd like the sofa to be, and they place it down for me. One of them is tall and blond, with a big smile and floppy hair that gives him a surfer vibe. The other is older, closer to me in age, and more serious-looking. He reminds me of Harrison Ford, which instantly makes me want to start quoting Star Wars scenes. I bite it back. It won't be amusing for anyone but me.

'I'm Sam,' the blond says. 'I live a couple of doors away, with my partner Becca and our daughter, Little Edie.'

'Is there a Big Edie?' I ask.

'There is, she also lives a few doors away. She's actually pretty small though. And ninety-nine. We had a huge birthday party for her over the summer. She rode through the village in a horse-drawn carriage waving like the queen! She liked that a bit too much, think it went to her head…'

The other man smiles at the memory, and nods. 'I'm Matt,' is all he says. A man of few words, which I always appreciate.

'Welcome to Budbury,' Sam adds. 'You'll find out everything about everyone sooner than you could possibly imagine.'

I feel a flash of alarm at that statement. I mean, I'm absolutely fine with finding out everything about everyone else – I am very curious about people and their lives, given that my job is basically making stuff up – but I'm not quite as keen on reciprocating. I like being an observer, not a participant. I should probably get that printed on a T-shirt, or have it on my gravestone.

Matt clocks my reaction, and I immediately get that he is a lot more sensitive than he looks. 'Don't worry,' he says quietly. 'They banned waterboarding last year.'

I'm not sure who 'they' are, and I have a few moments of Wicker Man worry. 'Are my fingernails safe?' I ask.

'Totally. They're sneakier than that. They'll woo you with cake. As long as you don't eat the cake, you'll be fine.'

Don't eat the cake, I repeat mentally. Don't eat the cake. That's definitely like the start of a good horror story – a quaint little village where the smiling locals ply the innocent new arrival with Victoria sponge, fattening her up for the sacrificial ritual…

Another man pops his head around the door, tall, brawny, blond, good-looking in an outdoorsy way. What is it with this place? This village is tiny – why are there so many attractive men? This one, I realise as he introduces himself as Cal, is actually Australian. He looks at me with a slight frown, and asks if we've met before. When I say definitely not – because frankly I'd remember – he laughs it off, and asks which room I want the double bed in.

The actual removal men that I have paid to do this job are currently taking a tea break, perched on the back of the open-doored truck, with a huge flask, blowing steam from their cups and watching as the others carry on working. To be fair they have driven from London, and I wouldn't mind a brew myself.

As soon as the thought crosses my mind, a woman with wild curly hair walks towards the house carrying a cardboard holder with two cups, and a picnic basket. This is terrifying. Telepathy? Mind control? Or just a happy coincidence? She knocks on the doorframe and walks right in. She's slightly round, super-pretty, and actually blushes when she sees all three men hefting furniture around.

'Oooh,' she says, grinning at me, 'it's like one of my fantasies come to life!'

Matt puts down the box he was carrying and comes over to kiss her. 'Go easy on her,' he says. 'She's new.'

'I don't know what you mean! Now shoo, get back to work. Maybe take your top off.'

She looks at me, and her eyes are sparkling. 'That's my husband, Matt. He's a dreamboat. Anyway, I heard you'd arrived – Katie sent a smoke signal from the pharmacy – so I thought I'd bring you some refreshments. I'm Laura, and I work at the Comfort Food Café. It's just down the hill – follow the road, you can't miss it. If you walk into the sea or fall off a cliff, you've gone too far. Call in any time, we're all very excited to meet you!'

Those words strike a new level of fear in my heart. I suppose I hadn't really thought about the flip side of living somewhere small. In London, nobody gives a damn who you are, and for sure nobody wants to talk to you. It's clearly going to be different here.

I keep my face neutral and manage a thank-you smile as I follow her through to the kitchen. She opens up the wicker picnic basket she brought with her, and the smell immediately hits me. Vanilla, sugar, cinnamon... Oh God, it's the cake! They've come for me!

She gestures towards the drinks, saying: 'We had no clue if you were a coffee person or a tea person or a tequila-in-the-day kind of person – no judgement if you are – so I brought both. Not the tequila, sadly. There are some basics here for you: milk, butter, some sourdough I baked this morning. Plus a special treat, our brand-new Autumn range!'

She pulls out a whole smorgasbord of baked goods, and arranges them on pretty lilac plates. As she swipes her hair back behind her ears, I notice that her cheek is smeared with flour. I get the feeling that it might be a permanent state of affairs. Like a birthmark she grew in later life.

'So, there's pumpkin spice cupcakes,' she says, pointing to the appropriate plate, 'and this is plum and ginger pudding – don't worry, I brought custard!'

I hadn't been worried, but she says this very seriously, in a reassuring tone. I smile, slightly overwhelmed by it all. 'And this is Dorset apple cake. Perfect for the season, and a local speciality. Lots of brown sugar and nutmeg and cinnamon, it's totally delish. What's your name?'

She segues into the question seamlessly, and I start to understand what Matt meant. Cake is the gateway drug to complete assimilation. Still, it would be churlish to be rude when the nice lady has walked all the way up a hill with a basket full of sin for me.

'I'm Sarah,' I say, adding a 'nice to meet you' as I stare at the pudding, my nostrils flaring at the smell.

'Are you talking to me or my cake?' she asks. 'Never mind, we're pretty much the same thing. Anyway. Welcome to Budbury. We're very friendly, and we don't bite. I have to get off to collect my girls from school, but please, pop into the café any time, and if there's anything you need at all, just let one of us know.'

'One of us?'

'Yes. We have a hive mind. Just stand in the street and shout. We'll all come running.'

She winks to show that she's joking, and disappears off with her wicker basket. She pauses outside, watching the men appreciatively as they work. Matt gives her a hug and she melts into him a little. I don't miss the fact that she gives his bottom a little slap as they part, and can't help but smile. That kind of togetherness has never been for me, but it's very pleasant to see anyway.

The removal men, along with their newfound helpers, make short work of the rest of the unpacking. I didn't bring everything I own because I wanted to leave the London flat habitable, and because my new home is on the petite side. After an hour or so, the lorry finally moves on – without a single beeped horn or angry motorist objecting to their visit at all. Unreal.

Matt, Cal and Sam stay for a few minutes more, asking if I need anything else. 'You'll probably decide you want the furniture moved around,' says Sam, raising his eyebrows. 'Women always do that.'

I raise my eyebrows right back – it's impossible to take offence at his playful tone, but I feel obliged to try. 'Right. Well, it's good that you've got us all figured out.'

'Lord no,' he replies, looking horrified. 'I grew up with a million sisters and I live with two women, but you all remain a mystery to me. Anyway. Hope you settle in okay. We'll see you around, in the pub or the café or whatever.'

'Thank you,' I say firmly, 'all of you. You've made it so much easier. I owe you all a pint.'

I have no plans whatsoever to spend a night in the pub with the villagers, but I'm sure there's a way I can leave some money behind the bar as a gesture of my appreciation.

By the time I am finally blissfully alone again, it is approaching evening. Thanks to Laura, I don't even need to go to the shops, and the night is my own. I stand in the middle of the kitchen, gazing out at my little patio garden, and enjoy a flush of contentment. It feels peaceful here, but there is a pharmacy nearby for emergency antibiotics in case I develop a flesh-eating bug, and enough people that we could rebuild society if a solar flare takes out civilisation.

My mind is a strange place, like Sally is constantly pointing out. I'd love to say that 'hope for the best, plan for the worst' is my motto, but it's actually just the second half. At least a few of those unloaded boxes contain emergency supplies that I will tuck away under my bed, just in case; I feel less anxious if I'm prepared. It might be crazy, but having a stash of multi-vitamins, first-aid stocks and water purifying tablets makes me feel secure. And Sally didn't think it was quite so crazy during the early days of the pandemic, when I was the only person in London with spare loo rolls and hand sanitiser.

I make up my bed and unpack essential toiletries, and then decide that it's time to go and explore. I have work to do, but it will wait for me until tomorrow. My bike is here with me for longer trips, but for now I'd like to walk. The drive from London was long and stressful, and I need to decompress. I love walking, especially at this time of day – that perfect moment between light and dark. I have unravelled so many tricky plot points during a walk, come up with so many twists and turns, conjured up the scariest of villains, fixed so many problems. In my fiction, obviously. I'm not quite so good at fixing problems in real life.

It's half six, and the little shops have all closed up. None of them have metal shutters over the windows, which is a nice surprise, and I enjoy browsing as I work my way down the street. There is a magnificent Halloween display in the storefront of the pharmacy, with models of vampires and werewolves all taking multi-vitamins and iron tablets, and a big felt black cat surrounded by antihistamines. A child – or a very bad artist – has drawn posters to go with them, in bright colours and rainbow-shaded block capitals. It's all very imaginative.

I glance into any homes where the curtains are open, catching glimpses of life unfolding – domestic routines that are both mundane and fascinating to me. I stroll past the pub, the Horse and Rider, and hear laughter as I pass. I speed up a little, just in case I get sucked in. I've had more than enough social interaction today.

I notice a small community centre, and a glass-screened notice board promises me all kinds of excitement: a Knitting and Crochet Club, a choir, gardening sessions, and an upcoming talk on fossils by 'our very own Sam'. There's a pumpkin-carving masterclass, and the chance to sign up for a coach trip to Bristol to see the pantomime in December.

I can't imagine myself at any of these events, but they make me smile anyway. There is also a small wooden sign directing me to a pet cemetery, but I decide against it. I love graveyards of all kinds, and enjoy piecing together the stories of people's lives from the few words that summarise their time on earth. When I was a teenager, I preferred hanging around in the local cemetery on my own to hanging out in the local park with Sally, drinking cider and lounging on the roundabouts. Neither of us especially wanted to be at home, because it wasn't an easy place to be – we just had very different avoidance techniques.

A pet cemetery might be a bit much for me tonight, though. I will inevitably cry about the loss of the beloved dogs and cats, because I'm a big softie when it comes to animals. And then my mushed-up mind will process it while I sleep, and I'll have terrible nightmares about zombie Labradors and armies of undead Poodles. Then I'll have to write it all down in the notepad I keep by my bed, because my 3am brain will tell me the nightmares might make good stories. Then I'll wake up in the morning and decipher my scrawl and realise it's all nonsense. This is a tried and tested series of events – I have a box of notepads full of such delirious scribbles.

I do as Laura instructed and follow the road down towards the sea. I can hear it calling me, and not just in my imagination – the village is quiet, and the sound of the waves is clear as I approach. I feel a little thrill, a sense that maybe I haven't made a mistake after all. I reach a small car park, the only vehicle still here is a white van emblazoned with the words Comfort Food Café. The name is entwined with a pretty design of trailing red roses, and beneath is what I presume to be their company logo: 'Making the world a better place, one cake at a time.' It makes me laugh, and then it makes my stomach rumble when I remember the treats that are waiting for me back home. Matt's instruction to not eat the cake is going to be completely impossible.

I glance up at the cliffs and see what I presume to be the café in question perched on top of them. A couple of paths lead up towards it, and although the inside of the café itself is dim, strings of multi-coloured lights dance around the building. It looks so inviting, like a little beacon of hope and hot chocolate gazing down at me. Maybe I'll go at some point, even if I am a little reluctant. I didn't come here to make friends, or to immerse myself in the community. Everyone so far seems delightful, and kind, and keen to welcome me, and while most people might want that, I don't. To me, it feels like the emotional version of nails scraping down a chalkboard. It's not that I hate people – I really don't – I've just learned that life is simpler if I don't get too close to any of them. Or let any of them slide too close to me.

I walk down from the car park, along a rough sandy path that takes me to the beach. I stand there for a few moments, watching the sun slowly sink into the sea, the darkening sky a swathe of deep blue, streaks of purple, the glimmer of stars beginning to twinkle above me. I stare, and I breathe, and I almost cry – it is so very beautiful it makes my heart swell. It's like I'm standing at the edge of the world, and anything could happen.

I sit on one of the big boulders that fringe the base of the cliffs, and I listen to the hiss and suck of the water on the sand. I sit there for a while, watching the day turn into night before my very eyes, and I allow myself a moment of complete and perfect peace. I do not get many of those, and I appreciate the ones that come my way.

I give it another ten minutes, letting my mind wander freely and feeling my body finally unwind after a challenging day. I stand and stretch my arms upwards, and close my eyes. The universe flows around me, and I welcome it. This is my fresh start. This is my new home.

This is where I will begin again.

Chapter Two

I'm just about to head back up to the village when I hear a voice shout: 'Ahoy there!'

I jump and curse myself for not having my keys gripped between my fingers like I would if I was walking in London. Then again, I decide, a vicious killer probably wouldn't shout first to get my attention – plus the voice sounded female. Not that women can't be vicious killers, but let's face it, history tells us it's a lot less likely.

I glance behind me, wondering if someone, or even something, has emerged from the sea – maybe a water goddess, or a mermaid! Nope, predictably enough. I look left and right, in case there is someone else on the beach I didn't notice. Also nope. There is only one option left – I am hearing voices.

'Up here!' it shouts again. 'At the café!'

I turn in that direction and see that there is a balcony facing out over the sea. I can only imagine how spectacular the view is from up there. On a clear day you can probably see to infinity and beyond. I see the rosy red glow of the tip of a cigarette, and it waves around like a little ghost spark. I have to assume that the ghost spark is in the hands of a human, one who is waving to me. She seems to realise that I can't really see her, and a sudden glow of light surrounds her face – the torch from her phone.

I'm not sure that's much better, because now there's a whole Blair Witch Project vibe going on instead. And I'm still too far away to make the face out properly.

'Are you Sarah?' she yells. 'And would you like a cuppa and a bite to eat?'

Damn. What is it with this place? How does she know who I am, and how does she know I'm hungry? Or maybe she always assumes people are hungry. Maybe everybody here shows their kindness through the medium of food. I freeze momentarily, not at all sure what to do next. My instincts tell me to flee, to run back into the night, to go and hide in my little safe haven. Except she obviously knows who I am, which means she knows where I live, and I don't really want to start my time here by being so very rude. I might not want to be deeply involved in the lives of my new neighbours, but I also don't want them to hate me. Then where would I be after the solar flares?

I wave back, no idea if she can see me properly or not – in the last few minutes it's become much darker, the moon kicking the sun out of its spot. 'Come on up!' she calls.

I'm still in two minds when I hear a little yapping sound accompanying her. 'My dog wants to say hello!'

That pushes me over the edge. I always trust people with dogs, which I know is a weak spot of mine. All a serial killer or twisted kidnapper would have to do to get me in his car would be show me a dog. I'm almost fifty, and still the kind of little girl who would fall for the 'Would you like to see my puppies?' trick.

I decide that I will hedge my bets. I will go and say hello, to be polite, but I will not go inside and make this interaction last any longer than it needs to. I head towards the paths, glancing up at the café as I go. From this angle it actually looks like it's hanging over the cliff. It would definitely topple off if there was an earthquake.

There are two paths, one with steps and one that is paved and winds around the slope, presumably for people with buggies and wheelchairs, or just people who hate steps. Right now, I am one of those people, because the slower ascent will give me more time to prepare myself for meeting yet another Budbury resident.

The climb up is actually pleasant, the path sided by handrails that are lit by pretty golden fairy lights, making the whole place feel like Christmas has come early. I pause and look out at the sea, smiling at the way the moon reflects on the shimmering water. It really is gorgeous. An owl hoots from somewhere more distant, and I take a deep breath as I continue on. Owls are fantastic creatures, I've always thought – they look really weird and nowhere near as cool as some of the other birds, but somehow retain an air of mystery. Life goals right there.

I reach the top of the path and walk through an iron archway into a garden. The top of the archway is curved with the words Comfort Food Café, metallic roses trailing in and out of the individual letters. Green and red and black, the effect incredibly pretty.

The string lights cast a merry glow over the sloping garden, highlighting the higgledy-piggledy picnic tables and the tubs and troughs of plants and flowers. The café itself is a sprawling one-storey affair, and there is a little annexe that has books in the window. I'm automatically drawn towards it, as ever unable to resist a bookshop, and admire the Halloween display. A little bookcase has been placed there, draped with spooky cobwebs, surrounded by miniature pumpkins. I spot the works of Stephen King, Anne Rice, Charlaine Harris, alongside some darker crime novels and some psychological thrillers.

I pull a face when I spot one of my own books on the shelf, because no matter how many copies I sell and how many languages I'm translated into, I will always feel like an imposter. I'm just a slightly crazy girl from Essex who managed to turn her morbid imagination into a job, and it still feels strange to see myself next to 'real' authors. My actual name is Sarah Jane Wallis, but I write under SJ Andrews. When I first got an agent, many years ago now, he suggested that having a surname higher up the alphabet helped because when people are browsing bookshelves, they get bored by the time they hit 'W'. No idea if there is any truth to it, but as I value my privacy, I'm glad we made that choice anyway. Hopefully Sarah Jane Wallis is much harder to track down than SJ Andrews.

I'm interrupted by the sudden opening of the café door, and a light being switched on. A little dog comes yapping towards me, definitely letting me know that this is her territory. The routine is spoiled a bit by the fact she is tiny and fluffy and white, a shaggy little bundle of fur and fury. Also by the fact that as she approaches me, she stops barking, drops to the ground, and rolls onto her back for a belly rub.

'She's a killer and no mistake,' her owner says, emerging from the café door. The dog leaps up again, runs around my ankles several times at breakneck speed, then dashes off to find a bush to pee on. 'Come on in.'

The woman turns back inside and leaves me there, obviously expecting me to follow. I am momentarily rooted to the spot. I had no intention of going in, and had planned on simply saying hello and then making my excuses to leave. Huh. My plans have failed. The dog yaps at me and runs back towards the door. She stops on the threshold, her fluffy little tail wagging, her brown eyes gazing up at me from behind a neatly trimmed white fringe. Damn. Who could resist?

I walk into the café, and it smells like heaven. Like everyone's favourite foods ever, mixed in with the lingering scent of coffee beans and cocoa. I close my eyes and inhale, my senses overriding my thoughts for once. When I open my eyes again, I'm confronted with a vision of female power. Seriously, this woman looks like she could have given birth to the Avengers, raised Wonder Woman, and colonised Mars in her spare time.

I'm five foot eight, but she is slightly taller than me, and while I'm on the slender side, she is wide and big and frankly magnificent. Her hair is loose, a long shimmer of wavy silver, kinked in that way that suggests it was recently in a plait, and her eyes are sparkling with a youthful energy that is at odds with the lines on her face. If I had to guess, I'd say she was at the least in her seventies, but she is one of the least 'old lady' people I have ever encountered: she exudes cheery confidence and gives me the kind of smile that makes me feel like everything in the whole world will be okay. I fall immediately and uncontrollably in love, and most definitely want to be her when I grow up.

'I'm Cherie Bloom,' she says, 'It's dark outside, so gin and tonic?'

I gape a little at that logic, then manage to reply: 'Uh, I'm Sarah. But you'd already guessed that. How did you guess that, by the way?'

'Well, I watched you walk down the hill via my spy satellite, obviously.'

My eyes widen, and she laughs at my expression. 'Oooh, your face! No, love, I just heard you'd arrived, and spoke to Laura after she'd popped in. Then I was out on the balcony having one of my herbal cigarettes, and saw you down there. She told me you were a tall, gorgeous strawberry blonde.'

'And you still recognised me despite that terrible and deeply inaccurate description?'

'I did. Now, drink, cake, chat?'

No, I tell myself. Do not get drunk. Do not eat the cake. Do not get sucked in. I was warned about this…

'Yes, please,' I find myself saying, unable to tear myself away. She tells me to sit tight for a minute, and disappears off into the kitchens at the back. I look around, and realise that the interior of the café is as interesting as its owner.

Apart from the usual and entirely expected stuff like tables, chairs and a serving counter, there is a complete feast for the eyes. Mobiles made from old seven-inch vinyl singles dangle from the ceiling, nets are filled with shells, and a vintage gold and black Singer sewing machine battles with a huge fossil for pride of place. I literally don't know where to look next, there is so much to take in – bookshelves, board games, squishy leather sofas, photos, posters, lobster pots.

I wander the room, touching the random items, feeling like I've just discovered Tutankhamun's tomb and all its treasures. My personal tastes lean more towards the 'less is more' approach, but this is amazing. It's all spotlessly clean, but also incredibly cluttered, and somehow it works perfectly. The windows are huge, and the views are stunning. Maybe sitting outside on the little balcony and smoking a 'herbal cigarette' is Cherie's happy place – it could definitely be mine. Without the cigarette.

Only half the lights are on so it's quite dim, adding to the air of wonder as I explore. I come across a framed picture of a middle-aged lady leading a yoga class, and laugh at the assortment of people she is guiding in downward dog. Yoga classes are often filled with a certain type of person, but this one bucks the trend. I'm still smiling when Cherie appears at my side and hands me a glass. One sip tells me there is as much G as there is T.

'That's Lynnie,' she says, 'we lost her a few years ago. She was quite the force of nature. She had a few issues with memory in her later years, and she used to turn up here and do impromptu yoga sessions. We all went along with it.'

'Ah. That explains a lot. You don't often see a crowd like this getting their Namaste on.'

Cherie smiles and points out a silver-haired man wearing a plaid shirt and green cords. He's looking up at the camera with impossibly blue eyes. 'That's my hubby, Frank. We lost him as well. We've really been very careless recently… Anyway, cake!'

I see the glaze of tears in her eyes, and give her the space to retreat into the kitchen. She emerges with two big slabs of chocolate fudge cake, and sets them on a table along with a jug of pouring cream. Clearly I am going to end up the size of the Michelin man if I stay here for long. I sit down, and the little dog immediately jumps onto my lap.

'That's Luna,' she says, smiling indulgently. 'I adopted her a few months ago. Be careful or she'll snaffle your chocolate cake, and it's not good for her.'

I nod as she passes me a spoon, the dog's eyes following it. 'I'm so sorry,' I say, 'about Frank. He looks like a lot of fun.'

'Oh yes, he was! We got together later in life – in our eighties, which is kind of the new sixties isn't it? What we lost out on in time we made up for in memories. I suppose it was quality, not quantity. I… I miss him every single day. I mean, I have great friends and I love this place, and I stay active. It's hard to be lonely in Budbury, but there are moments when I still manage it. Moments when everyone has left, and I'm upstairs in my little flat, surrounded by remnants of my life and the people I've lost. That, my dear, is when I start kidnapping poor innocent women who are minding their own business and having a nice quiet walk on the beach!'

I take the first bite of my fudge cake and almost have a *When Harry Met Sally* moment. I shudder with pleasure – this is heaven in a spoon – and Luna gazes at me with disgust.

'I don't mind being kidnapped if this is how you're going to feed me. Did you live here with Frank?'

This is one of the big contradictions about my personality. I am by nature solitary and introverted, but I am also extremely nosy and curious about other people's lives. It's confusing for me and anyone I meet.

'Long story, but no. I moved here after my first husband, Wally, passed away. It was a fresh start for me – Budbury is the perfect place for a fresh start, you'll see that for yourself. Frank and I were a slow burn, but when we finally did get hitched, I moved in with him at his farmhouse. He died suddenly, still working out in the fields, which is exactly what he would have wanted, the old goat. He'd have hated some long lingering illness that kept him indoors. He was one of those fellas who could have lost an arm in the combine harvester and called it "just a scratch", you know? I was happy enough there with him, but after he went, well … it felt wrong. It was too hard. So I came back here, to my happy place. And my sad place.'

'Just your *place* place?'

'Exactly! Anyway. Enough of me moaning. I won't need to dress up for Halloween; I can just haunt the café with my whinging! I think perhaps you've sparked it off in me, Sarah.'

'Yes,' I reply, licking cream off my spoon, 'I have that effect on people. They can be perfectly happy beforehand, then after a few minutes in my company, they're crying and wondering what the point of life is. It's a skill.'

She shoves my shoulder playfully, but she's a big lady and I almost fall off my chair. 'Get away with you!' she says, grinning. 'It's nice to have a new face around. Though actually, you're the second this month.'

'Oh. Now I don't feel special.'

She laughs, and stares off into the distance for a moment. 'We don't know much about the other new one though. He's very mysterious. Keeps himself to himself.'

She says this as though she cannot possibly understand such a ridiculous urge. 'Is that so bad?' I ask. 'Some people are more private than others. It doesn't make them evil.'

'I know that, darling. And don't think for a minute that I haven't noticed the way I've spilled my guts to you, and you've told me not one single thing about yourself! But … well, maybe it's the time of year. I get a Halloween-y vibe from him.'

'What does that mean?' I ask, frowning. 'How does a person have a Halloween-y vibe?'

Even as I ask, my imagination is filling in the blanks. Is he accompanied everywhere he goes by a black cat? Does he only come out at night? Does he have no shadow? Is he a time-slip soldier from the First World War? Does he do a horror-movie laugh like Vincent Price every time he leaves the room?

'I can't quite explain it. Why don't you come in

tomorrow and meet everyone else? We can fill you in on our theories!'

Everyone else? How many more people am I expected to meet? This village is tiny! Already today I've met Sam, Matt and Cal, Katie and Laura, and now Cherie... Frankly, that's my 'meeting new people' quota for a whole year under normal circumstances. It's ironic that I moved here to get away from the crush of humanity and I seem to be more surrounded than ever.

'Um, I'll see how I get on,' I reply, finishing up my G&T with an icy clink. 'I've got all my unpacking to do, and a lot of work to catch up, and—'

'And you're freaking out?'

'I can neither confirm nor deny. But for now, I do need to get back. I genuinely have stuff to get on with. Thank you for the cake. And the whole bottle of gin. And … take care of yourself, okay?'

I put little Luna back down, but she sneakily licks my face first. Either she's a very affectionate dog, or I had a stray smear of chocolate on my skin. I scrape the chair legs back and stand up. Before I can protest or make my escape, Cherie wraps me in her arms and gives me a world-class hug. It is impossible to resist, and I melt a little bit, my head clasped to her substantial shoulder. Her hair smells of joss sticks and sugar and a wisp of herbal cigarette. Like a doughnut stand at a music festival.

'See you tomorrow, Sarah!' she says, as I finally break free.

Not if I see you first, I think. The old ones are the best.

Chapter Three

I keep busy until the early hours, first setting up my little workstation in the spare bedroom. It's nothing glamorous, a desk, a laptop, endless stacks of notepads and Post-it squares, and a giant board. The corkboard looks like one of those evidence walls that obsessed detectives set up in Hollywood movies – scrawled cards, maps, pinned photos, names and dates, arrows and lines connecting them all. I'm not an obsessed detective myself, but DI Carina Shaw, my current lead character, is. She's currently hunting a serial killer who covered his tracks for decades, and only she could see the trail of bloody breadcrumbs.

Like most of my books, its content is dark, its characters tormented, and there is death, violence and a subterranean torture dungeon. What can I say? That's *my* happy place. I often throw in a hint of the supernatural too, like DS Shaw getting clues from beyond the grave from her murdered partner, or a villain who may or may not be possessed by a demon. They're not for everyone, my stories, and part of me wishes I could write something more cheerful and positive. Something with romance and rainbows and happy endings. Sadly, that's just not me, and anyway, the few sessions I had with a therapist years ago showed me that my writing is good for my brain. Apparently it allows me to purge trauma, perceived and real.

I have not experienced the kinds of trauma that my poor characters experience – I really drag them through hell and back – but my childhood was messy, my marriage was painful, and my relationship with my father is still difficult. I have struggled in lots of ways, and have always seen the worst in every possible scenario, which has unfortunately often turned out to be true. It's one of the reasons I left London.

Sally always fought her way out of every situation we faced when we were young; that's how she dealt with it all. She scrapped and sassed her way through my dad's drinking, the yelling and screaming that were the soundtrack to life at home. I internalised it and found my own coping mechanism by escaping into my imagination. I suppose it made us both stronger in our own ways – she became a doctor, and found the stresses and strains of life in a busy hospital a breeze in comparison. I turned my fantasies into a successful career. Maybe we should actually be writing our father thank you cards.

Dear Dad – thanks for being such a prick when we were kids – lots of love, Sally and Sarah xxx

I smile at the idea. He'd actually think it was genuine, and my mum would go along with it for an easy life. They've been married for over fifty years, despite showing every outward sign of despising each other. But hey, who am I to judge? Relationships are not my specialist subject.

The little back bedroom is actually the perfect size for an office, and from the pale blue paint on the walls and the little smiley face symbols that have been drawn on the inside of the cupboard door I'd say it used to belong to a child. Maybe one of Katie's. I like the smiley faces, and will definitely keep them. They feel like a good omen.

I sit and work for a few hours, and as ever it feels good to lose myself in a world that I can control. The real world remains stubbornly difficult in that respect, despite my best efforts. No matter how hard I try to be prepared, to protect myself, to stay safe, something always seems to sneak through. Maybe it will be different here. I really hope so, at least. Though a quick glance at my laptop, with its insanely long password and the black tape over the camera, warns me it won't be that easy.

I get a message from my niece Libby at about 3am, the ping of my phone disturbing me from a blaze of typing as Carina Shaw starts to put the puzzle pieces together and come up with a horrific whole.

Go to bed!

The text makes me laugh.

I will if you will 😘😘

I hesitate before adding the kisses. I've never quite got on with emojis. I never recovered from my nieces showing

31

me a series of innocent looking items – banana, aubergine, pineapple, doughnut – and then explaining what sexual acts they corresponded to. Sally had laughed her head off, but I'd been traumatised. Now I'm always scared that I'll send the wrong emoji, and people will think I'm a ketamine addict who likes going to swingers' parties. I also often have to close my eyes in the fresh produce aisle of the supermarket. Lord help me if in this little rural corner of England I ever happen upon an aubergine farm…

> I'm already in bed

She replies, and I picture her curly blonde head on her pillow.

> Just not asleep. Busy brain. Time for a chat?

I decide that I have got time for a chat. The words have been flowing, but my eyes are stinging and my wrists are sore and my back is aching from hunching over my desk. I feel like a coffee, but it is the middle of the night and I know from past experience that it is very easy for me to become entirely nocturnal. I hit call, hoping she's okay.

Libby and Lucy, like myself and Sally, are non-identical twins. And also like myself and Sally, they are very different, personality-wise. Lucy, though, as I've pointed out to my sister many times, is not quite as cruel to her quieter sibling as she was to me. Sally always shrugs and pulls a 'what's done is done' face, which still annoys me after all these years. Truth be told, she can still press my buttons. I'm not sure she's even aware she does it. I handle it better now, and speak up for myself when she goes too far, but I've always felt in her shadow. It's not the same dynamic with my nieces; they get along well despite their differences – contrast without as much conflict.

'Hello, Auntie dearest,' says Libby when she answers, her voice sleepy. 'Was I right? You were still up working, yes?'

'Guilty as charged, m'lud. Just got carried away. Why are you awake?'

'Lucy snuck out of the house to go clubbing with her friends. She's got a fake ID and everything. So I'm kind of jealous and also a bit worried about her. What if she gets her drink spiked? What if Mum finds out?'

I don't just mindlessly reassure her, because I know that doesn't work for the over-thinkers of the world. I have no clue why Libby is like this. I explain away my temperament with the way things were at home, but Libby's family life is stable, loving and fun, as far as I know. Maybe it's just genetics having a laugh at us all.

'Well, how many friends is she out with?' I ask. 'Boys or girls?'

'Mainly girls, some boys. And quite a lot of them I think.'

'Well, that's good, then. I know your mother has talked to her about spiking, because she's seen cases come into the hospital, and I know that I've always drummed it into the two of you to always keep an eye out for your mates. I'm pretty sure that other mums and mum-type people will have done the same for the rest of them. So, even if Lucy isn't paying attention – which I'm sure she will be – then someone else in that big group will have their eyes open.'

Libby sighs, and I can hear her turning over in bed. I picture her room, with its crammed bookshelves and messy desk and her huge collection of vinyl. The vintage movie posters on her walls, the collection of potted plants that make the place feel like a rainforest. I will miss seeing them as often, but in reality they are both busy these days. It's not like they're little girls who need their aunt to babysit any more.

'Okay, that makes sense. Thanks, Auntie. What about the other worry? If Mum finds out?'

'If your mum finds out she'll go ballistic, so just steer clear of the blast radius. She did far worse when she was that age, but nobody needs to mention that. She'll know it, deep down, and not go too hard on her. You okay? Everything all right at school?'

'Yep,' she says, stifling a yawn. 'Kind of. Well, it's crap, but that's nothing new, is it? It'll be over soon.'

Libby hates school. She likes learning, enjoys her A-level subjects, but has very little time for the social niceties and the tribal values of what she calls the 'battery chicken farm'.

'I'll come and visit soon, if that's okay?' she asks, her voice quiet, a touch of nerves. 'Is it nice?'

'Of course that's okay,' I assure her. 'And it is nice yes. It's new, which is always strange. And it's strange, which is always new.'

'Strange how? Good or bad?'

'I'm not sure yet. There is possibly a hive mind. The men are all too good-looking, and I've been bewitched by a woman in her eighties who smokes spliffs and seduced me with chocolate cake.'

'Oh. Well, that sounds like a most excellent adventure, Bill.'

'I'm sure it will be. Party on, Ted. I'll speak to you soon. Love you.'

We bonded years ago by watching movies from my childhood, and the Keanu classic has remained one of her favourites.

I hang up and check my phone for anything else. I don't have any social media at all on there, and only my family and close colleagues have this number. It's new, and I told everyone it was because I dropped my old one in the bath while I was reading a book called *My Best Friend's Exorcism* on my kindle app. That's not true, but it is the kind of behaviour that wouldn't shock them. The real reason I got a new phone was because I needed to change my number, and because I became paranoid about the phone itself having some kind of tracker on it. Crazy but true – modern technology has opened up all kinds of new and exciting ways to worry.

I'm holding my breath slightly as I examine the screen, looking for anything out of place, but there is nothing there that shouldn't be there. I let out a sigh, annoyed that my hands are shaking slightly. Annoyed with the whole thing.

I switch off my laptop and try to clear my mind of everything. Plot points I need to untangle, vague concerns about Libby, hoping I was right about Lucy's pals being sensible, freaking out about sleeping in a new place, feeling unsettled in general.

I go downstairs, and quickly double check all the locks and make sure the windows are closed. There was one open in the kitchen, but just the little one at the top. I switch off the lights and take myself to bed. I'm already in my pyjamas – have been since just before nine o'clock, because I'm rock and roll like that.

I pull the covers over me, and realise I need better curtains. Ones that will black out the moon, which is currently shining way too brightly around the gaps in the fabric. I glance around the unfamiliar room, the moonlight at least allowing me to pick out a few comforting sights: my bookshelf, as yet empty because the books are still in boxes. A stack of my clothes, currently heaped on a chair. My little bedside cabinet, upon which stands my glass of water, my reading glasses, and a small wooden cross. I don't believe in vampires quite as vehemently as I did back when I was little, but I've never quite recovered from *Salem's Lot*. Better safe than sorry.

Shit. Why did I think about that? Because now I know that, as soon as I start to drift off I'll imagine those creepy fingernails scraping on the windowpane… Stop, stop, stop! Do not let your mind take charge. Put it back in a box and tell it to go to sleep, right now. There is no such thing as vampires. There are no zombies on the street. This cute little house is not built on a graveyard, and it is not haunted. Nobody can hurt you. You are safe.

Just as I'm managing to calm myself down, giving myself the same pep talk I have given myself so many times, I hear it. The faintest sound of something scratching. I screw my eyes together, shake my head, fight back against the panic. No. I imagined it. There was no scratching.

I hear it again. Louder now. Impossible to ignore, impossible to put down to imagination. A rhythmic scrape, coming from somewhere nearby. Rats? Weresquirrels? Something more sinister … like the worst monster of them all, a human being?

I tell myself to move. To get out of bed. To grab the scissors I always keep in my cabinet drawer just in case I ever need a makeshift weapon. But no matter how many times I tell myself to move, my body stays frozen, my mind trapped and terrified.

The scratch comes again, and is followed by the long, slow creak of the bedroom door being pushed open. My hands grip the sheets, and my eyes are wide and staring. My heart is hammering in my chest, and I can barely breath. Get up! Run! Fight! Call for help!

Just as I manage to force myself to creep my hand out towards my phone, there is a solid thud on my bed. A thud, and a chunky presence next to my legs, and … a purr? Is that a purr?

I sit up, and see a pair of luminous green eyes staring at me. It's a cat. It's a bloody cat. A massive furry ginger cat with the tip of one ear missing. He licks his paws and stares at me, then purrs a bit more. My heart is slowly recovering, and I wipe the sheen of cold sweat from my face. This will seem funny in the morning, but right now adrenaline is coursing through my body, and I'm feeling that awful jarring sensation, like I've tripped up and everything inside me has been shaken about like a milkshake. I hold out a hand, and the cat licks it with a sandpaper tongue. He seems friendly enough. Not a zombie cat for sure.

I run my fingers through his thick fur, and he purrs some more. I'm relieved, but I'm also upset with myself. When will I ever stop freezing in the face of fear? I've spent so much of my damn life afraid you'd have thought I would have learned how to deal with it by now. How to override it and take back control of my own body and mind. Sadly, I haven't, and the fact leaves me filled with such a toxic mix of emotions – anxiety, self-loathing, anger. But mainly, a deep sense of sadness.

The cat rubs himself up against my palm, his purring deep and soothing. 'You almost gave me a heart attack,' I say, smiling at him. 'That would be a terrible way to go – scared to death in my own bed by a ginger cat. What's your name anyway…?'

He's wearing a collar with a little bell on it, which I'm sure he hates because it gives all his feathered and long-tailed potential victims the chance to escape. I probably couldn't hear it over the sounds of my heart pounding in my chest. There's also one of those little discs with a phone number and a name engraved on it.

I laugh out loud as I read. I look at this massive cat, who is by no means a young gentleman, with his missing ear tip and scarred lines of fur from the brawls he's been in, and decide that whoever named him must have a sense of humour.

'Tinkerbell?' I say, amusement dripping from my voice. He glares at me, as though he understands he is being mocked and is outraged at the indignity of it all. 'Tinkerbell!

Well, there you go. If you're still around in the morning, Tink, I'll call this number and see if your presence is required elsewhere. And I will not be feeding you, okay? This isn't my first rodeo. I know what happens when you feed cats who aren't your own.'

I was once adopted by a charming little tortoiseshell who appeared in my roof garden. We became best friends, and she stayed with me most days. One time she turned up with an injured leg, bleeding and hurt, so I took her to the vets. It cost me several hundred pounds to have that leg fixed, and we left together, she with a cone of shame around her head. A few days later, I saw her on the windowsill of a house a few doors down – a house where she clearly lived. To this day I laugh when I imagine her actual owners, wondering what the hell was going on when the cat turned up with stitches and a head cone. She stopped coming by after that; I suspect her family decided she needed to be an indoor cat for a while.

Tinkerbell looks at me as I speak, then lifts one leg and licks his bum. Right. Well. That told me.

I pull the covers back over myself, and settle down. I finally feel so exhausted I will probably pass out. With the comforting lump of the cat curled against my thighs, I finally fall asleep – my very first night in Budbury.

Chapter Four

The next day, the cat is gone. I have no clue how, because everything is locked up tight, but that is the Way of the Cat. They are mysterious creatures, and I suspect they have secretly mastered the science of teleportation.

I do some more unpacking, feeling more at home once my bookshelves are full, and do some basic shopping in the little grocery store. There are the usual suspect supermarkets a further drive away, but I enjoy shopping locally when I can. There is a little butcher's counter, freshly baked croissants, and milk that I'm told is 'fresh from Farmer Frank's Farm'. I wonder if that's the farm that Cherie's late husband owned, but don't want to ask. I've already been engaged in a lot more conversations than I'd expected to be engaged in.

I buy myself a beautiful bunch of deep red dahlias from the florist, because I decided long ago that I would never wait for anybody else to buy me flowers. They are gorgeous, and I'm carrying them when I call into the pharmacy, which is across the road from my house. I need to buy some antihistamines in case the cat becomes a fixture, and in case I develop an allergy. Yes, this is how my mind works.

It's a pleasingly old-fashioned place, with wooden cabinets and storefront windows that look at the very least Victorian. A little bell tinkles as I push the door open, and the smell of mint and cough sweets hits me. It's like walking into an apothecary shop, and I half expect to see someone mixing herbs with a pestle and mortar.

Instead, I see a very elderly lady lounging flat out on a bright red sofa that is designed in the shape of a huge pair of lips. She's draped along it, looking like she's about to be eaten, and is wearing a plastic crown. Another woman, dressed in a white coat, is kneeling at her side hand feeding her grapes. Right. Okay then. Things just got weird.

I'm about to turn back around and leave when Katie emerges from behind the counter carrying a glass of something fizzy and alcoholic looking. She smiles when she notices me, and says: 'Sarah! Nice to see you. Erm, Edie is Queen for the Day…'

The elderly lady – who I now see is very elderly indeed – sits upright and grins at me. Her blue eyes almost disappear into her wrinkles, and she straightens her wonky crown. 'Flowers!' she says, gazing at the dahlias. 'Thank you very much!'

She is a tiny woman, her grey hair short and tightly curled, her whole body encased in shades of beige. She raises an eyebrow at me and holds out a hand, and I feel like I have no option at all other than to hand the bouquet over to her. I almost curtsy, but catch myself at the last moment.

She cackles, an outrageously raucous sound coming from somebody so small and frail looking, and says: 'Oooh, I got you there, didn't I? Don't worry, I won't steal your beautiful blooms!'

She offers them back to me, and I find that I no longer want them. I want her to have them.

'No, please, Your Highness, I would be honoured if you would accept this small token of my esteem and respect,' I reply, bowing deeply. I have no idea what's come over me. It's probably the after-effects of that cake at the café. Or the cake I had for supper. Or the cake I had for breakfast this morning. Maybe it's simply seeing a woman of her amazing age laughing so hard she has tears in her eyes. What's not to love about that?

'Now, Auburn, you see, *that's* how you should speak to your queen!' she says, wagging a finger at the lady in the white coat. She stands up, deep red hair streaming over her shoulders. 'I was on my knees feeding you grapes, woman, what more do you want? You're not a queen, you're a dictator! It's time for a revolution... I'm going to order a guillotine from Amazon! I bet they've got them on Prime...'

Edie cackles some more, and Katie shakes her head in bewilderment.

'Don't worry,' she says calmly, 'it only gets more surreal. Auburn, Edie, this is Sarah. She's moved into the empty house over the road. My old place.'

'We're almost neighbours!' declares Edie, hoisting herself to her feet and looking up at me. 'Don't be knocking on my door complaining about my rap music, you hear? I've earned the right to play my Nicki Minaj records as loud as I like!'

I stare at her, not even remotely sure if she's serious or not.

'Kidding!' she announces. 'I'm more of a Missy Elliot kind of girl!'

'Ignore her,' says Auburn, clearing up grapes from the floor. 'She's messing with you. She looks all cute and harmless, but underneath she's pure evil. How are you settling in? Do you want some tea or some biscuits? Or a pumpkin scented candle?'

'Um, no thank you. And I'm settling in fine I suppose. Though I did get visited by a very large ginger cat last night.'

Katie pulls a face and looks embarrassed. 'Did he have part of his ear missing? And behave like your lord and master?'

I nod, and she says: 'That would be Tinkerbell. Technically he is my cat, but obviously he belongs to whoever he chooses. We haven't lived in that house for ages. We live over the fields, but he likes to keep an eye on the place. I'm so sorry.'

'Not a problem,' I respond, feeling a slight hint of disappointment. Maybe I'd secretly and irrationally been hoping that Tinkerbell was a stray and that he would adopt me. That we would rescue each other a little bit. 'He's welcome any time. Anyway … I'd better be going. I have work to do.'

I make a sharp exit before any of them can ask what I do

for a living, waving as I dash out of the door. I didn't get my antihistamines and I lost my flowers, but I escaped intact at least. The minute people find out what I do for work, they make 'Oooh, how interesting!' noises and ask me lots of questions. They often seem to think that it's a super-glamorous life full of parties and awards ceremonies and red carpets, but the truth is far more mundane. I do sometimes get invited to those kinds of things, but I say no; I prefer being at home, actually writing the books, rather than out in the world talking about them. Sometimes I just lie and say I work from home doing accounts for a cement supplier. That's so dull nobody ever wants to know a thing about it.

I let myself in, and as I close the door behind me decide that I should get some better locks. This one really is awkward and not very burglar-proof. I probably need to get a home security firm around to install an alarm as well. I haven't spotted the tell-tale plastic alarm boxes outside any other houses here, and I'm sure it's not exactly rife with crime – but it will make me feel better, especially if my guard cat isn't around.

I put my shopping away and work solidly for the next five hours. I don't even stop for lunch I'm so in the zone, and emerge from my fictional world bleary-eyed and confused. It's a strange life, spanning the real world and my imaginary one, and when I've been immersed in my writing for too long I actually start to wonder which is which.

I glance at my phone and see that it's already mid-afternoon. Idly, as I transition back to the here and now, I browse the internet for information on my new home.

Knowledge is power, right? The world wide web has made it so much easier to stalk people, which is one of the reasons I don't do social media and keep my profile as low as my work will allow. My publicist loves that about me.

I find the Comfort Food Café has an Instagram, and drool a little at the pictures of cakes and milkshakes. I discover that Cherie Bloom doesn't just own the café, but also a holiday complex nearby called The Rockery, as well as several other properties and businesses – so despite looking like she's lived her whole life in a VW camper van at Woodstock, she is clearly a successful entrepreneur too. I find a news archive piece about a Frank Farmer's death that fits with her account of it, and feel surprisingly sad. He was obviously a stalwart of the community, and I well up a little as I look at pictures of the man throughout his life – as a little boy at a street party for VE Day, as a young man winning awards for his prize-winning turnip crop, later on as the face of the Budbury Summer Fete committee.

There is a video clip from the funeral, the procession going all the way down the high street, past the very house I am sitting in – a miles-long stream of cars, trucks, tractors, combines and quad bikes, all beeping their horns and flashing their lights in farewell to a man who was clearly very well loved by the whole village. No wonder Cherie feels the loss so keenly. 'He leaves behind his widow, Cherie Bloom, his son Peter, and two grandchildren,' the article says. It sounds so simple, doesn't it? 'Leaves behind' – as though she will eventually catch him up. I suppose that's true, but the time in between seems to be making Cherie sad, and I hate that. I resolve that even if I'm not exactly

Mrs Social Whirl, I will make the effort to see Cherie. She is 'left behind', and if I can provide a bit of company when she needs it, then I will.

I move on in my internet journey, and discover that Matt, the Harrison Ford look-alike and Laura's husband, is also the local vet, and that Sam is a ranger for the whole of the Jurassic coast. Edie turns out to be Edie May, and she's had her fair share of time in the spotlight as well – running the local library, being in charge of all kinds of community events, and then helping to archive items from a nearby historic house called Briarwood. Briarwood now seems to be some kind of hot-house school for budding inventors and young scientists. That sounds like fun, and I wonder if I could go and visit one day. Maybe, like the cats, they've discovered the key to teleportation. Or invisibility. Or figuring out why when you drop toast it always lands butter-side down.

I read all of this within half an hour, and then drag myself away. For someone who is so fiercely protective of her own privacy, I really enjoy invading other people's, it seems. I amble down the stairs and make myself a cup of ginger tea to take outside. It's another warm, clear day, and at this time of year you have to grab them when you can – in the blink of an eye it will be torrential rain and snowstorms. I sit at the little table, and stay very still as I watch the robin perched on the branch of the lilac. He's watching me too, tiny shining eyes in a twitching head, looking for signs of threat.

'I won't hurt you, little pal,' I say very quietly. 'Just listen out for the bell around the cat's neck, though.'

I swear he seems to nod at that. I wonder if he's thinking 'yeah, that cat is a complete arsehole!' I wonder if robins think at all. So many mysteries in life.

I finish my tea and do a few stretches. I haven't unpacked my yoga mat as yet, and am starting to suspect that I might have forgotten to bring it. I try and do a little every day, because it irons out the kinks both physically and mentally. I've tried all kinds of sports and hated pretty much every single one of them. I can't abide the gym, with its loud music and clanking metal machines and huge men, and I'm very much not a team sports kind of person. I don't run unless I'm late or trying to catch a bus, and find any kind of organised exercise class to be a special type of hell. I love walking, and other than that and the occasional cycle, yoga is pretty much the only activity I've been able to maintain. Though I'm rubbish at the meditating bits at the end.

The robin flies away as I do my stretches, obviously correctly deciding that I'm a lunatic. I go back inside, intending to have some proper food and look for the mat. As I walk by the front door, I notice a little envelope has been pushed through the letter box. Getting mail like this is a novelty – my flat in London is in a serviced building with a doorman, and everything gets put into a lock box for me. And too often they were things I really didn't want.

I stare at the envelope, a tiny sliver of worry running through me. There was a man, in London, who I don't like to think about. Who made my life difficult. He used to send me notes, too. Even the sight of this one makes my nostrils flare.

No, I tell myself, shaking it off. This is not him. This is not London. This is not anything to be scared of. And even if it is, what good will ignoring it do? If by some grim miracle he is still looking for me, and has found me, then I need to know so I can deal with it. Last night, when I was lying in bed terrified, I let that terror paralyse me, and that is not an option for every single day of my life. I cannot let that happen.

I lean down, pick up the envelope. See my name scrawled on it. I open it up and find a small card bearing a picture of seashells.

YOU ARE CORDIALLY INVITED TO YOUR FIRST MEETING OF THE
BUDBURY LADIES COFFEE AND CAKE CLUB.
4PM AT THE COMFORT FOOD CAFÉ.
BE THERE OR BE SAD THAT YOU MISSED LAURA'S NEW
BLACKBERRY CHEESECAKE!
LOTS OF LOVE, CHERIE XXX

Oh crikey. A club? I don't do clubs. Even ones that offer coffee and cake. Over the years, I've tried to engage more with the world around me, but I've always come to the conclusion that I don't enjoy it very much. The fault lies with me, not others – it just seems to be the way I'm made. I was always like this, even when I was young, and it's probably why I started writing. I created my own world to engage with instead of risking the real one. I'm not socially inept; I just generally prefer my own company.

But, only a little while ago, I was promising myself that I would go and see Cherie again. I genuinely liked her. I felt a sense of security and peace with her that I haven't known since … well, possibly never. My own mum did her best, but life at home was a constant drama. My dad, a domineering drunk, was the lead character, and she played a supporting role. She was the placating wife who was either doing anything she needed to avoid confrontation, or sometimes causing it. There was always tension in the air, and kids pick up on that from a very early age. There was no tension at the Comfort Food Café. There was no sense of threat. It was nice, and warm, and … well, comforting. I suppose the clue is in the name.

I wonder how big this club is? I've met a few Budbury ladies here already. Maybe it's just them – would I be okay with that? Edie, Auburn, Katie, Laura, Cherie … that's only five. Five women, all of whom seem very nice and a whole lot of fun. Surely, I can cope with that? And if I hate it, if I start to feel too stressed or start to shut down, then I can leave. Nobody is going to hold me prisoner at the Comfort Food Café.

I decide that I will go. Even if it's only for half an hour. I quickly make a sandwich before I leave, because I cannot have another day where all I eat is cake. I'll have to swap the yoga for a Peloton if I keep eating this much cake.

By the time I leave the house, it is almost four. I don't want to get there early. Plus being late gives me the chance to lurk outside and check it out first. Always good to think these daring missions through thoroughly. James Bond wouldn't have needed to do so many skydives and ski off so many mountain tops if he'd just thought things through a bit more.

I walk slowly down the hill, already strangely comfortable with this little place. I've only been here for one night, but somehow it is starting to feel more like home than my London flat did even after years.

It's disarmingly warm for October, and I find myself tying my cardigan around my waist and smiling up at the sunshine. I stop at the bottom of the road and turn my face up, letting it gently heat my skin. It feels like an autumn evening in Spain rather than south-west England. My hair is long and on the wild side, and I scoop it up and tie it into a knot. It won't stay there for long, but it cools me down a little.

I resist the temptation to head straight to the beach instead, and climb the steps up to the Comfort Food Café. I can do this, I tell myself. Heck, I might even enjoy it.

Chapter Five

The door to the café is wide open, even though the sign on it is turned to 'closed'. This must be some kind of after-hours thing. Possibly there will be heavy drinking, and strippers.

Or, I think, as I take a tentative step inside, just a gang of women laughing their backsides off – which is actually a lot more fun. It's the kind of sound that should be bottled and used as a treatment by the NHS.

Cherie jumps to her feet when she spots me, and half hugs me, half drags me fully inside. Almost as though she knew I was a flight risk.

'Sarah, this is everyone. Everyone, this is Sarah!'

'Some of us have already met her,' says Auburn, the pharmacist. Or at least I think that's what she's saying, as she has a mouthful of cheesecake right now.

'Well pretend you haven't,' replies Cherie, ushering me towards a seat. The sunlight is flooding in through the huge windows, laying thick golden stripes across the red and white gingham tablecloth. 'And let me do the honours!'

She pushes me down into a chair, and I feel a blush rising as everyone looks at me. I have hair that weird shade between blonde and red, and very pale skin – as a result, the slightest nerves or embarrassment leaves me with a face that looks like someone's slapped me. It's delightful.

Laura emerges from behind the counter, and presents me with a slab of the promised cheesecake. She takes one look at me and gets me a glass of water as well.

'Hot flush?' she asks sympathetically. 'I know the feeling!'

I suspect none of these ladies would feel even slightly uncomfortable discussing menopause symptoms in front of each other, but frankly I barely like discussing it with myself. Not that there is a great deal to discuss as yet, but I know it is looming in the near future.

'Uh, no … I just go red really easily. Sometimes even when I'm on my own.'

'Serves you right for having that whole Nicole Kidman thing going on,' she says. 'It's just balancing it out. Coffee? Baileys? Wine?'

'Would it be rude to say all of the above?'

The women around the table all burst out laughing, and Cherie says: 'See? She fits right in!'

If I do, it will be for possibly the first time in my whole life. I've never fit in anywhere at all, and I suppose over the years I've stopped trying, and on the whole stopped caring. I have my work, and my sister, and my nieces, and I'm not lonely. Most of the time, at least.

Laura pours me a coffee, adds a glug of Baileys, and then pushes a bottle of Malbec towards me. I've been in worse situations. I feel a little rustling motion beneath the table, and see that Luna is down there, presumably minesweeping for crumbs of dropped cake.

'So, Sarah my love,' Cherie says, smiling, 'I shall now introduce you to the ladies of the Budbury Coffee and Cake Club. But before I do, the rules. The first rule of cake club is you do not talk about cake club. Except when you're at cake club, when we very much encourage talking. Now, this is Auburn, who is our local pharmacist. She's married to a hunky Dane called Finn, who manages Briarwood.'

'The place where all the boffins live?' I ask, eagerly. She nods, and wipes cream from her lips.

'It sounds really interesting,' I say. 'Do you think I could visit?'

She shrugs, and tells me that would be fine. 'Though I warn you, it's best to wear a hard hat and be ready to duck and cover. Things seem to be exploding all the time, or setting on fire, or breaking windows. It's like being trapped with a tribe of super-intelligent savages. Give me your number before we finish, and I'll be in touch.'

My number is usually a closely guarded secret, but I just bite my tongue and thank her. I'll think about it later. Nobody is going to understand why I'm such a freak that I won't tell them my number. They'll think I'm just being rude.

'Moving on, this is Laura, who you also already know. She's married to Matt—'

'Who is also hunky,' Laura intercepts. 'But admittedly not Danish.'

'Laura has two grown up children called Nate and Lizzie. Nate is at university in Liverpool training to be a vet, and Lizzie lives in London, where she is taking over the world one TikTok at a time. Matt and Laura also have six-year-old twins called Ruby and Rose. They live out at the Rockery with a psychopathic black Labrador called Midgebo.'

'Uggh. Twins. They're the worst,' I say, smiling to show I don't mean it. I notice the big age gap between her children, and assume there are different fathers involved. I will have to find out her story; I'm sure she has one.

'Completely,' Laura responds, deadpan. 'Other than sisters who are two years younger than you. They really are the worst…'

The slender brunette sitting opposite throws a spoon at her, and it clatters against Laura's forehead before hitting the table with a metallic bang. It leaves a trail of cream on her face.

'And this is Becca,' Cherie says. 'As you might have guessed, Laura's sister. They grew up in Manchester, and Laura moved down here for a fresh start. Becca came to visit and fell in love with our gorgeous Surfer Sam, and the rest is history. They live a few doors away from you with their daughter, Little Edie.'

'Nice to meet you, Sarah,' Becca says, ignoring the dramatic way Laura is sighing and wiping the cream from her face. 'Sam says hi. He's not allowed here. Chicks only. But I'm sure we'll all meet up in the pub at some point.

Even if you don't want to, it's hard not to bump into people around here.'

'I've noticed that,' I respond, filing away Becca's details. There is a lot of new information flying at me, but I'm good with that. My brain is used to compiling fact files about my characters, so all I have to do is treat these real-life women as though they're fictional, and I'll remember everything about them. I just hope they don't end up dead or missing, like most of my made-up people.

'Isn't it lovely?' says a dark-haired lady with sparkling eyes. Like Laura, she's slightly on the plumper side, but it suits her. 'My favourite thing about Budbury is how quickly everyone gets to know each other! You arrive as a stranger and within days, you're part of the fabric of the place!'

She's just described one of my worst nightmares, but I drag out a smile. I take a big gulp of that Baileys coffee.

'This is Maxine, known to all as Max,' Cherie tells me. 'She arrived here around this time last year to work in the café, along with her daughter Sophie, who is now at uni in Cardiff. She was recovering from a broken heart, and managed to get it well and truly mended by the very sultry Gabriel Moran. Together they now buy and do up properties, and live out on Gabe's farmhouse with two donkeys and a dog called Gary.'

I nod and wonder if she's finished. She is, and now everyone is looking at me expectantly. I feel a bit like I'm at some kind of self-help group meeting, where I'm going to be asked to stand up and introduce myself.

The blush is building up again, and I pour myself a glass of the wine. 'Um, hi, everyone. My name's Sarah.

I'm originally from Essex, and I arrived here via London. I have a twin sister and two nieces, and … that's about it really. I'm not that interesting.'

Auburn narrows her eyes and says: 'Cherie, she's resisting! Get the thumbscrews out!'

For a split second I actually worry she means it, but luckily I never find out because we are distracted by a new guest walking through the door. She's short, petite, and has a huge head of full-on ginger curls. She's wearing dungarees and hot pink Crocs, and stares at me as she walks towards the table.

'This is Zoe,' Cherie announces. 'She came to Budbury with her god-daughter Martha, who now lives in London with Lizzie. She lives at Frank's farmhouse with Cal, who is Australian, and runs the farm. Zoe manages the Comfort Reads bookstore next door, and her hobbies are sharpening pencils, alphabetising, and making sarcastic comments.'

There's a pause here, and from the looks on the others' faces, this is the point where Zoe would normally jump in with one of those sarcastic comments. Except she doesn't. She just stares at me, frowning. I have the sneaking suspicion that she knows more about me than I've just revealed to the group. She pulls a book out of her satchel, and I grimace inside when I see it's a hard back copy of my latest. DI Carina Shaw is my third series, and all the titles have the word 'missing' in them. This one is *The Missing Heart*, and the cover is suitably dark and ominous.

'It's you!' Zoe says, looking from the publicity shot on the dust cover to me. The photo is about ten years old, and I've refused to have any new ones taken – frankly I'd rather remain completely anonymous. 'You're SJ Andrews! Cal said you looked familiar. I have your books all over our house... Oh God, will you sign it for me?'

She looks incredibly flustered, and everyone is now looking at me even more intensely. I feel like screaming, and maybe launching myself out of the window and doing a duck and roll down the cliffs, never to be seen again.

'Of course,' I say, as she rummages in the bag and emerges with a sharpie. I do my now well-practised fake signature and pass it back. She sighs and hugs it to her chest.

'Authors are my rock stars,' she murmurs. 'And I'm one of your groupies! I can't believe you live here...'

I love bookshops and I love books, and I generally get on well with other people who feel the same – but I really don't want to get sucked into being some local celeb, or doing signing sessions, or getting invited to events. I did not come here for that, and I need to make it clear before Zoe's enthusiasm overtakes her.

'I'm here incognito,' I say firmly, feeling like a bit of a pillock as I speak. 'I don't really like publicity. I... Uh, I'd really rather not be on any social media or whatever, if that's okay with you?'

Lord, I sound dreadful – like a complete diva. I might as well put on a pair of sunglasses indoors and start saying 'no paparazzi, please!' as I swan around the village in a fur coat with two bodyguards. But it needs saying. The last thing I want is someone posting a picture of me on Insta.

'Are you in hiding?' Laura says, looking intrigued. 'On the run?'

I take a moment here and swallow my nerves. How much should I tell them? I'm freaked out by all this attention and really not enjoying this at all, but what is the alternative? Snubbing everyone? Packing up all my stuff and leaving? Moving from place to place, avoiding all contact with other people, until eventually I end up back at square one? No. That is another thing I cannot allow to happen.

'I kind of am,' I say quietly. 'There was a problem, back in London. A man. I don't really want to talk about it more than that right now, but I would appreciate it if you could respect my privacy.'

There is a surprised silence in the room. I've even surprised myself. Cherie reaches out and takes my hand across the table.

'Don't you worry about a thing,' she says reassuringly, squeezing my fingers. 'You'll be safe here, I absolutely promise you.'

Something about the certainty in her voice makes me almost believe her. Wouldn't that be nice, I think, to feel truly safe. Zoe nods, and adds: 'What she said. Don't worry, I won't be tweeting about our exciting new celebrity resident. To us, you're just Sarah. Our friend.'

Maxine pats me on the shoulder. 'We'll look after you, love. You can relax here. Nobody even walks down the high street without someone reporting it. And while I get that might feel a bit invasive to you right now, maybe try and view it as the world's best and most organic intruder alarm?'

'Yes,' Laura adds, pouring me some wine, 'nobody

sneaks by us. And we might call it cake club, but I reckon we'd all be pretty good in a rumble. You don't need to worry. You really don't.'

I realise, much to my horror, that I have started to tear up, and quickly swipe the moisture from my eyes. What the hell is going on here? What's happened to me? Not only did I open up to almost-strangers, but I'm close to crying in public!

'Thank you, all of you. And now please move on or I might actually explode. Is this the entire Ladies' Club?'

I'm desperate for an escape and they obviously sense that. 'We're missing my sister, Willow,' Auburn replies. 'She's currently living in Spain with her husband, Tom – he started Briarwood. They have a five-month-old baby girl called Ronda, after the place they were staying when she found out she was expecting.'

I've been to Ronda, and it is a magnificent hillside town carved into the side of a mountain. Not sure about it as a name, but as a place, it is stunning. I nod to acknowledge, and she continues: 'And Katie had to go home. She has three sons who need a lot of wrangling, and she's shacked up with my brother, Van, who's probably the most childish of the lot. Queen Edie is at her great-niece's house for dinner. Anyway … how about we move on to our agenda?'

'There's an actual agenda?' I ask.

'No,' Laura tells me. 'At least not officially. We don't even meet on set days, just squeeze it in as often as we can. We discuss super important things like the Halloween Ball at Briarwood, and Cherie's gourmet evenings in the café, and men. In particular, one man. Is it time?'

There's a flurry of people looking at their phones, and Becca announces: 'About five minutes to go. Time to take our positions, ladies.'

I have no clue what's going on, but everyone picks up their drinks and moves to tables by the window, where there is a clear and gorgeous view down to the beach. There's a breeze picking up, and the waves are crashing into the bay with more force than yesterday. I look forward to seeing this exact same vista in every different season, I realise – I don't want to ever leave. If that means a bit of adjustment on my part, then that is what I will have to do. You're never too old for personal growth. Or the *Twilight* movies, but that's just me.

'So,' Cherie says, gesturing to the window with her head. Her hair is in a big fat plait today, trailing over her shoulder in a silver and black fishtail. 'You know I said there's also a new man living here?'

'Yes. You said he was Halloween-y.'

Becca snorts out hot chocolate as she laughs at that, and Laura points at her and mocks as the liquid trails down to her chin. Sisters – the same no matter how many years they have on the clock. 'Halloween-y!' Becca says. 'What does that even mean? Does he have a carriage made from a pumpkin?'

'He could have,' Laura replies seriously, 'for all we know. I get what you mean, Cherie. He's mysterious, and dark, and brooding, and…'

'Sleeps in a coffin?' Zoe supplies, looking amused. 'Has a garlic allergy? Turns into a wolf when there's a full moon?'

'Again, for all we know, yes!' Laura answers. She sighs, looking distraught. 'None of us has even talked to him, and he's been here for three weeks! And there are stories, you know, going round the village.'

'What stories?' asks Auburn, frowning. 'And why haven't I heard them?'

'Well, Scrumpy Joe's wife, Joanne, told me she was driving past his place and she heard howling. Like, proper howling. And Leanne who runs the butchers' counter says he sounds exotic, like he might be from the States or Canada. And he buys loads of steak – pounds and pounds of rare, bloody steak!'

'So,' Zoe interjects, trying hard not to laugh, 'you think he might be … what … an American werewolf in Budbury?' I lose my own battle at that point and let out a stifled giggle. I wonder if I'll pop into that pub over the road from me, and they'll all stare and tell me to stay on the road?

'And anyway, of course the steak is rare and bloody,' Becca adds in. 'It's a butcher's shop, not a restaurant! That means nothing! Maybe he just eats a lot of protein… He certainly looks like he works out…'

They all pause here, and a communal smile seems to run from one woman to another. The debate suddenly forgotten. 'Hang on, I thought you hadn't met him?' I ask.

'We haven't met him, no,' Cherie tells me. 'But at about this time every day, he runs along the beach. And he does it *topless.*'

Laura nods vigorously, her curls bobbing around her happy face. 'It seems rude not to watch, really, when he's putting in so much effort. This is like our Diet Coke moment – you know, like that old TV advert? Except with cheesecake and booze, which is much better.'

'Oh' is all I manage to say. I feel slightly uncomfortable now. I'm not quite sure if it's because of the invasion of his privacy, or because if this was a group of men watching a woman go for a run, it would feel seedy. This doesn't, honestly. It just feels a bit silly … but still. I'm not especially enjoying the double standard.

'Here he comes!' says Laura, sounding insanely excited as she points through the window. I want to look away, or go to the loo instead, but something about the mood compels me to follow suit. Maybe it's all the talk of this man's alleged supernatural qualities, because I'm a sucker for even a hint of a mystery. Whatever the reason, I join in, staring out of the window.

I glance around and bite back the laughter. It is an amusing sight: a group of grown women, cups and glasses halfway to their lips, looks of anticipation on their faces as they wait. Laura in particular looks like she might be about to spontaneously combust.

I turn back to the window, and see what all the fuss is about. Oh. Wow. My goodness. I blink a few times, and work hard at not audibly sighing. That would be embarrassing after my vaguely self-righteous thoughts of just a few seconds ago. He is… Well, he is a work of art, to put it simply. Tall, broad-shouldered, dark hair. Powerful legs in action as he runs, his bare chest and pumping arms displaying the kind of physique you generally only get to see on television. He is eating up the distance, and all of our heads turn to follow him as he reaches the path that leads from the bay.

'Now he goes up into the village,' Laura says, her voice full of wonder. 'You and Becca could actually sit in your living rooms and watch this, you lucky cows!'

I laugh out loud, and can't imagine it: me sitting behind the net curtains, peering out and waiting for this man-God to jog past as the highlight of my day. It would be too humiliating. But maybe the upstairs window could work…

'Oh my God!' she says, jumping up to her feet in a flurry of discarded cake crumbs and excitement. 'He's stopped! He's not going into the village… He's coming here!'

She leaps away from the window and runs her hands through her curly hair, her face bright red. The other ladies all follow suit, dashing back to the original table. I stare through the glass and see that she is right: after a moment of hesitation, he is turning towards the café steps.

'Quick!' Auburn says, tugging at my shoulder. 'Come over here or it'll look like you were perving at him through the window!'

'Yes, Sarah,' Zoe adds, her tone dripping with sarcasm. 'Don't you know it's wrong to objectify men like that? Disgusting attitude!'

I'm still scurrying over to the other table when he appears in the doorway. He stands there, slightly out of breath, covered in a light sheen of sweat, sunlight cascading over his muscular shoulders.

'It's like a gift from God…' Laura mutters, as she waves at him. He smiles, and it is a stone-cold killer of a smile. There is a collective swoon, as he pulls the door open.

'Are you closed?' he asks, pointing at the sign. 'It says you are, but then I noticed the place was full. The windows were steaming up a bit.'

Yes, I think, biting my lip to keep the laughter back, that would be because of the sheer amount of lust flying around. Or, to be more polite, appreciation.

'No, no, we're never really closed!' Laura says, ushering him inside. Close up, he is even more jaw-dropping – a wide mouth, defined cheekbones, thick, slightly long hair. He has a top tied around his waist, and he tugs it back on over his head. Laura looks distinctly disappointed.

Luna yaps and then runs over to him. He immediately crouches down to give her a tummy tickle, and she rolls around in ecstasy.

'That's Luna,' Laura says, 'and I'm Laura. Let me introduce you to everyone…'

She goes around the table giving our names, and naturally enough when she gets to me, I feel my face blazing up. *Stop it*, I tell myself. *There's no need to be embarrassed. He can't read your mind.* Besides, in my experience, middle-aged women are completely invisible to young men anyway – we simply do not exist in their universe. Their eyes skim over us on the way to something more appealing and relevant. He is no older than his mid-thirties, possibly even younger than that.

His eyes, a really quite dazzling shade of green, linger on mine for a moment as we are introduced. I wait for him to skim past me, as expected, but he doesn't. A small smile plays on his lips, and for a second I worry that he actually can read my mind. Or that he's a hypnotist. Shit, what if he's a hypnotist? What if we all end up squawking like chickens every time somebody says the word 'marshmallow' or something?

'Ladies,' he says, giving us a small bow, 'it's a pleasure to meet you all. I'm Aidan. I run past here most days.'

'Do you really, love?' says Cherie, keeping an admirably straight face. 'Well, isn't that nice! Our door is always open. Unless it's closed, and that usually means we're in the pub. Can we offer you some cake, or coffee, or—'

'Anything at all!' finishes Laura, grinning up at him. 'You're living in the old Hazelwell place, out near Eggardon Hill, aren't you?'

'I am. It's beautiful. My own little patch of paradise. I'm from New York originally, and this is very different. Exactly what I needed.'

You can hear the States in his voice, but also a hint of British. At a guess he's someone who moved around as a child.

'Have you had any spooky experiences?' Auburn asks. She glances at me and adds: 'Eggardon Hill is the stuff of legends. Iron Age hillfort. Personally, I love it, but there are all kinds of stories. Hauntings. Ghouls. Cars mysteriously breaking down.'

I'm intrigued and vow to go and explore as soon as I can. I love things like that, and find ancient sites fascinating. I can look at stone circles all day long, and my mind conjures up all kinds of wonderful stories to go with them. My own mind is often a bit like my own Netflix. The upside of that is that it's free; the downside is that I can't switch it off, and the curse of having a vivid imagination is that you can imagine the bad just as easily as the good.

Before I was truly successful as a writer, I bought a ticket for the National Lottery. I lay in bed that night and fantasised about my new life as a millionaire, and it started well – financial security, freedom, world travel, multiple donations to animal sanctuaries – but within a few minutes, somehow my brain had taken me on a darker path – getting kidnapped, being pursued by con men, dying alone and scared in my Mayfair mansion. It was quite the ride.

'Nothing spooky so far,' he says, grinning. 'Other than the most supernaturally beautiful sunsets. Never seen anything quite like it. Anyway, I can't stay today. Just wanted to show my face. Next time, I'll come in with proper clothes on, and join you for a coffee. Zoe, Auburn, Cherie, Laura, Becca, Max, Sarah – I hope to see you all again soon.'

I can't believe he remembered all of our names, and from the way he looks at us all individually as he speaks, he's even matched them to the right people. Maybe there actually is something Halloween-y about him, like Cherie says. He definitely looks the part, with his piercing green eyes and all that muscle. Like he could be a weretiger or something...

He looks at me for a few more moments, and I start to wonder if I have cake smeared on my face.

'Sarah's new here too,' Laura pipes up, as he turns and walks towards the door. 'You should get together. Swap notes.'

What the actual F is she up to? I'm too surprised to even glare at her, and before I can splutter out a reply, Aidan smiles at me. That smile. It really is trouble. The kind of smile that turns women to rubble at ten paces.

'I'd love to,' he answers, his eyes meeting mine. I can't look away, no matter how much I want to. Definitely a hypnotist. He looks mildly amused at the blush that is now so bright I must look like a matchstick on legs. 'Perhaps we can watch a sunset together, Sarah?'

I manage a jerky nod, and he leaves, running back down the way he came, practically enveloped in a cloud of sex appeal and self-confidence.

'Oh my god, the way he looked at you!' says Laura, fanning herself with her hands and jumping up and down so her boobs jiggle. 'What just happened?'

'I have no idea,' I say, standing up, feeling a little unsteady. I am not happy with any of this, and realise I shouldn't have come. I should have stayed in my little house. 'But I'm not sure I like it. Laura, I literally just told you that I value my privacy – why would you do that? Why would you put me in that position?'

There is an awkward silence, and I feel momentarily bad about it. There is clearly no harm in these ladies at all, especially Laura – but even coming here was a big step for me. Making potential friends is a big step for me. Trusting anybody at all is a big step. And now I feel like I've been thrown under the matchmaking bus in a really inappropriate way.

I see Laura's face changing as she realises she's crossed a line. She glances at Cherie, and the older lady just raises her eyebrows in a 'you're on your own, kid' kind of way.

'Ohhhh... Oh no... I'm so sorry!' she stutters, her hands

flying to her face. She looks so stressed, and I'm worried she might even cry. 'I'm really, really sorry, Sarah. I didn't think. I just got carried away. He was definitely looking at you like he was interested, and—'

'He really wasn't, Laura,' I say as gently as I can, 'but even if he was, I really don't need to be set up on almost-dates with strange men. I know nothing about him, and after my last experience in the dating world… I know you didn't mean any harm, but please don't get carried away on my behalf again.'

She nods vigorously, and I now feel evil, like I've kicked a puppy. In fact, I now feel like I should apologise. Ugggh. People stuff is complicated. The real world is messy. Is it any surprise I prefer fiction?

'I won't,' she replies hastily. 'And again, I'm sorry. Please forgive me.'

'I've forgiven you already, Laura. I just… I'm really not interested in men right now.'

Not even, I tell myself, a man who looks like that. A man with a smile that could entirely possibly make me forget my own name, never mind my own rules.

Chapter Six

I stay for a little while longer, just to make sure I don't leave with any of us feeling awkward. I've said my piece, Laura has apologised, and that is that. I don't hold grudges, especially over something that I know she only thought of as a bit of fun. Over the years, as I've seen my friends and peers grow up and move on in life, I've noticed that some of them have been confused and in some cases almost challenged by me staying single. My sister being one of them – me getting married definitely had something to do with her encouragement.

I think if they're happy and content with their life, people want the same for others – which is really lovely in its own way. But 'content' doesn't look the same for everyone, and part of me really does rebel against the idea that a woman needs to be part of a couple to feel fulfilled. Maybe I just haven't met the right person, or maybe I'm just not made that way. I've always found being part of a couple stifling, and in my own experience it's taken away more than it's given. Possibly just more than I was willing to give.

I sometimes wish things had been different. I would have liked children, but it never happened for me with a partner, and I was never quite determined enough to make it happen by myself. The thought of being a single mum daunted me. I suppose I was convinced that I'd mess it up somehow. I realise now, as I head into my fifties and know quite a lot of parents, that everyone feels like that. There is no instruction manual, no magic formula for being a good mum. Maybe I should have done it, but there's no point even in wondering now – I will never know.

It's the mums with younger kids who drift off first from the coffee club, Laura and Becca both heading home. Becca, I learn, does not drink, so she is always the designated driver. 'I don't mind,' she says, shrugging her shoulders. 'Laura tips me in cake.'

Laura apologises yet again before she leaves, and I can tell she still feels a bit bad about it. 'It's okay,' I assure her. 'I know you were just trying to do me a favour. We're fine, honest, as long as you don't try and pimp me out again.'

'Are you sure?' she asks, looking slightly wistful. 'He was very nice. And so hot there was practically steam coming off him…'

'That was the sweat from his run, and yes, I'm sure.'

She nods in reluctant understanding, then disappears off with her sister, slightly tipsy after all her Baileys hot chocolates. Auburn goes with them, getting a lift as Briarwood is apparently 'up the world's biggest hill'. Zoe promises to drop me off a booklet about Eggardon Hill and other local legends, then heads away. Maxine is collected by her partner, Gabriel, who calls in to say hello. And by that I mean he says 'hello', and literally not one word more. He's strikingly handsome, in a wild and untamed way, with a smile that only comes out to play when he sees his lady. I might be the least romantic woman in the world, but the sight of that intense connection does make me sigh inside.

Eventually, I'm left alone with Cherie, and help her to clear up. We stack the plates and mugs in the big dishwasher and wipe over the tables. Luna assists ably by dealing with any cake spillage, like a furry four-legged hoover snuffling around between our feet. By the time it's all done, it's dark outside, and yet again I find myself alone with Cherie in the café.

She's wearing a magnificent flowing kaftan, black with gold trim, and her plait has come slightly loose. You rarely see ladies of her age with such long hair. She catches me looking, and says: 'If anyone sneaks up behind me and cuts this off, I'll lose all my strength. Like Samson.'

I can't imagine Cherie losing her strength. She is physically imposing, but she also exudes an air of confidence and security, of being totally comfortable in her own skin. Even the fact that she openly talks about sometimes being lonely, about missing her husband Frank, seems to make her stronger, not weaker. She embraces all that she is in a way I can only admire and possibly envy.

'I doubt it,' I reply. 'Samson was obviously a wuss in comparison. I suspect you're made of sterner stuff. Right, anyway, thanks for a lovely time. I better be going.'

'Are you sure?' she asks, raising her eyebrow. 'I have a bottle of Calvados upstairs…'

Calvados. Apple brandy. That sounds incredibly dangerous. I definitely shouldn't stay for Calvados.

'Okay,' I say immediately. 'Just the one, though. I have a lot of work to do.'

She smiles and replies: 'Attagirl. That's the spirit!'

I follow her through the kitchens, to a small staircase at the back. The steps creak as we make our way up, and with all the lights off in the main part of the building, it's very slightly spooky. Or maybe all this talk of Halloween and haunted hills has got the better of me. Despite my vivid imagination and interest in the supernatural, I've led a decidedly dull life on that front: I've never seen a ghostly face in the mirror other than my own, never encountered a poltergeist, never fallen through a timeslip in Trafalgar Square. I suppose there's still time.

We emerge into Cherie's little flat and I stare around in appreciation. It is small but perfectly formed, with skylights that frame square portraits of the dark, starry sky above. The sofa is covered with a red velvet throw with gold tassels, there are photos everywhere, and one corner is filled with a huge vinyl collection and an old-fashioned record player that looks as though it's lived a life and a half. As she gets us drinks, I stroll around and take it all in, the colourful knick-knacks, the incense burners and their little piles of ash, the shimmering bead curtain through into the kitchen. It's bright and bold and eccentric, the ultimate reflection of its owner.

I pause in front of a framed poster for the 1970 Isle of

Wight Festival. 'That was a good one,' she says, passing me a glass. I'm pretty sure you shouldn't drink Calvados in full tumblers, but there you go. I raise my eyebrows at it and she says: 'Well, you said one glass. You didn't specify the size. You're lucky it's not a pint.'

I snort out a laugh, because I already wouldn't rule that out. 'Were you there?' I ask. 'At the festival?'

'I was. I was at all of them. That was the year with The Who, The Doors, Hendrix… It's where I met my first husband, Wally.'

I glance at her tanned face, the crinkled laughter lines and the eyes that have almost disappeared into her smile, and can totally picture her there. 'Have you got photos?' I ask.

'Not many,' she replies, frowning. 'It wasn't like it is now, back then. These days, everybody takes pictures of everything, including their dinner. But this was pre-digital, and not many people had cameras. I have a few though, if you really want to see?'

'I really do. I warn you now, I'm sneakily nosy.'

'I've noticed. Okay, sit yourself down and I'll find a few snaps from the past. Any music preference?'

I tell her I'll let her choose, and within a few minutes she has joined me on the sofa with a small album on her lap, the mellow sound of Nina Simone playing in the background, the distinct hiss and crackle of well-played vinyl. Luna is snuggled up in a basket, but the occasional glance tells me I'm probably in her usual spot.

Cherie shows me a picture of her as a young woman, sprawled on a patch of grass, a cigarette in her fingers.

Her hair is rich and dark and shining in the sun, parted in the middle and draped with a coronet made of daisies. Her bell-bottom jeaned legs seem to go on forever, and are paired with a leather waistcoat that barely covers her assets. She is absolutely gorgeous, the very epitome of a carefree flower child.

'Wow,' I say, smiling as I turn the pages. 'You look stunning. And so happy.'

'I was … although the weather was pretty rotten, I seem to recall. When it was all over, I got separated from my friends on the way home. It was carnage really, pure hippy chaos, and I ended up hitchhiking. Wally picked me up, and it was the best thing that ever happened to me. Totally changed my life.'

She shows me a few more shots and tells me a few more stories, and she seems to be enjoying it. It's fascinating, really, this glimpse into her world – you can totally see those origins in the woman she still is today. The herbal cigarettes, the kaftans, the hair, this little flat that feels like somewhere the Beatles would have hung out during their guru meditation phase. Cherie is unlike anyone I have ever met before.

'So,' she says, propping her feet up on the multi-coloured pouffe in front of us, 'do you want to talk about it? The reason you were so worried about your privacy. I get that you're a bit of a public figure, but it was more than that, wasn't it? What happened?'

I stare at her, quite surprised at the sudden turnaround. One minute I'm listening to her tales of hanging out in rock bands' dressing rooms, and the next the spotlight is on me. I have never enjoyed the spotlight.

'This is the part where I should say "you don't have to talk about it if you don't want to", I know,' she adds, looking at my closed-off expression. 'But I think you probably should. If this is a fresh start for you, maybe you should clear the air with yourself.'

I'd never thought of it like that. Clearing the air is something we always do with others, isn't it? But she's right, in a way – maybe it's more important we do it with ourselves. Face up to our fears, forgive ourselves for the things we are ashamed of. Allow ourselves the same space and kindness as we allow others. Sitting here, in this cosy room, with this ageless woman, it makes sense. Going against a lifetime of self-conditioning, I decide to talk to someone about it all. I nod abruptly and gulp down way too much Calvados at once. I almost choke, and that wouldn't be a bad way to go – killed by strong French liquor.

'Um, well, there's not that much to tell,' I say slowly, trying to form my thoughts into an orderly queue. 'His name was Martin. We met in the park, and he was walking his dog. I always trust people with dogs, but I later found out it wasn't even his… He was walking it for his boss. He didn't tell me that. I suppose maybe that was the first clue – fake dog ownership.'

'Definitely a red flag. Go on.'

'Well, it was a cute dog, and we got chatting and he seemed very nice. Good-looking, but in an approachable way, you know. He told me he was a freelance web designer, divorced, in his early fifties. The only true part of any of that was his age. The rest was all made up. I still haven't figured out why he'd go for those things, if he was going to lie. I mean, why not say he was a retired astronaut or a Nobel prize winning poet or something?'

'I suppose,' Cherie responds, frowning as she thinks about it, 'that maybe you wouldn't have believed him? Sounds like he was trying to be an everyman kind of guy?'

I nod. She's probably right. I don't like talking about this at all, but I notice that it is easier than I expected it to be.

'Anyway, to cut a long story short, we started seeing each other. I'd been single for a very long time, and I suppose maybe I was a little lonely … or maybe it's just that I thought I should, you know, be with somebody. It was nice, having a person to do things with, go out for dinners, go to galleries, meet up for coffees. It was maybe a month or so into it that I started to notice a few strange things about him, stuff that didn't add up. Like he could never do Saturdays, which is odd when you're a freelance web designer, isn't it? And that I could never go to his place, because it was being redecorated … for a whole month. It's not like I was ready for marriage or whatever, but I suppose I was ready to be more intimate. To see what would happen next.'

His face is still so vivid in my mind – brown eyes that at first I thought were kind. An easy smile. The way all of that kindness and ease could disappear in the blink of a brown eye, and turn to contempt. It was like he had two faces, and they were the complete opposites of each other.

'What did happen?' Cherie asks, grabbing the bottle and topping up my drink.

'Nothing dramatic, nothing sudden. But I suppose I kept asking questions, and was getting increasingly confused by the answers. I had the opportunity to go on a work trip to Lisbon for a week, to meet my publishers there, and I asked him if he wanted to come. He said his passport was out of date, which again seemed odd. I asked him if he wanted to meet my twin sister, and he always cancelled – or sometimes found a way to make me cancel. Like not only didn't *he* want to meet her, he also didn't want me to see her either.

'Then a few things happened that made me even more concerned … like messages disappearing from my phone, and people later asking me why I hadn't replied; my old address book going missing. Entries on my calendar being deleted. The doorman in my building greeting him like an old friend, even though as far as I knew, they'd only met a few times. He was … creeping into my life, and very subtly trying to take it over. It was happening so slowly I could almost convince myself I was imagining it.'

Cherie makes a snorting noise, and shakes her head. 'That's what they do, isn't it? Men like that? Make you think you're going mad? I bet every time you talked to him about it, he looked all sad, like you'd hurt his precious feelings by daring to doubt him?'

'Exactly that! Later, I asked the doorman, and he said he'd been around quite a bit. He'd obviously somehow made a copy of my key and was letting himself in on days I wasn't at home. Which he knew because he'd also been rummaging around in my phone, and by extension, my life. Amazing how much we put on those things. I don't anymore.'

'Luckily, I barely know how to use mine,' she answers, grimacing. 'WhatsApp is the outer limit of my ability. But I know what you mean; it's like your whole brain is downloaded into your phone these days.'

'Absolutely, and it's not good,' I reply firmly. 'It's bad enough if you just lose it, never mind have it invaded. Anyway. This dragged on for maybe another month, with me getting more and more paranoid, him getting more and more controlling. Every time I got to the stage where I just wanted to end it, he somehow pulled it back. There would be some grand romantic gesture, a night in a swish hotel, my favourite flowers, whatever. He had some kind of sixth sense for when I was about to end it. I felt like I couldn't end it, like I was trapped. Looking back, I'm so angry with myself.'

'I don't see why you should be,' Cherie replies. 'It wasn't your fault. You were just being a human. He was being a monster. How did it all work out? Obviously, not well, from the fact that you've moved hundreds of miles away.'

'I didn't just move because of him, Cherie. I was ready for something new anyway, and I've always wanted to live by the sea. But I can't deny getting away from him was a real bonus – even though I still think about him way too often for my liking. Eventually, I did something totally out of character – I hired a private investigator. The way I saw it, either something was wrong, and I needed to know, or I was indeed just being paranoid and potentially ruining a good relationship with my own insecurities. Like he constantly told me I was.'

I had all kinds of pre-conceived ideas about what a P.I. would be like, most of which turned out to be completely untrue. For a start, mine was a woman in her thirties, fit and healthy and without any apparent tendencies towards alcoholism, depression, or wearing rumpled trench coats. She listened to what I had to say and nodded in a way that seemed to imply she'd heard this kind of story a few times before. She took some details and asked me what I was hoping to get out of this. The truth, I said, no matter how boring or how ugly. Just the truth.

It didn't actually take very long for it all to unravel. I told her when he'd be at mine, and one morning she followed him when he left. Cheryl, the P.I. is a very ordinary-looking lady, neither too big or too small or too pretty or too fashionable. Not noticeable in any way at all. I'm guessing that must be an asset in her line of work. She certainly seemed to have no problem trailing 'Martin' all the way back to a three-bedroomed semi-detached house in Wembley. Once she had that address, she was easily able to discover the rest.

I explain some of this to Cherie, who shakes her head in astonishment. His real name was Scott Jones and he actually worked in HR for an IT firm. He was married, not divorced, and had three children – one of whom played tennis at county level, and who he had to take to matches most Saturdays. He did not own a dog, or in fact even a cat. Everything he had told me was a complete fabrication.

A little more digging by Cheryl revealed that his

marriage wasn't exactly on steady ground, and that the police had been called to the property on several occasions to deal with domestic disputes. He had no criminal record, but her contact in the police force confided that they suspected there was more to him than met the eye.

I was horrified on so many levels. I felt like an idiot, for being taken in so easily. I felt like a gullible, desperate fool, one so keen to find a man that she would fall for a pack of lies. And I felt like a vile, morally bankrupt piece of trash for having slept with another woman's husband. No matter how many times I told myself that I hadn't known he was married, I still felt dirty and soiled by it. I would never, ever do that, not in a million years. It's one of the many things I will never forgive him for: making me break a deeply held rule, something that I was especially sensitive about since my husband was unfaithful to me.

While listening to Cheryl calmly present her report, I managed to hold myself together, at least on the surface. Inside, I was a mass of emotions – bitterness, self-pity, disappointment, fury, and good old-fashioned anxiety.

'I'd change all your locks, your passwords, your phone number, and get all of your IT devices professionally checked if I were you,' Cheryl had said, all business. 'We can't be sure what his motivation was, and you've said that there's been no financial intrusion, but that doesn't mean we can rule it out. You also need to consider whether to file a police report or not. The issue is, lying to a woman isn't actually a crime – although personally I think it bloody well should be!'

'Can you imagine?' I'd said, momentarily distracted by

the idea. 'They'd have to build new jails! I have… I have no clue why he's done this. What has he gained?'

'I can't answer that. Only he can. Could be he's playing a long game, and eventually he'd have asked you for something – an investment in his business, a loan, whatever. Could be he genuinely liked you, and like a lot of middle-aged men, was living out a fantasy life because he was bored of his real one. Could be that he's just a sick, twisted scumbag who gets his kicks by manipulating women. There's a lot to think about, and you need to make some decisions about how to proceed. I'd obviously suggest ending it immediately, and taking security precautions. Just because he doesn't have a criminal record doesn't mean he isn't potentially dangerous.'

I stayed in a hotel that night, while I tried to process everything I'd learned. I felt like a cliché. I needed to hide away and lick my wounds, and also come up with a plan. Ironically, he called me over twenty times that night. This was not unusual; if I didn't answer, he didn't just leave a message and wait for a call back, he just kept ringing. I suppose I'd gotten used to it, persuaded myself it was a sign that he was so keen to speak to me. In reality, it was a sign that he was unhinged and didn't like to have me out of his control.

The next day, when I went back to my flat, he was waiting for me there – outside, as though he didn't actually have a key at all. I didn't want him inside with me, and insisted that we went to a nearby café instead. Once we were there, I told him it was over. I told him I knew who he really was and that he'd lied to me. I had no idea how he was going to react. Part of me expected him to deny it, or to claim he'd done it because he had genuinely fallen for me and got in too deep. What I didn't expect was what actually happened.

He listened to my words, which I'd managed to speak with an amazing level of calm, considering the turmoil going on inside me, and then everything changed. His eyes, his face, his voice – it was like he morphed into a completely different human being. Even now, almost a year later, I can still see that transformation. It's burned into my eyeballs, a dark stain that I can never wash out.

'You arrogant bitch,' he'd said, his voice so low that nobody around us could possibly hear him. 'You don't get to end things with me! You're the one who was desperate. You're the one who started this. Locked in your ivory tower writing your stupid books, you couldn't wait to find a real man, instead of the ones you made up. And at your age, who the hell is going to want you anyway? I felt sorry for you, that's all!'

I just stared at him, feeling like he'd slapped me. I went to stand up, to leave before I gave him the satisfaction of seeing me cry, but he grabbed hold of my hand and held it so tight I could feel the little bones in my wrist grinding against each other.

'You. Don't. Leave. Me. Understand? This is over when I say it is, and not before.'

I was terrified, but also angry. Angry that this absolute arsehole of a man felt he had the right to treat me like this, to treat his wife like this, to treat anybody like this.

'You're wrong about that, *Scott.* It is over. If you touch

me again, contact me again, even so much as mention my name again, I'll report you to the police. And your wife, now I come to think of it. I'll tell anyone who will listen what you did to me.'

'Yeah? And how are you going to prove it? It's my word against yours. I'll just tell them the truth – that you were begging for it. Good luck proving I've done anything criminally wrong. My wife? Well, she'll be annoyed for a bit, but she'll forgive me in the end. She always does.'

He sniggered at that, and my overwhelming feeling in that moment was one of horror – horror that I'd been so thoroughly fooled. Horror that after years of solitary behaviour I'd gone against my instincts and finally let someone into my life only for them to turn out to be this hideous creature sitting across from me. How could I have got it so very wrong?

I ran from that coffee shop, into the rainy London streets, tears in my eyes, my heart pounding. I didn't go home for another week, not until the locks had been changed, the doorman briefed, and all my devices replaced. Even then, I didn't feel safe. The place was still filled with memories of him. Of him in my bed, of him drinking wine at my dining table while we ate dinner. Of us sitting together on the sofa watching movies. Of all the normal, day-to-day stuff that I had wanted to believe in, but that in the end had done nothing more than show me I was right all along – I shouldn't trust anybody. And more to the point, I shouldn't trust myself.

Cherie takes all of this in, remaining silent as I tell the story, lost in the past and my own regrets. I am surprised to feel tears on my cheeks when I finish, and even more surprised when Cherie reaches out and takes me into her arms. She holds me there, letting me cry for what feels like forever. I don't even fight it. It feels good. She is big and warm and solid and kind, and those are all wonderful things to have in your life. When I finally pull away, borderline embarrassed at the snot and tears, she says: 'You poor thing. None of it was your fault, you know that, don't you? Was that the end of it, then? Did he leave you alone?'

'No. At least I don't think so. I'd get anonymous cards through the post – you know, like sympathy cards for when someone has died. Once I got a delivery of flowers, and when I opened the box, every single one of them was dead. Lilies. He started leaving really awful reviews about my books on websites, under the name Martin Clifton, which is what he'd claimed he was called. He did other things, too. And … well, there were times when I thought I was being followed. I know I was probably imagining it, just stressed about it all, but I'd get that feeling, like I was being watched, you know?'

Cherie pats my hand and passes me a tissue from the box next to her. 'Understandable to feel like that, my darling, but also possibly true. Don't assume you were being paranoid. He sounds like exactly the kind of creep who'd do something like that. Has it carried on, all this time?'

'Again, I think so. I can't be one hundred percent sure, but there are constant small things happening. Maybe with less frequency. Maybe he's getting bored of torturing me. But only a few weeks ago, someone posted a photo of me on social media, my face attached to a naked woman's head. It was very obviously fake, but still, this stuff is embarrassing, and the online world can be cruel… I mainly stay off the internet, but my publicist noticed it. That could have been him, I suppose. Or it could have been your bog-standard online weirdo. I really, really don't like people knowing who I am.'

'Tough in your line of work,' she replies sympathetically.

'Yes. I just want to do the writing. Ideally, I'd be completely anonymous.'

She thinks it over for a few seconds, then asks: 'Is this why you didn't look too happy about giving your phone number out earlier?'

'You noticed that, did you? Well, yes, it is. When I took my phone in to the place Cheryl had recommended, they found he'd installed some basic spyware on it, so he could always know what I was doing, who I was talking to. A few weird things had happened with it, so luckily I only ever spoke to Cheryl on the landline or in person – unheard of these days, right? But it freaked me out. I was a cautious person before, but now … I don't think I'll ever believe anybody ever again. Nobody is who they seem.'

Cherie pulls another tissue out of the box, and gently dabs under my eyes. Then she places her palms on either side of my face, and gazes at me.

'That, my love, is complete crap,' she says seriously. 'Many of us are exactly what we seem. Others take a while to figure out. You've been through a terrible ordeal, and of course you're scarred by it. But that man is the exception, not the rule. Don't give up on the whole world because of him – don't give him that power. Nobody is perfect, for sure, but you have to be willing to see the good in people. To take a leap of faith every now and then.'

'If I took a leap of faith, I'd land in a cow pat.'

'Well, that's a very real possibility in this neck of the woods, my sweet, I won't lie. But give us all a chance. You never know. You might just surprise yourself.'

I nod as though I'm agreeing, but inside I'm really not. I absolutely hate surprises.

Chapter Seven

For the next few days, I keep myself to myself. I genuinely do have a lot of work to catch up on, and I'm starting to realise that living out of cardboard boxes is not a sustainable long-term lifestyle choice. I force myself to unpack the last of them, and that allows me to take stock of what I'm missing. Mainly, I think, I'd like to get a few more bits and bobs – some pictures for the walls maybe, or some house plants. I might even decorate, get some colour into the place. I feel like I could love this little house, so I might as well put some effort in.

My suspicions that I'd accidentally left my yoga mat in London turn out to be right. It's not been a huge issue, because I've been so busy since I got here that I've barely had time to even say the words downward dog never mind get into one. I order a new mat anyway. It's good for me, and I enjoy it. At some point my brain will feel like it's going to implode, and I'll need to start fixing it by twisting my body into weird positions. I'm not sure of the science behind it all, but it definitely works for me. Plus, I'm almost fifty – anything that stops my joints seizing up has got to be a win.

I clear the little patio garden of the leaves that are now starting to fall, and I add 'bird feeder' to my mental list of things I should get. I have no idea where to find all of these random items, but I remember Laura saying that Max renovates houses and is a whizz at interior design. Apparently, she's done all of Cherie's holiday cottages out at the Rockery. I'm sure she'll have some suggestions – maybe a local antique shop, or a market. Before I left her flat a few nights ago, Cherie wrote down everybody's names, phone numbers and addresses on a sheet of paper for me. It was delightfully old-school and analogue, and I have the list pinned up on the cork board in the kitchen.

Today, I decide, I will venture out. I've spent the last forty-eight hours doing edits on my latest book, which is always an intense time. I really do need to get into the real world again now, or I know from experience that I will be tempted to never leave the house again. I could get my groceries delivered and exercise in my courtyard, and shun all of humanity for the rest of my life. I'd be found here in a hundred years, covered in cobwebs, my dead, bony fingers still resting on my keyboard. The End.

I shudder at the image, because there is a grain of truth in it – I could easily turn into a hermit. It's yet another reason why I didn't buy a bigger property, somewhere more secluded. If I start going down that path I might never stop. My work and my personality are isolating enough without encouraging it.

I pick up the landline, a garish shade of red, and dial Max's number. She answers straight away, and sounds a bit breathless. 'Are you okay?' I ask. 'And, uh, this is Sarah by the way. Sarah who you met at the café. I hope you don't mind me calling.'

I suddenly feel like an idiot. Why am I bothering this person I hardly know when I could just use the internet to find things out? Isn't that what a modern woman does these days? Or is part of me secretly yearning to reach out a little, to see what happens if I take maybe not a leap of faith, but a baby step of faith? I saw what these women share, the easy way they communicate and support each other. The way they're all so different, but when they're together, all seem the same. I saw it, and perhaps here, in my fresh start place, I would like to see how that feels. I have never been blessed with a wide social circle, and the woman I've been closest to has been my sister – and it's fair to say our relationship isn't always silky smooth.

'Sarah! So nice to hear from you! And yes, I'm fine. I was just, um…'

She pauses, and I blush. I'm glad she can't see me. I have the awful feeling that I maybe just interrupted her having sex.

'Well, I know it's hard to visualise,' she continues, 'but I've just been chased around a field by a pair of naughty donkeys! I thought they'd look cute with witch's hats on, you know, with holes cut out for their ears? They disagreed. Violently.'

'Oh! Right. Well, that's good. I thought maybe you were … uh…'

'Mid-bonk? Sadly not, Gabriel's away looking at a house we're thinking of buying in Somerset. First Dorset, now Somerset – next it'll be Paris and Milan! How can I help you anyway?'

'Well, I've finally finished unpacking, and I've decided I'm probably going to decorate, and maybe buy some … well, I suppose the polite term would be bric-a-brac.'

'Oh, goodie!' she exclaims, and I picture her clapping her hands. 'Nothing says "home" quite like a bunch of carefully curated tat! You've come to the right woman. In fact, I was thinking of heading out to an antiques fair down the coast today, if you want to join me? I could pick you up in an hour or so?'

I remember that Max and Gabriel live in an old farmhouse outside town, and wonder out loud if I could cycle there. It's a gorgeous clear day and I've been cooped up inside for way too long. I haven't used my bike once since I arrived.

'Er, you could if you wanted to,' Max replies, sounding frankly appalled at the idea. 'But it is a few miles, and it is a bit windy, and it is a bit hilly… Are you sure?'

I tell her I am, and jot down her directions. They're very 'countryside' – turn left at the cattle grid, take a left at the water trough, straight across at the scarecrow, that kind of thing, but it seems straightforward enough. I'm on my way within thirty minutes, after a quick wash and brush up, feeling exhilarated as I fly down the country lanes. The October air is cool against my cheeks, but the physical effort soon warms me up, and I'm decidedly pink by the time I finally arrive at the house. Which, by the way, and sorry to be childish, is called Pumpwell Farm.

I can't quite keep the smirk off my face as I see the sign, and Max rolls her eyes in understanding. 'I know,' she says. 'I was the same. Right. Do you want to meet the donkeys? My dog, Gary, is away with Gabriel, or you'd be able to meet him too.'

I love the way she talks about the animals as though they are people who I absolutely need to be introduced to. I say yes to the donkeys, who I'm told are called Belle and Beast. Belle is horrendously ugly and screeches at me, waving her huge yellowing teeth in my face.

'Ah, she likes you!' Max says, and I have to give her a sideways look to check she's not joking. 'No, seriously – she hasn't tried to bite you, that means she likes you. She's mellowed out a lot since we adopted Beast. She was a temperamental old moo when she was living alone. Anyway. Are you ready for an adventure in the heady world of antiques?'

'An adventure? Will it be like an episode of Lovejoy? Will there be a roguishly handsome art dealer charming us over a pint of scrumpy?'

'Well, that's not happened to me so far, but who knows? I can see why you do the job you do, with an imagination like that. Every day must be a bit of an adventure in your head!'

I leave the bike by the front door of the farmhouse, as Max assures me there will be no passing bicycle thieves on the prowl, and we climb into her car.

'Not really,' I reply, doing up my seat belt. I'm

uncharacteristically excited about this trip, though – I really need to get out more. 'My life is very dull.'

'Ah, but surely your internal life is rich? I bet you tell yourself stories all the time!'

'I do,' I concede, as she drives us through picturesque lanes dripping with evergreen hedgerows and swirling autumn leaves, 'but they're not always nice stories. It's not all rainbows and unicorns and roguishly handsome art dealers. I'm more of a "worst case scenario" kind of girl.'

'I get that,' she says, tucking a strand of her long dark hair behind her ear. 'And life often has a way of proving you right, doesn't it? When I moved here, I was a mess. My husband had had an affair, and when he left me for the other woman, he took all my self-confidence with him.'

'I'm so sorry Max. I've… I've been there, too. It really hurts. And it definitely doesn't boost your belief in happy endings.'

'Look up!' she says suddenly, pointing ahead of us. 'It's a sparrowhawk! They're so pretty … but some little creature down here is about to have a terrible day…'

I watch the bird hovering on the wind currents, and I smile at its effortless grace. There are more wild creatures than you'd think in London, but seeing them here is somehow even more natural. In London, a sparrowhawk might be diving for a discarded sausage roll.

'Anyway,' she continues, 'I get that, too. I never expected to find a happy ending. Maybe I thought I didn't even deserve one, that I must be a crap wife and a crap mum and a crap human, or why else would he have done that to me?'

'I'm not sure, but possibly because he was a bit of a twat?'

'Indeed, eloquently put – I can see you're a wordsmith! He was a bit of a twat, but we're okay now. Much easier to be laid back about it all now I have Gabriel and I'm happier than I've ever been in my life. I genuinely didn't think it was even possible to be this happy, not without some class-A party drugs in your system. When I'm with him, I feel like I'm on ecstasy all the time!'

She sounds thrilled about it, but I'm not so sure that would suit me. I've always valued my self-control too much to do drugs, or to even be curious about how it would feel to abandon my inhibitions. It would be scary, for sure. Still… I remember the way Gabriel looked at her that day in the café. The way his guarded face came to light, the way their eyes seemed to sparkle for each other. Okay. Maybe that would be nice … but it's not for the likes of me.

'What about you?' she asks, her accent telling me she is originally from somewhere near Birmingham. 'Any romance on the horizon? Barring Laura's misguided attempts to matchmake you with… Oh God, what was his name? The American werewolf in Budbury?'

'Aidan,' I say quietly. How could she forget? Even his name is sexy. Not to mention the way he said it, his voice so deep and self-assured.

'Yes, that's it, Aidan. He doesn't live far from us you know. Closer to Eggardon Hill. You could even go home that way if you took a slightly different route.'

'Why would I want to do that?' I ask, frowning. 'I'm not

interested in him, and I'm one hundred percent sure he's not interested in me!'

'Um, I know. I just thought you were interested in Eggardon, that's all. Lady, you doth protest too much!'

I laugh and hide my face in my hands. I know it's blazing when I finally come out again. 'Okay,' I say, 'I admit he was cute. I'm only flesh and blood. But no, to answer your original question, no romance. I'm all about the self-love.'

'Self-love is important,' she agrees, nodding wisely. 'Just make sure you don't run out of batteries!'

That sets the tone for the rest of the trip really, and we laugh all the way to the antiques market. It turns out to be in a huge old warehouse in a small town on the Devon border, and is packed with an entire world of 'carefully curated tat'. Some stalls are offering genuine antiques with eye-watering prices and letters of provenance; others are flogging copies of Vogue from the eighties and collections of vintage Pez dispensers.

Max is in her element, veering from stall to stall, making small talk with people she knows. She bargains her way into two elaborate cast-iron fireguards that she says will be 'just perfect' for her latest project, and pays what seems like way too much money for a pottery badger.

'It's junk really,' she says, as she places it in her bag, 'but we have a badger sett in the woods at the back of the farm. Gabriel loves badgers, and he named them all after different types of lager. This one looks just like Estrella. Have you seen anything you fancy? Have you got a theme in mind, colour or otherwise?'

We talk my ideas over for a while, and I end up promising to look at her beloved Farrow & Ball paint card before I make any decisions. I'm kind of thinking dusky pinks, lavenders and mauves, and Max is practically salivating at the thought. She clearly loves her job. I end up buying a gorgeous oil painting of Lyme Bay, not done by anybody famous but still so pretty I can't take my eyes off it. I pick up a couple of lovely glass vases, some old leather-bound books about insects with amazing illustrations, and finally a crocheted toilet roll holder with a plastic doll's head on top. It comes complete with a free toilet roll, and you can't go wrong with that.

'Very retro,' Max says, eyeing up her purple ball dress and blonde hair, poking the matching woollen bonnet perched on her head.

'It's awful I know, but my nan used to have one of these in her bathroom. It's a really vivid memory from when I was a kid. I shall call her Loo-ise.'

I'm elated with my purchases, and truthfully also with the company. Max is laid back and fun, and although she does ask a lot of questions, she also shares as well, so I don't feel like I'm being interrogated. She fills me in on the background of the other ladies, and I find myself dumbstruck when she reveals the painful stories that so many of them have. None of it is a secret, she stresses, so I know she's not gossiping.

I would never in a million years have guessed that Laura had lost her first husband, widowed by an accident when she was so young, left with two children to raise alone. Or that Zoe moved here because her best friend passed away from breast cancer, and she took over the care of her teenage daughter, Martha. Or that Auburn and her sister Willow, the one who lives in Spain, nursed their mum through years of Alzheimer's at home.

'And Edie,' she explains on the drive home, 'Edie... Well, this is a strange one really. But you might notice that Edie sometimes takes extra food home from the café, or mentions her fiancé.'

'Fiancé? Crikey, that's optimistic – isn't she ninety-nine?'

'She is! And her fiancé was actually killed during the Second World War. She just ... sometimes thinks he's still around.'

I blink at this one. Edie seemed completely with it when I met her – all her marbles very much present and correct, despite her age. I turn it over in my mind and just shrug. 'Well, I don't suppose it's doing any harm, is it? And she seems happy enough with her life.'

'Exactly. That's what I decided when I found out. And who knows? Maybe he *is* still around...'

She says it in a spooky voice, and takes her hands off the wheel for a second to make wavy movements with her fingers. I assume the gestures mean 'supernatural' to her.

We move on to other topics, but I know that one will settle in my mind. The old lady who is nearing a hundred, and her dead-but-not-dead-to-her fiancé. The human psyche is an incredible thing, and we're all capable of convincing ourselves of the impossible, I suspect.

Max persuades me to come inside for a coffee, and we agree that I will call around with my car tomorrow to collect my treasures. Except the doll toilet roll holder – she's coming home with me in my bike's basket. She's too special to leave behind even for just one day.

Max and Gabriel's home is beautiful, and her obvious talent is on full display – the way she has perfectly combined the age of the old farm building with modern style, the two somehow complementing each other. She proudly places the pottery badger next to a jug that has been decorated with the face of a donkey. The rest of the room is pristine, and somehow these two deeply personal and deeply eccentric items make it even better.

By the time we've had a cuppa and I've used the facilities, it really is time for me to go. I plan to cycle home the long way so I can see this famous hill, and if I'm in the mood, I might even stay there to watch the sunset. It'll mean riding home in semi-darkness, but I have lights on the bike and I'm unlikely to be caught up in traffic.

'Be careful,' she warns me as I leave. 'Who knows what they used to get up to in an Iron Age hillfort.'

'Pretty much the same as people get up to now, I suspect, but without electricity or plumbing. See you tomorrow?'

With one final screech from Belle the belligerent donkey, I'm on my way. Max's instructions are fresh in my mind, and as predicted there are no other vehicles on the road. I get the feeling that me being here constitutes rush hour. The only other creatures I encounter are ones with wings, or farm animals in fields. I can't remember the last time I was in a place so secluded, and when I start to feel slightly spooked by it, I remind myself that the safest place to be is away from other humans. Crime rates are probably very low among herds of cows.

I find the path that leads to the hill and push my bike along it past late-season blooms. Blackberries droop from trailing vines, along with small purple-black fruits that look like damsons. There are sloes and rosehips and hazel, a tangle of wild foliage that looks like a forager's feast. The air is alive with birdsong, and the fading day is still warm enough for me to be wearing a light sweater instead of the heavier fleece that is folded in my basket.

I prop the bike up and clamber over a small wooden stile. The hill is steep, but the grass-covered sides are covered in ridges, giving it the appearance of having terraces cut into the slope. A small collection of sheep is grazing, staring up at me with curiosity as I pass. A quick look, and back to chewing grass.

It's hard to describe without sounding like a flake, but as I walk along, it's like I can actually feel the age of the place. The ancient history is practically singing out loud as I start to climb, connecting me to those who lived here thousands of years ago. How many feet have trodden these same paths, I wonder, over the last few millennia?

It's sneakily difficult going, and when I finally reach the top, I stand, hands on hips, and enjoy a moment of pure triumph. Wow, I think, gazing around me, this was very much worth it. Every step I took brought me here, to the top of the world. Where, again, countless people must have stood and gazed in amazement at what they saw before them.

The view is slightly different from each angle, a

patchwork quilt of luscious green fields, tumbling hills, and in the very distance the sparkling shimmer of the sea. I can hear no sign of the outside world, of traffic or people or alleged civilisation. It's just me and the sheep, and the sheer mind-blowing beauty of this magical place.

I take a sip of water and settle myself on the ground, my knees bent in front of me. It's getting cooler, and I let my hair down to keep my neck warm, wrapping my arms around my legs and hugging them in. The sun is huge in the sky, a circle of orange flame jostling through clouds streaked with pinks and purples. The colours are astonishing, rippling before my eyes, ever-changing. I am lost to its beauty, completely captivated. If I never see another sunset again, this one would be enough. I consider trying to take a picture of it, but I know I could never quite capture its magnificence. Better to simply sit, and watch, and remember.

It takes its time sliding down towards the horizon, huge fingers of gold spreading over the landscape as the sun makes its last stand. The fields and hills come alive, the sea sparkles, and the whole world feels transformed. It's so dazzling that I realise I've been holding my breath, enraptured by the sight of this perfect moment when day sinks into night.

I sigh out loud and shake my head. I don't care how tough the climb was. I don't care that I'm going home in twilight. I don't care that I'm now shivering. That was so worth it.

I'm about to climb back up to my feet when a voice comes from behind me.

'Beautiful, isn't it?'

I go suddenly dead still, my body and mind flicking straight from peace and serenity to sheer panic in a split second. My hands clench into fists, and my fingernails cut into the flesh of my palm. I suck in a desperate breath, and the familiar highlights reel runs through my mind: death, disaster, doom. They've finally found me, here of all places. Nobody will hear me scream apart from the sheep.

I know I should be choosing between fight and flight, but something about my fear response is broken. I always, always react like this. I don't fight, I don't flee. I just freeze. I bite the inside of my cheek to shock myself out of it, and manage to turn my head to one side.

'Hey, are you okay? I didn't mean to scare you. It's Aidan. We met a few days ago.'

His tone is calm and gentle, his words spoken in a deliberately reassuring cadence. He walks up beside me, his hands held out in front of him, like I'm a scared animal. I suppose I kind of am. The light is fading, casting his face in a strange otherworldly glow. He does indeed look, as Cherie might say, a bit Halloween-y.

I slowly start to relax, feeling the coiled springs of tension unravel themselves inside me. My fists unclench and my heart rate tumbles back down to that of a normal human being. I still feel slightly sick in my stomach, and I'm blinking a lot to try and clear my mind. I start to stand, as he reaches out a cautious hand to help me to my feet. I'm shaky and I appreciate it.

'I'm sorry,' I say, feeling embarrassed now rather than

terrified. 'I… Uh, well, I didn't recognise you with your clothes on.'

He laughs, deep and loud, his hand lingering on mine for a few seconds more than was needed. 'Well, I guess I can't argue with that. I'd offer to rectify the situation, but it really is getting cold out here. You look freezing. Are you sure you're okay? I should have made more noise, or shouted from a distance instead of sneaking up on you like that … but you just looked so peaceful, watching that spectacular sunset, and I didn't want to disturb your moment.'

As he speaks, he takes his fleece jacket off, and wraps it around my shoulders without asking. I should object, but it's so nice and warm that I don't. It smells good, masculine and clean, and my nostrils flare a little at the scent. It's only when I'm not shivering that I realise quite how cold I was.

'Thank you,' I say gratefully. 'You're a gentleman. I feel like an idiot now for leaving my jacket with my bike. And please don't apologise for scaring me. I… Well, frankly I'm easily scared. It's not your fault. Long story.'

His eyes meet mine, and even in the dusk they are bright and piercing. I could stare at those eyes almost as long as I could stare at that sunset.

'Right. Well, I love a good story. There's a pub not too far from here. Can I persuade you to join me for a drink?'

'Ah, no, I don't think so, thanks. I have work to do, and it's late, and—'

'And you can't think of any more excuses?'

He smiles at me, and I worry that my knees will actually

buckle. That smile should come with a health warning, and I suspect he's totally aware of how lethal it is.

'Well, Aidan, I don't actually have to think of an excuse, do I? I can simply say no.'

He looks mock-upset and holds his palm to his heart, staggering around as though I've shot him. It's silly, and it makes me grin.

'Please?' he says, once he's stopped playing around. 'Truthfully, I haven't spoken to another human being in two days. You'd be doing me a favour.'

Ha, I think, I know that feeling. Maybe he's a writer too, and spends his whole life cooped up in front of a screen. Apart from the beachfront runs. And the sunsets. And the trips into the village to buy pounds and pounds of rare and bloody steak.

'Well, when you put it like that, maybe,' I reply. 'As long as you answer one question.'

'Anything. I'm an open book.'

'Are you a werewolf, a vampire, or any other kind of supernatural creature? Because the ladies in the café have their doubts that you're entirely human…'

He laughs again, and it is obviously something that comes easily to him. I like that. I like people who don't overthink, who just embrace the moment. They have no clue how lucky they are.

'Well, now, that would be telling. I kinda like the idea that I'm a man of mystery. It makes me a lot more interesting than I actually am… Now, can I interest you in the pub, m'lady?'

Chapter Eight

We end up throwing my bike into the back of his jeep, which is huge, black, and smells of animals. I immediately like it, and think it possibly smells even better than the jacket I am still wearing. As he hoists it effortlessly into the big boot, poor Loo-ise rolls out of my basket.

He pauses and stares at it in confusion. Possibly horror.

'What the hell is that?' he asks, picking her up and peeking beneath her crocheted skirt to find the toilet roll she came with. 'Some kind of English voodoo doll?'

'Yes,' I reply, raising my eyebrows. 'Whenever I want to make someone in a purple ball dress and matching bonnet suffer horrendous pain, I stick a pin into this. I don't have much call to use it, there being a distinct shortage of women who dress like this in the twenty-first century.'

'Ha. Well, that's a pity – I'd like to bring back hoops and bustles.'

'I'm not sure they'd suit you.'

'That, m'lady, is where you're wrong,' he says, grinning at me as he closes the boot. 'I'd look hot as Hades.'

'What's with the m'lady thing?' I ask as I fasten my seatbelt. He flicks the heating on, and I see that the car is actually quite luxurious, despite the smell. 'I know I'm old enough to be your mother, but really, it makes me feel ancient!'

He glances across at me, and for once looks quite serious. 'I'm thirty-three. There's no way you're old enough to be my mother.'

Thirty-three. Good lord, he's a baby really. Not that it matters.

'Well, I'm forty-nine, so technically I could be. If I was an early starter.'

Which, of course, I very much was not. I was so shy as a teenager that there was no chance of me even going on a date, never mind actually having sex. It took me until I was twenty-one to down a bottle of tequila and seduce one of Sally's medical student pals. Well, I suppose it was less of a seduction, more of a drunken encounter that neither of us could clearly remember in the morning. I just wanted to get it over with so I wouldn't end up as the world's oldest virgin – or at the very least Essex's oldest virgin.

'Well, you know what they say,' he replies, easing the car onto the road, 'age is just a number. And believe me, when I look at you, I very much do not see a mother figure. M'lady is... Well, look, I don't know what it is. Other than it's classy, like you, and it was the name of Rebecca De Mornay's character in *The Three Musketeers*, and I watched it as a kid and really liked her...'

'Oh lord. It's worse than I thought then. We're separated by different versions of *The Three Musketeers*. Mine will always be the seventies one with Oliver Reed in it. This is a huge issue. What will we find to talk about?'

He navigates the car down the now completely dark country lanes, and I'm glad I'm in this beast of a jeep instead of cycling. I'd have made it home, I'm sure, but it would have been hairy.

'I don't know. Maybe we could watch the one Eva Green made a few years ago and see if we can find common ground?'

He slows down as a small, furry creature scurries across the road, and waits until it is safely on the other side. I see him smiling as he watches it go, his face lit up by the dashboard lights.

'Fox cub,' he says. 'Or juvenile, I suppose, at this time of year.'

'Really? Why this time of year?'

'Because they're born around March, and tend to get kicked out into the big wide world about seven months later. That was a young animal, possibly on his first foray into independence.'

'Poor thing,' I reply, staring off into the field behind the hedgerow but seeing no sign of it. 'How do you know so much about foxes? Can I tell the café ladies that you're a werefox?'

'You can if you like,' he replies, pulling up outside an old pub with a thatched roof and a sign that tells us it's called the Blue Bottle. 'As long as they don't expect to see my bushy tail.'

I let out a deeply attractive snort of laughter at that, and he winks at me before turning the engine off.

The pub is all dark wood and cosy corners, a fire blazing in the hearth. It's busy, but we find a corner table, and settle down with our drinks. A ginger beer for him, and a cranberry juice for me. We are wild and crazy folk, and no mistake.

'I'm not drinking because I have to drive,' he says. 'What's your excuse?'

'I'm worried that if I have a gin and tonic, I might end up at a karaoke bar doing my trademark version of Celine Dion's "My Heart Will Go On".'

'Really?'

'No,' I say, laughing gently at how absurd an idea it is. 'I've never done karaoke in my life. I'm too shy. I've just got a lot of work to do tomorrow.'

Plus, I think but don't say, I do not want to be the drunk woman to his sober man. It's all very well telling myself that I'm old enough to be his mother, but I still can't deny how attractive he is. Getting tipsy communally with the ladies is one thing. This is entirely another.

'What do you do? For work?'

'I'm a writer,' I reply, which is my standard answer. Sometimes people leave it at that, because it covers a multitude of sins. It could be anything from writing the warnings that go on the back of bleach bottles through to technical manuals for Skodas.

'A writer of what?' he persists. Damn him.

'Books, actually. You might not have ever seen one at your age. They're made of paper, with words printed on them. Very popular before information was downloaded directly into your brain.'

He tilts his head to one side and gives me a knowing smile. 'You're really keen on stressing this age difference thing, aren't you? Why? What are you scared of? We're just two strangers, new in town, having a drink…'

I meet his eyes, but quickly glance away. They're too bright, and I get the feeling they see too much. I'm suddenly very hot, and tug at the neck of my sweater. What am I scared of? Good question. Pretty much everything, as it turns out. I wish I was more like Sally. She'd take one look at Aidan and devour him verbally. She would flirt him to within an inch of his life.

'How are you finding it?' I ask, changing the subject. 'Life in Budbury? It's got to be very different from New York.'

'It is, and that is precisely why I love it. My mom is British, my dad American. I grew up in New York and worked there for most of my adult life.'

'And your work was?'

'Finance,' he says simply. There's a slight smile flickering on his wide lips, and I realise he's played me at my own game. Finance. That could mean anything from processing loan applications through to running Goldman Sachs. I'm curious, of course I am, but I refuse to be drawn. I just nod, and sip my drink, and wait to see if he has anything to add. He doesn't, at least not about that.

'And as for how I'm finding life here … well, so far I love it. My nearest neighbour is four miles away. Nobody pukes on the street or tries to steal your watch. The views are stunning, the air is clear, and this really interesting new chick just moved into the neighbourhood…'

I widen my eyes. 'Really? You should probably be having a drink with her then, instead of me. I'm very, very dull.'

His eyes roam my face, his smile slowly grows, and my cheeks redden in a way that seems to delight him. FFS, as my nieces might say.

'Somehow, I don't believe that for a second, Sarah. What kind of books do you write?'

I'm half tempted to say erotica, or steamy Regency romance, but he'd undoubtedly love that a bit too much. 'Books about the dark side of life,' I say simply. 'Crime, a hint of the strange. Mysteries, basically.'

'Right. Maybe you can set something around the hill. There's definitely a mystical quality to the place, isn't there? It feels like the whole area is so old. Makes you aware that we're just visitors, temporary blinks of an eye intruding on the landscape. Nature is in charge here.'

I nod, because he has explained it perfectly. In big cities like London and New York, you can forget that – you can be fooled by the tall buildings and clever technology and the rumbling sound of underground trains running through tunnels bored into the earth. There, it feels like we've wrangled the world into a shape we like. Out here, it's very different.

'Yes. I know exactly what you mean. And maybe I will. Most of my books are set in London, but maybe it's time for one of my detectives to retire to a sleepy coastal town, where they will, of course, be plunged into a world of murder and mayhem…'

'And maybe, if your detective is female and straight, she could hook up with a lusty farmhand? Or an intriguing stranger with green eyes and a habit of running around without his top on…'

I laugh out loud, because he actually looks slightly intrigued by the idea. He shrugs, looks slightly sheepish, and says: 'What can I say? I read a lot of romance when I was growing up. I was close to my British grandmother, and she had shelves full of them. Garish covers with dudes like Fabio on the front. Mills & Boon. Rakes and virgins, governesses and lords… I suspect it deeply influenced my view of the world.'

'Oh no,' I respond, amused. 'Adjusting to reality must have been hard?'

'Yeah. Real women were a lot more fun. Nobody in my granny's books got drunk after a Giants game and stayed out dancing until dawn.'

'And that's the kind of woman you like, is it? Party girls? I think you're going to be disappointed living out here…'

He takes a slow sip from his glass, and leans back in his chair. He surveys me, in a way that doesn't feel intrusive – more appreciative. He has a way of speaking with his expressions that I find intriguing.

'I suppose those were the kinds of women I liked back in my old life, at least at one stage. Now, I'm in a different head space.'

I always admire the way Americans can say things like

'head space' without sounding sarcastic. I've met a lot of people from the States through my work, and on the whole they are so much more 'in touch' with their feelings than we are, and not afraid to talk about it, either. Obviously, the idea of behaving like that myself makes me shudder, but that doesn't mean I can't see its value.

'Why? What changed for you?' I ask, genuinely interested.

He glances off to the side, and when he looks back, those mesmerising eyes are a little more serious. 'Oh, you know, the usual: heartbreak, despair, soul-crushing disappointment. It was a few years ago, but I suppose it made me reassess my life. That's when I decided that it needed to change, and I started to consider walking away from everything I'd ever known.'

'That's very big stuff,' I say gently. 'Your family?'

'Well, my dad, yeah. Have you ever watched *Succession*?'

I nod. Like most people who did, I'd been sucked into the toxic world of people I despised but couldn't stop caring about. Brilliant writing.

'Well, picture that, but with less familial warmth. My dad is the latest in a long line of cold, arrogant assholes who see themselves as a modern-day God. The business has been passed down the generations, getting bigger and more bloated with each new era. It was always assumed that I'd be next, and when I was younger, I went along with that assumption. I was privileged; I was rich; I was trained from childhood to step into his shoes when the time came.'

'But you didn't,' I reply, absolutely fascinated now. 'You moved to rural England, of all places. Or do you,

I don't know, run your evil global business empire from Dorset?'

He laughs again, and it eases the tension that had started to creep into his face while he talked about his background. 'No. I do run my own business empire from Dorset, which is a lot less evil and mainly involves me monitoring my investments and making sure enough money is coming in to pay my bills. I may have turned my back on that world as the heir apparent, but I still learned a lot, and I still kind of enjoy it. The moving, the shaking, the shuffling. The sense of competition. But these days, it's all just for personal use. I have no interest in *legacy*.'

Legacy. That's one of those words that normal people don't use, isn't it? Most of us are just trying to muddle our way through our own lives, without worrying too much about what we leave behind. My books are global best-sellers and have been turned into movies and TV shows, so I suppose they will live on for a little while, but I prefer the context of Eggardon Hill. Blinks of an eye. None of it matters at all when you look at it through that lens.

'Are you still close to your mum?' I ask, as ever consumed by a need to understand.

He nods. 'Yeah, sure. She lives in London now, so I get to see her. My sister too. There was a schism in the family, and the ones I care about are all on this side of the pond. It's nice being on the same continent as them, but I also needed to strike out alone for a while and figure it all out. I had my own place, near the New Forest, and I adopted a dog. Then another dog. And … well, let's just say I'm a dog person.

You've heard that saying, the more I learn about people, the more I prefer dogs?'

I nod. I have, and I agree. Though sometimes I feel like it would also work with 'the more I learn about people, the more I prefer earwigs.'

'Then I needed even more space,' he continues. 'And that's why we ended up here. I'd never even visited the property and land I bought. I just saw it online for sale, and something about it, I don't know, called to me? Does that sound insane?'

'Totally insane,' I reply, deadpan. 'And I did exactly the same. I was looking for a change, and I saw my little house on a website. I put in an offer without even seeing it in person.'

He raises his glass and grins at me. 'Well, we must both be crazy – or maybe it's fate. Here's to fresh starts!'

Chapter Nine

Tinkerbell visits me in the evening, and when I wake up he's sitting on the pillow next to my head, staring at me. Whiskers twitching, he stretches once he sees I'm awake, and jumps off the bed – presumably to disappear into whatever secret portal he uses to enter and exit my very well-secured home.

'Bye!' I shout as he slinks out of the door. 'Lock up on your way out!'

He doesn't reply. How rude. I follow suit and do some stretching. I'm nowhere near as elegant, I'm sure, as I clamber off the side of my mattress and reach my arms up to the ceiling. I have slept amazingly well, much better than usual, and actually feel refreshed this morning. Maybe, I think with a small smile as I go into a forward fold, it was the dreams.

Aidan dropped me off at home after our one drink, and despite all his flirting, he was a perfect gentleman. There was no angling for an invite in for a nightcap, no attempt at a goodnight kiss. I was both relieved and disappointed, and reminded myself again about the age gap. I suspect Aidan is one of those guys who automatically flirts with women, and has a gift for making them feel special. He doesn't mean anything by it, I'm sure.

While that made perfect sense while I was conscious, my sleeping mind had other ideas. Aidan visited me in my dreams, and he was not in any way, shape or form gentlemanly. I do a few side twists, aware that I'm even blushing while I'm alone. The memory of my night-time fantasies is enough to make me feel hot under the pyjama collar. I think it might have been him talking about his grandma's romance books, with the dastardly dukes and the lusty lords... Somehow they all got tangled up in my mind, and Aidan kept appearing dressed in full Bridgerton-style gear, galloping around on horses and rescuing me from ruffians. The rest was very much X-rated.

I have a moment where I feel borderline ashamed, because I could actually be his mother. He's not a child, not by any means, but still ... it feels slightly forbidden. He might be a gorgeous guy with an old soul, but he's still too young for me.

I did enjoy my evening with him, though, and found him to be interesting company – certainly better company than the person I'd spent the last few days with, i.e. myself. He told me more about his family, or at least the part of it he likes, and he is a well-travelled and cultured guy beneath the slightly wild appearance. 'I'll be happy if I never wear a suit again,' he told me. 'In fact I'd probably walk around naked all the time if the weather allowed. I was dressed up in tuxedos and paraded around at parties from the age of two, and it sucked.'

I ignored the nakedness reference, but was fascinated by the childhood and family life he described. Mine was so very, very ordinary: my dad was a school caretaker throughout my childhood, as well as a borderline alcoholic and a bully; my mum worked nights behind the tills in a twenty-four-hour petrol station. We lived in a small three-bedroomed semi in Billericay, and a weekend in Margate was considered an adventure. Every two years we'd go to Benidorm, where my abiding memory is of sunburn, scuttling around to find shade and refusing to wear a bikini because I was too shy. My mum and dad would start their day with a full English and then he would drink himself into oblivion. There's nothing wrong with any of that – Sally always had a whale of a time making friends and snogging boys – but for me it was torture.

I've travelled a lot as an adult, at times during the year when the sun was less likely to see me end up with third degree burns, and have seen many amazing and beautiful places, but the way Aidan talks, he is very much a citizen of the world rather than an occasional tourist. All of which makes it astonishing that he lives here, in this tiny patch of sleepy countryside. It's like finding an exotic butterfly in a world of moths, or a peacock in a flock of pigeons.

Despite his background, he is down-to-earth, easy-going, and surprisingly open. It was only when he mentioned his father that he clammed up. Something bad has gone on there, without a doubt. I try not to let my imagination fill in the gaps, which is difficult for me. A bit of an occupational hazard really.

I spend a couple of hours working, checking over the edits I've recently done, and when I'm satisfied, I send them back over to my editor. She will take a while going through them, and until then, I'm kind of at a loose end. I already have a few ideas for my next book, but I don't want to throw myself into it just yet. Maybe I deserve a few days off. I could sort the house out properly, do some more exploring, even pursue that ever-elusive goal – to just relax.

Before I can decide, there's a knock on the door, and I open it cautiously. I really should get a spyhole installed. No chance of peeking through the curtains without the intruder spotting me. Outside, I find my near-neighbour, Edie May. The one who is almost a hundred and lives with a ghost fiancé, apparently. She really is very small, and her tiny face looks up at me like a pale, smiling raisin.

'I come bearing exciting news!' she announces, as I invite her inside. Even I don't feel threatened by Edie, although that could of course be a terrible mistake. She would, after all, be the perfect assassin. Nobody would ever suspect her.

Once safely in the living room, she looks around as though studying for signs of change, and nods approvingly. 'Nice to see somebody living here properly. It was a rental for a long time, and once Katie and her nippers moved out, nobody stayed for more than a few nights. It was one of those … what do you call 'em? Bear D&Ds?'

'Airbnb?' I suggest.

'If you say so, dear. Anyway. Now we've got you for

keeps, and that's a marvellous thing. You must pop in for tea. I'm only a few doors down. But today, I have an invitation for you…'

She grandly passes over a silver envelope, and looks at me expectantly while I open it. It's printed on thick silver card embossed with purple velvet in a fleur-de-lys design. I run my fingers over it. It reminds of old-fashioned flock wallpaper. On the back, I see that my presence is requested at Briarwood House for a Grand Halloween Ball. The dress code is 'Supernaturally Stylish and Freakishly Formal'.

'I'm chairing the organising committee,' Edie tells me proudly. 'On account of I'm almost dead, and therefore very in touch with the other side.'

I stay silent, scared of responding in a way that might be offensive. She gives me a cheeky wink and adds: 'To be honest, all I do is boss the others around a bit and tell them made-up scary stories about the place. So, now you can sort your costume out, and there's a number on there for our WhatsApp group if you want to join. Now I just need to get one of these to that new young chap out by Eggardon, the one who's got them all in a tizzy…'

She looks at me speculatively, eyebrows raised. Is she setting me up, I wonder? Does she somehow know I was out with him last night? Can she dream-walk?

'Aidan?' I ask.

'The very same! No idea what his surname is though, do you?'

'I… Uh, I think it's Calloway?' I know it is, because he told me so last night. Thus allowing me to look up his family on Google, and invade yet another person's privacy in a totally hypocritical way. I'm not going to feel too bad about it; I'm sure he's done the same with me, and I've no doubt that Laura and the others will have done too. It's natural to be curious.

The Calloways, it turns out, have been one of the most influential families in the States for generations. Old money east coast, and currently headed up by Aidan's father, Benedict. Maybe I was prejudiced by what I'd heard about him, but I couldn't help thinking he did look like an arrogant asshole, just as Aidan described him. A handsome silver fox type to be sure, maybe in his sixties, but with dead eyes and a smirk. I came across a few pictures of Aidan at events and parties, and a story about his parents getting 'amicably' divorced. At that point I forced myself to stop. It was all getting way too personal and gossipy, and was probably all nonsense anyway.

Edie nods and gives me a little smile. 'Calloway. Well, I suppose I'll walk out to his place, or maybe go on my bike. I'm sure my hip will be okay…'

I'm alarmed at the thought of her doing either of those things, but I have the sneaky suspicion I'm being played anyway. Edie is clearly well loved by this whole community, and nobody would hesitate to offer her a lift, including me.

'I'm heading out to Max and Gabriel's place later,' I say, playing along. 'Would you like me to drop it off for you?'

'Would you mind?' she says immediately, digging in her bag and magically coming up with a matching invitation to mine. 'I had it with me just in case I encountered some kind soul... Anyway, I must be off. I'm going as a Bride of Dracula, and I have a dress fitting!'

I have no idea if that is true or not. It's impossible to tell with Edie. I see her off, smiling as I watch her walk steadily away on her sensible shoes. Everyone she meets on the street stops to chat, and I'd guess it might take her a solid hour to walk from one end to the other. It's not a bad way of life really, certainly very different from London, where even when you're young you can go weeks without talking to anybody.

I stare at the invitation, and wonder if he'll go. From what he said last night, he's had his fill of formal events, though this being Budbury, I'm guessing it won't be formal in any recognisable sense of the word. I also wonder if I'll go. I've enjoyed my forays into friendship since I arrived here, but I'm still not ready to fully commit. I'm still probably the kind of person who would cross the road to avoid chatting to anyone. I am the anti-Edie. I also have my niece's birthday bash to go to, between now and then, and that might use up all of my social battery for the month. In fact, after that one, I might have to lock myself in a dark room for a week to recover.

There's time to worry about all of that later, I tell myself. For now, I need to get myself to Max's place, collect my goodies, and find a way to deliver this invitation, that ideally doesn't involve me coming face to face with Aidan Calloway. I could do with a day or so to let the memory of those dreams fade away.

I head to Maxine's first, where I am greeted by a screaming donkey and the sound of a barking dog.

This turns out to be Gary, her little black mystery hound who was a rescue from Hungary. He looks like every breed of dog ever was put in a big mixing bowl and combined to create him. He's a friendly little chap once he's had a good sniff of me, though, and is definitely more outgoing than Gabriel. He nods at me when he comes into the kitchen for a coffee, and then disappears outside. 'He's a man of few words,' Max says, watching him go and smiling. 'Luckily I make up for it by being a woman of many.'

I suppose she has a point. I mean, I can be on the quiet side myself. What if I ended up with a guy who was just the same? We'd barely speak. We'd be silent over the dinner table and ignore each other on romantic nights out.

'So,' she says, spreading various colour charts and fabric samples over the big old pine table, 'I rooted these out for you. Obviously, it depends on your tastes and your budget, but these might give you a few ideas. If you need any help just let me know. Gabriel is super-handy and can do most jobs, plus I've built up a lot of good trade contacts now. And I'm always available for a shopping trip. Only for house stuff, though. Not clothes or shoes or whatever. If you need a new frock, you're on your own.'

I thank her for the help and add: 'Are you going to this Halloween Ball? I suppose I might need a new frock for that...'

'Oh gosh yes! Definitely going. And I'm making him come with me. There was a party at the café last year, and he skipped it 'cause he's a grump. I went as a sexy witch – well, a witch – and that was the night we ... ah ... connected, when I got back here.'

'Is that what the kids are calling it these days?' I ask, as I place the cards and samples in my bag.

'Okay, fair enough. It was the first night we tore each other's clothes off. So, kind of our anniversary really! The kids will all come back for it as well, the village teenagers who've moved away, mine who are at uni. It'll be fun. We're going as pirates. Gabriel doesn't know that yet, so don't tell him.'

I can't imagine a situation where Gabriel and I would ever make small talk. 'Aye aye captain. Your secret's safe with me. I have no idea if I'm going. It's not… I feel stupid even asking this because I'm sure I know the answer, but it's not a date type situation, is it? We don't have to go with partners?'

'No, Sarah. It's not like the prom in an American high school movie. There'll be a coach laid on from the café I suspect, because it's a bit of a hike to Briarwood. Something to look forward to, anyway.'

'If you say so,' I reply, heading to the doorway.

'I do say so. Stop being a Gabriel. It'll be hilarious. Singing, dancing, costumes, Cherie's famous Pumpkin Spice Punch and Murderous Martini. How could you resist?'

'I'd find it remarkably easy, I'm afraid, Max. Anyway. Thanks again, and I'll definitely be in touch about the house. It's only small so I don't want to get carried away. Lick of paint for now, I think. Plus, I'd like to get rid of some of the downstairs carpets.'

'I'll pop round some time if you like,' she says, walking me to the door, 'see the state of your floorboards.'

'I'm not sure I'm ready for that level of commitment, at least not until we've been out a few more times… Now, can you give me some directions to Aidan's place? Edie was threatening to cycle there on her bike to deliver his invite, so I said I'd drop it off for her.'

Gabriel, who is sanding down a pine door nearby, lets out a snort of laughter at that. Max joins in. Gary remains blessedly stoical about the whole thing.

'Edie doesn't cycle,' Max explains. 'But she is an absolute mistress of gentle manipulation. She has a way of persuading you to do things, without you even noticing. Gabriel is basically her slave, aren't you, love?'

'Yep. Happy to be, too.'

This is quite a speech for Gabriel, and I smile at the image of this taciturn man spending time with the old lady. Friendship comes in all shapes and sizes, I guess.

Max gives me instructions on how to reach Hazelwell where Aidan lives, and warns me that there's no handy post box on the main road, and also that it's not 'right in your face' like their farmhouse is. Apparently the house is so deeply hidden in the parcel of land around it that nobody's even seen it in recent times. I guess that all adds to the sense of mystery around him and fuels the gossipy fires. I must call in and see Cherie later, I find myself thinking, and give her the lowdown … if I make it that far, anyway. Maybe I'll just chicken out and post it to him.

Except … I also brought him a little gift, and now I feel like a complete idiot for that. I climb back into the car and give a beep as I leave – Max has explained that it is required countryside etiquette to beep when you come or go – and head out into the hills. I try not to think too hard, because all this ever does is wear me out.

It's a clear day, but the wind is noticeably stronger than it has been, and I see crisp brown leaves swirling from the trees. It looks like they're dancing around in little whirlwinds. The temperature is dropping, and I wonder how many days of sunshine we have left. It already feels like we're on borrowed time. Before long, I will be preparing for my first Christmas in my new home, which makes me smile. It already feels like exactly the refuge I was looking for. Peaceful, quiet, remote, by the sea – but with an unexpected amount of 'people' stuff to navigate. I really hadn't expected so much people stuff – coffee clubs and unexpected visitors and balls and men. Or one in particular. One I can't quite banish from my mind.

I see the wooden sign that points me towards Hazelwell, just as Max told me I would. I suck in a breath and make the turn. Why am I making such a big deal of this? I'm dropping a couple of things off with someone who is practically a neighbour, and then I'm going home. There is no drama to be found here, no moral dilemma. No cause for embarrassment or self-analysis. In, out, gone.

I tell myself this as I make my way down the narrow one-way track, my car edging between the overhanging greenery and bumping over the uneven terrain. I can see why he has a four-wheel drive.

I reach an open wooden gate and continue on down the path. I see his big black jeep parked just inside another gate, this one tall and closed to. I pull up and go to examine the gate. This one is much taller and made of metal. It's bolted but not padlocked or anything. I nervously push back the metal bolt, open it just wide enough to fit myself through, and close it again.

I glance around, finding myself in the courtyard of an old stone farmhouse that's not dissimilar from the one Max and Gabriel live in. It's pretty, in that way that older buildings are – acquiring character as they age. Off to one side is a wooden outbuilding in good condition – maybe a stable or some kind of store – and a huge pile of chopped logs. An axe has been lodged solidly into a big stump, and I shake my head to clear off the image of Aidan, shirtless, axe in hand as he works. I'm turning into a romance novelist. I don't think my agent would appreciate the change in direction.

I notice that there is a tall metal fence running around the perimeter, disappearing off into the dense woodland behind the house. I wonder if Aidan is security conscious because of his background. He literally comes from the kind of family that could be a kidnap risk. He seems very laid back, but maybe he has been raised to think about risk and danger and potential threats. If so, maybe he could give me some advice, because I've still made no progress in sorting an alarm system for the house.

I walk towards the door, my feet crunching on the gravel, and knock on it firmly before I can chicken out. I cast my eyes around, looking for cameras, but see nothing, not even a Ring doorbell. It's quiet out here, just the sound of the birds in the background and the whistle of the wind blowing through the treetops. I knock again. Nothing.

I feel suddenly quite spooked, realising how isolated I

am. I know there's a road on the other side of the land, but it's a long way from where I am right now. What if something's happened? What if he's been murdered and he's lying in a pool of his own blood? What if there's been an accident, or the house is rigged with a bomb, or he's about to emerge with bloodshot eyes, infected with a virus that makes him want to tear people limb from limb? What if the rumours were true, and he is a werewolf or a vampire?

What if you get a grip, you daft cow? I physically slap myself lightly on the forehead. It really is exhausting having this kind of brain. It's like a mouse in a microwave, being chased by a cat on acid. A never-ending carousel of mental chaos. Just because Martin/Scott turned out to be a genuinely nasty guy doesn't mean all my crazy fears will come true. I have so many crazy fears that it was really just a case of even a stopped clock being right. It was bound to happen at some point or another, and one bad experience does not a pattern make.

Feeling a little calmer, I knock once more and peer through the window. I consider trying the door, but that is a step too far. I'd never, ever leave mine unlocked, but if I did, I'd still be outraged if someone simply walked in without permission. For all of my creative explanations for there being no response, the truth is undoubtedly something a lot more prosaic, like he's out on his property somewhere, or in the shower. Or maybe he has spotted me already, and he's lying on the floor hoping I go away.

That humiliating idea takes root, of course, and I hastily pull Edie's silver envelope from my bag, intending to simply post it through the letterbox and leave as quickly as possible.

I'm just bending down to do exactly that when I hear the most bloodcurdling noise. A long, piercing ... howl. There's no other word for it. It's not just me imagining things. I freeze, and feel the familiar paralysing terror starting to creep over me. I force myself to stand up straight, and manage to suck in a long, deep breath, my nostrils trembling.

The noise continues, eerie and almost beautiful. At least it would be if I wasn't so afraid. Another howl joins in, a slightly different tone, and then another and another. They wail and yowl together, the plaintive notes climbing higher and lasting longer. They seem to tumble over each other, rising and soaring and falling in a glorious and heart-stopping song. It triggers a primal fear in me that tells me to run, run, run, but even though I know I should, I am rooted to the spot, feet in blocks of cement.

I don't want to look. I don't want to face whatever it is behind me. My heart is thudding in my chest, and I feel lightheaded and shaky. I've been scared before, usually without good cause, but this is it, I know. This is finally it. Eaten alive by wolves.

I turn my head slightly, and see blurs of movement in the treeline. Flashes of white, glimpses of lean bodies, the rustle of branches. The howling stops. The greenery is pushed aside ... and Aidan emerges. I stare at him, and more than half of me expects him to suddenly fall to the ground and morph into a gigantic slavering beast.

'Hey!' he shouts over, waving at me. Do werewolves

wave? Could he have changed back into his human form that quickly? Why oh why didn't I think to buy a gun loaded with silver bullets?

I don't even reply, because as he comes out from the trees, he is followed by four enormous animals. They stay by his side, jostling for position, all of them fixing their eyes on me in a way that makes me lose the ability to breathe. I love dogs, and I've always thought that wolves were exceptionally beautiful, but standing here confronted by them I realise that I underestimated their power. Each one of these creatures is huge, all massive paws and athletic muscle. And teeth, of course. They'll have lots and lots of teeth.

As Aidan continues to walk slowly towards me, three of them fall back, lurking instead at the treeline, watching carefully. They dig at the ground, and let out snarls, but they don't follow him. The fourth one, though… The fourth one has different ideas. It streaks towards me, eating up the ground between us, terrifyingly fast. I flatten myself back against the door, my hands hitting the wood. The envelope drops to the ground at my feet.

'Don't worry,' Aidan calls, jogging towards us now, 'she's harmless, I promise!'

I note the 'she', and a still hysterical corner of my mind wonders if it's his sister or his mother. If in fact his entire family are werewolves, and they all live out here in the woods together…

His sister/mother/aunt barrels into my legs, then snatches up the envelope I dropped. She holds it in her mouth and looks up at me, her bushy tail swinging from side to side. She's absolutely exquisite, mainly white with streaks and stripes of light brown, and striking amber eyes peering up at me from a mask of darker brown fur. She comes up past my knees, and her ears are twitching around like they might be antennae.

There is absolutely no sign of aggression from her, and as soon as my mind accepts that, my body starts to relax. I reach out a very slow hand in her direction, and she drops the envelope so she can give my fingers a good sniff. Her tail continues to wag, and Aidan is now right by her side, looking on. 'That's okay,' he says softly, I suspect more for my sake than the animal's. 'It's fine to touch her. She likes you, I can tell. Plus, Juno is a major goofball. She won't hurt you.'

I look up at him, see how calm he is, and nod. Okay. I can do this. I gently run my fingers through the thick fur around her head, and smile at how it feels. Like a combination of thick and silky soft. She leans into it, and I scratch behind her ears. A sensation of complete joy swoops through me, and I crouch down to get a better look at her. She licks my face, and then collapses down on the floor with her belly facing up. I laugh and give her the rub she so obviously demands. It feels incredibly special, being so close to this spectacular creature. A total privilege.

'I warn you, she'll let you do that all day,' Aidan says, as I reluctantly stand up. He's yet again not wearing a top, but the silly grin I have on my face has nothing to do with him, no matter how glorious his bare chest looks. I only have eyes for Juno. 'You want to come inside?'

'Only if she does,' I reply, and he laughs as he opens the

door. Juno prowls through and proceeds to give everything a sniff. I follow. The hallway is spacious with a paved stone floor. There's a wooden cabinet full of dog things – leads, harnesses, grooming brushes, plastic chew toys in the shape of bones, tug-of-war ropes. It smells like his car: clean, but with a distinct eau de canine. I inhale, loving it.

'Sorry about the stink,' he says, noticing me. 'Comes with the territory. Coffee?'

Juno pads through into what turns out to be the kitchen, and jumps up into an old sofa that is very obviously hers. She stretches out, watching us both with those amazing amber eyes. Aidan starts up a coffee machine that looks like it could be from a steampunk movie, and grabs a sweatshirt from the back of a chair. 'Sorry about the state of me, too,' he adds.

'No need to be sorry about anything,' I say hastily. 'I've turned up uninvited. And anyway, I love the stink. What… What is she? Juno? And will the others come in?'

'They're all Wolfdogs. And the clue's kinda in the name. They're a hybrid of wolf and domestic dogs, usually German Shepherds, Huskies, that kind of thing.'

'Wow. Is that… Um, I don't mean to accuse you of being a criminal, but is that legal?'

'As long as they're what's called third generation, yeah, here in the UK. Different rules in the States. My family always had Shepherds and Malinois, great guard dogs, super intelligent. When I moved to England, I came across a rescue centre that looked after these guys, and I was smitten. It took time and a lot of training – for me – but eventually I adopted Juno. Lucked out with her; she was only young when she was abandoned, so she was able to bond with me, and generally socialised well with humans. As you can see now, she's a killer…'

Juno raises one eyebrow at him and thumps her tail once, as though acknowledging that he is talking about her.

'What about the others?' I ask, fascinated. 'They don't come inside?'

'They do, yes, but they won't when you're here, not until they're sure about you. They're a little more wolf in their behaviour. All three of them ended up in the rescue as adults, and that can be hard for them. Like with wolves in the wild, they're pack animals, and their owners are their pack, their entire world. If that goes wrong, there can be problems. They're more likely to run at the sight of a strange human, and it takes them a long time to trust one. They're good with me, but I need to start introducing others into the mix now. It helps that they're together, but they've still got a way to go. It's… Well, it's a commitment. One I've made to them.'

He talks with such passion that I find myself looking at him in something akin to wonder. How many layers are there to this guy?

'What?' he asks, smiling in that knee-buckling way. 'Are you laughing at me inside?'

'No! No, I'm really not, honestly! I'm just… Well, you're a billionaire playboy philanthropist, aren't you?'

'Iron Man? Really? Cool as Tony Stark was, I'm not him. I earn my own money now, so I'm a way from being a billionaire, and I'm not sure rescuing Wolfdogs qualifies me as a philanthropist. Playboy … once upon a time, maybe. Not anymore. Now I only have eyes for one woman.'

He gazes at me, and it is intense. The man is stupidly good-looking and I gulp audibly.

'Don't worry,' he says, one side of his mouth quirking in amusement. 'It's Juno.'

I laugh in relief, and clasp my hand to my heart. 'Oh thank the Lord! You had me worried for a moment there! And I totally get it. I think I might be in love with her as well… Do you, you know, take them for walks? Or is that yet another stupid question?'

'I take her out, yeah. She's good with people, even though she can be a little nervy around too much noise, or too many new smells. The others are, yet again, a work in progress. I have them in their harnesses for an hour or so every day to get them used to it. I have muzzles if I need to take them to the vet or anything. But mainly, we run together. I have a decent amount of land, lots of good terrain where they can play and chase and dig. And a really high fence to make sure they don't escape!'

'I've never seen them before,' I say, 'Wolfdogs. Are they common?'

'More now than they used to be. *Game of Thrones* made them kind of popular. But they're not the easiest of pets, and a lot of times people underestimate what they're getting themselves into.'

I nod, and can completely see how the Starks's gorgeous direwolves in the books and TV show could have caught people's imaginations.

Aidan passes me a coffee and leans back against his

kitchen table. His hair is damp, I notice. And slightly long. It's hard to picture him in an expensive suit and tie, but I know that was his whole life not so long ago. I admire how he has completely changed his life and pursued something that makes him happy instead. I'd like to do that, except I haven't as yet quite figured out what that would look like.

'I'd like to meet them, the other dogs,' I say quietly, not sure if I'm overstepping. 'If you think it would be okay? I could be your … uh, your guinea pig.'

He considers it, and nods once. 'That could work. Juno likes you, which is a good start. Don't expect too much though – they're probably never going to be like she is. We'll make progress, and they'll settle, but it will be slow and sometimes frustrating. Persuading them the world is safe, that it's okay to trust again, won't be easy.'

I feel a sudden and unexpected sting of tears behind my eyes. I have more in common with the Wolfdogs than I could ever have thought, and I wonder if Aidan has somehow picked up on that kinship. He smiles at me gently. 'But I promise,' he adds, 'that they will be worth the time and the effort. They're damaged, but they're not broken. They just need someone to believe in them.'

It's too much. Too intense. Too close to home. I look away, staring at the now-snoozing wolf on the sofa, and squeeze the moisture from my eyes. I need a moment, and he gives that to me.

'Anyway,' I say, when I've regained control, 'I came bearing gifts.' I hold up the now soggy envelope. It's smeared in mud and has tooth marks on it. Aaah, Juno.

He opens it up, and his eyebrows rise when he sees the invitation.

'Wow,' he says quietly. 'I guess I'd better go. What do you reckon? Werewolf outfit? Too obvious? The vet from the village – Matt I think? – is due to come out here tomorrow to meet the pack, so I won't be able to maintain my air of supernatural mystery for much longer.'

'No, you won't – he's married to Laura from the café.'

'Ah. She was real nice. Are you going? To this ball?'

I bite my lip a little, and think it over. 'Truthfully, I don't know. I have another social event I have to attend in London before that, and I'm not sure I'll have much left in the tank. I'm… I'm not really a party person. Like I told you, I'm very, very dull.'

The smile again. Yikes.

'And like I told you last night, I don't believe that for a second. I for one find you deeply interesting.'

I can't deny it, my heart does a little hop, then adds in a skip and a jump. Deeply interesting? What does that even mean?

'In the same way you'd find a documentary on the history of the Black Death deeply interesting?'

'No. Not even remotely. You know the way I find you interesting. I can tell you do, because you're blushing. It's cute.'

'Aidan, I'm almost fifty. Cute is not an appropriate word!'

He laughs and holds his hands up in surrender. 'Eye of the beholder, Sarah, eye of the beholder! But if you prefer, I'll use a different word … like gorgeous, or beautiful, or good old-fashioned hot. Now, what else have you got for me?'

'What?' I ask, momentarily confused. I'm not really used to flirting with men. Certainly not in such an open way, and certainly not with guys like this. It's very discombobulating. English men are usually a lot more reserved.

'You said you came bearing gifts, plural. Or was the other one simply the pleasure of your company? If so, I'll take the deal.'

I shake my head and look in my bag. 'Do you ever stop being charming? Is it automatic?'

'Not at all. This is all for you. Besides, I'm conducting an experiment: I'm trying to find out exactly how red your skin goes, and if I can keep it that shade the entire time you're here.'

I feel my cheeks flame even deeper in response, and I scoop out the book I rescued from my shelves for him. A very well-read copy of *Rivals* by Jilly Cooper. I slam it into his chest in mock disgust. 'There! That's for you, because you said you liked romance novels, and because you now live in the English countryside… Jilly is the absolute best. Though I'm not sure you deserve it.'

He flicks through the book, and grins at me. 'I've heard of Jilly Cooper, though I haven't read any. Isn't she supposed to be pretty racy? It looks like you've read the heck out of this one, Sarah…'

'I have. No shame, no guilt. That would be my desert island book. Anyway. I have to get going.'

I have to get going because being around Aidan is both delicious and disconcerting. I feel off balance with him, and

I've never been the kind of woman who enjoys fairground rides. He is younger than me by a distance, but I still feel like he is the one in charge. It takes away some of my self-control, and I've worked very hard for it.

I go over to Juno and bury my fingers in her luscious fur. She gazes at me down her long muzzle, and I swear she seems to smile. I give her a final cuddle, then head to the door.

'Thank you,' he says, holding up the paperback. 'I look forward to reading this. And to seeing you on Friday.'

'Friday? What's happening on Friday?'

'I thought Juno and I might come and visit you. Or maybe you could meet us for a walk? I mean, I know you have zero interest in me as a man – you are "old enough to be my mother" after all – but I thought you might be interested in me as Juno's dad…'

I narrow my eyes at him. It seems very unfair and also quite ruthless to use the dog against me. Despite that, I find myself agreeing to take his phone number.

Chapter Ten

I call round to the café later that afternoon and find Laura and Cherie clearing tables at the end of what has obviously been a busy day. Every table is strewn with plates and mugs, and both of them look traumatised.

'Coach party of OAPs,' Laura says, standing with her hands on her hips and stretching her back. 'So many of them, it was like the granny apocalypse…'

'And what's wrong with OAPs, madam?' Cherie asks, snapping a tea towel at her. 'You'll be one yourself one day!'

'If I'm lucky,' Laura retorts, and a flicker of sadness crosses her face. I remember what Max told me, about her husband dying. I wonder how you come back from that? How you trust the universe to not screw you over again and again? She definitely seems to have done it though, and I admire her for that.

She snaps herself out of it, and passes me a roll of bin bags. 'Make yourself useful while you're here. I'll pay you with a pumpkin spiced latte and a Bakewell tart.'

'I'm going to be the size of that marshmallow man in *Ghostbusters* if I carry on eating this much cake,' I say, setting to work. Laura and Cherie both snort in amusement.

'Doubt it,' Laura replies, looking me up and down. 'You're one of those *ectomorphs*.'

'I beg your pardon! How dare you!'

'It means your body type is long and lean. My body type is Teletubbie. Did I mention that I hate you?'

'Well, you've got killer boobs. I've always wanted bigger boobs. None of us are ever happy, are we?'

Cherie, with a body type that is entirely her own and defies all categorisation, adds: 'I'm just happy mine is all in one piece, and I can still get off the loo without a pull rail. You're gorgeous, Laura.'

Laura gazes down at her admittedly plump but perfectly curvy physique with a sigh. 'Thank you. I suppose I do eat a lot of cake. And Matt doesn't seem to mind…'

'Matt adores you, sweetie,' Cherie says, looming over her. 'And you'd be grumpy if you didn't eat the cake. You'd make all our lives a misery.'

Laura gives this some thought, then grins. 'You're right. So, in reality, me eating all the cake is a selfless act, designed to improve the quality of life of those around me. I'm practically a saint.'

'Well, once we get the cleaning done, you can go back to polishing your halo,' Cherie quips. They're a great double act, these two. You can tell they've worked together like this for years. I know from Max that she used to work here too, but now concentrates on the property business with Gabriel. Apparently, even though they've advertised for a replacement, they still haven't found 'the right person'. I'm led to believe that this is some kind of mystical process, and when that right person comes around, Cherie and Laura will 'just know it'. It sounds more complicated than choosing a new pope.

We finish off the work, and against the backdrop of the big dishwasher, Laura whips up the promised spiced lattes. Within minutes, we are sitting by the window, hot drinks and treats in front of us. Luna is outside in the small field next to the café, running around with a chaotic black Labrador – Laura's dog, Midgebo, I'm told, who has been banished after scoffing a whole tray of paninis.

'He's happy out there with Luna,' she says. 'There's a kennel with bedding. They've got space and water. On busy days there are often quite a few dogs in there. It's fun.'

I nod, and my mind wanders back to Juno and the other Wolfdogs. The sound of their howls, the way her fur felt beneath my fingers. The way Aidan looked at me when he spoke those words – 'damaged, not broken.'

'I went to Hazelwell today,' I announce, earning surprised looks from both of them. I laugh at their shocked reaction, and brace myself for the assault.

'What?' Laura shrieks. 'You went to see our gorgeous jogger? Without telling us? Matt is due out there tomorrow so I was hoping to have a scoop… Oh well. Go on, tell all!'

'You might as well, love,' Cherie adds. 'We'll lock you in the oubliette if you don't.'

'What's an oubliette?' Laura asks, frowning. 'And do we have one?'

'It's a dungeon where you put people to isolate them,'

I reply. 'From the French for *"oublier"*, to forget. I had one in a book once. An apparently normal suburban bank worker had one dug into his garage floor...'

Laura shudders. 'How horrid. Give me Bridget Jones or a nice Marian Keyes any day. I love a happy ending.'

'There was a happy ending,' I tell her. 'His seven kidnapped victims were all rescued before he released the poison gas. Admittedly, some of them were missing body parts, but they all survived.'

'That', Laura says, pointing at me with her spoon, 'is not my idea of a happy ending. You can make it up to me by telling me all about your visit to Hazelwell. Did he have his shirt on?'

'Not to start off with, no. But I did find out why your friend heard howling. He has dogs. Really big dogs that are part wolf. They're... Oh, they're so beautiful! Though I admit I was a bit scared to start with. He adopted them from a rescue centre.'

Both women sigh, and yet again I have to laugh. They have the exact same soppy expressions on their faces, and I get it, I really do. He's a charming, good-looking guy who loves animals. The only way he could be better would be if he decided to become a fireman as well.

'Edie says she's invited him to the ball,' Laura says, her gaze dreamy. 'I wonder if he'll come. I wonder if he'll wear a top. I mean, I do like him bare-chested, but I bet he'd look good in a tuxedo too. Or a cape, you know, like a super-swish Count Dracula?'

'Maybe you can ask him,' Cherie says, nodding at the window. 'Here he comes, making his regular appearance...'

Had I forgotten that he runs past here at this time every afternoon, or did my subconscious mind persuade me that this was the exact right moment for me to pop in to the café? They can be sneaky things, those subconscious minds. I glance subtly through the glass, refusing to full-on stare like some desperate cougar. Cougar. God, I hate that word. It sounds so predatory, doesn't it? Men have been cougars for time immemorial, but nobody came up with a derogatory term for them.

He gives us a wave as he passes, and part of me wonders if he will gallop up the steps again and come in to say hello. I suspect the others are thinking the same, because they look disappointed when he runs on past, sticking to his usual route up to the village. I think perhaps I'm disappointed too, but I manage not to look it. Cherie and Laura are far less guarded with their feelings.

'Ah well,' Cherie says, slapping her hands down on the table. 'That was our fun for the day, I suppose! Bloody hell, I'm knackered… We really need to get some help around here. I keep trying to retire but end up being dragged back in!'

'Rubbish,' Laura says firmly, clearing our plates. 'You'd be bored rigid. You'd just sit upstairs and listen to Joni Mitchell and cry into your kaftan. A woman like you isn't made for retirement, Cherie. Right. I'd better be off. Becca's picked the girls up for me. She's giving them their tea… They always come home raving about having their tea at Becca's, and you know what, all she ever does is fish fingers or frozen pizzas! Here's me, slaving my fingers to the bone making them delicious and nutritious home-cooked food, and what do they prefer? Ready meals!'

'They're only six, hon, give them time,' Cherie replies, scraping back her chair and rising majestically to her feet. 'And do you want to take some of that Bakewell home with you?'

'Good thinking, Batman! Have you asked Sarah here what her comfort food is?'

Cherie starts packaging up slices of tart, and I notice she automatically does some for me as well. I may never need to cook again. 'It's one of our little quirks,' she explains, passing it over to me. 'We like to find out what each of our regulars' comfort food is, and we try to always have it in stock. My favourite is Sam's: chicken and mushroom flavour Pot Noodles!'

I ponder this question very seriously, because both of them are gazing at me as though it genuinely is the most pressing issue on their minds. I run through childhood dinners, treats and forbidden fruits, and cast my mind back over the many fancy restaurants I've been to in more recent years. I really can't come up with one single item.

'Umm … this is shameful I know, but I'm not sure I have one,' I say eventually. 'I think for me, it might not be one single comfort food. Maybe it would be a comfort meal?'

They both look confused, and I try to explain. 'Okay, so, when I was a kid, we didn't eat together a lot. Different work shifts, plus just generally a sense of not being bothered. And when we did, it was … a bit of an ordeal, let's leave it at that. I remember watching TV shows and seeing these images of big family meals, even on the adverts, everyone sitting around a table, chatting and laughing? It just didn't seem real to me. And then I suppose, apart from the few years I was married, I got used to cooking for one, which I don't mind at all. But…'

'You still have a yearning for it?' Cherie asks, placing a comforting hand on my shoulder. 'For that big family Sunday lunch feeling?'

I nod. 'I do. Is that pathetic at my age?'

I wonder if maybe it is? It's strange, but I never even realised I did 'have a yearning for it' until I was asked to think about the subject. I thought I was perfectly happy eating by myself every day. Something about this place, though, just has a way of unravelling all your secrets, even the ones you keep from yourself.

'Not at all, darling. It's what we all want, isn't it? Those simple pleasures – sitting with those we care about and breaking bread. It's easy to think this is just a café, that what Laura and I do is basic, but it's really not. People have bonded by sharing food and drink and shelter for as long as humans have existed. We might not be sitting around a fire in a cave anymore, but we still turn to each other for safety and love and support. And family, you know, comes in many different shapes and forms. Take Laura here – no blood relation, but if I'd ever had a daughter, I'd have wanted her to be nothing like her at all…'

Laura tries to look offended, but can't stop herself laughing. 'You're a cow, Cherie Bloom! And no, Sarah, it's really not pathetic. And even if it was, we wouldn't mind. We're all pathetic sometimes. Right. I really do have to go now. Becca will be giving the kids tinned rice pudding for their afters, and they'll think it's the best thing ever…'

She's turning to leave when the door to the café opens, and we all fall silent as Aidan walks in. He has his top on for once, and he smiles as he enters. In his hands is a small bouquet of bright sunflowers, their vibrant petals an unusual shade of orange-tinted yellow.

'Hi, Cherie, Laura,' he says, heading towards us. We're all frozen in place, staring at him. We must look ridiculous, but I'd guess he's used to this kind of thing happening to him. He draws closer, his eyes holding mine. 'Sarah. These are for you. When the sunlight hits your hair, it's almost exactly the same colour. Enjoy, and I'll see you soon. Juno sends her love.'

He passes me the flowers, and I manage to mutter a surprised 'thank you'. He gives us all a nod, and he's gone as quickly as he came. I'm left standing there, staring at the flowers, feeling totally taken aback. I'm very aware that Laura and Cherie are sharing significant glances around me, but I don't really know what to say.

'I usually buy my own flowers…' is all I manage.

'Well, that's as may be, my love, but isn't it nice for someone else to do it every once in a while?' Cherie says, admiring the bouquet.

'Oh my God,' Laura says, her voice low and excited. 'You're… Sarah, you're being wooed! I know you said you weren't looking for anything like that, but you're being wooed!'

I look up at her, feeling the frown develop on my face. I realise that I've been standing here smiling, like some

143

lovestruck teenager. She's right. I did say I wasn't looking for anything like that, and I meant it. I'm just getting carried away with all the attention. It's flattering, and I'm only human, but I need to stay grounded.

'I don't get wooed,' I reply, shaking my head. 'I've never been wooed. I just don't give off that kind of vibe. I'm a woo-free zone.'

'Well,' she says, sliding her coat on and giving me a look, '*someone* seems to disagree. Why don't you just go along for the ride, enjoy it, and see what happens?'

Ha, I think, laughing inside. That comment is living proof that she barely knows me at all. We say goodbye to Cherie, and Laura walks with me up to the village. She chatters away, and I answer when required, until we reach my house. She doesn't immediately continue on to her sister's, but stops by my front door and puts a hand on my arm.

'I know I come across as a middle-aged airhead,' she says, and before I can protest, she continues, 'and I do witter on. But believe me when I say I understand pain, and loss, and the way that sometimes in life, you can be surrounded by people and still feel isolated. You're not me, and I'm not you, but Budbury is Budbury. Try not to be too cynical about it. It really is a place where very special things have been known to happen.'

Her words are so heartfelt that I can't possibly argue. I just nod, and promise her I'll try. Maybe I even will, I think, as I head inside and put the flowers into one of my new vases. They look beautiful on the dining table, and I find myself standing there staring at them, a big dumb grin on my face. I'm so distracted that I almost jump out of my skin when my phone rings. Ha, I think, feeling the adrenaline flood my body, serves me right – I forgot to be on high alert for a moment there.

I see my niece Libby's name on the screen, and happily answer it. 'Hey, Libs,' I say, 'how's it going?'

'Surprise, it's me!' my sister says instead. 'You've not returned my calls, and I had a sneaking suspicion that if you saw my name pop up you might not be as quick to answer…'

Damn her. She's right. I love my sister dearly, but we are very different people. She's always been so confident and outgoing, and she loves to talk. Literally for ages, about absolutely nothing. She started working part-time when the twins were born, and really should consider going back to longer hours now – she has way too much time to fill. She's called several times since I moved, which would be nice if it was to hear my news, but it's actually been to talk about her own life, to moan about the world, and to complain incessantly about the demands of organising the twins' birthday party.

'Sally, what a terrible thing to say!' I reply. 'Even if it is true… Sorry, I've been busy.'

'Doing what?' she asks, and I hear the sound of glasses in the background. I smile as I picture her in her kitchen, grabbing a wine glass and pouring a Malbec. Sally has never cared much for what she's supposed to do, yet another trait that is both infuriating and admirable.

'Oh, you know … work, making friends, being wooed.'

'Work, I believe. But making friends? Being wooed?' she

says, sounding comedically shocked. 'That doesn't sound like you at all! Are you making this up?'

It's slightly annoying that she immediately asks that, assuming that I'm incapable of change. She is probably right, but still. I could fill her in on the café, on the ladies I've met, on Aidan, but I really can't be bothered. I will tell her everything when we see each other, or the next time we are alone together. For now, it's easier to just go along with her.

'Yes,' I reply. 'You know me. Solitary bee all the way.'

'I do. Anyway, I needed to talk to you about the party…'

I grimace. Of course she does. I listen for the next fifteen minutes as she discusses catering, a problem with the DJ, and the fact that she's hired both a photo booth and a photographer for the night. I let it roll over me in a blur of words, sitting on a chair and admiring my sunflowers as she talks.

This party has taken on a life of its own, and I think in some ways it is as much for her as the girls, as well as their friends. It sounds like all of Sally's pals are coming, plus extended family on both sides. I understand that, I really do – she's the one who birthed them, and raising twins is not easy. Them turning eighteen is significant to Sally as well, and I can understand why she's gone all in with it – it's a celebration for parents too. I just wish she hadn't turned into Partyzilla, raging on about the smallest of issues, currently griping about the ever-expanding guest list.

'At least I know you won't be causing me trouble, sis. You won't be making special requests for seating arrangements, or insisting on vegan canapés, or asking to bring a plus one.'

Good old reliable me, I think, never any trouble. What a trooper Sarah Wallis is. Quietly divorced with no fuss. Always available for babysitting. Working from home like a dependable little drone. Doesn't even mention her bloody stalker, for goodness' sake. I take up practically no space at all, especially compared to Sally's expansive life of kids, hubby, career, lunches, skiing trips and a million and one petty dramas. That's the dynamic that has always existed between us, and I've been happy to take the back seat. But suddenly, I feel a flash of annoyance.

'Why', I ask, reaching out to stroke the velvety-soft petals of the flowers, 'would you assume that I won't be bringing a plus one?'

I hear the wine being glugged, and then she says: 'Well, because you live like a nun, babe. Let's be honest, you didn't exactly set the dating world alight when you lived in London, did you? So I can't imagine it's much different in deepest darkest Dorset. Do they even have men under eighty there?'

It's not Sally's fault that she doesn't know about Martin/Scott, obviously. It's mine for not telling her. She probably would have been super supportive, and knowing her, offered to go round and put his windows in. But there is a reason I didn't tell her, and it's only partly to do with my own sense of shame and humiliation. It's also to do with the fact that she always does this: reduces my life and what happens to me to a one-sentence summary that feels incredibly dismissive. She's always overshadowed me, and that is something I came to terms with long ago. In fact I even welcomed it, because it meant nobody paid me much attention at all.

But really, here we are, almost fifty – and she still doesn't seem to see me as a fully formed human being. I'm still just her lame little (by twenty minutes) sister.

'Actually, I do want to bring a plus one,' I say assertively. You have to really push to make Sally hear you. I fight the urge to add, 'If that's okay with you?'

I've played a big part in Lucy and Libby's lives. I've been a good aunt. I've loved them, nurtured them, taken them on trips, showered them with gifts, looked after them when their parents went away for romantic weekends. I've even gone and given a talk to their English class, the memory of which still makes me cringe. I've listened to countless complaints from Sally, and provided a spare room when she's had huge rows with Ollie. I've basically always been there, a supporting actress, always on hand, waiting in the wings until I was needed. Why the hell wouldn't I deserve to bring a plus one to the bloody party?

A pause, and then: 'Right. Well, I suppose I can make that happen, Sarah … but really, couldn't you have warned me earlier? It's very inconsiderate to drop that one on me so late in the day.'

She sounds irritated, and so am I. But I also know that one of the reasons she is irritated is because she is stressed. The party is her camouflage, but I suspect things aren't great with her and Ollie. She's actually barely mentioned him recently, which is a sign; she usually relentlessly lists the things he's done to piss her off, then laughs and says something like 'but hey, I still love him, the old goat!'

Add to that the fact that our parents will stay with her while they're in town, and that never improves anybody's stress levels. She gets on with them better than I do, but it will be one of her concerns. Sally has her anxieties too. She's just much better at hiding them than I am.

I take a deep breath, determined not to let it escalate, and reply: 'Well, let me know. Look, I need to go. Work calls.'

'Of course. Speak soon. Love you.'

I hang up, and wonder why I just did that. Why did I deliberately cause a problem where one needn't have existed? I suppose it was the result of a lifetime of her taking me for granted and assuming she knows everything about me. I've not been in my new home for long, but I already feel like the people here know me in a completely different way from my sister. Maybe I'm starting to see myself through their eyes and liking what I see.

The only problem now is that I need to find a plus one … and that will come with its own set of complications.

Chapter Eleven

I am sitting in a clearing in the woods around Aidan's home, on a picnic blanket, sipping coffee from a flask. He is lounging at my side, gazing up at the trees above us. Sunlight is filtering through the green-and-brown canopy, dappling earth that is heavy with fallen leaves, twines of flowering ivy curling around solid trunks. We are surrounded by the colours of nature – rich autumnal golds, vibrant deep reds, the whites and creams of mushrooms and wild clematis. The air is fragrant with the smell of it all, the melodic twitter of birdcall our soundtrack.

It could be any normal picnic in the woods if not for the fact that we are currently being stalked by wolves. Juno is with us, happily alternating between running around with her pack-mates, and depositing herself in a panting ball of fur by our side. She's very interested in the picnic basket in front of us, but is well enough trained not to simply attack it.

'Laura's dog ate a whole tray of paninis the other day,' I tell him.

He laughs, and says: 'Labrador by any chance?'

'Yes. A very naughty one, obviously. Juno looks like she'd quite like to raid the picnic basket too.'

'She probably would. I'm going to get some chicken out and feed her a scrap soon. And then bit by bit, the others might be brave enough to come in. They'll be tempted by the meat, and they'll see Juno interacting with you, and me interacting with you, and start to relax a little.'

I nod and cast my eyes around the little clearing where we've based ourselves. One of the Wolfdogs is sitting watching us, his fur a silvery grey with dark markings. He's called Argent, and he seems the most likely candidate for coming forward. The others are still further back.

Aidan sits up, and I tear my eyes from the dog to look at him. I watch as he calls Juno over and feeds her a treat. Then he passes them to me, and I do the same. She is remarkably gentle, and I feel a rush of warmth towards her.

'If one of them does come over, try to relax,' he says. 'Don't make any sudden movements. It's okay to talk. And by the way, did I mention how much I love your hair?'

My cheeks flame, predictably enough, and he smiles at my response. 'Um. You can't tell me to relax then say things like that.'

'Ah, but I can,' he says, stroking Juno's ears. 'That day I came across you at Eggardon Hill? You were watching the sunset. I was watching you. The colours set your hair on fire, and I could almost feel the heat.'

Oh my Lord. This man. I've very much stopped thinking

of him as a boy, because his personality simply doesn't allow for it. He's too experienced, too worldly, too confident. He sometimes makes me feel like a girl, though, and I can't make my mind up whether I like that or not. I definitely shouldn't, but I have a sneaky suspicion that I do.

'I don't know how to respond to that,' I say, shaking my head, now suddenly conscious of my loose hair on my shoulders.

'No need. Your blush is doing it for you. So, Argent is coming over. Just carry on as you are. Don't try and coax him or call him, just let him do what he feels comfortable with.'

The other dog lopes towards us hesitantly, one step forward then a couple back, like he simply can't make his mind up. Juno lets out a little yip, maybe of encouragement, and when he gets close enough Aidan holds out a small chunk of chicken. Argent gobbles it up, looks at me curiously, then runs away. He disappears off into the woods to join the others, and although I know they're close, I can't quite see any of them. I presume if I got up and left, they'd all creep out to see Aidan.

Aidan himself is now grinning ear to ear, and it's infectious. He's clearly delighted.

'That was fantastic,' he says. 'I didn't think any of them would actually come that close! Even if that's as far as we get for today, it's progress. Thank you. It's… Well, I guess it's nice to do these things with someone. I like my own space, and my mom says I'm a "lone wolf" myself, but I start to go slightly too feral if I'm alone for too long.'

I can't ever imagine a man like Aidan being short of

company. But then again, looking from the outside in, maybe people would say the same about me. Yet here we both are, carving out our solitary paths in life, bumping into each other in this remote corner of the world.

'Me too,' I admit. 'I have a terrible tendency to disappear up my own backside for days on end. Some of it's the nature of my work. Some of it's the nature of me, I suppose. I'm not very good at … you know … people.'

He reaches out and tucks a strand of hair behind my ear, and the unexpected contact makes me jump. I try to hide it, but of course he notices.

'I'm sorry,' he says quietly. 'I didn't mean to do that.'

'It's okay. I was just surprised. Like I said, I'm not good at people.'

He looks on as Juno runs into the woods, and replies: 'You're doing just fine with this particular person. I'm a patient guy.'

'I get that, Aidan. But I still don't quite understand why you think I'm worth waiting for. We barely know each other. You could… Well, let's not lie, you could have any woman you wanted, looking the way you look, being the way you are.'

He raises his eyebrows and laughs. 'Being the way I am?'

'Yeah. Confident. Flirty. Touch of the tortured soul. All that stuff.'

'Wow. I'm going to start putting that on my résumé. As to the rest of that, I call bullshit. Technically, we barely know each other. But I've told you more about myself in a week than I have anybody else in a year. I felt it as soon as we met, a pull, an attraction. Admittedly, to start with, it was just because you look great, but now? Now, I like you. You're funny. You're smart. You're interesting. I think you like me too. And I want to see where this goes.'

I want to tell him he's mad, that he's imagining it. But I can't. It's all true, and I've felt that same pull, much as I'd like to deny it.

'Are you sure I'm not just a challenge? I bet you're used to women falling at your feet. Perhaps this is just the novelty of me remaining upright.'

He laughs and says: 'I love the way you put things! And yeah, maybe that's part of it, but what's wrong with that? It doesn't mean that as soon as I persuade you to become not-upright – I'll leave that to your imagination – I'll lose interest. I'm not that guy.'

'Okay,' I reply, not quite knowing how to deal with all of this. Maybe a touch of honesty would help us both. 'But you should know this about me: I have baggage. The emotional kind.'

'I'd be worried if you didn't. So do I. Maybe we can unpack it together.'

My eyes widen at the idea, but then I ask myself, would that really be so bad? Why do I feel ashamed and embarrassed about the things that have happened to me? Why do I always somehow manage to take on the blame when other people treat me badly?

'Maybe we can,' I say quietly. 'Maybe we can. I get … nervous, I suppose. I'm easily spooked. It takes a lot for me to peek out of my shell, and in the past, whenever I've done that, I've ended up being hurt. I'm not in a great rush to go through that again, so I make no promises. I can be your friend. I can help you with the dogs. Anything else… Well, I have no clue if I'm even capable of anything else right now. I don't want to lead you on in any way.'

He nods and looks away for a moment. 'All right. I can handle that. But tell me one thing. I'm not imagining it, am I? That there is this spark between us? Because if I am, tell me now, and I will stop pursuing anything other than friendship. Because I'm also not *that* guy.'

'What guy are you, exactly?'

'I'm the guy telling you he likes you. I'm the guy telling you he thinks you're beautiful. I'm the guy telling you I can't stop thinking about you.'

Oh, I think, feeling the heat rise inside me. *That* guy. It's not just my face that is hot right now; it's my whole body. My eyes run over his broad shoulders, his long jean-clad legs, his thick, dark hair. I don't think I've ever met a man I find so attractive. Even looking at him makes me breathless.

I could take this as a way out, I know. He's asked the question, and I need to answer it. I could simply tell him that yes, he is imagining it, and leave it at that. But I would be lying, and I really don't think I could bring myself to do that.

'No,' I answer simply. 'You're not imagining it.'

He turns to look back at me, and gives me the smile. His green eyes sparkle, and he looks so damn perfect that if a magical rainbow suddenly appeared behind him and a choir of angels started singing his theme tune, I wouldn't be at all surprised.

'Good. I won't push. We'll go at your pace. Friendship first. Hot, wild sex and screaming orgasms later.'

He winks at me, and I laugh so loud I startle birds from trees.

'Who knows? Anyway. Now we've cleared the air and laid down some boundaries … how do you fancy meeting my entire family?'

Chapter Twelve

The next two weeks pass in a slightly bewildering blur. I paint the downstairs rooms of my house, and am thrilled with the result. Despite many lovely offers of help, and of course the temptation of seeing Aidan carrying out manual labour and possibly even wearing a tool belt, I do it myself. The house is small and I like decorating. I enjoy all of the dull and tedious processes of it – the cleaning, the masking tape, the careful placement of the dust sheets, then the actual act itself. It's really quite zen in its own way.

It also makes it even more satisfying to sit in my little cocoon of a home in the evening, reading a book and enjoying the peace and quiet. It feels more like *mine* now, somehow. Maxine has been round and declared my floorboards in decent condition, ready to be sanded down and painted or varnished, depending on my tastes. That's a job for later, because it will involve someone else with better skills than mine coming into my home. Gabriel, I would feel safe with, but somebody completely new? I'm not ready for such craziness.

I have paid a visit to Briarwood, and been given a guided tour by Finn, Auburn the pharmacist's husband. He had the air of a slightly weary father, even though all of his charges are technically adults. The house itself is a grand affair, perched on a hill overlooking the village, obviously once a very noble place. I'm told it went from being a base during the war to being a private boarding school for children whose parents were either not around, or not interested in looking after them. One of the orphaned youngsters who lived there grew up to be a businessman and inventor called Tom Mulligan, who bought the place after it had fallen into dereliction, and restored it.

Now, he uses it as a hot-house residential for bright young things to experiment and hone their skills. It's like Hogwarts for engineers. Tom himself isn't around, because he is married to Willow, Auburn's sister, and lives with her in Spain. At least I think I've got all of that right. There's a lot to remember about this place and the way everybody is interconnected. It's like a very benign spiderweb of relationships.

I have been to Edie's house for tea, a few doors down from mine, and was surprised to be greeted in the living room by a life-sized cardboard version of the dancer Anton du Beke. Edie's favourite, apparently. She is a mine of information about the village and its past, as well as an absolute hoot.

I have visited with Cherie on several occasions, and she has called in here as well. I think she likes having someone to sit and chat with, someone else who also doesn't have a partner or children. The last time she came, we stayed up until the early hours, drinking the sloe gin she'd brought with her and talking nonsense. It was such a lot of fun, I kind of wished we could just move in together. That is the first time I've ever thought that about anyone, even my husband, Will. When we lived together, I always felt protective of my space, keen to keep a bubble of my own territory.

I've worked on my edits, sketched out a rough plot for my next book, and done some boring life admin like filing accounts. I've been busy, in a non-stressful, non-urgent way.

I have also continued to be very steadily wooed by Aidan Calloway, much to the café ladies' delight. The more restrained of them, like Katie and Zoe, are interested but polite. The more raucous, like Laura and Auburn, are pretty much committed to the idea of me allowing myself to be seduced, just so I can provide them with a full report. 'You need to take one for the team,' Laura said. 'As part of your initiation into our sisterhood.'

She said that last part very seriously, conjuring up images of them all donning robes and making me drink chicken's blood out on the moors at midnight. Not that there are moors, but you know what I mean.

Aidan himself is taking it all in his stride, obviously used to the attention of women and happy to be in their company. A few days ago, we called in there together after a long walk along the cliff tops, damp from a sudden torrential rainfall and seeking refuge. Laura offered to run his clothes through the tumble dryer, and I could barely make eye contact with her. She has no shame at all, and even though he declined, she spent the rest of our visit humming *I Heard It Through The Grapevine* by Marvin Gaye. It took me a moment, but then I remembered; it was the soundtrack to the old advert where the super good-looking guy strips off his clothes in the launderette.

So far, he's taken me out to a gorgeous gastropub a few towns over, joined me on a visit to an art gallery in Lyme Regis, and cooked me dinner at his place. The man is infuriatingly accomplished. We've continued to work with the dogs and are making progress; they are starting to ignore me now rather than run away from me. It's a start, at least.

I'm still borderline confused as to why he is bothering with me at all, but maybe that says more about me than it does about him. He continues to be a perfect gentleman, and seems genuinely satisfied to accept friendship with a healthy side helping of flirtation for now. There was a moment, when he dropped me off after dinner, when I thought he might try to kiss me. He opened the car door for me, and as I climbed out I tripped over my own feet and staggered against him. He immediately caught me and held me steady, our faces inches apart, our breath mingling in the cool night sky, my body pressed against his.

I felt excited and trapped at the same time, and my expression must have reflected that. He smiled, dropped a gentle kiss on my forehead, and said: 'You look like a startled deer with those big brown eyes. Don't worry, Bambi – you're safe with me.'

As he drove off into the night, I stood on my doorstep,

lost in thought. My emotions were very mixed, but the overwhelming one was disappointment. Even the soft brush of his lips on my skin had excited me, leaving my pulse racing in a way I'm really not used to. I was so distracted I stayed there, in the open, alone at night, for whole minutes without even considering whether an axe murderer might be on a rampage looking for victims.

Even now, days later, thinking about it makes me flush. It also makes me wonder why I'm resisting this thing, this attraction. My body is extremely keen on taking it further. As ever, it's just my stupid brain holding me back. That and the fact that I like living in Budbury, and I don't want to mess it up. When things go wrong with Aidan – and in my usual optimistic way I assume they will – I don't want to have to avoid him, or for us to feel awkward around each other.

I try not to think about it now, as I get ready for Libby and Lucy's birthday party. I'll just end up stabbing myself in the eyeball with my mascara. Then my eyes will water uncontrollably, and I'll end up having to do my whole face again. I have form for this kind of thing.

I haven't exactly got the steadiest of hands right now. I've spent the whole afternoon with my sister, and my nerves feel like someone has doused them in petrol and then thrown on a hand grenade. I'm absolutely frazzled. She was stressed and highly strung, and as a result finding fault in absolutely everything. We were at the venue – a hotel near their home in Islington – all afternoon, and by the end of it I suspect the manager was ready to cancel the booking and take the financial hit.

Sally, in all fairness, is not normally awful to deal with. She is normally charming and enthusiastic, her caustic comments usually landing on the right side of bitchy. Today, though, she is really not herself. She sniped at everyone she came into contact with, nothing was good enough and the whole world was against her. I have no idea what is going on with her, and maybe it will all pass once the party is out of the way, but today has not been great. Everything from our parents to the balloon arch to the caterers came in for criticism. Everything except Ollie, I couldn't help noticing.

Even though I've been with her for hours, helping as best I can, lugging tables around and putting up giant poster photo montages of the girls, she still announced: 'Why do I always have to do absolutely bloody everything on my own, all the time? Why?'

I was clearly the invisible woman, taken for granted as usual. I let it slide, because she was almost crying as she spoke. That weird woman combination of anger and sadness that makes us look weak, when we're actually furious.

I felt sorry for her, and I was worried. Could it just be the stress, or some kind of delightful menopause mood swing thing? Or is there something bigger lurking beneath the surface? Sally has always been good at pretending everything is fine, even to herself. She's the kind of woman who would hit the dance floor during the end of the world, and bust out a quick Macarena as civilisation crumbled around her.

'Are you all right?' I said at the end of the day, as we had a quick drink before getting ready. 'You seem a bit ... stretched?'

She glared at me, narrowed her eyes, and said: 'Yes. Well. Let's just hope I continue to stretch, eh? Let's just hope I don't run out of stretch and completely snap! Who is it you're bringing tonight anyway? Is it some old biddy you met at the W.I.? Or a chubby farmer type in wellies who smells of cow shit?'

'You think they're the only kinds of people I could meet in the countryside?'

She stood up, grabbed her bag, ready to leave. 'I'm amazed you've met anybody at all, Sarah. I assumed you'd just batten down the hatches never to be seen again! You've never been the best at engaging with the real world, have you?'

I stared at her and bit my tongue. She was lashing out at me because she's upset. Or possibly, because it's just the way things go between us. I finished my drink and replied: 'No, I really haven't. I'll see you later, with or without Worzel Gummidge.'

She nodded, barely registering my sarcasm, and left. Our mum and dad were already back at her house, so I was glad to stay here. I spent a pleasant hour or so replying to emails and watching videos of Golden Retrievers on my phone, enjoying my own company. A day spent with my sister is always enough to remind me why I live alone.

I've brought my dress and make-up with me, and there's a very swish ladies' powder room where I'm currently glamming myself up ahead of the big event. I went to the salon earlier and had my hair done with what I was reliably informed was 'pin curls'. The lady told me that once I was set, I could take out the pins and I'd be party-prepped and ready to dazzle. It seems too much to hope for after an afternoon of moving furniture, but the pins are in fact all still in.

My dress is new, a simple fitted sheath that goes just below the knee, made from a silky fabric in a deep shade of forest green. I run my hands over it as I stand in front of the mirror, feeling suddenly uncertain. It's more fitted than I'm used to, hugging my body in a way that makes me feel a little exposed. It's strapless but the top feels pretty secure. I make sure to test it out, though, by jumping up and down, jogging on the spot and doing some very vigorous dancing while singing Footloose out loud. That results in no slippage, no hint of a potential wardrobe malfunction, and only a minor case of being out-of-puff.

Is it too much, I think, gazing at my reflection? Is it too young for me? Is it too dark on my pale skin? Why am I even thinking about this so much?

I don't often get dolled up. My job sounds glamorous, but the reality is that I spend a lot of time alone in my pyjamas. Yes, there are events and parties and public appearances, but I've cut those back to the bare minimum and developed a kind of work uniform for them. Smart black trousers and matching jacket, plain shoes, minimal fuss. I probably look like an FBI agent from a movie, now I come to think about it. That fits with my writing and it's relatively little trouble, but it's not exactly alluring.

Tonight, I realise as I stare at this stranger in the glass,

I'm aiming for alluring. It doesn't take a genius to figure out why, and I immediately blush. I've applied my make-up with a lot more care than usual, I'm wearing a fancy new frock and slinky black heels. I tug out the little pins that have been strategically placed in my hair, and as promised it rolls down my shoulders in a whoosh of waves. I fluff it up with my hands, and stand back to survey the finished result.

I look completely different. I look like a fashionable, attractive, confident woman. If only, I think as I apply some lipstick, I could actually feel like that as well. This all feels like I'm playing a part, like a kid dressing up in her mum's wardrobe. It's not the real me, but maybe that's a good thing. Maybe the real me has been hiding in the shadows for too long. Maybe the real me is a bit of a wuss. The fake me looks pretty kick-ass. I don't think I'll mind being her, at least for a night.

I spritz on some perfume and fight down the urge to simply run away. This is a celebration of my wonderful nieces' eighteenth birthday, and I will not skip it. I will tolerate my parents and their toxic jibes; I will not overreact to my sister, and I will not plot a great escape because Aidan is coming and that is also freaking me out. I will do all of this because I love Libby and Lucy, and because I am Not A Wuss. I abbreviate it in my head to NAW, which makes me laugh. I should get it tattooed somewhere subtle, like my forehead, just so I never forget.

My ponderings are interrupted by the arrival of a gaggle of giggling teenagers. They pour into the room, filling the pink-and-marble space with their youth and chatter and clattering heels. Lucy is one of them, tall and slender, her red hair gleaming.

'Auntie Sarah!' she exclaims, coming over to hug me. 'You look amazing! What happened?'

'I don't know,' I reply seriously. 'I think I might have been kidnapped by the makeover police. Happy birthday, sweetie!'

It's not their actual birthday for another three days, but who wants a party on a Tuesday?

She thanks me, and I emerge out into the lobby and then our function room. While I've been completing my transformation, quite a few guests have turned up. I spot Libby with her own little group of friends, and blow her a kiss, and find Sally at the bar holding a glass of champagne. She's staring at it like it holds the answers to all the mysteries of the universe.

'Oh. There you are,' she says, glancing up at me. 'I thought you might have done a runner.'

No comment at all about my dress or the way I look, even though I can tell she's noticed. Okay, I think, I've kind of had enough now. I am NAW, after all.

'Is there something going on with you, Sally?' I ask, grabbing my own drink from the tray. 'Or are you just being a cow for no good reason?'

She gapes slightly, and I know from experience it could go one of two ways now. Either she'll cave and apologise, or go nuclear. She pauses, then shakes her head.

'Sorry, sis. Just… Just a cow, I suppose. Too much stress. Mum and Dad have been pains in the arse, and Dad has already started on the whisky. "To toast the girls' big day," he said. As though he ever needed an excuse. Do you remember our eighteenth?'

I nod grimly. It's not the most idyllic of childhood memories. There was no flashy party like this, just a group of our friends gathered in the local pub. It was the kind of place that sold egg and chips, and showed horse racing on a big screen. My dad had got absolutely obliterated and ended up having a physical fight with one of his drinking buddies at the bar. They had disagreed about something stupid, probably to do with football, and because they were both hammered it got nasty very quickly. Dad ended up decking him onto the pool table, scattering the balls and knocking our friends out of the way as he did it.

I was mortified and just went home and cried. Sally was mortified too, but she always handled things better than I did. She made a big joke of it, and somehow ended up looking even cooler. That party became the stuff of legend in our school, the stories about it getting wilder and wilder until it resembled one of those huge saloon fights in a Western movie.

'How could I forget?' I say, spotting my parents over in the far corner of the room. I'll have to speak to them at some point, but not right now. 'This won't be anything like that, Sally. Your girls are lucky; they've got the best mum in the world.'

She looks at me, and I see a faint sheen of tears in her eyes. 'You think so? I don't know. I always feel like I'm messing up. Lucy is vaping, even though she thinks I don't know about it, and Libby's scared of her own shadow, worried all the time. I just want them to be happy...'

'They are,' I assure her. 'They're just not perfect. Neither were we. You've done a great job with them. You really have.'

'Thank you,' she says quietly. 'And you look gorgeous, by the way. I feel quite frumpy standing next to you. I'm not sure I like it.'

'Ha! You couldn't look frumpy if you tried.'

This is completely true. Sally is curvier than me, with curly blond hair and a great smile. One of those 'light up the room' smiles, although I haven't seen much of it tonight.

'That's a good point,' she responds, with a hint of her usual sass. 'Thank you for reminding me. Now, I suppose I'd better go and mingle.'

The room is fairly full now, a mix of excited-looking teens and adults. Ollie is chatting to my parents, and I say a silent prayer to whoever might be listening that my dad behaves himself tonight. He's seventy-four now and he has slowed down a little. He talks about his prostrate a lot, and only goes to the pub four nights a week instead of seven. But he's still a big, robust man, still as domineering as ever, and I never quite relax when he's around.

I'm sure Ollie has heard all about our eighteenth many times over, and will hopefully be on alert for any signs of aggression in my father. The trouble with my dad, though, as it often is with bullies, is that he can unpredictable, jolly one minute, vile the next. In a split second his eyes narrow and his voice changes, and then anyone who knows him prepares to duck and cover. I shudder a little at the prospect of spending time with them, and then remind myself I'm NAW.

I might not be a wuss, but I'm also in no rush to dash over there and start receiving my traditional interrogation. My answers will go something along the lines of: 'Yes, I'm still single.' 'No, I don't think moving to Dorset was a mistake.' 'Yes, it is lovely seeing the twins.' And 'No, I don't regret not having children myself.' The last one isn't entirely true, but I don't trust my parents enough to be vulnerable around them.

The truth would be that while I don't sit around pining or weeping for the babies I never had, it is a little lump of sadness I carry with me. I would never let them see that, though. I have always maintained that it was a deliberate decision, not because I have never had a relationship that felt secure enough to bring a child into. When I was married to Will, we both said we might try for a family 'in a few years, when the time is right'. Sadly, the time never was right, and at my age that ship has well and truly sailed.

I look at Lucy hitting the dance floor surrounded by her friends, and at Libby engaged in an intense conversation with a cute nerdy-looking boy with a long grunge-band hairstyle, and smile. At least I have them. I have been privileged enough to be a second mum to these magnificent creatures, and I don't think it would be possible to actually love them more or be prouder of them if they were my daughters instead of my nieces. In fact, I know it wouldn't.

I sip my champagne, and scan the room. I wave to people I'm familiar with – old friends of Sally's, mums I vaguely know from doing school runs in days gone by, colleagues from her and Ollie's work – and then tell myself to stop. I'm quite obviously searching for Aidan. I glance at my phone and see that it is only just after eight. The party officially started at half seven. He is not really late; he is just fashionably late. I have taken the astonishing step of actually giving him my mobile number, and there is no message from him. I have to assume that he is simply a little delayed, and have a bit of faith that he will be here soon. Huh, I think, snorting in amusement at myself – since when have I been any good at having faith?

Right on cue, one of the main reasons for that walks right up to me, a pint in hand. My dad is a tall man, beefy even though he is now older. My mum is at his side, the complete physical opposite. She looks like a little sparrow in comparison to his bird of prey. Always pretty, always neatly turned out, my mum looks fragile on the surface.

Appearances can be deceptive, though, and she is not a weak little woman. When she wants to, she stands her ground. She just rarely seems to want to. She usually defers to him, but when she is in the mood, she gives as good as she gets. They've never seemed happy together, and my childhood was punctuated by their ever-escalating rows. I thought that was normal until I spent time at friends' houses and saw their mums and dads laughing with each other, no glowering in sight. Still, as my mum would be the first to point out, who am I to comment on other people's relationships? I've certainly never been any good at managing my own.

I plaster on a smile and give her a kiss on the cheek. I turn to my father, and immediately carry out a risk assessment. Anybody who has grown up with a drinker knows to do that straight away. Within seconds, you learn how to spot the signs. How to differentiate between 'three pints in and still within normal limits of behaviour', and 'absolutely smashed and about to go full-on lunatic'. It's always fun, waiting for the moment when Jekyll and Hyde trade places.

Right now, he's hovering between the two. Sally said he was hitting the whisky at her place, and he's been here long enough to have topped that up with at least two pints of lager. We'll be okay for a while longer. If he shows any signs of messing up Lucy and Libby's party, I decide, I'll take him down myself. No idea how, but I'll manage it.

'You look nice,' my mum says, reaching up to touch my hair. The unspoken 'for a change' hovers between us, or maybe I'm imagining it. She's been dying her hair a bright shade of red for years, ever since her natural copper tones started to fade. 'I was told you were bringing a *date*?'

My dad snorts a little, and his lager jiggles in his glass. 'I'll believe that when I see it,' he says, gazing around the room. 'Maybe you've scared him off, like usual.'

My dad, for some reason I don't quite grasp, has a theory that I terrify men. Apparently having a successful career, being financially independent, and not being desperate to mind-meld into a couple makes me intimidating. He once told me I was an 'ice queen' and gave off 'frigid' vibes. He's a charming man.

The irony of all this is that Will left me, not the other way around, and as for me being the scary one… Well, I'm sure Martin/Scott would disagree. What my dad, and possibly others, perceive as me being cold is actually just me being afraid. It is the social equivalent of huddling up in a ball in the corner and hoping nobody hurts me. I could never in a million years explain that to him. He would laugh and tell me to toughen up. Or 'just be bloody normal for once', which was one of his favourite catchphrases when I was a kid. Looking back now, as an adult, I suspect my mum agreed with him. She certainly never objected.

While I have done a lot of growing up and changing, in the decades that have passed since I left home, there will always be a small part of me that thinks they might be right. It's one of the reasons I don't enjoy being around them. They make me feel even more vulnerable.

'Maybe I have, Dad,' I say, not ready or willing to rise to his bait. Sally joins us, and I see her eyes flicker between my father and me. She is also scanning for those signs, hyper-alert to threat. I give her a reassuring smile to let her know I'm okay, and that this isn't going to get out of hand.

'It's going great, Sal,' I say, gesturing to the now-packed dance floor. 'You've done a great job.'

'Cheers!' she says, raising her glass. 'I have, haven't I? Are you guys all right?'

'We're fine, love,' Dad says. 'But bloody hell, the prices in this place!'

'The bar's free, Dad,' she replies, shrugging. She knows as well as I do that logic has no place in my dad's universe.

'I know that, but I looked at the list. Eight quid for a pint?'

Sally and I swap glances, and I guess we're both thinking the same, that the free bar was a mistake. The cost alone might have put him off otherwise. I sigh inside, because every time I'm away from them, I forget how exhausting this is. Tip-toeing around his moods, constantly searching for flashpoints. He's like an overgrown toddler who never matured, and we all indulge him because we're scared of the consequences if we don't. I catch my mum biting her lip, and I wonder what she was like before she met him.

'Not to worry, Alan,' she says, patting him on the arm. 'Anyway, tell us about this man you're bringing, Sarah!'

She's deflecting attention onto me to avoid conflict, and I don't especially love it.

'Well, he's invisible for a start,' my dad interjects, laughing at his own joke. Sally rolls her eyes, but also sneaks a look at her watch. It is now almost half eight. Maybe he's not just fashionably late, I think, feeling the slow thud of disappointment sink in. Maybe he's just not coming. And who can blame him? I didn't exactly sell it – 'Can you pretend to be my date for the night to stop my nightmare family picking on me? Pretty please?'

I know he was heading into London to see his own family, having arranged for a friend to come and stay with the dogs. It's a woman who volunteers at the rescue he adopted them from, so they're familiar enough with her for him to sneak away for a couple of nights. Maybe he got caught up in something with his mum and sister. Maybe he's stuck in traffic. Maybe he simply changed his mind…

I feel much more upset than I would have expected at the idea of Aidan having let me down. I have no right to expect anything from him. Flirtatious as our relationship is, we are not actually a couple. He owes me nothing. All I've given him is some time and my phone number. And while they both feel like big commitments at my end, I know I'm especially weird about such things. Despite my father's tender encouragements, I've never quite figured out how to 'just be bloody normal'.

I'm trying to formulate a reply that answers their questions but also hides the slightly sick feeling I have in my throat, when Sally taps me on the arm.

'For the love of all that's holy,' she mutters, her head nodding towards the entrance. 'Who on earth is *that*?'

I follow her gaze, and my mouth falls open. It's Aidan, but it's a version of Aidan I've never seen before. He pauses in the doorway, dressed in an exquisitely tailored navy-blue suit that emphasises the length of his legs, his broad shoulders, his perfectly flat stomach. A white shirt is open a couple of buttons at the top, and his hair has been trimmed, the thick dark tresses shining beneath the lights. Some men wear suits well, but Aidan stands there like he was born in one. He looks unbelievable – like a model, or a Hollywood actor about to walk the red carpet.

We're not the only people noticing the new arrival. All around the room, women are sneaking peeks at him, some of the teenagers giggling and shoving each other, the mums smiling in appreciation. The nerdy grunge boy Libby is chatting to is openly staring at him, and even my mum looks taken aback.

Just as the music segues into 'Moves Like Jagger' by Maroon 5, he spots me, waves, and strides right across the dance floor. Everyone parts to let him pass, some of them gawking after him as he goes. Lucy is definitely checking out his ass, and pretend-fans her face with her hands as she does. She incorporates the action into the chorus, which is pretty neat.

Leaving a trail of distracted women behind him, he closes the distance between us. I manage to shut my mouth, but my eyes are still wide as he approaches. He's giving me the smile, and it is even more effective than usual. My knees literally go weak, and I lean back against the bar for support. Hot damn, he is gorgeous. I think Laura would literally explode if she saw him like this.

'Babe,' he says, his accent more pronounced than usual. 'You look … stunning.'

He swoops me into his arms and presses me close, his fingers twining into my hair as he holds my face a few inches away from his. I lose the power of speech, and he whispers into my ear: 'Just go with it, Bambi…'

My arms wrap around his waist, and our bodies melt into each other. His green eyes are shining – probably in amusement at my bewildered expression – and he gives me a barely-there wink. Then he kisses me. It is long; it is lingering; it is good enough to turn me into liquid. I have not been kissed for a very long time, and I have not been kissed quite like this in my entire life. It sets all of my senses alight – the way he looks, the touch of his lips on mine, the scent of masculine cologne. My hands creep up to his shoulders, and I cling on for dear life, wrapping my fingers around his neck.

By the time he pulls away, I'm breathless for all kinds of reasons. Our eyes maintain contact even after the kiss has ended, and I gaze up at him and blink. The man has kissed all the sense out of me.

'Wow,' Sally says, reminding me that the rest of the world exists. 'I feel like I should applaud…'

Aidan looks across, as though seeing her for the first time. He disentangles from me, but keeps my hand firmly held in his. I squeeze it, needing the support.

'You must be Sally,' he says, giving her the smile, but only a watered-down version. He keeps the big guns for me. 'I'm Aidan Calloway. Delighted to meet you.'

He holds out his other hand for Sally to shake, and she actually blushes. Now, for me this would simply be a sign that I was awake, but Sally never blushes. She sees embarrassment as a sign of weakness and usually refuses to have any dealings with it at all. At a guess, though, Aidan's sheer gorgeousness has undone her.

'And I'm Sarah's dad,' my father says, staring at him with a touch of belligerence. He's used to being the biggest man in the room, but Aidan has a good few inches on him and uses them well. To be fair he's also just snogged his daughter right in front of him.

'Sir,' he says, in such a polite tone that not even my argumentative dad could find fault with it. 'A pleasure. And who's this? Another sister?'

He uses such a flirty tone with my mum that she also blushes. Good lord, the man has ruined us all. She lets out a coquettish giggle and slaps him lightly on the arm. 'Get away with you,' she says, clearly delighted. 'I'm Sarah's mum of course!'

Sally is still staring at him, uncharacteristically lost for words, shaking her head slightly as though she's trying to wake herself up. I know exactly how she feels. I'm still reeling from that kiss. From that closeness.

When I came up with this stupid suggestion, we didn't actually discuss what this evening would look like in terms of physical contact. Maybe naively, I didn't even consider it. I just had this half thought-out idea that it would stop my parents and my sister from seeing me as a tragic spinster. Maybe I anticipated a bit of handholding, or an arm around the shoulder, just to make it look real.

What I hadn't anticipated, though, was being melted into a puddle of tangled nerve-endings, with every cell in my poor confused body screaming for more. That must have looked real, surely? It most definitely felt real. And wonderful. Was it wonderful for him too, or is he just acting? What the heck is going on?

Maybe it's this befuddlement that renders me incapable of doing what I really should be doing – whisking Aidan away from my family before anything can go wrong. He's done his bit – boy, has he done his bit – and now we should slink away to a quiet corner for the next few hours and stay out of trouble.

Except that's not quite how things seem to be working out. That entrance of his, plus that kiss, attracted a lot of attention. I can feel people's eyes on us. I've never especially enjoyed the feeling of being watched, and I grab another glass of champagne to help calm my nerves. I pass one to Aidan without asking, and he kisses me on the cheek in thanks. God. This is going to get overwhelming very quickly if he keeps touching me like this.

Both my nieces descend upon us, as well as their dad, Ollie. Introductions are made, and I can tell that they are all smitten. Aidan is as socially adept as I am reluctant, and he shines in the spotlight – gone is the laid-back wolf man running around the village topless, and in his place is this super-stylish, supremely confident master of the universe. He told me about his former life, but I suppose I hadn't been quite able to visualise it. Now I can, and it's quite the spectacle.

Libby says a shy hello, and Lucy hugs him, making the most of every moment. She laughs as she pulls away, and says: 'Blimey, Auntie Sarah, you've done all right for yourself, haven't you?'

Even Ollie is clearly in the grips of some kind of man-crush, shaking his hand and grinning like a loon. 'Is that Tom Ford?' he asks. 'The suit?'

'It is,' Aidan confirms. 'I hope that's okay? I was told tonight wasn't too formal…'

His suit, of course, looks like it belongs on a mega-yacht, along with its owner. You can practically see Ollie wondering what Aidan's idea of 'formal' looks like if this is casual. Within seconds, Aidan has been pumped for information by my whole family. I look on in amazement as he navigates it all, telling them the truth but in a way that somehow doesn't really reflect the Aidan I know. Yes, he works in finance. Yes, he's recently bought a 'crash pad in the countryside', and he was indeed born in the States, but somehow, none of that feels real or authentic. It's impressing the hell out of my lot, but at the same time, I prefer my Aidan.

Even as I think the words, I feel like an idiot. There is no 'my' Aidan. He is putting on a good show here, giving no hint of the fact that he has abandoned his once-glamorous life for a reclusive existence in the back of beyond, surrounded by Wolfdogs. I see that side of him, and enjoy that side of him, but it doesn't make him 'mine', in any way, shape or form.

I'm still so impressed by his transformation that I barely react at first when my dad swigs down the last of his pint and narrows his eyes slightly. He rubs his chin, though, which is often a sign of impending trouble. That's usually the way he prepares to say something awful. Something awful that he will then justify by shrugging and saying 'Well, I'm just telling it like it is!' He seems to think this excuses every horrible thing that comes out of his mouth, and that it somehow makes him some kind of folk hero fighting for the cause of truth and justice, rather than just a twat.

'Aidan,' my dad says, his voice taking on that 'everyone, listen to me' tone that automatically puts my back up. 'It's a shame you didn't meet our Sarah ten years ago, son. She should have popped out a couple of babies like Sally did, given us some more grandkids. Suppose she's probably too old now, so no chance of that.'

There is a stunned silence as he speaks, as he 'tells it like it is'. Why he felt the need to say that, to embarrass me, I will never know. He probably doesn't know himself, other than he likes to be the focus of everybody's attention. Whether that's for negative or positive reasons seems to be irrelevant to him.

Beyoncé's 'Crazy in Love' booms incongruously in the

background, and even my mum looks taken aback. She steps away from him, as though trying to distance herself from the comment, and Ollie stares at his shoes. Aidan, to give him credit, is the first to recover. Maybe it's because he didn't grow up in my dad's shadow, and therefore isn't as anxious about him as we are.

I feel his hand tighten around mine, and he tugs me very slightly closer, so we are just about touching. I'm used to taking crap like this from my dad, but I have to admit it's nice to not feel alone for once.

'Your daughter is an intelligent, kind, beautiful woman, Mr Wallis,' he says, his voice firm but even. I can tell he's angry, but I doubt any of the others could. 'She's built a career from her sheer talent, she works incredibly hard, and she makes time to be a good friend, sister and aunt. Personally, I don't think I've ever met such an amazing lady. I don't care about her age, and I don't want children – there are already plenty of those in the world, many of them in need. I'd also point out that there is a lot more to Sarah – to all women – than simply producing babies. They weren't put on this planet just to act as breeding mares. Now, could I get you another drink, sir?'

My dad splutters a little, completely out of his comfort zone at somebody daring to disagree with him.

'Hear hear!' says Lucy, clapping her hands. 'Auntie Sarah, he's not just hot, he's a feminist!'

Everyone apart from my father laughs at this, and I feel a sliver of tension creep into my jaw. Is this the point where Dad decides to try and fight his way out of a corner again? I can tell Sally is worrying about the same thing. Aidan stands a little taller, and uses those extra inches to look even more capable. He is a lot younger, a lot fitter, and would never hurt a man in his seventies. But my dad doesn't know that. I see the cogs turn in his brain. Offering him a drink was genius; it gives Dad an out and allows him to save face.

'Yeah, go on then,' my dad says, obviously deciding to take it. 'I'll have another pint, thanks pal. Eight quid, mind!'

'That's okay,' Aidan says, smiling. 'I can afford it.'

'The bar is *free*!' Sally replies, rolling her eyes in exasperation. It makes us all laugh again, and the moment of danger passes. For now at least.

Aidan orders us all drinks, and passes them around. I watch him with wonder, surprised yet again by another layer being revealed. When he's done, he puts his arm around my shoulder and pulls me in next to him, dropping a sweet kiss on the bare skin of my shoulder.

'Thank you,' I whisper, as everyone else chats among themselves. 'Nobody has ever stood up for me like that before.'

'You're welcome,' he whispers back. 'I've dealt with a lot of assholes in my life. Your dad doesn't even make the top ten. And by the way, I meant what I said earlier. You do look stunning.'

Chapter Thirteen

The party is a huge success, and both the girls have a blast. The dance floor is packed all night, with the DJ mixing up modern songs I've never heard in my life with classics for the whole group. Aidan further impresses with some slinky moves, as well as some very energetic jumping to One Direction's 'What Makes You Beautiful'. Even Libby giggles around him, coming out of her shell in a way that warms my heart. He leads us in a line dance to 'Achy Breaky Heart' that should be uncool, but all of the teenagers absolutely love.

The last song of the night is 'Wicked Game' by Chris Isaak, which is surprisingly popular with the younger crowd as well as the oldies. 'It was in *Friends*,' Libby tells me – which is also surprisingly popular with the younger crowd.

As the song starts, Aidan leads me onto the dance floor and holds me in his arms, effortlessly guiding me in a slow and sensual shuffle that I lose myself in a little too easily.

I rest my cheek against his chest, inhaling his cologne, and wrap my arms around his waist. He's so tall he makes me feel dainty, even in my heels, and I let myself enjoy the moment.

'Thanks for this,' I say, as we swirl. 'It's… Well, you were perfect. Apart from being late.'

I feel his chest rise and fall in laughter. 'I wasn't late. I was waiting until the time was right. The right amount of people, the right song … maximum impact.'

I look up at him, grinning in surprise. 'What? You were lurking outside? And "Moves Like Jagger" was the song that said "Go, go, go!" to you?'

He smirks and replies: 'What can I say? I'm a showboater – or at least I used to be. I guess I kind of missed it. The suit, the power plays. Making beautiful women swoon with my amazing kisses.'

'You make yourself sound like James Bond! And I didn't swoon.'

He swoops me backwards in an unexpected dip, then easily brings me back up. My heart is in my throat as I thud slightly against his body.

'You would have done,' he says, 'if I hadn't been holding you so tight.'

I'd like to argue, but we'd both know I was lying. That kiss was spectacular. 'Smug doesn't look so good on you, Mr Bond,' I settle for saying. I'm lying again. It all looks good on him. I'm so unsure of everything right now. I'm dressed up, on a dance floor, in the arms of a man who is sixteen years my junior, in front of my whole family. Even more amazingly, I just don't care.

The song is drawing to a close, and I know the night is at its end. That whatever magic spell has been cast will sadly be broken. I feel a sudden and wholehearted kinship with Cinderella.

'This reminds me of clubbing when I was younger,' he says, as the room gets brighter. 'When the lights came up and you finally saw who you were dancing with, you know?'

'Not really. I wasn't a clubbing kind of girl. I was more of a "going to the library" kind of girl.'

'Just as sexy in its own way. Come on, let's say goodnight to your folks.'

He leads me by the hand to the huddled group of my parents, Ollie and Sally, and the girls. My dad is silent and wavering slightly from side to side. That's his 'drunk but trying not to look it' stance, and it's not a bad one; he's usually concentrating so hard on not falling over that he doesn't have the time to be an arse. The downside is that he sometimes does fall over, and he's a big unit to shift.

Libby and Lucy give us both hugs, and Libby whispers: 'He's lovely, Auntie Sarah. Totally bodacious.'

I have a moment of guilt at this whole charade. I've never claimed that Aidan and I were serious. I just told Sally he was a new man in my life. Which is true. But after his Oscar-worthy performance tonight, they're all going to be very disappointed when it 'just fizzles out'.

That, I decide, as my family disappears into the night in a flurry of coats and kisses, is a dilemma for another day. I look around as the DJ packs up his gear, and tired-looking staff patrol the room collecting glasses and scooping paper plates into bin bags. I wonder what they do with the balloon arch once the party is over? And what about those giant light up numbers that make up the 18? Do they go to some sad party graveyard, joining in with all the abandoned 21s and unwanted 60s?

Aidan slides my coat over my shoulders for me, which makes me feel weirdly sophisticated. He is so smooth when he wants to be… Needless to say I've never known a man quite like him. We walk together to the foyer and out into the cool night air. It feels welcome on my skin after a night of stress, dancing, and an unexpected amount of physical contact with Aidan. Plus, possibly one too many glasses of champagne.

I pause in the street, and once the relief of the drop in temperature fades, I realise that I am very much not looking forward to the next part of the evening.

'What's wrong?' he says, gazing down at me. 'Your face just fell. What did you think about?'

He notices way too much, this man. I bite my lip and consider lying, telling him that he imagined it, or that I've just remembered I need to work tomorrow. But when I see the genuine concern in his eyes, feel the gentle touch of his hand on my arm, I simply can't bring myself to do it.

'I was supposed to be staying at my flat tonight. But I really don't want to go there. I think … I think I might check in at the hotel instead.'

'Why don't you want to go there?'

'Long story. I'm just… Well, it's been a nice night. I'm in a safe little bubble and I don't want to burst it.'

He turns this over, then replies: 'You wouldn't feel safe in your own flat?'

I shake my head, suddenly sad and a little overwhelmed. It sounds so ridiculous when he says it out loud, and I'm annoyed with myself. I lived there until recently. Why am I suddenly so reluctant to return? I think it's because I've felt so much better since moving out, since I relocated to Budbury. It's like I didn't even know how tense it was making me, living there after everything that had happened, until I left. The thought of going back to that – to looking over my shoulder, being obsessed with the alarm system, even barricading the front door with the armchair so I'd know if anybody got in – is weighing heavily on me.

'What about if I come with you?' he asks. 'Would that help?'

Would it? In many ways I do feel safe with Aidan. He is calm and kind, soothing to be around, and I have no doubt at all that he could handle any physical challenge that arose. But I'm not a princess who needs protection, and in other ways he makes me feel quite unbalanced. He disarms me, and has a way of sneaking past all my emotional alarms and barricades. In some ways that is just as concerning.

'How about this?' he says, when I don't reply. 'We head back there and I come in for a coffee. I promise not to use my evil James Bond skills to try and seduce you. I'll just stay until you feel like you want me to go.'

'What if I never want you to go?'

'Then that's fine too. I'll stay with you the whole night if that's what you need. I'm here for you, Sarah.'

How does he always know the right thing to say?

He has a habit of unravelling me that is so unnerving. But maybe being unravelled every now and then isn't such a bad thing, I tell myself. Maybe if I'm unravelled, I can knit myself back up better than new.

'Are you sure?' I ask. 'It might be cold. And there's no milk.'

'I've survived worse. Cab or walk?'

'Cab, in these heels.'

He glances down at my feet, and then lets his eyes move slowly up my legs, over my body, and finally back to my eyes. The deeply appreciative look on his face makes me feel very, very warm again.

'They suit you,' he says, his voice a little more gravelly than usual. 'But I like you just as much in your sneakers.'

I'm starting to think he might not be human. The way he looks, his charm, always knowing what I need to hear … he could be an android. A high-level government experiment, or a new generation AI overlord developed by a top-secret crime syndicate. Because of course both of those would be keenly interested in testing out their new product on a middle-aged author from Essex.

'I know what you mean,' I reply, trying very hard not to blush at the compliment. 'The suit is great, but your running gear is just as nice.'

He raises an eyebrow. 'I usually run without a shirt. Pervert.'

I laugh, and obviously lose my battle with the blushing.

Aidan hails a cab, because he is the kind of guy who magically conjures up cabs as soon as he needs one, and as we drive back to St John's Wood I send a selection of photos from the night through to Cherie. Aidan looks on, grinning at the line-dancing shots.

'I enjoyed it tonight, Sarah. The girls are lovely. Your sister was a lot of fun.'

'And my dad was a pain in the bum?'

He shrugs and pulls a face. 'Hey, I'm the last one to judge. Families are tough. You can love 'em, but that doesn't mean you have to like 'em. Me and my dad… Well, I'll tell you that story one day. It's a humdinger. It calls for popcorn.'

I glance up, filled with curiosity. I like knowing about other people's lives, especially his. It certainly makes a nice change from obsessing about my own.

'Your face looks like a giant question mark!' he says, smiling.

'Well, you can't say something like that and not expect me to be interested. I'm a very interested person.'

'Is there any danger I'll end up in your next book?'

I've been asked this many times over the years, whether my characters are based on real individuals. The truth is that none of them are directly modelled on anybody I know, but I do use elements of those I've met – not just people I'm close to, but chance encounters as well. Conversations overheard on the bus, chats in the supermarket queue. Random psychos who stalk vulnerable women. That kind of thing. I always say that writers are like magpies – we spot the bright, shiny things and carry them away with us. Except, you know, in our minds and not in beaks.

'Not directly,' I reply honestly. 'Though I might steal your eyes.'

He frowns and looks confused. I like the fact that he's caught off-guard for a second. 'My eyes? And what do you mean, steal them? I know what kind of books you write…'

He's correct. It's entirely possible that I could create a morbid plotline around an actual eyeball collector. He could have an apprentice, and I could call it The Pupil…

'I just mean that you have lovely eyes. I might give them to a character.'

'Ah. Well, thank you. And make sure he's the love interest.'

'Not a lot of love interests in my books, but I'll bear it in mind.'

Cherie pings back a reply to the photos, saying that Aidan should invest in some cowboy boots and start a line-dancing club at the Comfort Food Café. He laughs, and says he'll take it under advisement. I chat to Cherie for a few messages, knowing that she's up late and alone. She was the only person I told about Aidan coming with me to the party, and against the odds she's kept it quiet. She at least deserves an update on how it went.

Before long we have arrived, and Aidan beats me to it to pay the driver. It feels odd having someone do that. I've always been financially independent, and stubbornly insistent on it. It is a small thing, but the fact that I find it intrusive says more about me than it does about him. I've always found it difficult to let people in, but I suspect I've become even worse in the last year. Since Martin. Budbury is undoing a little of that resistance, I think, and I'm not sure yet if that's a good thing or not.

My apartment is located on the top floor of a rather

grand Victorian building. The lobby is quiet at this time of night, but we are greeted warmly by Frederick, the night-duty doorman.

'Nice to see you back, Miss Wallis,' he says, looking at Aidan with the barest flicker of curiosity. 'No, uh, problems while you were gone.' He nods at me while he says this, and I know he's referring to Martin. I'm relieved that he hasn't been spotted here, but also know that it doesn't necessarily mean anything. He is cunning when he wants to be, and managed to hand-deliver notes to my door even after the staff were told to look out for him. All it takes is a busy time, or for the person on reception to be distracted, and he could easily sneak through.

I wonder if Aidan picks up on the interaction, but if he does, he doesn't comment. I'm silent in the lifts, feeling the tension in my belly build as we rise through the levels. My place is the only one on the top floor, and as the lift opens up onto the landing, I hesitate before stepping through. Had I been here alone, I would have chickened out at this point. I realise that I have reached out to grab Aidan's hand without even noticing, and he gives my fingers a reassuring squeeze as we walk towards my flat.

I have only been away for three weeks, but it is enough for the sights and smells of this building to feel slightly alien. I've never felt especially comfortable here, but it was in a good location, had the nice roof garden, and was private and secure. At least I thought it was, until I invited in trouble. Now, it just feels like stepping into potentially hostile territory. I walk along the thickly carpeted floor as though it is littered with land mines.

I pause outside the front door, biting my lip as I unlock it. My hands are trembling as I slot the key in, and push it open. The alarm activates in a slow beep, telling me it is still on and that nobody has been inside, and that helps to calm me as I type in the code.

We go through into the long corridor, Aidan behind me. Without even asking, he puts the security chain on. Perceptive. I gaze around, inhaling the slightly musty smell that places get when nobody lives in them, and flick on the lights.

'You've got mail,' he says, bending down to pick up an envelope from the mat. He holds it towards me, and I immediately recognise the handwriting. It's from him. He's been here, again.

I freeze on the spot, unable to reach out and take it. Unable to move at all. I feel the familiar terror creeping over me, the sickening way my vision blurs at the edges, my fingers curling into tightly balled fists.

Aidan steps towards me, then stops when he takes a good look at my face. 'You're okay,' he says quietly. 'It's just me and you. You're safe. You want me to take a quick look around?'

I manage a tight nod, one quick jerk of my chin. 'I'll come with you.' I have no option. I can't bear the thought of standing here alone for even a second.

The movement helps, because my body is forced to take in air. I slow down my breath as much as I can, knowing that it will have a controlling effect on my insane fear reaction. It's very hard to panic and do deep breathing at the same time. I keep my eyes on Aidan, his big, solid form walking slightly ahead of me. He glances back every now and then, checking in, and I feel a little better each time.

The first room off the hallway is my office, which is now a little forlorn without its desk and shelving. Next come the bedrooms. One is pretty much empty, because I took most of my stuff with me, and the other is a small guest room mainly used by the girls when they came to stay. It has two single beds, and a few posters on the walls. One from *Mamma Mia* that we got after we saw the musical, the K-pop bands that Lucy used to obsess over, and Libby's preferred indie classics, vintage Blondie, Nirvana, Arctic Monkeys.

Without me needing to ask, Aidan opens the wardrobe, and crouches down to look beneath the beds. He also checks the window locks are still tight, and investigates the en-suite. On into the main bathroom, with its pretty white and green tiles, the shelving crammed with toiletries. He examines the inside of the airing cupboard, and makes sure the window is secure.

Down to the open plan living room and kitchen, and the patio doors that lead out to the roof garden. All of it is thoroughly checked, every cupboard door opened, every dark corner lit, the remaining sofa vetted. Martin is not hiding in the house, and my relief is now mingling with a touch of embarrassment. Nobody likes to be seen at their most vulnerable, when their behaviour is based on dread rather than logic.

He unbolts the patio doors, and pushes them open. I turn on the outside lights and the terrace is illuminated. I smile at the familiar sights out here: the table and chairs where I've spent so many hours, the barbecue I cracked out for the twins' amusement every summer, the low-maintenance shrubs and plants that are now looking a little neglected. I'll have to arrange for someone to come and tend to them over the spring, I think. I can't let them fade and die. It's not their fault I don't want to live here anymore.

Aidan prowls around the perimeter, looking inside the small shed that contains nothing but a few gardening tools and some bags of soil. He comes back to me and says: 'I think that's everything. How are you feeling now?'

His face is half in shadow, and he reaches out to smooth my hair away from my face. 'Better. Thank you. I feel like an idiot.'

'Don't. It's not often I get to feel macho, living on my own with a bunch of dogs. You did me a favour. Gave me the chance to earn some man points.'

'Are there points?'

'Yeah,' he says, grinning. 'When you've got enough, you can claim a ride-on lawn mower, or an electric chainsaw. It's real nice out here, by the way. I love the countryside, but something about the city at night is beautiful in its own way, isn't it?'

I look out across my little corner of London. Stars in the sky, moonlight on the rooftops, traffic glittering into the distance, every brightly lit window telling its own tale. I nod. I've always thought the same. I've spent many evenings sitting out here with a glass of wine, making up stories about the lives going on all around me.

'It is. But I'm also bloody freezing now. Come on in, and I'll make us both a cocoa.'

As soon as the words are out of my mouth, I decide they make me sound like a grandma. But hey, what can I say? I'm not the kind of cool person who whips up a vodka martini while listening to jazz albums. It's more likely to be hot chocolate and a good book.

Within a few minutes we are settled on the sofa, forced to sit close to each other because there is only one. The doors to the garden are locked, the heating is on, and we have blankets thrown over us as we nurse our mugs of cocoa.

'So,' he says, keeping his tone neutral, 'do you want to talk about it? No pressure if not. I'm happy to provide security services for free.'

It's understandable that he asks. And opening up to Cherie helped, made it all feel like less of a guilty secret. I have nothing to feel guilty about, and maybe the more I talk about it, the less shameful it will feel. None of this comes naturally to me, though, and he seems to know that. He stays silent, sipping his drink, his face behind a cloud of steam.

'I had a relationship,' I begin, hoping I can condense it this time, and possibly not cry. 'It ended a year ago, but it did not end well. The man in question used a fake identity and was actually married with children. He… Uh, in modern parlance I suppose he was a gaslighter. He made me feel like I was going mad, while at the same time infiltrating not just my physical and emotional life, but also my … my space. He got keys made to this place, installed spyware on my phone, and he invaded pretty much every aspect of my privacy.'

There. I'm getting better at this. Aidan's nostrils flare and his eyes narrow, and I can see that he is upset. He nods, taking it all in. 'How did you find out?'

'The traditional way. I hired a private eye! I'd started to have my suspicions by that stage, and she confirmed them. A lot of this stuff would have been hard to prove; he never stole anything, or physically hurt me, and he could have argued that he was innocent of all of it I suppose. Anyway. I ended it, but he didn't take that news gracefully. Since then, he's kind of … pestered me. Small things on the surface, but enough to remind me that he's around. That he's still watching. That I haven't quite broken free of him.'

He glances at the coffee table in front of us and the white envelope that threw me into such a panic. 'Like that?' he asks.

I nod and reach out for it. I'm finally calm enough. Inside the envelope I find a birthday card, for an eighteen-year-old girl. There is no message inside it. With shaking hands, I pass it to Aidan.

He examines it, and I see the little muscles of his jaw flex before he speaks. 'I see what you mean. This by itself isn't threatening. But because it's from him, it's basically saying 'I know things about you and your life'. It's another intrusion. I'm… Damn, Sarah, I'm so sorry this happened to you. It explains why you can be so jumpy.'

'Don't count on it,' I reply, managing a smile, 'I was always a little on the nervous side. Just the way I'm made, I guess.'

'Is this why you moved away? To escape him?'

'That was one of the reasons, but not the only one. And

I'm glad I did. I'm enjoying life in Budbury. I'm enjoying the café, and the community, and the … other attractions.'

He tilts his head to one side and gives me a killer smile. 'Well, who can blame you? I'm glad you moved there too. I just wish this wasn't still hanging over your head. You never wanted to go to the cops? Get a restraining order?'

I shake my head, feeling the usual sense of disquiet when I think about it. 'No. I maybe should have done. Partly, I wasn't convinced he'd done anything serious enough for the police to listen to me. Partly, I just wanted it to go away, you know? I wanted him to go away. Going through it all via the legal system would have dragged out the violation. And beneath all of that, I suppose there was an element of me blaming myself for what happened. For trusting the wrong person.'

Aidan nods, and his face is grim. 'I get it. It wasn't your fault, though, and these jerks play on the fact that women tend to do that, to find fault with themselves, to take responsibility when things go wrong. My sister had a similar experience a few years ago. This guy she'd met had her convinced she'd asked for it, had her doubting herself and her own judgement all the time.'

'I'm sorry. What happened there?'

'My dad happened. He came through. When I found out what this guy was doing, I wanted to go round and beat the crap out of him, but my dad … well, I suppose in some ways he's cleverer than I am. He got him fired, persuaded his landlord to evict him, and then his new place was raided by the police, who found a ton of cocaine in his closet.

I have a suspicion it wasn't his. My dad is a ruthless bastard, but in this case, I didn't object.'

My eyes widen at the story. 'Wow. Well, he might be a bastard, but at least he believed her. My dad would probably accuse me of leading him on.'

'Yeah. I can see that. But your dad, as discussed earlier, is an asshole. Look, I'm going to stay here tonight, okay?'

A sudden rush of thoughts and feelings hits me all at once. I stay silent and try to pick my way through them.

'Don't say no,' he adds, looking at me intensely. 'I'll sleep on the couch, and I promise I won't flirt past your comfort zone. I just want to be here with you. Please, don't say no.'

I smile, and reach out to twine my fingers into his. It feels strangely natural, having him here, and I have to fight down the urge to question that. Just like with Aidan's sister, one of the biggest victims of this whole thing has been my belief in my own judgement. It wasn't just that I stopped trusting other people; I stopped trusting myself. That's something I very much need to work on.

'I wasn't going to say no, Aidan. I was going to say thank you.'

Chapter Fourteen

The rest of the night was actually a lot of fun, with both of us seeming to decide that we had dealt with enough heavy issues.

I put on a pair of deeply enticing flannelette pyjamas, baggy, washed a million times and in a faded shade of pale blue, and took off all my make-up before emerging back into the living room. It was a far cry from my foxier earlier self, but was more genuinely me. Aidan took one look, laughed, and said: 'You're so hot right now. Where did you get those PJs? Was it Victoria's Secret?'

I threw a pair of balled up fluffy bed socks at him, as they were the only items of clothing in the flat that stood a chance of fitting him. Turned out even they were too small, and the poor man was forced to sleep in just his boxers.

We talked until the early hours, catching up on important topics like our favourite movies, first kisses, childhood pets and whether pineapple is a valid topping for a pizza. It's so not.

In the end, we both slept in the small room that the twins usually share, in single beds that are barely a foot apart. He was way too long to be comfortable on the sofa, and I assured him that I'd be able to restrain myself from 'jumping his bones', as he put it.

We laughed a lot, maybe inspired by the teenaged décor, and it was exactly what I needed. He was flirtatious as usual, but I never felt at all uncomfortable. The only physical contact was actually kind of sweet. He reached out his arm as we were drifting off to sleep, and we held hands for a while. Considering how anxious I felt when I walked into the apartment, it was quite the turnaround – and all thanks to him. Instead of spending the night in a hotel, or coming back here alone and being completely freaked out, I ended up falling asleep with a smile on my face, feeling completely safe and relaxed.

I woke up a few minutes ago, and I still have a smile on my face. I roll over onto one side, and look at him. A few stray fingers of sunlight are creeping through the curtains, falling across the gorgeous man lying across from me. It's like he's a work of art being lit up in a gallery.

He's half kicked the covers off, and is naked apart from his black boxers. While he's still sleeping, I allow myself the indulgence of taking it all in, the defined muscle of his chest, the broad shoulders, the meaty curve of his thighs. I blush as I let my eyes roam over his body, feeling slightly indecent but not quite able to stop. He really is something.

'Like what you see?' he murmurs, opening one lazy eye and peering at me. I immediately hide beneath the covers, face blazing, while he laughs long and hard. 'I could feel you looking at me, Sarah Wallis. It's outrageous, really. I'm not just a piece of meat, you know!'

'I know! I'm sorry!' I bleat from beneath the covers. 'Please go away so I can come out of the covers and not die of shame!'

I hear movement, and he replies: 'Okay. I'm heading to the bathroom. This is your chance to run.'

The door to the en-suite opens, and I hear the shower switch on. I try very, very hard not to imagine him in that shower. Not to picture the water cascading over his shoulders, his hair wet against his skin, his gorgeous backside on full display… Yeah. I'm failing. I sigh and go to the other bathroom to do the same myself.

I stand beneath the jets, washing my hair and wondering what it would be like if he was in here with me. Wondering what it would be like to touch as well as look. To soap each other up and wash each other clean. To be kissed like I was kissed last night…

'Stop it,' I say out loud. 'You're a dirty old woman!'

Once I'm done, I dress in jeans and a nice sweater in lovely shades of brown and orange. It always feels like a good thing to wear in autumn – like camouflage. I raid the freezer for some bread, toast it up while I make black coffee, and open up a fresh jar of jam. Laura was making jam the day before I left, and the café was saturated with the delicious aromas of blackberries, plums and sugar. I'm looking forward to going back, I realise. Back to Budbury, the place that now feels more like home than anywhere else I've ever lived.

Aidan emerges into the room with damp hair, wearing his clothes from last night. He still looks sensational.

I pass him a coffee and some breakfast, and say: 'I'm sorry I hijacked you. I'm sure you could have been staying with your mum and sister, getting looked after.'

'Don't be sorry. I had a great time. What's your plan today? I'm going to call in at their place in Kensington and get changed. They'll be waiting to grill me on why I'm doing the walk of shame, and I can't promise to keep it all a secret once they start waterboarding me…'

I raise my eyebrows, while sipping my drink. 'There's nothing to tell, is there? It was just a performance for my family. It was all fake.'

'If you say so,' he answers, staring into my eyes. Damn him. He knows exactly what effect he has on me, and he enjoys it. I turn away, suddenly having an extreme need to wash the plate I just used.

'I'm going to pop in and see my sister for an hour or so, then head back down to Dorset. Thank you. For last night. All of it.'

I sense him standing behind me, close enough that I could lean back and nestle into him. He smooths my hair away from my neck and drops a single kiss on the side of my cheek. 'You're welcome.'

Yikes. Every time this man touches me, I melt. His fingers, his lips, the slightest contact and I lose all brain function. It's very unsettling, and also really quite wonderful.

I grab my bag and recheck all of the window locks before we leave. The low buzz of the alarm activating sounds out as I close the door behind me. I have no idea when I will be back here. I really can't imagine staying in the place alone ever again. I have fairly regular meetings in London for work, but moving forward I guess I'll book a hotel, or crash at my sister's. I should probably just put the flat on the market, and say goodbye to that part of my life. It's a big decision, though, throwing all my eggs into the Budbury basket, and not one I'm quite ready to make yet.

My car is in the underground car park, and Aidan insists on walking me there. I'm actually quite pleased, because it's a bit creepy. I never liked it, even before any of the other stuff happened. You can't write the books I write and feel comfortable in a secluded subterranean car dungeon, even if there are cameras.

I'm offering to drop him off at his mum's when I first feel it – the sense that I am being watched. I trail off in the middle of a sentence. I'm holding my car keys so tightly they dig into the skin of my palm. My eyes range around the place, but my body remains still.

'What is it?' he asks, his voice quiet, one hand on my shoulder.

'I think… No. I'm being silly.'

'You're not being silly. Come on. Trust your instincts.'

I look around some more, and then spot a single red rose, the stem tucked beneath my windscreen wipers. It would be pretty if not for the fact that it is desiccated and dead. I suck in a hiss of breath. He's been here. He knew I was at the party and he knew I'd stay in the flat, and he knew I'd come down to the garage. What he didn't know, of course, was that I'd have company.

I wonder if he's still here? Is he lurking, watching, waiting to enjoy the sick satisfaction of seeing me react? Does he want to witness me falling to pieces, see my face go pale, smirk at my fear? I think the answer to all of that is yes. I've always had that strange feeling when I've felt him nearby, a kind of tingling sensation. Previously I've always talked myself out of it, but Aidan is right. I need to trust my instincts.

'You think he's here?' Aidan asks, following my gaze from the rose to the places he could be. The stairwell, the door to the emergency exits, the ramp that leads out to the road. The other parked cars. I know there's a black spot in the CCTV in the corner to the side of the stairs, where the cameras are focused on the door instead. I made it my business to ask a few questions once it all happened. If I know that, then there is a chance that he could know that.

I nod at Aidan and his face changes. It's subtle, but his lips clamp together, his eyes darken, and he looks around us in the way that an animal would look for its prey. I remember what he said about wanting to beat the crap out of the guy who messed with his sister, and see how protective he is. I could learn to love that about him, but right now I think I need to learn how to protect myself. I am sick of this. Sick of living my life sneaking around, always anxious, always second-guessing myself. Sick of being scared of shadows. Sick of freezing when I should be fighting. Sick of *him*.

I place my hand on Aidan's chest, over his thudding heart, and smile up at him. 'Stay here, okay? I know you've got my back, but I don't want you dragged into this.

Satisfying as it might be to see his smug face smushed in by my big strong hero, that's not the right way to go.'

I see him struggle with the idea, but eventually respect my wishes and nod. 'All right. For now. But I'd feel better if you didn't leave my sight, and just shout if you want me to come and smush him for you.'

I stand on tiptoes and kiss him lightly on the cheek. 'That's very sweet, but I know you're just after those man points.'

'Damn right. I'm almost there for the lawn mower.'

Our eyes meet, and for a moment the rest of the world and all its bullshit simply fade away. That moment gives me the strength to move.

I stride confidently and quickly towards the dark corner beside the stairs, realising that I'm going to look like an absolute idiot if there's nobody there. I am scared, but I'm also fizzing with anger. Something about this whole scenario has suddenly changed for me. Maybe it's Aidan. Maybe it's Budbury. But for some reason, I find that I can move, I can push past the paralysis.

'Scott Jones!' I say loudly. 'I know you're there, you creepy little man! Come out and face me!'

I know Aidan is a matter of metres away, leaning against my car, alert and ready to intervene. That is reassuring, but somehow, I don't think it will come to that. Scott Jones *is* a creepy little man. Everything about him was a lie, and he gets his kicks from messing with women's minds. That makes him a failure and so much weaker than I've ever realised. How sad must he be to live like this? He has a wife, children, a job, but he needs to do this to feel good about himself? It's pathetic, but for some reason I've never seen it like that before.

He takes a step from the shadows, and for a moment as I see his face, shielded beneath a baseball cap, the fear threatens to overwhelm me. The snarl on his lips, the cruelty in his eyes – it all makes me remember that day in the coffee shop when I finished it, and the way he grabbed my arm so viciously.

No, I tell myself sternly. You will not freeze and you will not flee. This time, you will fight.

I throw the dead rose in his face, and he swerves to dodge it. 'No more,' I say firmly. 'This ends now.'

'Or what?' he asks, taking a stride towards me. 'You'll get your pretty toy boy to rough me up? I'd love to get that on film. When did you start cradle-snatching anyway?'

'Since the men my own age turned out to be spineless arseholes who can't take no for an answer. I'm not here to debate with you, Scott, and I don't think you're in a position to lecture me on my relationships. I just wanted to tell you, face to face, that this is over. I'm taking everything to the police. I have records of it all, and as we speak, my friend in the Met is logging a case file.'

None of this is true, but it could be. It should be.

'I've done nothing illegal,' he says, looking infuriatingly smug. I really would quite like to smush him myself, but perhaps Aidan's dad had the more sensible idea. There is more than one way to skin a Scott.

'That's debatable. But it's for them to sort out. I'm told there's at least enough for a restraining order and for the police to visit you at home. Plus, you know, given my profile and all, a court case might attract some media attention. That would be embarrassing for me, but I'd survive. For you, I suspect it might be a lot worse. Do you really want your daughters to know what kind of man you are? Your boss? You might even lose your job…'

'Are you threatening me?' he hisses. He's trying to look tough, but I can see him pale slightly. He's not used to this version of me. Neither am I.

'Yes, I am,' I reply simply. 'Now I'm going to leave, and I'm never going to see you or hear from you ever again. Goodbye, Scott.'

I turn and walk away, shaking inside but maintaining the illusion of strength. Bloody hell, that felt both terrifying and awesomely good. And actually, now I think about it all, I will speak to the police, or at least to my investigator's contact there. Even if it doesn't result in legal action, they need to know about it. They need to know so they can keep an eye on him. I might not be the first woman he's done this to, but I'd love it if I was the last.

I reach Aidan and his eyes flicker over me, like he's inspecting me for damage. Adrenalin is zinging through my body, and I suddenly feel light-headed. I've just faced up to something that usually breaks me, and I have lived to tell the tale.

I nod at him, and say: 'I'm fine. All good. But can you drive? I might need to throw up sometime very soon…'

He hugs me and kisses the top of my head. 'Sure thing,' he says softly. 'Anything you need, warrior princess.'

Warrior princess. I like the sound of that.

Chapter Fifteen

Aidan stays in the city for another night, but I make the drive back to Budbury. I've enjoyed seeing my nieces and my sister, but life in the capital just doesn't feel right for me anymore. I've made more genuine friends in less than a month in Dorset than I did over decades in London, and I'm happier away from it.

I am still very much a work in progress, but there is at least progress. On my first day here, when I moved in, I was built entirely of barriers. I hated the idea of going to the pub, of meeting new people, of joining in with anything at all other than the bare minimum social interaction required.

Now, I voluntarily go to the café on a regular basis, and I actually say hello to people on the street. For me, this is the equivalent of a total personality transplant. Part of me suspects I've been drugged or brainwashed in some way – I still recall Matt's warning about the cake, and I've eaten an awful lot of the cake. Still, it's nice to have options, to be able to lock myself away and work, or mooch around my little house in solitude, knowing that only a few steps away there is always somebody to chat to, to laugh with, to simply pass the time of day. This might be normal for other people, but for me it is something of a revelation.

Then, of course, there is Aidan. I really don't know what to do about Aidan. Not that I need to do anything at all. He has proved himself to be a profoundly good friend in a short space of time, but he has also made it clear that he wants more than friendship. The memory of that kiss, no matter how performative it was, is burned into my mind. But also burned into my mind is the knowledge that I have never been good at relationships.

In fact, I've managed to fail at every single type – from rare and uncomfortable one-night stands all the way through to marriage. I'm not friends with any of my exes, and my husband Will and I stopped speaking the minute the ink was dry on the divorce papers. If I let this thing with Aidan develop beyond what it is now, then I can't help thinking that I will lose him. Is it worth the risk? Yes, I find him crazily attractive, and yes, my libido has definitely given him the seal of approval, but really, is it worth it? If we become lovers as well as friends, how do I salvage the latter when it inevitably goes wrong?

I know that's a defeatist way of looking at things. Maybe it won't go wrong. Maybe we'll live happily ever after and adopt Wolfdogs together until we're both old and frail and the dogs need to pull us around on mobility sleds. Except, of course, that will be much sooner for me than it will for him.

Is that what this is really about? The age difference?

The deep-rooted belief that I can't actually give him what he needs long-term, as opposed to what he thinks he wants short-term? A man like Aidan should have it all. He shouldn't be lumbered with a woman like me. I'm not only significantly older than him; I'm also emotionally stunted. Will once told me my walls were up so high, he felt like he needed grappling hooks just to try and communicate with me. Maybe that's still true.

I'm thinking about all of this perhaps more than usual, because I'm due to meet Aidan in the pub this evening. We haven't seen each other for a few days, and he messaged to invite me out for a drink. It's the twins' actual birthday today, so it feels appropriate.

I call them before setting off to make the arduous trek all the way to the other side of my street, and it doesn't help that all they talk about is Aidan. I try and downplay it a little, but they're both excited for me. It's very sweet, and I feel like a bit of a fraud. I think they'll be more disappointed than me when we 'split up'.

I hear some yelling and door-slamming in the background, and cringe at the thought of Ollie and Sally having a row on the girls' special day. I distract them by inviting them down to visit over Christmas or New Year, and they immediately disagree on which. Lucy insists it has to be Christmas, because there will be no cool NYE parties in the countryside; Libby prefers New Year, so she can avoid all the cool NYE parties in the city. I leave them to sort that out themselves and for a while we talk about their upcoming school trip to Athens. Libby studies Art, and

Lucy studies Classics, so it's something they're both looking forward to.

After that, it's time to go. I lock up behind me, but realise that I don't feel anywhere near as paranoid as normal about leaving the house. Since my showdown with Scott Jones in London, I feel so much better. Cheryl, my investigator, has passed on a file of information to her colleagues in the police, and though I've been warned nothing might come of it, I do at least feel like I've done something positive. I have the suspicion that he won't bother me again. Or maybe just a hope. If he does, then I will deal with it. I have to start believing that I can. I need to be Not A Wuss in all aspects of my life.

Even, I think, as I pause outside the pub, when it comes to Aidan Calloway. I know I am building this up into something it doesn't need to be. I am creating drama and disaster out of thin air. It's fine to do that in my work – it's what I get paid for – but in my personal life? Not quite so cool.

I seem to be spending a lot of time persuading myself that getting closer to Aidan would be A Very Bad Thing. But what if I'm wrong? What if I decided to be brave, like I was with Scott? What if it turns out to be a Very Good Thing? *Bloody hell, I'm annoying.* I need to stop thinking and start doing. Aidan is great. He's gorgeous and he's funny and he's kind, and he wants me. Lord knows I don't have a clue why, but he does. Why am I being such an idiot about it?

I need to go with the flow and see what happens. Be more organic. Actually walking through the door into the pub would be a really good start to that.

I push open the door and am immediately greeted by a wall of sound. Laughter, chatter, glasses clinking. I've never actually been in to the Horse and Rider before, and I look around in curiosity as I step inside. There's a long, traditional wooden bar decorated with horseshoes, a roaring log fire, and approximately a million people.

I walk through the main room, excusing my way through the crowds as I look for Aidan, eventually finding him in a small side room. I see that he is not alone. Zoe and Cal are also here, and from the looks of the copper-topped table in front of them, have been for some time. Zoe stands up and waves her arms around when she sees me, and Cal immediately asks me what I'm drinking. When I try to object and offer to get a round, he looks deeply hurt and says: 'I can't let you do that – don't you know I'm Australian?'

I have no idea how his national pride is tied in to going to the bar, but there you go. I ask him for a glass of red wine, noticing with amusement that Zoe already has a stack of pint glasses in front of her, and he leaves.

It's only when he's moved out of the way that I see Aidan properly, trapped in a corner by another fireplace, grinning at me. Next to him, I now notice, previously hidden by Cal, is a drop-dead gorgeous young woman. She has a shiny dark bob, huge brown eyes, and a petite but curvy figure that's obvious even in her perfectly ordinary jeans and T-shirt. She looks to be in her twenties, and has that fresh-faced, natural prettiness that speaks of long hikes in the woods, treks on mountain trails, and dancing 'til dawn.

Aidan manages to stand up and move a stool out of the way, clambering over a backpack to reach me. He hugs me and kisses my cheek. I find it easier than normal not to melt because I'm too busy wondering who the hell the new addition is.

'Sarah, this is Melody,' he says, gesturing to the girl. 'She's been looking after the pack for me while I was away, and decided to stay on a few nights.'

Ah. All becomes clear. So, I now know who she is, but I still feel a little uneasy, caught off balance. She stands up to say hello, and nothing in her demeanour is anything other than open and friendly. So why do I still want to shove her out the door? Am I actually jealous? If I am, then I need to have a strongly worded conversation with myself, because I have zero right to be.

Cal and Zoe come back with a load of drinks, Cal carrying four pint glasses in his huge hands. He passes them out, and everyone other than me seems to be on beer. Zoe gives me a glass of Pinot, and I straight away feel like the odd one out. Like I'm their maiden aunt sipping a small sherry while they drop ecstasy and head off to a warehouse rave.

This, of course, is ridiculous. Although she is so small and funky she can pass for much younger, Zoe is somewhere in her forties, and Cal isn't far behind. There is no reason for me to feel like this, but I do. The unexpected appearance of Melody (what kind of a name is Melody?) has definitely tripped me up. I walked in here intending to be full-on NAW, and now I feel like I'm actually a full-on W. I sip my wine and smile and chat, but all the time I'm wondering when I can slink away and go home.

Melody is, unfortunately, as nice as she is pretty, and she talks animatedly and with passion about her work as a conservation officer in the New Forest, as well as her volunteering with the rescue dogs. It's interesting hearing her speak about them, and she obviously knows both Aidan and his pack very well. I suspect, from the easy way she laughs with him and the way she touches his arm when she speaks, that she knows him intimately. Or at least has done.

At first, thinking about that confirms that I am actually jealous, unfair as that is. But a few minutes after that sting fades away, I'm left with something altogether more familiar: sadness.

I hold it together just fine, taking part in the conversation and laughing in all the right places, but inside I am retreating. I'm very skilled at appearing engaged with the outside world while simultaneously running away from it, and tonight's is a vintage performance. I get in my round – my dad drummed that into us from being kids – and only start making 'going home' noises when I near the end of that glass.

Aidan looks disappointed, and the others all try to persuade me to stay a little longer. 'I've got to be up at the crack of dawn,' I tell them, 'to get ready for an online meeting with my publisher.' It's a big fat lie. All I have to do tomorrow is a bit of admin, and hand sign a big box of promotional hardbacks for the PR team.

The truth is, I can't stand seeing him with this bright young thing by his side. She is age-appropriate; she is sweet and lovely; she is a Wolfdog guru, and she is the kind of girl who could grow old with him, not before him. I'm going to bow out of this scenario gracefully. In a way I'm glad this has happened; it stopped me from doing something wild and reckless that I may well have come to regret. Frankly, I regret even thinking about it. It was like a virtual door opening in my mind, only to slam back shut in my face.

I make my goodbyes, and escape into the chilly night air. I spot a car parked up near the pub, an unbearably cute vintage VW Bug in red. The back windscreen is decorated with stick-on pictures of wolves howling at the moon, and the name of the rescue. God. Even her car is cool.

I scurry across to my home, my little refuge, and fight with the key as usual. I can't wait to shut the world out again. I've just about managed to open the door when I hear Aidan calling my name. I freeze briefly, and wonder if I can get away with pretending I haven't heard him. It's a tough lie to sell on a tiny street empty of traffic noise, but I give it a go. I'm into the hallway and about to close the door when he reaches me. Damn.

'Can I come in?' he asks. I consider saying no, but that really would be churlish. He's done nothing wrong, and I'm not angry or annoyed. Not with him anyway. I gesture him through and follow him into the living room. I make a show of yawning, as though I'm not in fact planning on sitting up working for the next few hours to distract myself.

'What's wrong?' he asks bluntly, sitting down on the sofa as though to make it clear he's not going to be fobbed off.

'Nothing at all!' I reply, slightly surprised that he even

noticed. I'm normally much better at hiding it when I'm upset. Maybe the ignoring him when he shouted gave it away. Damn. Must always carry earbuds in future. 'Why would you think that? And shouldn't you be looking after your guest?'

'Melody's fine. She's with Cal and Zoe, and anyway, she's a big girl. She backpacked around India on her own, I'm sure she'll cope with the pub.'

Of course she did, I think bitchily. I'm sure she's deeply spiritual on top of everything else, and probably much better at yoga than me too… God, I hate myself right now.

'Something's not right,' he says. 'Has something happened? With him?'

I realise that he's worried about the situation with my stalker, and I feel like an idiot for not understanding that straight away. Of course he is. I sit down on the chair opposite him, and decide that this is one of those occasions that calls for a touch of truth.

'No, honestly, that's all fine. I just… Is Melody an ex?'

He looks genuinely stunned, and then looks genuinely a bit smug. 'Are you jealous, Sarah?'

'Yes. No. Maybe.'

'I see. Well, that cleared that up. Look, Mel and I … I suppose it's a friends with benefits thing. When we're both single and both in the mood, we hook up. We enjoy each other's company and we both like sex. It's nothing serious, and we're both cool with each other saying no when it doesn't feel right. But these days, it's definitely just friends, not benefits. I promise.'

He looks so earnest as he speaks, leaning forward so he

is closer to me. 'I have no interest in Melody. I'm only interested in you.'

'I still don't get it, Aidan. I'm too old. I'm too difficult. I'm … just not right for you.'

A flicker of irritation crosses his face. I've still got the magic.

'Sarah, it's not up to you to decide what is or isn't right for me. I might be younger than you, but I'm a grown ass man who knows his own mind. Stop being condescending.'

'I'm not! I'm… Okay, maybe I am, a bit. I'm sorry. And maybe the problem lies with me and not you, but that doesn't mean it isn't real. I'm not friends with any of my former partners. Admittedly that's not a long list, but I'm not. I value our friendship, Aidan, and I don't want to lose it. I don't have enough trust to expect this thing between us to work. I'm sorry.'

He puffs out air and runs his hands over his face. 'I get it,' he says. 'Trust is a tricky beast. I have my own issues on that front. You know I have a difficult relationship with my dad?'

I nod. I've always been curious about that, but he's very gently parried any questions I've asked.

'We always clashed a little,' he continues, staring into the distance. 'Once I was past adolescence, it was like we were somehow competing, I guess. Stags in the forest, macho bullshit. Little things, like who could run faster, who could drink the most whisky, who could bench press the heaviest weights. Who made the biggest deals. It was the way he raised me, and it was one of the many toxic traits I was keen to get away from.'

'What happened?' I ask, because I can tell there is more to this story.

'He won, I guess. Him and my mom split up when I was eighteen, but they genuinely kept it pretty amicable. Some of that was for the sake of me and my younger sister, Charlotte, but some was because they simply treated it as a kind of deal – they had rules, and respected them. It was, in a weird way, pretty civilised. Right up until he stole my girlfriend.'

'He did *what*?' I ask in shock.

'Stole my girlfriend. Francesca. We'd been together for three years, and everyone expected us to get married. Hell, I suppose I expected that too. Except she ended up marrying Calloway senior instead. They'd been sneaking around behind my back for months by the time I found out. To this day, I'm not sure which betrayal hurt most – hers or his.'

Wow. It takes a lot to make my dad look good, but I think he's just managed it. I reach out and place my hand on his knee. 'Aidan, I'm so sorry. That's the big schism you mentioned?'

'Yeah. It was too much for my mom. It completely fractured the balance of their relationship. She decided to move back here, and Charlotte came with her – she'd had her own problems, as you know. I stayed there for a while, trying to figure it all out. Maybe thinking I could win Francesca back.'

'Is that what you wanted?'

'No,' he replies, the hint of a bitter smile on his face. 'I actually didn't. I suppose I just wanted to *win*. Once I realised that, I decided to leave too. For a while he was furious, because I was lined up to take over the business. But since then he's had another son with her, so I'm off the hook. My dad will probably live forever anyway.'

'That's dreadful. I'm not surprised you left.'

He nods and continues: 'I suddenly understood that I didn't even want the business, or the pressure, or that lifestyle of always having to prove myself to someone who basically wanted me to fail. I was lucky. I had enough independent wealth to be able to walk away. I think I'm actually grateful, to be honest. It was a wake-up call. Made me realise I needed to change pretty much everything about my life. If it hadn't happened, maybe I'd have ended up like him. Once I was away from him, from that whole world, I started to repair the damage, build myself back up.'

I remember something he said to me the first night we really talked. 'Damaged, not broken,' I say. He quirks his lips in a more genuine smile, and his green eyes are intense as they look up at me.

'Exactly that, Sarah. And now you know. I understand that trust doesn't come easy. But one of the things I decided, while doing that rebuilding, was that I wouldn't let what happened take away my ability to trust. That I wouldn't let myself become so scarred by cynicism that I couldn't ever love again. What happened with my dad and Francesca was heart-breaking. But hiding away from love? That would be a tragedy.'

I lean back in my chair and think about what he's told me. I'm now even more impressed with him as a human being – to show such strength, such optimism in the face of fairly conclusive proof that the world sucks. He might be physically younger than me, but he is far wiser, and far braver.

'Can I be honest with you?' I ask quietly.

'Always.'

'I'm not as courageous a person as you, Aidan. I'm trying, I really am, but to some extent it's going against my nature. Moving here, making friends, being part of a community, none of it is straightforward for me. And then you come along, and frankly you scare me. No, that's not a strong enough word... You terrify me. You've seen how I react when I'm frightened, the way I freeze.'

He nods. 'Yeah. I noticed it that first time, at Eggardon Hill.'

'Well, it's not just physical. I think I react the same way emotionally too. I enjoy spending time with you, Aidan, and I know there's a connection here. I'm not going to pretend that I don't find you attractive either, because we both know I'd be lying. But I'm not you. I don't have that same willingness to be open to love. Friendship, yes, definitely. And who knows, with time maybe that will change. But I know myself well enough to accept that maybe it won't. I can't let you wait around for me to be different. I might never be different, and you deserve better. This... This isn't going to happen.'

He looks as though he wants to disagree, but he nods and stands up. 'Well, I kind of regret asking you to be honest now. But okay. I hear you, Sarah.'

He looks sad, and I hate that I might have played a part in that. I walk hesitantly towards him, and say: 'Is it okay to give you a hug? I think maybe we both need one.'

He opens his arms, and I step into them. We cling on to each other, taking and giving comfort, and I sigh into his chest. The mood changes subtly, and he sweeps my hair away from my neck with gentle fingers. I feel his breath against me, then his lips lightly touching the sensitive spot behind my ear. My body takes on a life of its own, pressing against him, thrilled by the contact. By the scent of him, the feel of his arms holding me so close.

'You know I could change your mind, don't you?' he whispers, the words a warm caress dancing over my skin.

'I know... I know you could. Please don't, Aidan.'

He sighs, and I feel his reluctance as he pulls away. He looks at me, gives me the heart-melting smile, and shakes his head regretfully.

'That kiss, at the party?' he says slowly, his voice heavy and gruff. 'That was real. I meant it with every part of me.'

He leaves, and I fall back onto the chair, drained and trembling. Have I just made a huge mistake? Have I sent him back to the pub to be consoled by Melody? And if I have, is that any of my concern?

No, I tell myself, it's not. Aidan is my friend, and I need to draw a line under anything else.

Chapter Sixteen

I distract myself by staying busy. I start my new book, which as ever feels like an insurmountable task. At the beginning, it's like I'm at the bottom of Kilimanjaro looking up, wondering how I'll ever reach the top. Then, step by step and word by word, I always seem to get there. This will be the first book I write here in Budbury, and I hope it doesn't affect me too much. What if I start lovingly describing lemon meringue at crime scenes, or making my super-villain a donkey? My readers expect darkness and gore and terror, not daisy chains and cupcakes!

Luckily, so far, so good. Or bad, I suppose. DI Carina Shaw is going to be up to her neck in serial killers, suspicions and deeply worrying omens. In the very first scene, a crow flies straight into the windscreen of her car and lies twitching out its death throes on her bonnet. If that isn't a portent of doom, I don't know what is.

It actually feels good to be writing something new, to get back to a familiar routine. It's only familiar up to a certain point, though, because these days, once I've finished, I actually emerge into the real world and do that most horrifying thing of all – socialise.

I joined Laura, Matt, Becca and Sam for a pub quiz at the Horse and Rider, which we won on a tie-break. We all looked very surprised when Matt, the vet-of-few-words, displayed a superior knowledge of the works of Ed Sheeran. He shrugged and said: 'I have the radio on a lot at work… cultural osmosis.'

Laura poked him in the ribs, laughing as she responded: 'You told me you always listen to Classic FM, you big, massive Ed Sheeran fan, you!'

I went over to Max's place for dinner with her and Gabriel, though that mainly involved Gabriel eating and then immediately leaving so we could chat. He looked terrified that we might invite him to stay.

Aidan brought Juno around to visit me as part of her socialisation, and she immediately peed on the kitchen tiles. We just stared at each other and burst out laughing, Juno jumping all over us and looking very pleased with herself for being so entertaining.

As we cleaned it up, he said: 'Sorry about that. Maybe next time, we'll take her straight through into the yard.'

'Not a problem at all. Could have been worse.'

'Why don't you have a dog of your own?' he asked as he washed his hands, watching Juno frolic around the courtyard. 'You're a natural with them.'

'Good question. I mean, I work a lot, but I work at home… I suppose, Aidan, that I can't even commit to a dog. Does that make you feel better?'

He pretended to consider it, then shook his head. 'Nah. Not really. But I'm sure I'll survive. Do you want to come out to Hazelwell and do a woodland walk with me and the pack sometime soon? You can pee on my kitchen floor if you like, get your revenge.'

I've taken him up on the offer of the walk, but not of the revenge. The other dogs are getting much braver around me, occasionally running up to sniff my hand or take a treat from me. The weather is just about holding back winter, with a drop in temperatures at night but still some sunshine during the day. It's a glorious time to be in the woods, with colours changing around us, the perfectly camouflaged dogs winding in and out of the tree trunks.

I'm glad to have cleared the air with Aidan, to have cemented that things are staying firmly in the friend zone. Even though I can't resist sneaking admiring peeks at him as he runs and plays with the pack, looking as at home in the forest as he did in his Tom Ford suit, I know I've made the wise choice. I have been Captain Sensible and I'm sure I'll thank myself for it at some point. Melody went home the day after I met her, and I haven't asked if they picked up where they left off. It is none of my business and it would hurt a little too much. I'm better off not knowing.

All things considered, I'm relatively content with life as it is. It has definitely exceeded my admittedly very low expectations when I moved here.

This afternoon, I've finished work early and am heading to the café to discuss 'all things Halloween'. I suspect this is code for 'drink a bottle of absinthe and eat apple crumble', so I shall have to be on my guard. I go for a walk along the beach first, glancing at my phone to check that I'm nowhere near the Aidan Watch Danger time. I wouldn't want to spoil Laura's fun, if she's sitting up there with a pair of binoculars.

There's quite a breeze blowing today, and the sky is a dull grey, streaks of sunlight breaking through the clouds to shimmer on the water. I walk as far as the old boat house, enjoying the sound of the waves rushing in to land, and gaze further down the coast, where the red and gold of the distant cliffs curve into the edge of the world. It's so very beautiful, I get a little thrill every time I'm down here.

I make the now-familiar trek up the steps and walk through the wrought-iron arch that welcomes people into the Comfort Food Café. As soon as I get near to the door, I smile at the sound of laughter coming from inside. Looks like they've already started on the absinthe.

I open the door and am hit by a delicious blend of warmth and sugar, vanilla and spice. Cherie is standing in the middle of the room, dressed in a clown suit, complete with giant red feet. That would be terrifying enough by itself, but she's also wearing a huge curly red wig and brandishing a curved machete. I stop in the doorway and give some thought to running all the way back down the hill. Luna obviously feels the same, and is sniffing at the shoes suspiciously.

'Bloody hell,' I say, as I edge inside, 'you look horrible!'

'Thank you, sweetie, how kind of you to say,' she replies, waving her machete at me. 'I feel horrible too. This wig is itchy as hell.'

Laura is doing something behind her back and pops her

head around to say hello. 'Just making an adjustment,' she explains, waving a sewing needle with almost as much menace as Cherie does the machete. 'We had to get a super-size clown suit and I'm taking it in. There's no consistency in Halloween clown costume sizing these days...'

'Was there ever?' I ask, joining Becca at a table and pouring myself a glass of wine.

'Yes, probably, in the eighties, when everything was better...'

'What are you going as?' I ask Becca, who is sipping a pumpkin spice latte and nibbling on a biscuit in the shape of a bat. I'm working on the assumption that Cherie is wearing her outfit for the Halloween Ball, but I could be wrong. It could be something she's planning on wearing on a trip to the supermarket for all I know.

'Me and Edie – big Edie – usually go as something together. This year we're zombie ballroom dancers. It's Halloween week on Strictly, and that's a big deal for Edie. Auburn ordered her a load of fake scars and spray on blood, and she's found an old ball gown on Vinted. She's a demon on Vinted. I'll be the man. It's easier; I can recycle the suit I used when we were "brutally murdered Laurel and Hardy" last year...'

I nod. Of course. It's amazing how quickly I've adjusted to these concepts.

'I'll be a ghost, as usual,' Laura shouts from behind the solid bulk of Cherie's killer clown. 'Last year, I swore I'd have lost a load of weight by now, so I could be a sexy vampire of whatever, but that doesn't seem to have happened. Back to the sheet with eye holes for me!'

Laura is by no means enormous, but as ever with women, it's all about confidence. Cherie is a big lady, too, but if she wanted to wear a thong on the beach, she would, because she is comfortable in her own skin. Laura, like most of us, isn't quite so blessed.

'What about you?' she asks, popping her head out again. 'What's your costume?'

I'm silent for a few moments, feeling all of their eyes on me. It is actually quite scary, all of this scrutiny.

'Um … I haven't got one,' I confess, guiltily. 'I've been busy.'

Cherie shakes her head, and her red nylon curls bob threateningly. Laura looks crestfallen, and Becca tuts, though she also looks amused at my predicament.

'You've got to come,' she says. 'This is Edie's gig, and if you don't come, she'll notice. You'd need a really good excuse to get out of it. Like losing a limb, or finding a time machine and accidentally going back to the Bronze Age.'

I kind of like the sound of that option, and set it aside to think about later. 'I know,' I say. 'I know. And I will come. I just haven't sorted a costume.'

'Yet?' Laura says, raising an expectant eyebrow.

'Yet,' I confirm, starting to panic. I wonder if I can get something off Amazon that will land tomorrow.

'Good,' she says, going back to her sewing. 'Hands off the ghost sheet though. That's mine. I can't have you turning up looking like a sexier ghost sheet.

'Right,' she adds, standing back and admiring her handiwork, 'that should be fine. I wouldn't suggest any limbo dancing though, Cherie. You know what happened that year you tried it dressed as Cat Woman.'

'Pah, if I want to limbo dance, I'll limbo dance, love. I don't care if the crotch splits!'

My eyes widen at both the idea of Cherie as Cat Woman, and of her as a crotchless clown. The mind absolutely boggles.

Laura drifts over to the window, picking up a glass of Prosecco on the way. 'It's Aidan time…' she mutters, gazing down to the beach. Cherie catches my eye and raises her brow. I shake my head – no, there is nothing new to report, and certainly nothing I want to share. I don't even have it in me to go and watch the show. I can't insist to the man that we can only ever be friends, and then perv over him as he runs past.

I pretend I need the loo and leave them to it. I sit in the ladies and flick through Halloween costumes online, my heart sinking when I realise that most of them are sold out, or can't be delivered until next week. What use is that, I think, angry with myself and with the Lords of the Internet. Maybe I can make something. Or maybe Max can take me to a vintage store. Or maybe I can jump off a cliff and hope I rise from the dead, in which case, costume sorted.

By the time I go back into the café, Katie has joined us. She looks exhausted and is slumped in her chair, clutching a coffee mug for dear life.

'Are you okay?' I ask, as the others make their way back from the window.

'No. I have three male children and they are savages. I will never be okay.'

227

Oh. Well. I don't really know what to say to that. Katie is usually a very non-dramatic person. She must have had a really bad day.

'Is there anything I can do to help? I can babysit. Or dress up as Nanny McPhee?'

'They'd eat Nanny McPhee alive. But thanks for the offer of babysitting. I might take you up on that one day. For the time being, wine will have to do.'

I realise that her coffee mug is in fact full of booze. 'What are you going to the Halloween ball as, Katie?'

'A physical representation of that painting, The Scream. Or, failing that, I'll just stick on a witch's hat and hope for the best. The kids are excited though. Well, the older ones are. The baby isn't even one yet, so he's not expressed strong views about anything other than milk and Tinkerbell's tail. He hasn't been bothering you, has he?'

'The baby or the cat?'

'Either. They both have supernatural powers.'

'Tinkerbell pops in every now and then, but I don't mind at all. Would you like … uh, a spa break?'

She looks up at me and laughs. I don't know why. Is that innately funny?

'No, I mean it,' I insist. 'I got given a voucher ages ago and I'll never use it. I think it's got your name written all over it. It's for two, but hey, there's no rule that says you can't go alone…'

'Oh. I see. Thank you. Well, I'll think about it. That's very kind.'

The others join us, and Laura gives Katie a big hug

before she sits down. 'You look knackered,' she says. 'Kids playing up?'

The conversation turns to children and their challenges, along with plenty of disclaimers from the mums in the room about how much they actually love their offspring, and how they couldn't imagine their lives without them. I catch Cherie's eye and she smiles over her glass. Nobody means to exclude us, and listening to the stories is funny, but it's not something we can contribute to very much either.

Cherie disappears to the balcony to smoke one of her special cigarettes, and I wonder what Aidan is up to. I know he ran past, and he usually then heads straight to the village. Maybe he's popped into the butcher's for some treats for the dogs. Maybe he's called into the pub. Maybe it's none of my business. Why am I even thinking about Aidan? I should be thinking about more important things, like my Halloween costume.

I glance at my phone, wondering if there's any kind of emergency help line for people in a Halloween crisis. Or if I'll have to drive to a real town somewhere and find an actual shop. Could I get away with some devil horns?

I hear the door to the café open, followed by a slightly surprised silence. I look up just as Laura says: 'Aidan! And Aidan's friend!' Luna scampers over for her traditional fuss, gazing up at the new arrival from beneath her furry fringe.

I stare from Aidan to the person he's with, my mouth dropping open and my brain struggling to catch up with my eyes. What I'm seeing does not compute with reality.

Not only is Aidan here, thankfully with a top on, he's not alone. He's with my *sister*. I blink, just in case I'm hallucinating, but the vision doesn't clear. Sally is still standing there, her blond curls windswept and a big leather overnight bag at her feet. She's looking around the place with a slightly stunned look on her face, and Aidan meets my eyes. He gives me a little shrug, and then comes over to kiss me on the cheek.

It's not the same full-on assault on the senses as the kiss at the twins' party was, but it is enough to make my café friends stare in disbelief. Laura's eyes look like they're going to fall out of her head and Becca raises her mug as though congratulating me. Katie's mouth forms a surprised little 'oh', and you could hear a pin drop in the room as everyone other than Cherie clearly wonders what the hell is going on. I can almost imagine Laura's thought processes: 'Who is this stranger with Aidan, but more importantly, why is Aidan kissing Sarah? Sarah said she wasn't interested!' She will be literally exploding with curiosity.

Cherie already knows about the pretend date we put on for my family in London, and she is looking on in amusement, sitting with her machete on her lap and enjoying the show.

Bugger. Sally is here. Sally thinks we're a couple. Aidan is keeping up that pretence. He is maintaining the story we spun, but in as respectful and friend-zone-rated a way as he can. These thought processes all take place very quickly, and my nice, ordered life explodes in the space of about twenty seconds.

'Sally, what are you doing here?' I ask, finally finding my voice. I'm still trapped in disbelief, not quite accepting that she is standing in front of me. Sally lives in London. I live in Dorset. It's like my two worlds have collided and I'm squashed in between them. Flat as a pancake.

She snaps out of her own reverie and turns to look at me with a very confused expression. The Comfort Food Café will do that to you on your first encounter – it's a feast for the eyes, for sure. I suppose I've got used to it, but I still remember walking in here, almost a month ago now, and being fascinated by the exotic clutter of the place.

'Oh, I… I thought I'd come and stay for a bit. And then you weren't in. And then I bumped into Aidan and he said you might be here. Is it okay that I came?'

She sounds fragile and uncertain, and that is cause for concern with Sally. I can't remember ever hearing her sound fragile and uncertain. I suddenly don't care about anything else, so I walk over to give her a big hug. 'Of course it is. It's lovely to see you.'

It would have been nice to have some warning, but I keep my mouth shut about that. Maybe it was a last-minute decision.

'Do you want some wine?' Cherie asks, offering her a glass. Sally is fixated by her, and nods mutely. I suppose giant killer clown Cherie is even more intimidating than normal Cherie.

'And some cake?' Laura suggests. I smile as I see them offer this complete stranger their usual consideration. They don't know her at all – I haven't even introduced her properly yet – but they can see that she is connected to me, and possibly they can see that she is shaken. They are reacting the way they always do – with kindness.

Sally nods again, and Laura gives me a look as she heads off to the kitchen. 'I'll be talking to you later, Sarah,' she says sternly. Oh dear. This is going to get messy. I suddenly understand how Laura's twins must feel when they've been caught doing something naughty.

Aidan touches my hand, and I turn to look at him, my back to Sally. He pulls what Libby and Lucy would call a 'WTF face', and I have to hold in a laugh. What a pickle we've got ourselves into. I mouth the words 'Thank you' and he responds with a whispered 'You're welcome'.

'Babe, I've got to make a move,' he says to me, loud enough for my sister to hear. 'I need to get back to the dogs. Sally, it's nice to see you again.'

She watches him as he goes, then sighs as she looks back to me.

'Dogs? He has dogs as well? How perfect can one boyfriend be?'

Chapter Seventeen

After a few glasses of wine and lashings of cake, I take Sally back home. She stares down at the coast from the café garden, a dusky evening of cloud-smudged stars, and sighs. 'It really is nice here, isn't it? I've never thought I could leave London, but I can definitely see the appeal…'

I gulp back a moment of dread that I'm not especially proud of. I'm sure she has no intention of actually moving here. It's just a thing she's saying, surely.

Once we're back at the house, I grab extra blankets from the cupboard and make us both some cocoa. She looks a little wired, and I don't think more wine is going to help with that.

'So,' I say, once she's inspected the place and settled on the sofa, 'what's going on, Sal?'

'What do you mean? And is it a problem? Am I not welcome?'

I recognise the tone. It means she's looking for a fight,

and I'm determined not to give her one. She tends to lash out when she feels threatened.

'Always. You're my sister and I love you. You can stay here for as long as you like. But I can tell there's something wrong. Is it Ollie?'

She glares at me and snaps: 'What do you mean, is it Ollie?'

'I mean exactly what I asked. Don't be like this, Sally. I'm on your side.'

She snorts, but then rubs her eyes with her balled-up fists. 'I know. I'm sorry. I'm being a dick.'

'That's okay. I'm used to it.'

This at least makes her laugh and breaks down some of her resistance.

'Yes, it's Ollie,' she says. 'Of course it's Ollie. Things haven't been good between us for a while. He's always working, or playing golf, or listening to bloody podcasts. Seriously, I can't remember what his head looks like without his earphones on. We spend more time apart than we do together, and when we are together, all we seem to do is bicker. It's bearable with the girls around – they're like a buffer zone I suppose – but they're away on their school trip at the moment.'

Plus, I can't help thinking, before too long they will be leaving for university. Libby's applied to Oxford, and Lucy has her heart set on Edinburgh. There has been talk of a gap year, but for Sally, that might be even worse. What if they disappear to Cambodia or whatever? I can't see Libby doing that, but Lucy – definitely. Them leaving is going to be a tough thing for Sally to adjust to. With twins, you get double the work and then double the sorrow when they finally fly the nest. Add in marital problems, and that's not a good spot to be in.

'Do you think there's someone else?' I ask. 'With Ollie?'

'Not everybody cheats just because Will did, Sarah! And it's not like you two were ever really close, was it?'

Ouch. That was below the belt, and I bite my tongue before I can come up with a retort. I was never an especially confident person, but after Will's repeated infidelities, I was even lower on self-belief. It's not fair of Sally to trivialise it, but I will give her a pass because she's so upset.

'Okay. I'm sorry. What do you think the problem is, then?'

She sips her cocoa, and I see tears shining in her eyes. 'I'm sorry again, Sarah. I shouldn't have said that. And yes, I've wondered if there's someone else, of course I have. I think I would even understand that – God knows I've been tempted myself. The longest conversations we have these days are about the girls, and I can't actually remember the last time we had sex… It's like he's just switched off. He finds strangers on the internet talking about hip replacements more interesting than me!'

This is indeed a damning indictment, even for an orthopaedic surgeon.

'I just needed to get away for a bit,' she continues, swiping at her eyes like she's angry with herself. Knowing Sally, she probably is, for being what she will perceive as weak. 'The house feels so empty because the girls are away, and he is barely there, and when he is it's like I don't exist… Oh God, Sarah, what if we end up like Mum and Dad? Staying together even though we hate each other?'

The weight of that hits me, and I can see how scared she is by the idea. I don't blame her. It doesn't take a psychiatrist to understand that is one of the reasons I've avoided relationships. As ever, Sally and I responded differently to our childhood issues – she threw herself into marriage and motherhood almost defiantly, determined to make a happy home. So far, she's made it work, whereas I withdrew after my first attempt. Possibly even before then.

'You won't,' I say firmly, reaching out to hold her hand. 'Never. The very fact that you're asking that question shows you won't. Mum and Dad are … well, they're a special case. I promise you, if I ever think you're heading in that direction, I'll hire you a divorce lawyer myself!'

She laughs a little and shakes her head. 'Thank you. I bet you would as well. He's not evil or anything, and I know I'm probably overreacting, but everything feels so … grey. Maybe it's the bloody menopause too. I don't like it so far.'

'I don't think many women do. You're a doctor. Can't you get your hands on some good drugs?'

'I might look into it,' she agrees. 'I've always resisted the idea, which is really stupid when there is help out there. I suppose I thought I'd just wing it through sheer force of personality. Turns out that mood swings and hot flushes turn me into a bit of a bitch.'

'Even more of one?'

She throws a cushion at me and laughs properly. Progress.

'Don't bite my head off, Sal, but have you tried talking

to Ollie about this? Not fighting or whatever, but just sitting down and explaining how you're feeling? Being honest?'

I've been experimenting with this technique recently. Aidan has responded to it, and I've felt better for not lying all the time. The irony is not lost on me, as I look at my poor sister and her sore eyes. I need to tell her the truth, I think. I need to tell her that Aidan and I are not a couple. Not just fudge it and say we're splitting up, but confess the whole silly scheme. If nothing else, it will amuse her.

I'm about to do exactly that when she replies to my question.

'Sarah, I appreciate having somewhere to stay for a few days, but really, why would I take relationship advice from you? You have no idea what it's like to be married for over two decades, or the pressures of being a parent. You might be loved up right now, but based on your track record, it's not likely to last, is it? Do me a favour and don't try to fix me, all right?'

I stare at her, and feel my irritation levels rising. This roller coaster is starting to exhaust me: snark, apologise, snark, on repeat. Yes, she's upset. Yes, I love her. And also yes, I have wanted to throttle her many times during my life. Right now, I can just about restrain myself from manual strangulation, but I can't quite bring myself to tell her the truth about Aidan either. I hate the fact that she thinks she has me boxed off, firmly in the 'rubbish with relationships' category. Even if she probably is right, I hate it. Nobody likes being written off, do they?

'Okay,' I say simply, forcing myself not to let this escalate. 'Whatever you need, sis. I've got a fold-out sofa bed in my office, will that be okay for you? Or would you prefer the couch?'

She stretches out, and tests how long it is before confirming that she'll go for the fold-out. That isn't especially convenient for me, because it is, you know, my office, where I do my work. My work, obviously, has never been as important as hers. Which it kind of isn't, because she can save lives and I just create fictional ones, but it's still annoying. She's proud of me, while at the same time always slightly disparaging about it. Crikey. This is going to be a real exercise in self-restraint.

I tell her I have to sort a few things out, and head upstairs. As I go, I remember something I need to tell her.

'Sally!' I shout back down. 'If you've got antihistamines with you, you'd better take one. I have an occasional cat visitor.'

Sally loves dogs and cats, but is very allergic to the latter. I hear her groan and root about in her bag. The part of me that is still thirteen secretly hopes that she wakes up with Tinkerbell sitting on her chest and her eyes streaming.

The first thing I do when I get upstairs is call Aidan. It goes straight to voicemail, but the reception out in his little corner of Dorset is hit and miss at best, especially if he's out in the woods. I message him instead, knowing he'll pick it up later.

> Thanks for rescuing Sally! I had no clue she was coming. She'll be here for at least tonight, possibly the rest of the week.

I leave it at that and set about relocating my laptop and

all essential notepads into my bedroom. I've only just started plotting, so the big corkboard is currently empty. I fold out the sofa bed and find fresh sheets from the airing cupboard, as well as an extra pillow – Sally always likes an extra pillow. I move the desk lamp onto the little table that is next to the bed, so she can switch it on and off without moving, then close the curtains. I light my sea-salt and rosemary scented candle, carefully placing it to avoid burning the house down, and pop fresh towels on the desk. There, I think, standing back. It's about as cosy and nice as I can get it without having had any notice. I'd give myself a million stars on Tripadvisor.

I'm about to go back downstairs when Aidan calls. I scoot along to my own room and shut the door, whispering hello as I do.

'Sorry, I was feeding the hellhounds,' he says. 'You okay?'

'Yeah, all good. She's downstairs, fifty per cent drunk, fifty per cent sad, and one hundred per cent annoying.'

He laughs, and my heart trips a little as I imagine him leaning against his kitchen counter, dogs milling around, making himself some dinner. I really wish I was there with him.

'Sisters, huh? Has she said why she turned up like that?'

'Not in detail. I think she just needed a time out. She was under a lot of pressure in the run-up to the party, and the twins are away in Greece. She was seeking refuge away from her own life, I think.'

'Well,' he says, one of the pack baying in the background, 'we've all been there, right? What do you want to do about us? I kept up the act earlier, but I didn't know if I was doing the right thing or not. Do you still need me to be your fictional boy toy or not?'

'Boy toy? That's a terrible term! And … um … I couldn't ask that of you. Not after I—'

'Brutally rejected me and broke my poor heart?'

His tone is joking, but I also know that I did hurt him, and I hate that. He's done nothing to deserve it. 'Did I really?'

'Well, you definitely put a dent in it, Sarah, not gonna lie. And look, I don't mind if you don't. If she's only here for a night, then no stress. If it's longer, I'll call round and serenade you in the street or something. Naked, with a red rose between my … lips.'

I laugh at the image and reply: 'Well, let's see how it goes. And thank you.'

I say goodnight and hang up, then sit on the edge of my bed for a few moments. My cheeks are on fire and my mind has disappeared into a place that is very much not the friend zone.

I'm still picturing Aidan naked when my sister screeches up the stairs: 'Sarah! How do you get the bloody telly to work?'

Duty calls.

Chapter Eighteen

Three days later and Sally is still here. She is by turns frustrating and lovable, and I really need a crash course in how to train your twin sister. We have not lived together since she went to university. Once she was settled in Manchester, she rarely came back, not even for the holidays. She preferred to spend her summers working in a chicken processing plant and sofa surfing, which tells you a lot about our home life.

I made my own way in the world, a little later, and we eventually both ended up in London. Obviously, I've stayed at her place overnight, but it's always been with the girls and Ollie around. I've usually been there to provide childcare, which I was always pleased to do. We were both permanently busy, and we've never been the kind of close to go on mini-breaks together. Plus, as soon as the twins were born, Sally became a buy-one-get-two-free deal. I was more than happy with that.

Now, after spending such a solid chunk of time with her,

my patience tank is almost empty. Part of it might simply be that I feel like my territory has been invaded. I'm used to living alone, and having her mess and her noise and her constant sniping around isn't good for my sanity. Some of it is tiny, like finding her hair-entangled bobbles everywhere, and some of it is just plain rude, like rearranging my kitchen cupboards because they 'didn't make sense', or changing the passwords on my TV apps to ones that she could remember. She also draws cartoonish penises in the steam on the bathroom mirror, though I have to admit that one makes me laugh.

The home invasion has also expanded to the Comfort Food Café, where she has launched a charm offensive on all of 'my' friends. Sally is far more fun than I am, far easier to be around. I can acknowledge how childish it is to be jealous, but watching her sit and laugh with the other ladies, immediately switching on to their wavelength when I had to work at it, definitely triggers something buried deep inside me.

It takes me back to our youth, to the school days when she was the popular kid and I was the shy nerd. Maybe not that much has changed, now I come to think about it. I'm still a shy nerd; it's just that adult me is a lot more accepting of who I am. Having Sally around is challenging that, and I need to get a grip. She's going through a tough spot, and this isn't about me.

Today, Ollie has finally called her – after she's been gone for two nights. She predicted that he wouldn't even notice she was gone, and it turns out she was right. As soon as she mouthed the word 'Ollie' when her phone rang, I retreated to the kitchen. I thought maybe she'd go upstairs to take the call, but I ended up trapped in there, trying not to listen.

Once the yelling started, I headed outside into the little patio garden to distance myself even further. It's lashing it down today, the first truly grim weather of October, a flood of torrential rain that is flattening the leaves of the plants and creating puddles on the courtyard. Nice weather for ducks, as my mum would say. I shelter as best I can by the doorway, but I still get wet very quickly.

I bob my head back inside and hear that she is finally silent. I rub my hair with a towel, and make us both coffee before nervously emerging into the living room. There is every possibility that I'll get both barrels of her frustration.

Instead, she is curled up in a ball on the sofa, her phone on the floor, crying. It is like a thump to the heart seeing my vivacious sister so reduced. I sit down next to her, and pass her the coffee.

'How did it go?' I ask.

'How did it sound?'

'Umm ... not great. But I couldn't really hear you, I promise. What did he say?'

She laughs bitterly. 'He said he's been busy, and had assumed I was sleeping in the spare room – I mean, I do do that sometimes because he snores like a steam train, but never for two nights in a row! I think he only actually noticed because we ran out of milk...'

'I'm sure that's not true,' I reply, not at all convinced that I'm right. I'm very fond of Ollie, but he has always been on the self-obsessed side. So has Sally, to be honest. I've always wondered how they made it work. I think the girls have been their unifying bond, and now Sally is facing up to the reality of life without that human glue.

'Well, whether it is or not, he doesn't seem that bothered I'm gone. I told him I'd run away with my tennis coach and he just laughed and said: 'I bet you're with Sarah, aren't you?' Because apparently I'm predictable, as well as undesirable!'

I pat her hand and make soothing noises as she cries. Some of this sounds petty, but I can see how genuinely distressed she is. Sally would be the first to point out that I know nothing about marriage, but even *I* understand that no woman wants to feel superfluous to her husband's needs.

'You're neither of those things, Sal,' I reply. 'You're disturbingly unpredictable, and I bet you *could* have run away with your tennis coach if you'd wanted to. You're still gorgeous—'

'He's gay actually, but thanks for the vote of confidence. He – Ollie, not the tennis coach – didn't sound bothered at all. He said I should just take a break if I needed to, and we'd talk about things when I get back.'

I nod and stay silent. Nothing I could say at this point will help. I picked up on the yelling at her end, even if I didn't get all the words. At a guess, I'd say that Ollie didn't follow her script and get dragged into the big dramatic fight that she was looking for. She's now interpreting that as him not being bothered. I have no idea if she's right or not.

'Do you want me to talk to him?' I suggest tentatively. 'Maybe it's just a communication thing. You know how men can be. Ollie's used to being the king of his ortho empire. Maybe he's just struggling to explain himself...'

She looks up at me with tear-swollen eyes, and seems to consider it before finally shaking her head. 'No. He can go screw himself. If he wants me to come home, he needs to convince me. I'm not willing to just trail back there with my tail between my legs and be taken for granted all over again. I'm not even fifty, and fifty is the new forty these days. I'm not old enough to be ignored! No, let him stew. I'll just stay here.'

Oh goodie, I think, being very careful not to let that flash of 'Please God, no' show on my face. The last thing she needs is to feel rejected by me as well as by him.

'That's fine,' I say. 'Now give me a hug.'

She does, and wipes her face on my jumper at the same time. Then she immediately pulls away, and grimaces. 'Why are you so wet?' she asks.

She doesn't wait for an answer and immediately moves on. Sally is like a shark in that respect – always forwards. I know she is in an emotional crisis, but I also know that her way of dealing with that will be very different from what mine would be. Mine would involve solitude, weepy music and possibly ice cream; hers will involve action.

'So,' she announces, 'I think I'll stay for this Halloween Ball of yours. Edie has invited me – isn't she marvellous? – but I thought I'd be gone by then. I'd better get a costume sorted. I wonder if I can still pull off sexy nurse... Yeah, course I can! What are you and Aidan going as? And where has he been the last few days anyway? Laura was really surprised about you two, you know. Why did you keep it a secret?'

Oh my, I think, buying myself time by drinking some of the cooling coffee. The webs we weave. Layers upon layers of not-quite-truths. I haven't told my sister that Aidan isn't my actual boyfriend, and I haven't been able to explain it all to Laura either. We haven't been alone together, and I feel like such an idiot I don't know where to start. I asked Cherie if she'd tell her, but she'd just laughed and said, 'Oh no, my love – that's very much your mess to sort out!'

So now I have a fake boyfriend, a live-in twin sister, and a friend who is disappointed in me for not telling her that I had a boyfriend. Which I don't. It's getting as twisty as one of my plots, but hopefully without the murder and maiming.

'Oh, you know me,' I respond. 'I like to keep myself to myself.'

'That's what I told her. I said you'd always been a bit of a hermit, an emotional hoarder.'

An emotional hoarder? Is that true? Will I die one day, buried beneath a pile of emotions that I've kept stacked on mental shelves and crammed into mind cupboards? Crushed by all my repressed *feelings*?

'Anyway, what are you going as? Are you doing a couple thing? You know, Bonnie and Clyde or whatever…'

I can honestly say that I haven't given my Halloween costume much thought since Sally arrived. She's the kind of person who demands all your attention, and it was a lot for me to adjust to. Between her and work, I haven't had a lot of spare time. What little I've had has been filled with taking deep breaths and counting to ten.

We met Aidan in the pub for a drink last night, but we didn't really get the chance to talk. There was a big group of us, and I was feeling like a huge fraud because we were behaving like a couple when we're not. I'm going to have such a lot of explaining to do once this whole mess is over. I desperately hope that Ollie and Sal sort out their marital problems, because I really don't think I can keep this up much longer.

I haven't answered her question, and she fixes me with a stare, her head tilted to one side. 'Or is going as a Halloween couple too much of a commitment for you, Sarah? Please don't tell me you're already running away from him, shutting him out like you always do! I never even got to meet that last guy, Martin, you dumped him so quickly!'

I get up so abruptly I slosh coffee on my legs. Sally doesn't know what happened with Martin, and that is not her fault. But I still feel stung by the way she judges me so easily, and automatically assumes that it was me who was the problem.

'That was a complicated situation, Sally. Anyway. You're right, I really do need to sort out something for the ball. I'm going to go and see Aidan about it. Will you be all right on your own for a bit?'

'Yes. I'm not a child. I'll just pop over to see Auburn in the pharmacy if I get bored. She said she has a stack of Halloween face paints in. Maybe I could be a sexy corpse bride…'

Within seconds, my sister has flipped from sobbing about her failing marriage to planning world domination. I'm not fooled for a moment – I know her pain is still there, just beneath the surface. But I also know that if she is choosing to distract herself from it for now, then that is up to her. Besides, I really do need a break.

I grab my raincoat, and message Aidan from the hallway.

> Halloween costume crisis. Help!

Within seconds he has replied.

> Can you get away for a few hours?

> Definitely yes!

> I'll pick you up in twenty minutes.

I don't even hesitate. I head outside into the rain. Even that has got to be better than staying in with Sally.

By the time he pulls up in his jeep, I'm both slightly soggy and slightly tense. Why did I call him? Why did I reach out to Aidan, when I keep telling myself – and him – that we shouldn't be together? There are many answers to that question, but the one I keep coming back to is this: I'm an indecisive idiot.

I actually hesitate before getting into the car, and he gazes up at me as I hover between the pavement and the open door. 'Yes or no? Staying or going?' he asks. 'Are you singing that Clash song in your head?'

'I wasn't,' I reply, deciding on 'yes', 'but I am now. Urgh … Sally was driving me mad. And I genuinely need a costume. But now I feel like I'm a horrible user calling you when I need you.'

He turns the engine off, turning to face me. His expression is a perfect blend of exasperation and amusement, his green eyes sparkling. He nods and says: 'I see. Have I ever struck you as being an especially weak-minded person? Feeble, even? Without any thoughts of my own in my pretty little head?'

I bite my lip. 'No. Quite the opposite. You have way too many thoughts.'

'Okay then. So, would I be here if I didn't want to be?'

'I don't know. Maybe you feel sorry for me?'

He runs his hands through his hair and laughs out loud. 'My God, you really are impossible! How's this for a deal? We go shopping. We find Halloween outfits, because I'm also sadly lacking on that front. We have an enjoyable day together, where we avoid discussing anything deeper and more meaningful than our upcoming social engagement. Then I drop you off home, refreshed and ready to deal with your sister, and I go back to my dogs. Who by the way are a lot less complicated.'

I sneak a glance at him and see the way the rain has moulded his T-shirt to his body, slicked his hair against his neck. I tell myself off for noticing these things, and remind myself we are just friends. He is a good friend, helping me out. Nothing more.

'It's a deal,' I reply.

Chapter Nineteen

The night of the Halloween Ball is finally here. The whole village is alive with anticipation. The café has been closed for the day, because Laura and Cherie were sorting out the food for the party, along with Max's daughter, Sophie, who has come home from uni for the event.

A lot of young people have migrated back to Budbury for the weekend, and they bring a different energy with them. Ranging in ages from late teens through to mid-twenties, it strikes me how happy they all seem to be back with their grown-ups. I suppose if I'd had a mum like Laura or a dad like Cal, I'd want to spend time with them too.

I know it's not been plain sailing, that there has been loss and pain, but the overwhelming feeling is one of warmth and contentment. If I'd been lucky enough to have children, I'd be delighted that they were still interested in leaving their big city lives in places like London, Liverpool, Manchester and Cardiff just to come back to this tiny little place in the middle of nowhere. Even Sally is impressed, and says she hopes Lucy and Libby feel the same once they fly the nest.

I wish they were here tonight, now I come to think of it. Libby would start off shy, but eventually she'd love it here, with all these friendly and delightfully eccentric people. Edie just might be her spirit animal. Lucy would immediately latch on to Max's kids or hang out with Zoe's Martha or Laura's older ones and have an absolute blast. Hopefully there will be a similar vibe if they come down at Christmas.

I am putting the finishing touches to my make-up and doing a final inspection of my outfit. I'm in my bedroom, which doesn't have a full-length mirror, but I'm making do. Sally has, predictably enough, commandeered the one bathroom in the house, as she has since she arrived. Tonight I don't mind, because I can hear her singing in there. She sounds more upbeat than she has in days, as she merrily slaughters Whitney Houston's 'I Wanna Dance With Somebody'.

Ollie has called her a few more times, admittedly once to ask her where she keeps the iron, but he's sounded slightly more concerned each time. Perhaps it's finally sinking in with him that this might not be something he can ignore and hope it goes away. I bloody well hope so, at least, for all of our sakes.

I'm running a brush through my hair – or actually my wig – when she walks into the room.

'What do you think?' she asks, spinning around in a little circle. 'Still got the magic?'

'If by "magic" you mean an impressive cleavage, then yes, you look just as good as a slutty nurse as you did years ago!'

That's not one hundred per cent true – she is slightly thicker around the waist, and her face bears the passage of time as you'd expect – but she does look terrific. Blood, hopefully fake, is spattered all over her chest and stomach, and she's wearing fishnets and high heels, just like real nurses do. She nods and punches the air in victory, before looking me up and down.

She lets out a small whistle, and says: 'Wow. That looks … strangely hot on you.'

'You think? It's not a bit too much?'

'It's Halloween! No such thing as too much! You already have the lovely pale skin, and your red lippie is gorgeous. Just let me do a bit more eyeliner for you…'

She brings up a picture on her phone, and looks from it to me, nodding. Sally was always better at girl stuff than I was, so I put myself in her hands as she works. It's actually kind of nice. Maybe we'll bond.

'There. That's better. The dress suits you, but you should really get a push-up bra.'

Right. Well, maybe we won't bond after all. I actually did get a push-up bra, but I'm not going to embarrass myself by admitting that to her.

She finishes fussing with me, then insists we have a photo shoot. Some are of us together, and some are very much shots of her boobs that I know she'll be making sure she posts on her family group chat to make Ollie jealous. It's only just after six, and we've arranged to go to the pub for a drink first. There is a coach to take us from the village and back, but I've volunteered to be our designated driver for the night. Aidan's place is a little more remote, and at the very least I owe him a lift. Possibly for the rest of his life.

There's a knock on the door, and I feel a little flutter in my belly. I glance at myself again, and in the space of three seconds flat I decide that I look awful, then that I look great, then that I look like an idiot. What was I thinking? I should have gone for Laura's ghost sheet idea. Sally notices my expression, and grins at me.

'You look eminently fuckable,' she says, making me laugh. 'Are you nervous? You seem nervous. Aidan is going to flip, don't worry!'

'I'm not nervous,' I lie, trying to convince myself. Truthfully, I feel jittery for no good reason. Aidan is not actually my boyfriend and I don't need to impress him. So why am I staring at myself in the mirror, wondering what he's going to think?

Sally trots down the stairs, and I hear her exclaim when she sees him. 'Oh my god! Aidan, you look divine. You two are going to be the hottest couple at the Halloween Ball!'

She sounds like a teenager, and I wonder how much of Lucy and Libby has rubbed off on her. It makes me laugh though, and I take a deep breath and run my hands over my waist and hips to smooth down the dress. I suppose I'd better go and face the full horror of the night ahead.

As I appear at the top of the stairs, he is right there at the bottom, gazing up at me. I falter and grab hold of the handrail to steady myself. He looks so damn fine I almost lose my breath. It might just be a costume, but he wears the double-breasted pin-striped suit like a god. His dark hair is slicked back, and even the stupid fake moustache somehow looks good on him.

All of that is pretty delicious, but it's the way he's looking at me that is really sending my pulse racing. He is watching my every step as I descend, his eyes on mine, the heart-melting smile on his lips. When Aidan looks at me like this, so direct and so intense, I lose my grasp on reality. He has a way of making me feel like we're the only two people in the entire world.

He holds out his hand for mine to grasp as I reach the final step, and lifts it to his lips. I hear Sally sigh a little as he kisses my fingers and says: 'My darling Morticia. Stunning, as always.'

'Gomez,' I say, nodding at him. 'Looking pretty snazzy yourself.'

We stand there for a few moments, holding hands and smiling at each other. Or maybe it's longer than that, because Sally says: 'Earth to the Addams family! Earth to the Addams family! Are we going to the pub or are you two just going to gaze into each other's eyes all night? It's disgusting!'

I laugh and the three of us head across the road. The weather has been kind today, cold and sunny, but by this time of the evening all traces of the sun have disappeared. We're left with an inky blue sky, a scattering of stars, and the mildest of breezes.

We only stay in the pub for half an hour, because we're under strict instructions from Edie not to be 'fashionably late'.

'At my age, I like to start early and be in bed before midnight, dear,' she told me. 'It's not so much that I'll turn into a pumpkin, more that I might fall asleep in public and that dreadful Becca would take pictures of me drooling and post them on Instagran.'

'Instagram?' I asked.

'No, it's a special one for old crones…'

Nobody likes to disappoint Edie, so before too long I shepherd my already slightly tipsy sister into my car and drive us up to Briarwood. I suspect she's gone full teenager tonight and been on the vodkas before we even left the house. 'Pre-drinks', as Lucy always call it when she meets up with friends before a party.

Briarwood is the perfect place for a Halloween Ball, full of brooding Gothic charm, perched high on its hill and surrounded by mysterious woodland. Tonight, somebody has set up a spectacular light show, probably one of the tech geniuses that call Briarwood home. Huge red and green projections are flickering over the building, casting glowing images of pumpkins, cats and witch's cauldrons. Every window is lit up with pulsating red strobes, and the place looks spectacular in the darkness.

'Wow,' says Sally as she clambers out of the car, 'I wonder if someone's sitting in a space station telling NASA about this?'

We walk through into the lobby and are greeted by an unnerving number of Minions. There are dozens of them, bouncing around the hallway in a blur of yellow, taking coats and handing out glasses of sparkling red liquid. I'm guessing that they're the residents, and this is confirmed when I see Finn, the manager, dressed as Gru. Or as much as he can be, considering that he's a handsome blond dude.

One of the Minions shows us through to a side room that is packed with food and drink. I've seen some of it in its research stages, and the café ladies have really outdone themselves. The whole buffet is Halloween themed, from the jelly with eyeballs in it to the sandwiches cut into the shape of gravestones. There's a spectacular black and red layer cake decorated with marzipan spiders, and a mummy made entirely out of cheese. It almost looks too good to eat, but I spot a group of kids sitting under the tables already tucking into loaded plates.

Ruby and Rose, Laura's twins, wave up at us, both covered in green face paint. I'm not sure what they're supposed to be, but I'm probably not cool enough. They're with Becca's daughter, Little Edie, who is Doctor Who, and Katie's older boys, one of whom is a vampire and one of whom is just wearing a onesie with a dinosaur hood. Low maintenance. I like it.

We drift through to the main ball room, running the gamut of some very overexcited Minions, and find a lively version of the 'Time Warp' underway. Cherie is in the middle, along with Edie, and there's something weirdly fascinating about watching the giant killer clown and almost-a-century-old woman in a bloody zombie outfit dance in a line. I stare on as they do their pelvic thrusts.

'I'll never un-see that,' Aidan murmurs, shaking his head.

'I know,' I whisper, as Sally leaves us and runs over to join in. Obviously. Aidan takes my hand and puts it through his arm like an old-fashioned gent. It's a very Gomez and Morticia gesture, and I'm happy to be led over to a table. Within a few minutes, we're joined by Cherie and Sally, and a Minion delivers glasses of Murderous Martini to us all. I have a tiny sip, just to please Cherie, but then stick to water.

'You two look magnificent,' Cherie announces, raising her glass to me. 'The perfect costume. I always had a bit of a thing for Gomez. He was such a romantic…'

Aidan slides his arm around my shoulders. 'Easy to be romantic when you have such a beautiful wife,' he says, smiling at me. I feel a blush on my cheeks, which is decidedly un-Morticia. *This isn't real*, I remind myself. This is him pretending. This is all a show for Sally. As soon as she leaves, we can go back to normal. Whatever the hell that is.

The night goes with the kind of swing I've come to expect of Budbury, and within an hour of us arriving, the whole place is packed. Laura is, as promised, wearing a sheet with eyeholes cut out of it, and she ambles over to admire my dress with its long black velvet skirt and dramatic flared sleeves. 'Next year,' she says determinedly, 'I'll be able to wear something like that…'

Max has succeeded in getting Gabriel to come with her, and he looks almost unbearably hot in his frilly white shirt, britches and pirate hat. She can't keep her hands off him, and I don't blame her; he's giving off a totally Pirate Poldark vibe.

Zoe's costume makes me laugh. She's wearing a sensible grey trouser suit with Doc Marten boots, a rumpled grey overcoat, and a deep red knitted scarf around her neck. It might not be immediately obvious to most people, but I notice straight away – she's actually come to the party dressed as DI Carina Shaw, my fictional heroine. Carina has a whole selection of brightly coloured knitted scarves that her mother makes for her in the secure unit where she's lived for the last twenty years. Long story. Zoe waves from across the room, and I give her an amused thumbs-up.

Sally throws herself into the party with great gusto, burning up the dance floor and taking part in everything from apple bobbing to a vigorous game of pass the parcel where every layer reveals something ghoulish. She emerges with a plastic skeleton hand, which she proceeds to enjoy poking me with every five minutes.

There's a bit of a surprise after the first few hours, when the music turns off, the lights go down low, and Edie takes to the microphone. Her lovely little face is now covered in scars and fake bites, and her pink ball-gown is tattered and torn. 'One two three, testing testing…' she says. 'Is there anybody out there?'

A huge cheer goes up in the room, and then she continues: 'Good! So, tonight, my friends, we have a very special treat for you all… A mysterious guest, all the way from distant lands!'

A spotlight appears, lighting a path from the doorway through into the room. A woman walks into it, tall and slim and dressed in a traditional frilly Spanish dress. Her hair is pinned up and twined with roses, and her face is painted white and red in a striking Day of the Dead design. She strides over to Edie, and takes the microphone from her.

'*Buenas noches, amigos!*' she says. 'And happy Halloween!'

At the sound of her voice, more cheers go up, and I see Auburn get up from her chair so fast it falls over. She's joined by Van, her brother and Katie's partner, and they run together to the front of the room. They throw their arms around the new arrival and hug her to within an inch of her life. As Auburn is dressed as a blood-spattered Ariel from *The Little Mermaid* and Van is wearing a huge Count Dracula cape, it looks pretty terrifying.

'Is that Willow?' I ask Cherie, seeing the delighted smile on my friend's face. I know Willow used to work at the café too and that they were close. 'It is, my love. It's been hard keeping her visit a secret, but it was worth it! Look how happy everyone is!'

She's right, I think, looking on. Laura has torn off her sheet to throw her arms around Willow, and even the normally reserved Katie is getting in on the act. Cherie ambles over to join them, and the music starts up again. How lovely to be so missed, I think. So much a part of this world. I know she's been living in Spain with her husband and baby, but there's no sign of them. Probably too loud for a baby.

Aidan's hand slips into mine under the table, and I glance up at him in surprise.

'You look wistful, Morticia,' he says, leaning in close. 'You okay?'

'Yes, of course. I just… Well, it's nice, isn't it? This place, and the way it holds people so close? Does that make sense?'

'It does, and yes, it is. I've never known anywhere like it. I suspect Budbury is magical all year round. Did I tell you how beautiful you look, by the way?'

'You did,' I reply. 'And you know you did. You just want to make me blush again.'

He winks at me, ensuring that I do, then says he's off to find more drinks. He kisses me on the forehead before he goes.

I can't take my eyes off him as he walks away, and I'm only brought back from my lustful trance when Sally pokes me on the shoulder with her skeleton hand. I turn back to face her. She's sipping on a Murderous Martini.

'I've never seen you look at a man like that,' she announces. 'Not even Will, and you actually married him. Could it be that my sister is finally in *luuuurrrve*?'

I am shocked by the very idea and shake my head vigorously, feeling my Morticia hair swishing over my back. 'No! Of course not!'

'Why do you sound so horrified? It's nice! It's lovely! It's delightful. It makes the world go round, didn't you hear?'

'I did hear, but I never believed it. I'm sure the world goes round because of something complicated to do with the astrophysics of the solar system.'

'Pah! Trust me, I'm a doctor. *Love* makes the world go round, not physics. In fact, I have you to thank for reminding me of that. It was seeing you and Aidan together at the twins' party that made me realise just how unhappy I was with Ollie.'

I freeze, my blood turning cold in my veins. 'What do you mean?'

'I mean that I saw the way Aidan looked at you. Saw the way he, I don't know, cherished you even. Every time he laid his hand on the small of your back, or held you in his arms, he was just so … respectful. Loving, but respectful. Like he couldn't believe his luck, like you were a precious object. Not gonna lie, I was a bit jealous. Things hadn't been good with me and Ollie for ages, but that pushed me over the edge. I want that, too. I want to be seen the way Aidan sees you, and if Ollie can't do that, then … well, then I suppose it's over. I'd rather be alone than settle for second best.'

I desperately wish I hadn't agreed to drive now, because I really could murder a Martini. If I'm interpreting this correctly, then one of the reasons my sister has walked out on her husband of twenty years is because of me. Because of Aidan. Because of our charade. I grab my water and gulp some down. I have to tell her. Awkward as this is, I can't allow my silly games to influence such a major life decision. What if this separation sticks? What if my darling Lucy and Libby lose their stable family home, at least in part because of me? No. I wouldn't be able to live with myself.

I reach out and grab her hand, making sure she's looking at me and not at the dancefloor. Admittedly that's hard, because a whole room full of people is doing the Michael Jackson 'Thriller' stomp, and it's quite the sight.

'Sally, listen to me.' She turns back, grinning. 'None of it was real,' I tell her.

'None of what was real?'

'None of me and Aidan. We're not a couple. He's not my

boyfriend. I'm not in love and he doesn't cherish me... It was all an act. Please don't judge Ollie by a lie.'

She frowns, looking understandably confused. 'More detail please.'

I sigh out my tension and swallow down the embarrassment. This needs to come out.

'Aidan is a friend, nothing more. In fact I barely know him. I asked him to be my date, to pretend to be with me, because I wanted to come to the twins' party and for once not be the loser of the family.'

'That's how you feel? Like the loser of the family? You, the one who has the world at your feet and a career we're all in awe of?'

I nod, surprised at the comment. 'Yes. Me, the one who got divorced and can't make a relationship work and never had kids. The one you all think is a bit of a freak. You all have me tucked away in a little box, and I suppose I wanted to break out of it.'

She opens her mouth to object, but closes it again. 'Actually, okay. I see where you're coming from. I can see why you felt like that. But Sarah ... you brought a fake boyfriend to my daughters' birthday party? You introduced him to the girls, to our parents?'

I hold my face in my hands. I feel so ashamed of myself. Not only did I lie in the beginning, but I also let it drag on for this long. I look back up.

'Yeah. I did. Aidan is... Well, Aidan is a great guy, but it is not and never has been a relationship.'

She stares at me and asks: 'How are you defining relationship? You said you're friends?'

'Yes, but nothing more! I know he kissed me at the party, but that was all for show ... and now I feel like an idiot. You mustn't base any of your decisions about Ollie on me and my pathetic little need to appear cool.'

I expect her to be angry and annoyed, to shout at me, or at the very least to ruthlessly mock me. I've just given her the best ammunition she's had in years.

What I very much don't expect is for her to laugh. Long, hard, and genuine. To the point where she has tears rolling down her cheeks and is holding her sides. I look on in confusion as she chortles.

'Oh, sis,' she says, once she's able to breathe again, 'you really are brilliant, you know! I never would have expected you to do something like that. Me? Yes, I'd do anything for attention, we all know that. But you? You'd usually do anything to avoid it! Oh god, this is so funny...'

I'm relieved, I suppose, in a way, but also a little affronted that I'm now a laughing stock. I guess I deserve it.

'I'm glad I'm entertaining.'

'Oh you are. You really are! Mainly because you're talking complete bullshit, and you don't even know it!'

Now I'm even more confused. She slurps the last of her Martini, leaning back in her seat. She crosses her arms across her chest, which hoists her boobs up even further. She's veering into *Carry On Nurse* territory now, but the look on her face is serious.

'Look,' she says, 'bringing a fake date to a party is weird. Introducing him to your family is weird. But what's even weirder is the fact that you don't see that it's not actually fake at all. You're kidding yourself. The way he treats you?

The way you look at him? That *kiss*? You can't fake that kind of fire. This is real. You just won't let your way-too-clever brain accept that yet. You say we all put you in a box? Well, I hate to break it to you, but you're doing the same to yourself. You decided long ago that you don't like people. That you don't do relationships. Well, I've got news for you sister – look around. See your new life. See all the friends, the community. See the gorgeous man who is clearly into you. It's real. It's happening. And it's *good*.'

I'm about to splutter my objections when she holds up a hand. 'Let's ask Aidan!' she says, as he sits back down. Oh God, I think, my cheeks blazing and my heart sinking. This is so humiliating.

'Ask me what?' he says.

'Nothing!' I answer quickly. 'Nothing at all!'

'Ask you what your intentions towards my sister are, young man,' Sally says, pointing a skeleton finger at him. 'Sarah here has confessed her sins. She's told me the whole date at the party was a set up and that you're not a couple at all. But I don't buy it. I think the fake is the fake bit. What say you?'

Aidan takes a moment to process that convoluted statement. Then he nods slowly, smiling the smile, turning to look from me to my sister again. 'Yeah. You're right. None of this is fake for me, Sally. I absolutely adore your sister. I'd be her real-life Gomez in a flash if she let me.'

I stare at him, dumbfounded. Sally laughs, delightedly. 'Told you so, sis! Now, how about getting your head out of your arse and going with the flow for once?'

Go with the flow? Has she ever met me? Both of them

are looking at me in anticipation, but I'm given an escape route from the most unexpected of sources. Striding towards us, looking hot, bothered and very nervous, is my sister's husband Ollie. He's dressed in his surgical scrubs, which are spattered with fake blood. Or, I suppose, given his profession, it could actually be real. I glance at my phone and see that it's almost ten. He must have jumped in his car and driven here as soon as Sally sent those pics of her as a sexy nurse.

I grin and wave to him over Sally's shoulder.

'Don't try and avoid the question!' she says.

'I'm not avoiding the question. I'm waving to your husband. The sexy surgeon heading towards us.'

She frowns and looks deeply confused, then turns around. Ollie reaches our table, and despite the noise and costumes and chaos around us, only has eyes for his wife. Her mouth is open in shock, as she stands up to face him. Her hands go to her hips, and she says: 'What are you doing here?'

'I've come to see you,' he says, his gaze flickering over her. 'To tell you I'm sorry I've taken you for granted. To tell you I'll do better. To take you home.'

She hesitates, glaring at him with hostility. I know she's probably thrilled at the big romantic gesture, but I also know my sister and how stubborn she is. She won't back down this easily.

'Go on, Sal,' I say, nudging her. 'Why don't you get your head out of your arse and go with the flow?'

She gives me some severe side-eye, but eventually softens.

'Okay, Ollie. I'll agree to hear you out. That's all I'm promising at this stage.'

He sags a little in relief and joins her at the table. Aidan and I make a sharp exit, and get caught up in dancing to the *Ghostbusters* theme tune with the rest of Budbury. That suits me down to the ground, because you can't have a serious discussion while you're dancing to Halloween hits, and it gives me a break from what was becoming an awkward conversation.

Still, as I watch him bang hips with Cherie's killer clown and tell Laura that he's not afraid of ghosts, I can't help smiling. When did I ever feel this alive? When did I ever blush so much? When did I ever yearn to feel a man's hands on my body the way I do Aidan's? I've barely known him for a month, but I cannot stop thinking about him. I've confided in him more than I have in my own sister, and I've felt myself grow and change under his influence. Am I kidding myself, like Sally says? Am I faking the fake?

It's a lot to think about, and it's impossible to have a clear mind in this kind of atmosphere. Instead, I go with the flow in a different way – I simply enjoy myself. I dance and eat and chat both to my friends and to people I've never met before. I feel a swell of social confidence in this place, that is very unusual for me, and I don't actually fear being rejected or mocked. I suspect it's because everyone here is already so eccentric themselves that all of my quirks seem relatively run-of-the-mill. No such thing as normal in Budbury.

When we finally head back to the table, we're both a

little dishevelled. My wig is sliding to one side, and Aidan's moustache has been lost completely.

Ollie and Sally are holding hands and have obviously done a lot of talking. Ollie nods at us and says he's going to get some food. Aidan goes with him, presumably to give us a minute alone.

'So,' she says, leaning back in her chair and looking very happy. 'Ollie and I are booking into a hotel for the night instead of going straight home. He's seen the error of his ways and promised me a future of romantic city breaks, dinners out and flowers every Friday. Or at least, he's promised to actually talk to me and limit his time listening to podcasts. Thanks for the hospitality, but I think I'll be getting out of your hair. You can have your bathroom back and stop pretending that the deep breathing is a yoga technique rather than you trying not to murder me…'

'How ever could you think such a thing?' I reply, feigning shock. 'But what about your stuff at my place? Your clothes?'

'Stuff my stuff! I've got my purse and my phone with me. The rest isn't essential. As for clothes, I don't really expect to be wearing any for a while…'

She lets out a little laugh, and it makes her look twenty years younger. I get the feeling that she and Ollie will be just fine. The gesture felt big and dramatic, but that's the way Sally is. As she constantly reminds me, I know nothing about marriage, but even *I* get that there are going to be ups and downs. Hopefully these two will now be entering a long-lasting 'up'.

We stand and she gives me a huge hug. 'Think about

what I said, Sarah. Aidan makes you happy. You light up when you're around him. Don't turn your back on that because you're overthinking it. I know you. You'll have used everything as an excuse not to let him in, the age gap, your history, even his sheer unbelievable hotness … but come on, woman! Give it a chance!'

I nod and tell her I will. She makes the rounds of the room, saying goodbye to her new friends, and disappears into the night with Ollie. I immediately feel both relief and sadness. Aidan appears by my side as I watch them go.

'Will you miss her?' he asks.

'Yes. But we were reaching critical mass, and some kind of big row was probably inevitable had she stayed. I've always felt a bit … I don't know, disjointed around my family. I've always felt like they didn't really understand me.'

'And now?'

I look up at him and fix his slightly wonky bow tie. 'Now I think maybe she is more perceptive than I thought. Or maybe I'm not as mysterious as I thought.'

'You, my darling Morticia, are the very definition of mysterious…'

He whisks me into his arms and back onto the dance floor. It's a slow song, and I recognise it from the twins' playlists – 'Vampire' by Olivia Rodrigo. The lyrics are dark, but the rhythm is a sensual mix of swirling crescendos and driving beats. I melt into him, my hands twined around his neck, my fingers touching his hair. I lean my face against his chest and lose myself in the moment. The music. The mood. The man.

All around me, I see other couples doing the same, as well as the younger crew singing along to the chorus as they sway. Laura has shed her sheet and is gazing up at Matt; Sam and Becca are shuffling around together, and Cal has actually lifted Zoe up mid-twirl, the Doc Marten boots inches from the floor. Cherie is sitting off to one side tapping her giant clown boots, and zombie Edie is fast asleep next to her.

I smile at my friends and at the sheer silly loveliness of them all. I remember how reluctant I felt when I first moved here. How convinced I was that I would remain an outlier, keeping a polite distance. Now, it's hard to imagine life without them all. I suppose I've changed, impossible as that might have seemed.

And maybe, I think, as Aidan's breath whispers against my skin and his hands caress my back, I can change some more. Maybe I can stop denying myself the pleasure that is very much right in front of me, mine for the taking.

As the song draws to its delicious close, I look up at Aidan. His green eyes hold mine, and I thrill at what I see in them. He wants me, and perhaps it's time to stop wondering why and simply do what Sally suggested. Go with the flow.

'Would you like to come home with me?' I ask quietly. I feel the instant reaction in his body, the slight tightening of his arms around me, a quick intake of air making his chest rise and fall. He pauses, and for a second I worry that I have made a terrible mistake. That his flirting was just that – flirting.

'No problem if not,' I add quickly. 'I just … um…'

Oh God. I wish the dance floor would open up and swallow me whole.

'Of course I'd like to,' he says, kissing my forehead. 'One hundred per cent yes. It's just… The dogs. I know they'd be fine – they have shelter and water and food – but … I've never left them alone overnight. I know I'm a sucker, but I wouldn't want them to be distressed, you know?'

'I know,' I say, because it's so obvious once he says it. His commitment to those beautiful animals is one of the things that makes me like him so much. 'It's okay.'

'I suppose…' he adds. 'I suppose you'll just have to come home with me instead…'

Chapter Twenty

One of the dogs howls as we drive into Hazelwell, the sound echoing from the tree line, eerie in the moonlight. I park up and watch as Aidan gets out and walks towards the door. All of them run towards him, a couple from the woods, one from the shelter, and Juno from the house. They swirl around him, tails wagging, shoving their magnificent heads under his hands.

I take my Morticia wig off and fluff up my real hair, glad of the cool night air against my skin as I quietly get out of the car. Juno runs straight over to me for love, and Argent follows a little later. The other two, Frost and Mabel, look up at me with twitching noses. I always feel a bit sorry for Mabel, because the others have such cool names. But as she's a dog, I don't suppose she's bothered.

I walk slowly over towards them, and neither of them runs away back into the woods. This is a victory, and Aidan looks thrilled – even more so when all of the dogs follow us inside. This is the first time the whole pack has come into the house while I've been here, and I am also delighted. Maybe we're all making progress in our own ways.

We spend a little time with the dogs, and Aidan puts on some music and pours me a glass of wine. He throws some logs on the fire, and basically lets me relax. I am, of course, nervous, but I allow myself that. This is a situation where nerves are entirely appropriate, and in their own way luscious – the tingling feeling in my tummy, the jittery dash of energy when our hands brush, the sense of anticipation.

After the dogs have fully settled, safe in the knowledge that their alpha is home, he stands up and holds out his hands. I place mine in his, and he pulls me effortlessly to my feet. I've shed my heels and slide comfortably into his embrace.

He puts his thumb beneath my chin and gently turns my face upwards to look into his eyes.

'You're trembling,' he says softly, his other hand on my neck beneath my hair. 'Are you scared?'

'Yes,' I murmur, leaning into him.

'Don't be. Nothing is going to happen here that you don't want to happen.'

I nod and tentatively run my hands over his back. His jacket has been thrown on the couch, a plain white shirt beneath. 'I know. But … if you leave this up to me, then nothing will happen. And I want it to, Aidan, I do. I'm just … unsure. It's been a while.'

I expect a flippant comment, something along the lines of 'Well it still works the same as ever'. But he just nods, and caresses my cheek with his palm. It's not just that it's been a while. It's also that I've never, ever felt this way around a man before, and it is unravelling me in all kinds of ways. It feels dangerous and delicious all at the same time.

He takes my face between his hands and leans down to kiss me. It begins gently, slowly, almost delicately. Like he is giving me the chance to change my mind. When I don't – when my fingers tug his shirt loose and slide onto his bare back – everything changes.

The kiss deepens, our lips dancing together in a way that starts a fire inside me. My hands explore his body, running over the soft skin and the steel muscle that lies beneath it. He twines his fingers into my hair, pulling me closer, kissing me with even more passion. I'm crushed against him, our bodies flush against each other, and I feel the hardness of him pressing against me. If I'd ever doubted that he wanted me, I no longer can.

I push my hands between us, fighting for enough space to undo the buttons of his shirt, desperate to see him and touch him. He shrugs it off, breaking our kiss long enough for us both to take a breath.

He smooths my hair back from my face and runs his hands over my back. He finds the zip of my dress, and pulls it down, pushing it from my shoulders. His eyes roam over me hungrily, and his expression makes me weak at the knees.

'God, you're so damn beautiful…' he mutters, unhooking my bra and gently stroking my breasts. I suck in a shocked gulp of pleasure as he runs his thumbs over my nipples, his pupils huge, his face as serious as I've ever seen it.

He slides my dress down over my hips, and it puddles

on the floor around me. I have a second where I feel exposed and vulnerable, and then his hands are on me again and I forget all of that. I forget everything apart from this man, and the way I feel beneath his touch.

He swoops me up into his arms, cradling me against his chest, and I don't even feel threatened by that. He is big enough and strong enough to make me feel safe and small and so, so eager.

'I'm taking you upstairs,' he says, nuzzling into my neck, kissing the tender flesh and sending spikes of excitement running through me. 'The dogs are looking a little too interested…'

I glance down, see that he's right. All four of them are watching us with curiosity, heads tilted and ears pricked. Juno's tail thuds slowly against the floor.

'Good idea,' I say. 'I love the dogs, but some things should remain private.'

'They should. Now, hold on tight…'

He gallops up the stairs with me held against him, and I squeal like a little girl the whole way. He's laughing by the time he pushes open his bedroom door and lays me gently on the bed. I glance around, see a masculine but comfortable room painted in shades of blue, stacks of books on the floor, colourful artwork on the walls.

The sheets are cool and soft against my skin, and I stretch out against them. All of my nerves have disappeared. All of the embarrassment I usually feel at being almost naked with a man has gone. Something about Aidan does not allow those feelings to show themselves. Instead I am suddenly confident and playful. Teasing, even.

His eyes follow every move I make, a small smile dancing on his lips.

'I knew there was a sex kitten in there somewhere,' he says, tugging off his belt and his trousers. I stare at his magnificent form, hardly able to believe that this is happening. That the melting feeling in my tummy is real. That the need flooding my body is going to be fulfilled. That after a month of foreplay, I am finally ready.

He climbs onto the bed, and straddles me, trapping me beneath him. He plants a palm either side of my head and pins me down with his intense green eyes.

'I want you more than I've ever wanted a woman in my life,' he says, his voice a low growl. I rub myself against him shamelessly.

'Well, here I am,' I murmur, running my hand over his perfect backside. 'Yours for the taking…'

Chapter Twenty-One

I'm momentarily confused when I wake up in the morning. I'm somewhere new, and at first, when I come back to consciousness, I'm slightly startled. My eyes take in a different view, and my ears hear different sounds, and my skin is aware of different sensations.

The confusion lasts only a few seconds before it's replaced by a sense of profound contentment. The memories of the night before rush back over me, and I blush immediately.

I have never known myself to be so uninhibited, so wild, so free. So lost in physical delight. Honestly, it feels a little like the first time I have ever truly had sex. The other times, the other men, were so insignificant in comparison. I genuinely didn't know that my body was capable of giving and receiving such pleasure. Making love with Aidan was literally a mind-blowing experience. In fact I'm not sure my mind will ever recover. I'm a person usually driven by my brain, by my thoughts, by logic, but last night my mind was nowhere to be found. Last night my body was in charge, and it was a revelation.

Is that what it's like for other people? Is this what I've been missing out on? How have I never known about this? I'm almost fifty and I've slept with a grand total of five men. It is not a lot, but it is enough for comparison. The verdict is that before Aidan, I might as well not have bothered. He made me feel things I'd never felt before, took me to heights I'd never dreamt possible, and then held me in his arms as I fell asleep.

He is lying next to me still, one of his legs flung possessively over mine, one arm above his head. His hair is messed up and his chest is slowly rising and falling in a deep sleep. I wriggle onto my side and stare at him, remembering the time back in my flat when he caught me doing exactly this. Except now I'm allowed to touch as well as look. He has given me permission, and just as importantly so have I. I reach out and let my hand trail over his shoulder.

His eyes slowly open, and when he focuses enough to see me, his face breaks out into the most gorgeous smile I've ever seen from him. And I've seen a few.

'Hey,' he says, quietly. 'You're still here.'

'Wasn't I supposed to be?'

'I hoped you would be. But I also thought maybe you'd disappear in the night.'

'That doesn't sound like me,' I reply, laughing inside. That so sounds like me. 'And anyway, I was too tired after all that … activity.'

He runs his fingers through my dishevelled hair, and I

have a brief moment of self-consciousness. I must look a mess, what with last night's make-up and this morning's bedhead on top of the fact that I haven't brushed my teeth. He kisses me, and I immediately forget all about such matters. He doesn't seem to mind. Within seconds, he is letting me know pretty directly that he doesn't mind at all.

One thing leads to another, and the next half hour passes in a blur of mutual pleasure. When he finally gets out of bed, he struts towards the window, bare-ass naked and without an ounce of embarrassment. In fact he obviously knows I'm watching, and gives a little shimmy as he opens the curtains. Pale sunlight pours into the room. I wonder what time it is.

'I need to see to the dogs,' he says, tugging on joggers and a T-shirt. 'Then I'll be back up with coffee. Sound good?'

'Sounds amazing. Though I probably need a shower.'

He pauses in the doorway and grins at me. 'Well, you could take a shower. But in the interest of transparency, I'm planning on getting you good and dirty again very soon…'

I blush and hold my hands to my face. Why is it that after everything this man has done to me, after everything I've done to him, he can still make my cheeks flame?

He winks at me, clearly very satisfied with himself, and disappears from the room. I lie there for a few moments wondering if I should pinch myself. Is any of this real? Is it all a dream? Can it actually be happening?

I practically float along the landing to the bathroom, and although I don't have a shower, I use the facilities and rub my teeth with a bit of paste on my finger. It's better than nothing. I look at myself in the mirror and almost don't recognise the person staring back at me. Yes, my hair is a mess, and yes, Morticia's eye liner is no longer a straight line, but there is a sparkle to my eyes that was not there yesterday. I smile at my reflection, and say: 'Brazen hussy. Going back for seconds, are we?'

Of course I am. Although technically I'm going back for fifths. It was a busy night, and neither of us got a lot of sleep. I climb back under the covers and try not to think. When I start to think, I inevitably end up in trouble, and I don't want to come down from this high. I don't want to analyse or define or worry about what it all means. This was wonderful, spectacular sex. With a man I like. I don't need to overcomplicate it or poke it until hornets fly out. It is okay, I tell myself, to simply enjoy the moment.

That's not one of my specialist skills, so I distract myself by trying to wrinkle out some creases in my next plot instead. By the time Aidan comes back bearing delicious-smelling coffee, I'm frowning.

'You okay?' he asks, looking at my expression as he passes me a mug. He pulls his top off, and my eyes roam his perfectly formed torso. Cor blimey. It's like I've fallen into an alternate reality.

'I am,' I reply, as he climbs in next to me. 'I was just thinking about work. Tricky plot point.'

'Ah, I get it. That's cool. I thought maybe you were having second thoughts and actually considering knotting the sheets together to climb out the window.'

'Would I really need to do that? Couldn't I just leave through the front door? If I wanted to leave, I mean.'

'And do you?' he asks, quirking an eyebrow at me. It sounds like a genuine question, and I remind myself that this is new for him, too.

'Not right now. But I'd be lying if I said I was good at dealing with stuff like this.'

He laughs and shakes his head. 'Stuff like this?'

'Yeah. You know. Stuff.'

'Right. That makes it much clearer. And I know you're not good at it; that's why I made the crack about you climbing out the window. I thought maybe you'd freak out. That all this "stuff" might be too much. All this love, to give it its correct term.'

I stare at him, completely taken aback by his use of the L word. Only two men have ever used the L word on me. One of them was my husband, who went on to have multiple affairs behind my back, and the other was Scott Jones, an already-married psycho stalker who was living under a fake identity when he said it. Two men loved me, two liars who shattered me in different ways. That is not a good track record or something I expected to hear from Aidan. It trips me up, and my anxiety levels spike. What if Aidan turns out to be like them? He's shown no signs of that, but then again, neither did they to start with…

I can see that my silence is hurting him, and I bite my lip in an attempt to stop myself spiralling.

'You don't have to say it back, Sarah, but I needed to say it myself. I'm in love with you. I was already pretty far gone before last night, but now … well, there's no hope for me now. I love you.'

His phone rings on the bedside cabinet. He glances

down at it and shakes his head before swiping to ignore it. It should have given me the split second I needed to formulate an appropriate response to what he's just said. Unfortunately, it doesn't, and I'm still gaping at him when he looks up at me.

'You know,' he says, sipping his coffee, 'most women wouldn't look absolutely disgusted at me telling them I love them. Like I said, you don't have to say it back … but do you really feel that horrified?'

He sounds genuinely upset, and I give myself a mental slap around the head. 'Of course I'm not horrified. But I'm also not … most women.'

He looks deep into my eyes, and whatever he sees there makes him frown. I think he sees I'm shutting down, backing off. He knows me well enough to see the signs. I can't bear the disappointment on his face, but I don't know how to fix this. I don't know how to be normal. Right now, I don't even know how to speak.

I want to explain myself, to tell him that the men who declared their love for me were the ones who inflicted nothing but pain. I want to tell him that I like him, at the very least … but for some reason, I'm freezing. It's similar to the response I have when I'm physically afraid, or when somebody takes me by surprise. I know my face doesn't quite reveal it, but inside I'm currently paralysed.

'No. No, you're not, are you? Will we see each other again, or was this just a one-night deal for you? No pressure, but I'm a huge fan of the truth when it comes to matters of the heart.'

Of course he is. He lost his last partner to his own

overcompetitive father. Who wouldn't prefer honesty once they'd had that happen to them?

'I'm not sure,' I manage to mutter, the only few words that I can string together under this level of scrutiny. It's the truth. I genuinely hadn't looked beyond this moment. In fact I was trying very hard not to.

He nods and runs his hands over his face, sighing. 'Okay. You're not in the mood to talk. I get it. I told you I was a patient man, and I guess I'll have to be.'

I suddenly feel a flash of irritation. It comes from nowhere, and I'm not sure it's totally fair – but neither is this. I never promised Aidan love. I never lied about myself. He knew exactly who I was when he took me to bed. Everything was absolutely fine until he started lobbing the love bomb in my direction. The irritation frees me up a little, and ironically the first words I'm able to speak are ones I regret saying.

'I'm not one of your Wolfdogs, Aidan. You don't need to be patient with me, or feed me treats until I trust you. I'm not a project to be managed.'

'No, you're not like one of my dogs, I agree,' he answers, looking annoyed now. It's the first time I've seen that expression on his face, his eyes flashing and his lips compressed. 'You're more stubborn than they are. We've got something special here, Sarah. Really special. I'm not asking for a lifetime commitment. All I'm asking is that you give it a chance. That you don't give up on it before we even try.'

I can hear the sharp edge in his voice, and I don't quite believe how quickly this has turned sour on us. Just minutes ago, I was lying here naked, looking forward to spending the morning with him. Now, we seem to be on the verge of our very first argument … and I'm still naked. That, at least, is something I can control. I climb out of the bed, taking the top sheet with me, wrapping it around me and awkwardly looking around for my clothes.

'They're downstairs,' he says, his tone dark and his nostrils flaring. 'And why are you hiding away from me? I saw your body in glorious detail last night, Sarah. I kissed every inch of it.'

I know he is hurt – that he expected more of me, that he expected better – but I am now completely overwhelmed, and anything that comes out of my mouth is only likely to make matters worse. His phone rings again, and he knocks it off the table and turns back to me.

'Are you leaving now?' he asks, obviously making an effort not to raise his voice. I wish he would. I deserve it. Last night was a blip, a freak occurrence. This morning I'm back to being the real me. The freak of nature, the emotional cripple, the scared, stunted little creature who can't even trust a man, never mind let them love her or love them in return. I'm a failure, as ever.

'I am,' I reply, holding on to the wall for balance. 'And I'm sorry. I'm a mess. I think you got it wrong, Aidan. I'm not just damaged. I'm completely broken.'

I run down the stairs, praying he doesn't follow me.

Chapter Twenty-Two

I run out of the house in my bare feet, the tiny gravel stones of the courtyard digging into my soles. I don't care. I just need out.

As soon as I'm safe in my car, I lock all the doors and take a couple of deep breaths. I'm reacting like I'm being chased. My pulse is racing and my skin feels hot to the touch. My stomach is tied up in knots, and I feel like I might vomit. I can't let him see me like this. It wouldn't be good for either of us. Once I'm calm enough and my heartbeat has stopped thundering in my own ears, I put on my shoes and drive away.

The countryside lanes are awash with rain and the sky is threatening. There was sunshine first thing this morning, but now there seems to be nothing but grey clouds. Pathetic fallacy, I think, but then remind myself that the weather has better things to do than reflect my moods.

I realise I'm driving too fast when a pheasant whooshes out from a hedgerow, a blur of golden brown and green, flapping its wings and swerving to avoid me. It steals my breath again and I slam on my brakes.

I keep the car still in the middle of the road while I recover. It's unlikely anybody else will be driving these roads at this time of day. At least I hope so. Once I feel calmer, I restart the engine and this time I take it easy. I force my mind to stay in the here and the now, rather than skittering off back to Hazelwell and the look on Aidan's face as I walked out on him. I need to concentrate, because it won't help anybody if I crash the car. Or maybe it will, I think darkly, instantly ashamed of myself. Ashamed of my weakness, my vulnerability. My constant battle to not be *me*.

It takes me twice as long to get back to the village as it normally does, and when I finally park up, my hands are shaking on the steering wheel. I rest my head against it for a moment, then get out. I glance around me, checking for signs of life, but see nothing. They must all be sleeping off their hangovers. I'm glad; I couldn't handle small talk right now.

I do my traditional battle with the key, and as I let myself into the house, Tinkerbell appears and winds himself in and out of my legs. I crouch down and plunge my fingers into his thick, soft fur. He purrs and gives me the cat equivalent of a hug. Then he runs out of the door, leaving me alone again.

The house is silent and cold, and seeing the remnants of Sally's stay makes me even more sad. She drove me crazy, but I wish she was here now. I wish I had her to talk to. I'd tell her everything, from beginning to end. All the things I've hidden over the years, all the pain I've hoarded. Then maybe we'd get drunk, or break out the Ben & Jerry's, and everything would feel better.

I pick up one of her abandoned hair bobbles from the floor, and smile at the curly blond strand twisted around it. I hope she's had a good night with Ollie and has woken up full of resolve to make her marriage work. At least one of us should have a tick in the relationship box.

I climb up the stairs, bone weary, and force myself to take a shower. I throw the Morticia dress in the bin, and scrub at my face under the jets. I'm way too old for play-acting, for pretending to be somebody that I'm not. I'm not Morticia and he is not Gomez. I'm not good for him. I can't move at his speed. I don't have his certainty. I'm basically rubbish, and am starting to think that I always will be.

After I towel dry my hair and pull on some comfy clothes, I do a little yoga to try and recalibrate. It doesn't really work, but I'm sure my hips will thank me for it anyway. I'm achy and sore in places I didn't know I had, because last night and this morning my body got a very new kind of workout. I close that train of thought off straight away and head into the kitchen to forage for food.

Huh, I think, standing in front of the fridge and staring at it. If I stare for long enough, maybe something will magically appear. Sally ate me out of house and home, and today is a day when I should really re-stock. All I have is sliced lime for her vodka, and the crusts of the loaf because she doesn't like them. The freezer is filled with sensible items like frozen broccoli, but this really does not feel like a frozen broccoli kind of day.

In fact, this feels like a giant cake and a hot chocolate

kind of day. Now, where could I possibly find those things? I grab my coat and head out into the sleeting rain.

The Comfort Food Café is technically closed today, for Halloween Ball related reasons, but I'm pretty sure that Cherie will be at home and that she will not mind me turning up and scrounging from her. I could, of course, just drive to the big supermarket on the retail park a few miles away, but frankly I don't want to. I was not impressed with my driving skills earlier today and I'm not keen to get behind the wheel again. Besides, I can admit to myself that I'm looking for more than food. I'm looking for comfort. This, at least, is some kind of progress I suppose.

By the time I fight my way up the path to the café, leaning into the wind like I'm drunk, I'm soaking wet and my hair is scarier than last night's fright wig. The door is closed but not locked, in typical café style, and I let myself in, shouting her name as I go. I hear a little woof from upstairs, then the scampering of tiny paws on the steps. Luna comes shooting out of the kitchens to greet me, followed not long after by Cherie herself.

I do a double take when I see her, because although she is wearing a full-length hot-pink silk kimono, she hasn't taken her clown face paint off yet. Her cheeks are covered in patches of white, her lips are massive smeared red smudges, and her eyes are multi-coloured bruises. At least she's wearing her own hair.

'Good morning, my precious!' she says, sounding way too chipper. 'How are you this morning?'

I take my coat off and hang it up to drip dry on the hooks in the corner. 'I'm hungry and I'm sad.'

'Oh dear,' she says, frowning. 'Well, you've come to the right place. Upstairs or down?'

'Where is the cake?'

'Definitely down.'

'That's where I'll stay, then, if that's okay?'

She walks over and wraps her arms around me. Even with the scary clown face, she still gives the world's best hugs. I let myself cling on to her for a few moments, blinking back tears.

'Of course it's okay,' she answers. 'Look in the fridge and see what you fancy, I'll be down in a minute.'

I walk through into the kitchen, past the huge old coffee machine. It's a temperamental beast that regularly breaks down and has to be bashed with hammers. It obviously needs replacing, but for some reason she keeps it. I suspect that it has meaning to her, some sentimental value that makes it more than a coffee machine. I glance at it with curiosity, wondering how many hot drinks it's dispensed over the years, how much warmth and comfort it has shared.

I stare into the huge fridge and whistle at the sheer amount of food in there. This is definitely the place to be after those solar flares and the collapse of society. After a bit of poking around and the rearranging of plates and bowls, I emerge with an apple and blackberry crumble and a jug of custard. I pop them in the microwave and the smell of cinnamon and cream fills the room.

Cherie emerges from the stairs, bearing fleecy blankets and a packet of face wipes. 'You go and get snuggled on the sofa,' she says, 'and I'll bring over the hot chocolate. I'm assuming it's a hot chocolate occasion?'

I nod and do as I'm told, wrapping the blanket around my shoulders. The sofas are in the corner of the room, surrounded by bookshelves that are overflowing with paperbacks, guides, board games and colouring pads. I idly pick one up, along with a carton of crayons. I find a picture I like – a giant teapot made of squares like a patchwork quilt – and start to colour it in.

Within a few minutes Cherie is over with a tray holding bowls of steaming crumble and tall glasses of chocolate with cream, marshmallows and crumbled up Flake. Perfect. She sits down opposite me, the sofa slumping under her weight, and starts to dab at her face with the wipes. Scary clown starts to disappear bit by bit.

'Can't believe I slept in this,' she says regretfully. 'I suspect drink might have been taken… So, what's going on, my lover? I didn't see you sneak away last night. What happened to upset you like this? You're normally an even keel kind of girl.'

'I'm not, actually,' I say, abandoning my colouring and scooping up some cream with my spoon. 'I've just perfected looking like it on the surface. Underneath, I'm a mess.'

'Aren't we all, darling? Some people are just better at hiding it than others. Go on, spill. Tell your Auntie Cherie everything – you're safe here.'

I nod, and against the odds I believe her. She has shown me nothing but kindness, and I suppose I've come to trust her.

'I… Uh, I spent the night with Aidan.'

Her eyes pop open in surprise, and then a huge smile creases her face. 'About bloody time. So why the sadness? Was it that bad?'

I gaze out of the window, looking down at the moody and magnificent sea crashing onto the sand. 'No. It was … wonderful. Amazing. Perfect. Right up until the moment he told me he loves me.'

Cherie sips her hot chocolate and looks at me over the rim of the glass. She has a cream moustache now instead of a killer clown face. She thinks about it for a few seconds, then replies: 'And I'm guessing from your appearance here this morning that that's not a good thing? You don't want him to love you?'

I shake my head. 'No! It's too soon! It's too much! It's… What if it's the beginning of the end?'

'Okay, now you've lost me. Generally speaking, sleeping with a man for the first time and him saying he loves you is the beginning of the beginning.'

'Not in my experience,' I say bitterly. 'In my experience, when they say that, they're lying.'

She knows my history and she doesn't jump in to judge or tell me I'm being unreasonable. I will forever love her for that, but I'm already doing it to myself.

'You've had some shoddy experiences, my love, and no mistake. But tarring Aidan with the same brush isn't really fair now, is it? And do you think that maybe, just maybe, you're reacting like this because you love him too, and that's much scarier than anything else that can happen at Halloween?'

I buy myself some time by shovelling a huge spoonful of

crumble into my mouth. Despite the circumstances, I can still take a moment to appreciate how delicious it is. 'You or Laura?' I mumble.

'That one's all Laura, made with fruit from Frank's farm.' The woman's a genius, I decide. She should get some kind of award, an MBE for Services to Happiness.

I finish up, and Cherie is looking at me in amusement. 'Finished stalling?'

'Yes, I suppose. I can't love Aidan. He's too young for me. He's too good-looking for me. He's too nice for me.'

'I see,' she replies, nodding wisely. 'And he's said all of that, has he?'

'No. He's said pretty much the opposite. But it's still all true.'

'You're gorgeous, Sarah. And despite your best attempts, you're also very nice. I've noticed how sneakily kind you can be, spending time with me, offering to help out with Katie, talking to Edie for hours on end about Briarwood.'

'Those are pleasures, not chores. And I'm still too old for him.'

She snorts, and the remaining cream flies off the top of her drink. 'Bah! What a load of rubbish! You're, what, sixteen years older than him?'

'Yes. That's a whole adult human being older.'

'It's still rubbish. I'd have expected you to be more of a smash the patriarchy kind of woman, Sarah. Would anybody bat an eyelid if it was the other way around? If you were a man seeing a woman sixteen years younger? No, they bloody wouldn't! So stop being so … sexist. Besides, Aidan strikes me as an old soul, and you're behaving like you're immature. So maybe you can meet in the middle.'

I narrow my eyes at her and point the spoon in her direction.

'I didn't come here to be abused, you hag.'

'No, you came here for comfort, which I'm happy to provide. I'm not so good at lying though. Honesty comes with the cake. I'm on your side, darling, always, but that doesn't mean only saying what you want to hear. How did you leave it, with Aidan?'

'Not well. I kind of ran away. And he's called a couple of times since, but I couldn't make myself pick up. Crap. That does sound immature, doesn't it?'

She nods, and turns to her bowl of crumble while I think it all over. Could she be right? Could I be in love with Aidan? How would I know?

'I don't think I've ever been in love,' I tell her, my voice quiet. It's a tragic thing to admit at my age. 'I thought I had. I was married, and there was Martin… But looking back, I don't think I was.'

'I see. And what makes you think that?'

She winks at me. She knows exactly what she's doing, and I hate the path she's leading me down.

'Aidan,' I admit, shaking my head. 'I can't stop thinking about him. When we're together, I feel nervous, but in a good way. And I feel content, but in an excited way. And when we're apart, I … I'm always thinking about when I'll see him again. Even before we spent the night together, I suppose I was already doing that.'

'Does time away from him feel like time wasted?'

I nod, biting my lip. It kind of does, if I'm brutally honest. I do my work and I see my friends; and I've been there for Sally. But underneath all of those layers of busy, all those layers of otherwise occupied, my mind is always on him. Always wishing I could be near him.

'And how does he make you feel? Three words. Don't overthink. Just go for it!'

Ha, don't overthink… She might as well tell me not to breathe. Still, I close my eyes, take a deep breath, and let instinct take over.

'Special. Excited. Safe.'

Wow. I blink my eyes back open, and Cherie is looking unbearably smug as she eats her crumble. I throw a cushion at her, which she easily dodges.

'This is not what I expected when I came here!' I bleat. 'I just wanted some sympathy. And cake!'

'Well, I don't know what you're moaning about, you got both, didn't you? Just a bit of extra insight as well. You're welcome. No need to thank me. Now, what are you going to do about all this?'

I slump back against the squishy leather of the sofa and bury myself deeper in my blanket. Luna sits next to me, and I give her a little stroke.

I'm suddenly exhausted. And confused. And completely uncertain. This is all too complicated, and a cowardly part of me wishes I'd never come here. I should have just stayed in London, where nobody ever talks to you or forces you to face up to home truths. If I hadn't moved here, I wouldn't have met Cherie or Laura or any of the café ladies. I wouldn't have met Aidan, and then my life would have been a lot simpler.

And, I have to admit, a lot less inspiring. I've become braver since I moved to Budbury. I've opened up and blossomed in a way I never expected. And just possibly, I've fallen in love for the first time ever. I don't really regret any of those things, but it is still a lot, and I'm very tired.

'I don't know, Cherie. Honestly, I'm wiped out. Physically and emotionally. You've given me a lot to think about, and right now I'm just too confused and exhausted to do it justice.'

'Then go home and have a sleep. Let your batteries recharge. Then sort it out, love, please. I told you Budbury was the kind of place that specialises in second chances. Don't be that horse.'

'That horse?' I echo. She's lost me now.

'Yes. That really stupid horse. The one that gets taken to water but doesn't drink it. Drink the water. Be in love. Enjoy your life, sweetheart, because believe me it goes by quicker than you'd imagine, and I can guarantee nobody ever regrets letting more love into their world.'

I'm not totally convinced about that, but it was a good speech, and she obviously believes every word of it. She's lost two husbands, and still has that passion for love. There's not an ounce of cynicism in her body, and I wonder if maybe I got her portion somehow.

I nod, standing up to leave. She hugs me and we say our goodbyes. I promise to stay in touch and let her know what, if anything, happens. I make my way back home through the wind and the rain, and do exactly what she suggested – I go to bed.

I don't have the most restful of sleeps, but I do sleep. At least the passing of time seems to suggest that I have, even if I still feel tired. I peep through the curtains and see that it is dark out there now, and my phone informs me that it is just after 6pm. My phone also tells me that Sally has made it home with Ollie, along with a series of winky face and devil horn emojis.

Aidan has called again at about midday, and once more at about three, but after that hasn't bothered. He might have the patience of a saint, but I suppose even he has his limits.

I lie in bed for a while, stretching both my body and my mind. Was Cherie right? Have I been hiding the truth from myself? Am I in love with Aidan? I recall those three words, and say them out loud, over and over again. Special. Excited. Safe. Wonderful, wonderful things to feel. And Aidan makes me feel all of them. So why have I turned my back on them? What the hell is wrong with me? Don't I want to feel special and excited and safe?

I have never really let anybody through my defences like this. I have never given anybody the whole of my heart. I have never let anybody take care of me, or fully committed to caring for them. I have always held back, I see now. My connection with other men was never strong enough to break down the barriers I'd built over too many years of feeling threatened, feeling uncomfortable, feeling like the odd one out.

It is strange to be changing all of that at my age. But I think I have to. Lying here, I realise that I'm missing him already. That like Cherie said, every moment away from him feels wasted. Yes, I've been a solitary person for most of my life, but does that make me happy? Content, yes, but happy? Not really. I'm okay, but I'm not joyful. With Aidan, I'm joyful. It's not just the physical, though goodness knows that was amazing; it's the emotional. When I'm with him, I feel different.

When I'm with him, I feel better. I feel like my whole being is smiling.

That should, of course, be the moment when some kind of mental light bulb pops in my head and I embrace my new future. But I'm simply not built like that, so it takes a little longer. That is all right, I tell myself as I head downstairs and make myself a ginger and lemon tea. This is a big decision, and it is not in my nature to rush.

I lean against the kitchen counter and watch the robin in the courtyard garden. The rain has paused, and he is out there in all his red-breasted glory, head tilted on one side, eyes shining. He's probably wondering what I'm going to do about Aidan. Maybe he's my guardian angel robin, sent to watch over me in times of need. I laugh at the idea, and he immediately flutters away. So much for that.

I finish my tea, put the tea bag in the bin, and then very carefully and very slowly wash my mug. After that, I grab my coat and my car keys, and practically run out of the house. I need to see Aidan. I need to tell him I'm sorry. I need to tell him that I love him, too. I might add in some extras, like 'I've been the world's biggest arsehole', or 'you complete me', or I might just kiss him until he has to forgive me. Whatever I need to do, I am going to do it. After all this messing around, this now very suddenly feels urgent. It's not so much a bulb going off in my head as a whole field of flood lights.

I dash towards the car, and see Becca walking down the street with Sam and Little Edie. They all stare at me as I run, and Becca asks: 'You okay? Need any help?'

'No, thank you though! I'm just off to do something reckless!'

'Oh good,' Becca replies, grinning. 'That's the spirit! Say hello to Aidan for me…'

I laugh and start the engine. I drive carefully to Hazelwell, because I remember how close I came to an accident earlier today. There is very little traffic, but the roads are wet and it's very dark out on the countryside lanes. Streetlights are not a regular occurrence, and the night sky is clouded, hiding the twinkle of the stars and the glow of the moon. Tiny flying creatures are illuminated by my headlights, and I remember the young fox we saw that first night we properly spoke. It feels like a different lifetime. The one before I let Aidan sneak into my world.

I am tense but also exhilarated. My hands grip the steering wheel so hard my knuckles are white, and I have to keep reminding myself to breath. I am determined to say my piece, to let him know that I want to try and make a go of this thing between us. I need to say it, and I can only hope that I'm not too late. A little paranoid part of me wonders if I am. What if I pushed him away one too many times? What if he's decided I'm more trouble than I'm worth? The man told me he loved me and I ran away. Then I refused to answer his calls all day.

No, I reassure myself, that will not happen. Aidan is not an idiot like me. He will listen, and he will understand, and he will forgive. That is the way he has behaved towards me ever since we met. With kindness and integrity and … that smile. Lord, that smile.

It makes me grin to myself even thinking about it, and the last mile or so of the twisty-turny journey seems to last forever. I pull up outside the gates to the house and switch off the car engine. I hear one of the dogs let out a howl, and I know that at least one of them has heard me. Right. Action time.

I have my apology all planned. I have my 'I love you' ready to go. I've looked at this from every possible angle, and this is what I need to do. I want to be happy, and for the first time in my life, I also feel like not only do I have a shot at that, but I deserve it as well.

I get out of the car, still grinning, and walk through the first gate and up to the second. The lights from the house are shining out, and they fall on Aidan's big black jeep, parked where it usually is. I freeze when I notice something else right next to it.

An unbearably cute VW Bug in bright red. I edge slightly closer, gripping the metal bars of the gate, staring through. It's close enough that I can see the stickers in the back window. The pictures of the wolves howling at the moon.

The curtains to the living room window are open, and I see Aidan in there. Then I see Melody, walking towards him and wrapping her arms around his waist. He returns the embrace, holding her tight. They stand like that, engulfed in each other, for what feels like eternity. The room looks cosy, and I imagine the romantic music, the roaring fire. The bed he is clearly about to take her to.

That's when I blink and retreat away from the gate so quickly I almost fall over. I've seen enough and have no desire to watch what happens next between them. I can far too easily imagine.

I stagger back to my car, desperate to get away. To get away from this place, from the fact that Melody is here. His friend, who also comes with benefits. I remember him telling me about their arrangement, how they were there for each other when it suited them both. And now there they are, clear as night, enjoying their benefits already.

I was wrong, I tell myself bitterly. Wrong about it all. He has run out of patience. I have pushed him away one time too many.

I have lost him.

The sad thing is, I think, as I drive away again, that I can't even blame him.

Chapter Twenty-Three

After that, I do the only sensible thing. I go home, alone, and drink a bottle of wine. I allow myself one night to throw a pity party. I listen to songs like 'Winner Takes It All' and 'Nothing Compares 2 U', and my personal favourite, 'I Just Don't Know What To Do With Myself'. Both the White Stripes version and the Dusty Springfield classic. It kind of sums up exactly how I feel, perfectly capturing the sense of emptiness that has descended on me.

I thought I'd known heartbreak before. I thought I had known betrayal before. But it turns out I was wrong, because Nothing Compares 2 This. I feel absolutely dreadful, physically and emotionally sick, in a way I've never experienced.

I torture myself with images of Aidan and Melody, of their love-making, their walks with the dogs, the simplicity and warmth of their relationship. The flip side of having the kind of imagination that allows me to write books for a living is this: it's almost impossible to control. The fantasies take on lives of their own, and before long I have them married with kids. A boy and a girl, obviously.

I feel such a mix of things – humiliated, stupid, regretful, and above all, sad. Just very, very sad. For that very brief time, I genuinely hoped. It was like being shown a rainbow, then going back to life in shades of beige.

Knowing that at least some of it is my own fault doesn't help. It would be easier if I could write Aidan off as a bastard, but I can't even do that. He tried so very hard with me, and each time I slapped him down. I rejected him because of my own insecurities, my own fears. My inability to communicate. My basic crapness. I had my chance, and I blew it.

I'm surprised at how quickly he's moved on, but I imagine how hurt he must have been. After spending the last month courting me like a gentleman, wooing me, supporting me in every possible way, I finally show him some encouragement. And then, the morning after, when he tells me that he loves me, I become monosyllabic, then angry, and then I run away. Add to that the fact that for the rest of the day, I also ignore his phone calls. If a man did that to a woman, we'd call him all kinds of rude names. It would be a shooting offence.

After all of that, after me rejecting him, he has taken solace in the arms of his friend with benefits. The one who has always been there for him. And why shouldn't he? I haven't been much of a friend to him at all.

Cherie messages me asking how I am, and I simply tell her I'm tired and staying at home tonight. That is completely true, even if it's only a small part of the story.

I don't want to talk to her about what has happened right now, possibly ever. This is a small place, and I don't want to have to leave it. I don't want things between Aidan and me to become so awkward that it is impossible for us both to live in Budbury.

That might be a forlorn hope, I know. How am I going to react the next time I see him? How will I possibly manage to behave like a normal human around him? I can't imagine being at the café and seeing him run along the beach. I can't imagine bumping into him in the pub, or hearing about him from the others. What if Melody becomes more of a fixture and she starts hanging around as well? I think then, maybe, I would have to leave. I'm not sure my poor fragile heart could take it.

Before I go to bed – or more precisely, before I pass out on the sofa – I listen to a few more empowering tracks in an attempt to plant some positivity in my brain before I sleep. 'I Will Survive', obviously, 'Roar' by Katy Perry, and the modern classic that is Miley Cyrus's 'Flowers'.

It doesn't seem to do much good. When I manage to prise my eyes open, freezing cold because I've kicked off my blanket during a restless night, I feel far from empowered. I'm okay for approximately thirty seconds, before I remember. Then I feel like a pile of bricks has landed on my head, crushing me into dust. It's awful and I don't know how to deal with it.

I suppose ordinary women have their hearts broken when they're much younger. Sally started when she was about fifteen. I've always been a little too careful with my heart, I guess, and now I'm paying the price. I'm like someone who has never been exposed to a germ suddenly being doused in a vat of viruses; I have no immunity at all. This might actually kill me.

I roll off the couch and onto the floor, and begin the gradual process of putting myself back together again. Or at least trying to. I take a couple of ibuprofen with a black coffee, and let that sink in before I crawl up the stairs and have a shower. I try to do normal things, like check my emails and look at work, but I'm not really in the right head space.

My office is still set up as Sally's bedroom, so I decide that dismantling that will be a mindless enough task to keep me occupied for a while. I put the sheets in to wash, fold up the sofa, and clear the detritus she has left behind. For a woman who I know keeps a very tidy house herself, Sally is a very messy guest – I think she reverted to being a teenager while she was here. It's the only explanation for the half-drunk glasses of juice, the empty crisp packets and the dirty plates that have accumulated.

I gather up the clothes that were on the floor, and decide that I will wash those too. Then I will pack them all up in her overnight bag and drive to London to hand deliver them. And maybe I'll never come back here again...

No, I tell myself firmly, I will not do that. At least not on the very first day of dealing with this new situation. Aidan is very much linked to my Budbury experience, because I met him pretty much as soon as I moved here. When I think of this place, I think of him. Is that something I can overcome, I wonder? Can I build new routines, new habits, new neural pathways, ones where he doesn't appear everywhere?

I move my laptop and work notebooks back into my office, and assure myself that I can. That I will be all right, eventually.

The problem is, I'm a rotten liar. Especially, it seems, when I'm lying to myself. I sit in front of my desk, the place where I usually find solace, and I feel the tears rolling down my cheeks. I swipe them away, annoyed at my own weakness. I need to get a grip.

I idly google 'How to recover from a broken heart', and almost laugh at my own silliness. It won't help to join an online forum where I talk to strangers about how my man did me wrong. He was never really my man, and he didn't do anything that wrong. The best bit of advice I find is to keep busy, and try and look after myself physically as well as mentally. And, of course, to reach out for help if I feel like I'm becoming overwhelmed.

I already feel overwhelmed. This is all so new to me that I'm confused by my lack of mental focus. Will's cheating hurt me deeply, but in some ways the divorce was actually a relief – I could start to heal, start to rebuild, and go back to the solitary life that I'd always preferred. The situation with Martin was obviously very different and deeply damaging to my mental health. I was already a jumpy person, and he took that and turned me into someone who never had a minute's peace. But if I set aside the lying and the stalking, how hurt was I, really?

I'd thought I wanted more with him at the time. I'd thought maybe it could work between us – barring the fact that I didn't know his real name of course. But when it ended, was I heartbroken? I was nervous, I was anxious, and I was disappointed. I was saddened that he'd behaved like that and I was humiliated that I'd fallen for it, but heartbroken? No.

This feels completely different from what I've encountered before, and I'm flailing around in misery. How do people deal with this level of pain? How do they come out the other side? I genuinely feel like I'm in agony.

I have no idea what to do with myself, and I hate that. I can usually think my way out of things, or at least attempt to. This, though, has nothing to do with logical thought processes. This is raw and painful and huge.

I glance at my phone, and see that it isn't even eleven. I have a whole huge day yawning ahead of me. I also, I notice, have another message from my sister.

> Hope all is good, sis! Thanks for putting up with me. Forgot to send you this link from the twins' party.

I click through, for want of anything else to fill my time, and find that it takes me to a website that has tiny thumbnail shots of all the photos taken on the night. There had been a photographer buzzing around taking group shots and family portraits, as well as a booth full of ridiculous blow-up props and silly hats.

I flick through and am ashamed to say that my eyes barely register the ones of my nieces and my family. They scoot straight to the pictures that feature me and Aidan. Us at the bar, raising glasses of champagne. Us on the dancefloor. Us wearing big plastic sunglasses and playing inflatable saxophones. Us having fun.

Damn. I'm crying again. I reach out and touch the screen, wishing it was him. I look into his bright green eyes. 'I love you,' I say, aware that I'm acting crazy but apparently unable to stop. 'I love you, but by the time I figured that out, it was too late. How is that fair? Shouldn't I have had some kind of deadline? Was I that easy to replace?'

An image of Melody comes to mind. Young, pretty, uncomplicated. Yes, it seems, I was that easy to replace.

Chapter Twenty-Four

The next three days are both incredibly productive and incredibly lonely. I throw myself into my work once I feel capable, and absolutely smash my all-time record for words per day. My agent and my editor are going to be amazed at how quickly I deliver this next book, assuming that all of the 30,000 words I've written aren't complete gobbledigook. It's entirely possible that I just wrote 'Aidan' 30,000 times, because he is still very much on my mind.

I keep replaying that moment when I got out of the car at Hazelwell and saw them in each other's arms through the window. I'm mad at myself, but I'm also now a little mad at him. How strong could this relationship ever have been if he could go from my arms to another woman's in the space of a day? No matter how much of a bitch I'd been, that seems too rapid to be respectful. Maybe I didn't actually mean anything to him at all. Maybe once he'd slept with me, the fun of the chase fizzled out. Maybe he actually only said all that love stuff because he knew it would freak me out, knew that it would scare me off. Maybe it was all part of the plan.

Do I really think that? I ask myself, as I finish off my work for the day. Do I really think he could be that conniving, that cruel? I'd like to hope not, but as I've proved time and time again, I have terrible judgement when it comes to men. Moving forward, my plan is A) not to have anything to do with men, or failing that, B) let somebody more intelligent, like the Scarecrow in *The Wizard of Oz*, make all my decisions for me.

I sigh and close down my laptop. The urge to Google him has become almost irresistible recently. I have no idea why, and I'm fighting it. The best thing for me to do is keep busy, just like the internet told me to.

Work has been one way to occupy my mind. I've also started to decorate my bedroom. Despite my mood being black, I've gone for a very pale green, and I plan to add lavender gloss on the woodwork. For the last two nights, I've been up until the early hours either writing or painting. I'm very, very tired, but only by being physically exhausted do I stand a chance at getting any sleep. If I don't wear myself out to the point of collapse, I just lie awake, torturing myself about everything. My mind is like a whirling dervish, torturing me with images of Aidan, with ghosts of what might have been.

I know Cherie has been worried about me, and yesterday she called in to drop off supplies. All the café essentials – cake, sandwiches, freshly squeezed juice, and of course hugs. I didn't tell her the dirty and humiliating truth of what happened, just that things haven't worked out.

I could tell she wanted more, not out of nosiness – or at least not just nosiness – but out of concern. I suspect she thinks I might creep back into my shell again, and she might be right. I hope not, but I have my doubts about my faith in humanity these days.

I've just put on my painting clothes – old jogging bottoms and a baggy sweatshirt – when I hear a knock at the front door. I give some serious thought to ignoring it, but all my lights are on and my car is outside. It's like I have a giant sign on the front door saying: 'Sarah's home!'

I head down the stairs, attempting to tame the tangled mess that's my hair by running my hands through it. As I do, my fingers get stuck in a tangle. My personal grooming has taken a swan dive over the last few days. I had a shower this morning, but then obviously forgot to connect brush to hair at any stage.

I suck in a deep breath before I open the door, ready to at least fake being okay. All that changes when I see who it is. Damn, I really should have invested in that peephole. I've felt much more secure since I confronted Scott Jones. But there are other kinds of threat – like finding a certain friend-with-benefits standing on your step.

Melody smiles at me, her eyes flickering over my appearance and faltering slightly. What the hell is she doing here? I know I have absolutely no right to feel any resentment towards this woman – this girl, actually, because she is still in her twenties and definitely young enough to be my daughter – and yet I kind of do. I kind of want to punch her on the nose, in fact. I won't, because I'm a civilised human, but I really want to.

Once that initial rush of anger passes, I'm still left with questions. And sadness. A huge, great big smothering blanket of sadness. I'm such an idiot.

'Hi Melody,' I say, crossing my arms in front of me. This is my territory and I don't like her being in it. 'What do you want?'

She looks slightly taken aback by my less-than-welcoming attitude but recovers quickly. Melody, I remind myself, once backpacked around India on her own. She's not going to be intimidated by a paint-spattered middle-aged woman who looks like she's been dragged through a bush backwards, forwards and sideways.

'Hi Sarah, I was wondering if you could help me? Help Aidan? He was supposed to be back by now, but his flight's been delayed, and I really have to get on the road. I don't want to leave the dogs alone, and I know they'll be fine with you…'

'His flight?' I repeat dumbly, having no clue what she's going on about.

'Yes. You know, from New York?'

I stare at her, feeling deeply confused. 'You'd better come in.'

She follows me through, taking in the pretty living room and its organised clutter, heading over to the shelf that contains copies of all my books. She runs her fingers over them, and smiles as she says: 'I didn't want to come across as a fan girl that night in the pub, but I love your books! Carina Shaw kicks ass!'

'Um … thank you. She does, doesn't she? Could I get you a drink, or cake? I have a lot of cake…'

'No, I'm fine, thanks. Anyway. I think he's on the plane now, or somewhere he can't see his messages at least. I have no clue when he'll be back, but like I said, I need to be going. I should have left hours ago. Would you be able to pop over? I've got the keys with me?'

I sit down on the sofa with a bit of a thud, and look up at her. I have nothing to gain by pretending to be anything other than what I am. Bewildered.

'Melody, I'm really sorry, but I don't know what's going on. I thought you were here staying with Aidan for … uh … well, you know…'

She frowns and sits in the chair opposite me, her eyes huge in surprise. 'Gosh, no! Absolutely not! Not since he met you, Sarah, you're all he's been focused on. I'm here for the dogs. To look after them while he was in New York with his dad.'

'With his dad?' I echo, shaking my head. Melody bites her lip and looks at me thoughtfully.

'Okay, I don't know what's going on here, Sarah. I thought you two were together. Or at the very least close. I didn't get much of a chance to talk to him before he left. What's the score?'

'We were close. And we were together. And then we had a big fight, and I left, and then you turned up with your benefits…'

She throws her hands up in the air and laughs. 'Now I'm even more lost! I turned up because he asked me to. His dad had a heart attack and he had to fly to New York to see him. The only benefit I brought was looking after the dogs. He's not the kind of man who enjoys benefits with another

311

woman when he's into someone, and I'm not the kind of woman who sleeps with a man who is taken.'

I nod, struggling to process all of this, feeling slightly reprimanded. I remember his phone ringing several times that morning while we were fighting. And I know he tried to call me, also several times. Okay, the only message he left was one tense-sounding 'please call me back', which didn't tempt me, but now I know he was probably upset. He has a difficult relationship with his dad, but he is still his dad. And I hadn't exactly been open and loving towards him.

I feel a rush of regret, and a dreadful sinking feeling in my stomach. I wasn't there for him when he needed me, and I jumped to all the wrong conclusions because of my own stupid insecurities. I didn't give him the benefit of the doubt, not even a tiny bit – he paid the price because the other men in my life acted like jerks. Basically, I've been a terrible fool.

'How is his father?' I ask quietly.

'He's all right. It was only mild, more of a warning shot apparently, but his dad was desperate to see him. I think it was a bit of a wake-up call, and hopefully they might have sorted out some of their issues. Like I say, he's on his way back. I assumed he'd been in touch, that you knew…'

I didn't know. I didn't call him back. I didn't tell him that I love him, when perhaps he most needed to hear it. I saw this perfectly nice woman giving him a consoling hug, and I leapt into the abyss of doubt. It's understandable that I was upset, but unforgivable that I never questioned what my anxious, battered brain told me.

If I'd called him back, then maybe he would have asked

me to look after the dogs and Melody wouldn't even have been here. I've made such a mess of things.

I shake my head and feel tears swim in my eyes. Melody is instantly by my side, holding my hand. I now feel even worse for all the mean things I've thought about her over the last few days.

'Come on, it's okay. It'll be all right! He's really, really into you!'

That sounds so like something one of my nieces would say that it makes me smile. 'Maybe he *was*…'

'He still is. Have a little faith. One row won't change all that. It was hectic, getting that call about his father, booking a flight, having to get to London. Then dealing with his family and that whole drama. I have no idea how that all went, but it can't have been easy. But he's on his way back, and you can see him soon and sort this all out.'

She wipes the tears from my cheeks with gentle thumbs, and I tremble a little with emotion. 'You're so nice, Melody.'

'Why thank you, Sarah. Are you okay? Can I get you anything? Call a friend for you?'

I realise as she asks that yes, for possibly the first time in my life there are friends she could call for me. That I do not need to be alone with pain – hoard it, like Sally said. Cherie would come, or Laura, or Max, or any of the other lovely ladies.

That is a wonderful and comforting thought, but I only really want to see one person. I only need to see one person. And he's possibly somewhere over the Atlantic.

'I'm all right, or at least I will be. I'm sorry. This all just caught me a bit unawares. And yes, I can go around there. I can look after the dogs.'

She's been nothing but considerate, but I see a flash of relief on her pretty face. 'That's great. I was so worried about leaving them. They've had their dinner, so don't let Juno trick you into giving them more, okay?'

I laugh – Juno does do that – and walk with Melody to the front door. She pauses on the threshold and gives me a hug. I'm now, it seems, a person who happily hugs.

'It'll all be okay,' she says confidently before she gets into her now more bearably cute VW Bug.

Chapter Twenty-Five

I check every live travel information source that I can find, looking for incoming flights from New York to London. There are more than you'd think. Several are delayed by storms on the other side of the Atlantic, and I can't quite figure out if he's boarded, landed, or given up on the whole idea. I wonder if I should message him, but eventually decide that this is a conversation that needs to be had face to face. It's hard to grovel via WhatsApp.

Armed with the keys, I set off to Hazelwell. I don't want to waste any more time, and the longer I spend at home, the more chance there is that I could change my mind and chicken out completely. I now know I was wrong to feel rejected and betrayed, but that doesn't mean it wipes out the feeling entirely. I can still feel the aftershocks of that pain, reminding me of how much is at stake here.

I want to see Aidan and try to figure things out, because the time I've spent with him has been the most euphoric and wonderful time of my life. But the flip side of that is the pain. The agony of thinking I'd lost him cut me deep, and I'm terrified of feeling that again. I'm taking a risk here, exposing myself to that roller coaster all over again. At the moment I'm running on adrenalin and hope, but if I allow myself to sit down, to think, to worry about consequences, then I might well never leave the house again. That struggle has always been real for me.

Even as I stand on the doorstep, looking at my car, I have my doubts. What if he hates me? What if he kicks me out? What if he does neither of those things, and we get together, but three years down the line when I'm all in he decides to trade me in for a younger model? What if, what if, what if… I might have built a career on what ifs, but it can also derail me in situations where I need to be brave. And right now, I need to be brave.

I make the now very familiar night-time drive to Hazelwell. I park up, feeling a slight shiver of anxiety at the thought of being here alone for the first time. It is so secluded, so very dark, the wind whispering through the trees like a hungry ghost.

I go through the first gate and unlock the second. I'm not one hundred per cent sure how the pack is going to react. They are used to me, but they will be missing Aidan. I'm not at all scared – I know they wouldn't hurt me – but I'm also not sure they will welcome me either. Apart from Juno, of course.

I hear barking from inside the house as I let myself in. There is a large hatch in the back door so they can come and go as they like, so I don't know which of them are at home. Juno comes skittering along the hallway, crashing into me and jumping up to lick my face. She's a big animal, and I gently push her away, then crouch down to stroke her and rub her ears.

'Beautiful girl,' I murmur, as she lets out plaintive little bleats. 'At least you're glad to see me, huh?'

Argent follows, loping low and tentatively towards me. I fuss over him, and see the other two peeking through from the kitchen. They don't back away as I walk in their direction, and I'm so pleased that I head straight for the treat jar.

'I know you've had your dinner,' I tell them, as they all lurk around my feet, looking up at me with their amazing eyes, all shining colour and intelligence. 'So don't even think about howling for more… You can have one of these each, and then later maybe there'll be something juicy and meaty in the fridge…'

They all accept a treat, and follow me around as I walk through the house. I look at Aidan's framed family photos, his battered guitar, his piled-high bookshelves. His little office, set up with his computer and a landline. I sniff the fleece jacket he's left hanging up on the back of the door, hungrily inhaling the scent of his cologne. God, I miss him.

I make myself a mug of tea and drink it outside, watching the dogs chase each other and play. I stay near to the house, though, because I'm really not brave enough to go into the woods by myself. The dogs don't seem to want to either, and I enjoy seeing their antics. They all look so goofy and young when they're messing around like this. I can't believe I ever found them threatening at all.

I go back inside, and Juno comes with me. I leave the

rest out there; I know they are used to coming and going at will.

I glance at my phone and see that it is getting late. I yawn and rub my eyes, suddenly overwhelmed by fatigue. I have not slept well for way too long, and it is catching up with me. I think maybe it's also because I am here, in this place, where I feel safe and warm and protected. Maybe now I am here, and now I know the truth, my brain is finally telling me to relax.

I try to check on flight information again, but the signal is dropping in and out, as it usually does. I don't suppose there's anything to be gained by it anyway, other than being prepared.

Eventually I simply sit down on the sofa and try to read a book, or at least turn a few pages. Juno jumps up next to me, snuggling in, and I try to stay calm. It'll do no good if I'm like a coiled spring when he finally walks through the door. The last thing I remember is the words starting to blur, and me putting the book down on my lap 'to read later'. After that, I'm sucked into a delicious black hole of a deep and for once dreamless sleep.

It's probably the sound that wakes me. The sound would probably wake me even if I was dead. All four dogs are whining and woofing and being very vocal in their delight, because their human is home.

I'm splayed on the couch, the book on the floor, my brain still groggy. He is standing above me, his hands on the dogs but his eyes on me. I'm suddenly aware of my paint-spattered clothes, my unbrushed hair, the fact that I probably look like I've escaped from an institution. Again, I realise belatedly that I don't seem to think like normal women. Shouldn't I be in a slinky negligee and drenched in perfume?

'How's your dad?' is the first thing I ask, clambering to my unsteady feet. He looks tired too, but also phenomenally gorgeous in smart jeans and a crisp white shirt. His green gaze is inscrutable, and I can't tell at all from his expression what he's thinking.

'He's okay, thanks. We… Well, it was good to clear the air. As much as we could. I tried calling you to tell you, but you didn't answer. Eventually I suppose I got the message and gave up.'

I rub my hair back from my face and bite my lip. I deserved that.

'I know. And I'm really sorry.'

God, I sound so lame. Before he was standing here in front of me, I had all kinds of speeches prepared. I had the perfect words to tell him what I want to tell him. But now he is here, in all his glory, and I am so uncertain. I have gone with the flow, and now I am drowning.

'About my dad?'

'About everything. About the way I left things. About being me.'

He frowns slightly and shakes his head. 'Don't do that. Don't make this a thing about how you're just broken. I hate it when you do that.'

'I know,' I say, gulping. 'And I won't. But I'm trying to explain and I'm not doing very well. So, imagine that I'm a lot younger.'

He raises his eyebrows. 'Sarah, I'm too tired to have yet another conversation about your age.'

'No, no, honest, that's not what this is! Imagine I'm so much younger that I've never been in love. Imagine I've never understood what it feels like to need somebody. Imagine everything that's happened to me since I met you has been new, happening for the first time…'

'You're not a virgin, Sarah.'

'No, but emotionally, I kind of am. Or at the very least I'm … I don't know, immature. This is nothing to do with our ages. Because, frankly, you're the grown up here. You're the one who is wise enough to know what he wants and to ask for it. You're the one brave enough to talk about love, despite everything that you've gone through. I'm … a baby. A big, fat, crying baby.'

His lips start to twitch, and I see a flash of amusement in his eyes.

'You're not fat,' he says. 'But maybe you were a bit of a baby.'

The dogs are still winding around his legs, tails whacking, shoving their heads beneath his hands. I push my way gently through them so I'm standing right in front of Aidan. I place one hand on his chest, over his heart. I feel it thud beneath my palm, and look up into his eyes.

'I got scared, Aidan,' I say simply. 'I was scared and confused, and I ran. I regretted it so much. I did come back to tell you that, but Melody was here…'

I see him put it all together, and he nods in understanding. 'And you assumed she was … consoling me?'

'I did. And I know I was wrong, and I also know that if I'd bothered calling you back in the day, none of it would have happened. So, I've suffered like I've never suffered before, but I have nobody to blame but myself.'

'You suffered, huh? How?'

He lays his hand over mine, and that small amount of contact makes my heart leap. It gives me the encouragement to go on.

'I suffered because I was miserable without you. Because I thought I'd lost you, and that broke me. Because I don't want to go back to a life without you in it. Because I love you too, Aidan. With every part of me, I love you. And if you can forgive me, if you can bear to give me another chance, then I promise to show that to you every single day. I won't be perfect, but I will do my very best.'

He slides a hand around my waist and pulls me towards him. I land against his body and dare to hope.

'I knew you were here,' he says, his eyes running over my face. 'Melody messaged me, plus your car was outside. I knew but I didn't know what to expect. I walked in, and you were surrounded by the pack. They were all asleep with you. Juno on one side, Argent on the other. Frost and Mabel at your feet. You were just lying there, in my home, curled up in the middle of my dogs. It made me realise that they're actually *our* dogs now. It was… It was the most beautiful thing I've ever seen.'

'Really? I wasn't drooling or anything?'

'Maybe a little,' he says, moving closer and nuzzling my neck. 'But I don't care. It was perfect. Seeing you, seeing them, it was perfect. It was exactly what I needed to see.

And of course I'll give you another chance. Of course I'll forgive you. That's what we do for people we love.'

I sink into him, the joy and the relief flowing through me in an almost physical sensation. He loves me. He still loves me. I lift my lips to his and kiss him. His arms tighten around me, and we lose ourselves in the moment.

The dogs howl around us and our world is finally whole. Three words come to mind: Special. Excited. Safe.

Acknowledgments

Thank you for joining me on a trip to Budbury – I hope you enjoyed it! I loved writing about Sarah and Aidan, as well as catching up with old friends at the Comfort Food Café.

As ever, it wasn't a solo mission – I had a lot of help along the way. Thanks must go to my wonderful editor Charlotte Ledger, and the whole fab team at One More Chapter. They not only make my books better, but make sure they land in the hands of as many readers as possible. Thanks also to my excellent agent Hayley Steed at Janklow & Nesbit, as well as Mina Yakinya.

My friends are always there for me when it counts, and I couldn't do life without them. In particular, my author pals make me feel a lot less alone as I navigate my way through the maze of writing yet another book.

My family make me smile and laugh and count my blessings every single day. I am a lucky woman in so many ways.

Mainly, thanks to you, my wonderful readers, for coming on another adventure with me! Hopefully I'll see you next time...

Read on for an extract from *The Comfort Food Café*!

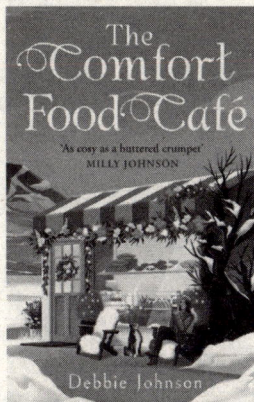

Welcome to The Comfort Food Café!

It's been a tough year for Maxine Connolly – so tough she's almost given up on finding her happy ending. But then she discovers The Comfort Food Café, shining like the star on top of the Christmas tree and welcoming her in to its cozy, cake-filled embrace for hot chocolates dripping with whipped cream, melty grilled cheese toasties and the funniest bunch of regulars she soon calls friends.

Then there's gorgeous local Gabriel Moran, who looks at Max like she's a present he can't wait to unwrap. She can't help but think that, maybe, he's just what she wants for Christmas too…

Available in paperback, eBook, and audio!

The Comfort Food Café

AN EXTRACT

Chapter One

Dear Laura,

First of all, I have to be honest: I'm writing this on behalf of
my mum, Maxine (though everyone calls her Max). She has
no clue I'm sending this email, and she'd probably kill me if
she did, but I'm willing to risk death to do this, because
something about your job advert made me think it was
perfect for her. You know when something just makes you
tingle because it's so right, like all your spider senses have
been set off, but in a good way?

I was considering coming up with a dramatic back story
to catch your eye—like our father is a gambling addict and
lost our family home in a high-stakes poker game at a
casino in Montenegro, or Mum has just come out of a
decade-long coma after a freak unicycle accident.
Something with oomph that would make her stand out
from the crowd.

In the end I decided that would be a fib too far. I'm already being shady, sneaking around behind her back, without lying about her as though she's not interesting enough in real life. I think that's already one of her problems: she doesn't think she's interesting anymore, and it won't help if her own daughter fictionalises her as well. She's had a few years of Totally Crap Things happen, and now she seems to have deflated. She's a bit like one of those squashed helium balloons that got stuck on a bush, and it makes me really sad for her.

The other day, we were watching *Dracula*—you know that old version with Keanu Reeves and Gary Oldman in it? Though she told me off for calling it the 'old version', because apparently 1992 was only five years ago in her head… Anyway, I'm sure you know the one. She said, after it finished, that if she was in a story like that, she wouldn't be Dracula, or Van Helsing, or Mina, or one of the glamorous vampire chicks. She wouldn't even be Renfield, she said—she'd maybe be in with a chance at being the servant who empties Renfield's slop bucket at the asylum. That's how much she sees herself as a background character, and I absolutely hate it. Everyone should be the star of their own story, shouldn't they—or at least the co-star?

That all sounds a bit depressing, I know, but I wanted to explain why I'm doing this. My mum needs a change, badly. She needs to get away from her life and make a fresh start, somewhere new, where she can stop seeing herself as dull and unimportant. She needs to feel useful, not like Renfield's slop bucket slave. At the moment she's forgotten all the good things about herself, like how kind she is, how funny she is, how she's the type of person who keeps a pocketful of pound coins every time she goes into town to give to homeless people. How she always stops and chats to them when everyone else tries to walk as far away as they can.

How she's always the one who gives up her seat on the bus, or helps a mum carry a buggy up the stairs, or offers to pay for someone's shopping if they've forgotten their purse. This stuff used to make me roll my eyes and feel embarrassed when I was younger, but now I see these little things for what they are: the signs that my mum, my lovely mum, is a really decent person who deserves better than what life has given her recently.

I'm nearly nineteen now, and all my friends still think she's the best and wish she'd adopt them. Everyone always hung out at our house—she was the mum who'd always give us lifts, or provide pizza, and bring the mattresses downstairs so we could have a movie night sleepover in the living room. The 'treat box' was never empty, and she always had a smile on her face. She rarely lost her rag, even when someone had puked Malibu and Coke on the dog (true story). She'd just pull a face and say 'well, we've all been there...'

Stuff like this should be more important, shouldn't it? It should get more respect in the world. I mean, she's never been famous or had a high-flying career, but she's so kind and brilliant and nice, and I think that makes her extraordinary.

If you're wondering why she's going through such a low

spell in her life, it's not one big dramatic thing. It's like a cavalcade of crap, a snowball of shit that's built up and up until it's basically squashed her (excuse my language but they're the mildest words I can use). I'll tell you about it, but this isn't in order—it all kind of smushed together anyway.

Her mum, my nana, died about a year and a half ago. It wasn't a tragedy—she was in her late seventies—but Mum had looked after her for years after her dad passed away. So she didn't just lose her mum, which would have been bad enough—I think she lost a bit of her purpose as well. She'd been caring for her for so long and suddenly she was gone, and that left a big nana-shaped hole in her heart and her life.

Then a while ago, she got made redundant from her job in a supermarket. I know it doesn't sound exciting, and honestly, when I was younger, I was a bit embarrassed when she used to turn up at school in her uniform (yes, I seemed to spend a lot of time being embarrassed; I think this is a normal girl thing). I suppose I wanted my mum to be more exotic, like a movie star or a footballer's wife or even just someone who worked in an office and wore high heels.

Thing is, she loved her job—loved all her regulars, and chatting to everyone who popped in, and telling me tales about the 90-year-old man who bought flowers for his wife every Friday, and the woman who was addicted to wine gums but hated the green ones. She used to say all of human life was there, and most of it fancied a four-pack of Carlsberg and a giant bag of Wotsits. She really enjoyed it, especially the old people who used to come in for 'their bits'; she said she could tell sometimes she was the only person they spoke to all day.

Then that thing happened where the supermarket brought in self-service tills instead, and swapped the humans for machines. I mean, I suppose we're all used to that now, but I never use them on principle, because I've seen the other side. Not just my mum losing her job, but my mum getting upset at the thought of all those old people struggling to scan their ready meals for one and trying to chat to a screen. I'd never even thought about the human side of it all before, just thought they were convenient, and if I'm honest, I was glad I didn't have to stand in a queue behind those old dears and their endless chat to the people on the tills. I'm a bit ashamed of that now.

So, she lost her mum and lost her job, and also my older brother Ben went off to uni in Manchester. This was a bonus for me, because he's an absolute arse and we get on about as well as Will Smith and Chris Rock at the Oscars. For some weird reason, though, she actually likes having him around, and when he left she was really sad. I caught her once sitting on his bed and crying, clutching a pile of dirty socks and soggy towels he'd left on the floor. I don't understand why she misses him—I mean, it's not like it was me who left, the far superior child!—but she does. Must be a mum thing.

This was all bad enough, but even worse was my dad— or as he's also known, The Biggest Twat in the Universe— walking out on her. People, even Mum, keep telling me this is a 'complicated' subject. That marriages are complicated, life is complicated, relationships are complicated. They say this like it excuses literally any kind of behaviour. I know I'm only eighteen and three-quarters, and therefore have less life experience than a garlic naan, but I still think that's bullshit. Like, can you imagine this excuse being used anywhere else? 'Yes, m'lord, my client was indeed found covered in blood, carrying the murder weapon, and wearing a T-shirt that said "Guilty as Charged!" on the front, but in his defence, it was *complicated*.'

In this case, it wasn't that complicated. My dad left my mum—left us all, let's be blunt—and moved in with a woman he'd been seeing behind her back for almost two years. So basically, while she was still looking after, and then grieving for, Nana, and saying goodbye to Ben, and getting shafted by self-service machines, he was sneaking around like love's middle-aged dream with a woman who runs a cocktail bar in town. That was about ten months ago now, and she's still reeling.

He's tried to dodge all of the responsibility for this, to the point where he seems to be blaming everything, from my mum to Guinness to global warming, for the choices he's made. Anything other than admit he's in the wrong. He's taken the things that make my mum special, and used them against her: she was too wrapped up in worrying about the kids, too concerned with other people, too busy caring for Nana. Too preoccupied to pay him enough attention.

Basically he's a giant baby, and doesn't even see how self-obsessed he is. At one point he even muttered the immortal words 'Well, you can't deny you've let yourself go a bit, can you?' Unfortunately for him, I was outside the room and overheard this gem, then walked in and slapped him across the face. He was horrified; Mum was horrified; I suppose even I was. But using the Rule of Grown-Up Life, I can just say 'Well, it's complicated', and get away with it, can't I?

I mean, it *is* complicated. I miss my dad but I also despise him. I love him but I also have no respect for him. Because of him leaving, we had to sell the house I grew up in, and now live in a much smaller place. Our whole lives have been tipped upside down, especially Mum's. She's made the best of it, but the best isn't exactly awesome.

So now he's run off, and Ben's away, and I'm at home seeing her very quietly and very slowly fall apart. She's even doing that in a kind way, as though she doesn't want to inconvenience anyone, and she probably thinks she's fooled me. Anyone who didn't know her as well as I do would think she was fine.

She's one of those people who always says good morning to random strangers, and knows everyone's life story on the dog-walking route, and always has a smile ready. On the surface, she's Little Miss Sunshine—but I know better. I hear her crying in her bedroom late at night, and see her looking at her own body as though she can't believe it's hers. She stays cheerful until she thinks I've left the house, and then sinks into blank-faced misery. I know this because I forgot my headphones once, and came back in without her knowing. It was horrible and I snuck straight back out because I knew she'd be upset if she knew I'd seen her.

She's doing her best to put on a good front, but her confidence has gone. It's one of the reasons she hasn't applied for a new job yet, and is living off her redundancy. It's like she can't see her own value anymore. She's still a great mum. She forgets her own issues as soon as I have one, and sometimes I even make them up to give her something to fix. But I can tell she's completely grey inside, when she used to be rainbow, if that makes sense. It's like she's become the Invisible Woman, and I want her to be seen again. I want her to see herself again.

I know I've gone on a bit—you did say 'heart and soul' to be fair—and some of this has been a bit heavy, and probably all of it is inappropriate. So I also wanted to tell you some of the positives, which might even be relevant. Well, the empathy bit and the good listener bit are definitely covered—those are her defining characteristics. Dad used to wind her up and call her the 'empathy sponge', because she got so involved in the way other people might feel—except he saw it as a bad thing, obviously, because he was like an empathy void instead.

She's a good cook; she's raised a family, and we always ate well. She can bake, and do a mean Sunday roast, and seems to enjoy feeding people. I love cooking too, and sometimes there's a scuffle in the kitchen about who gets to make dinner—so you might even get a BOGOF deal.

My mum is really hard-working, and one of those irritating people who lives that whole 'if a job's worth doing it's worth doing right' ethos. And she's really good at making a home. I don't know how to describe this—she just has a knack for it. She's always up a ladder doing the decorating, and she loved giving our rooms a new look, and her idea of heaven would be taking a blank canvas house and making it into a home.

When we moved into the new house, it was pretty grim. It belonged to an older man and it hadn't been painted since about 1902. Everything was really ugly and grimy and it felt like the place where hope comes to die. She got to work straight away and transformed it—and within a month it didn't feel like that. It didn't feel like somewhere crap we'd been forced into because of Dad's roving penis. It felt like our home, where we'd always lived, clean and fresh and comfy. Not sure that's any use in a café, but it's a really nice thing about her, and something she genuinely loses herself in.

Anyway. That's that, I suppose. Except, full disclosure, it's probably not just her who needs a fresh start. It's me as well. Everything that's gone on has affected me too, plus I split up with my boyfriend and messed up my A-levels. Maybe they were all connected, I don't know, but everything seems to have gone massively wrong. I didn't feel ready to leave Mum and go to uni anyway, and I wasn't even sure what I wanted to do, but it's never nice to fail at things, is it? I might do resits at some point, and my school said they can set me up with some online courses as well, so all is not lost—I could rediscover my inner genius in Dorset! I just know that maybe a change of scenery will be good for both of us, away from the past, and everything that reminds us of all that stuff that's gone massively wrong.

So, that's it, Laura. If you have any questions—like 'who is this crazy person?'—then feel free to ask! Even if I never hear from you, it felt weirdly good to get all of this written down. Cathartic, to use a fancy English A-level word.

Sophie Connolly xxx

Want to find out what happens next?
Available now in paperback, ebook and audio!

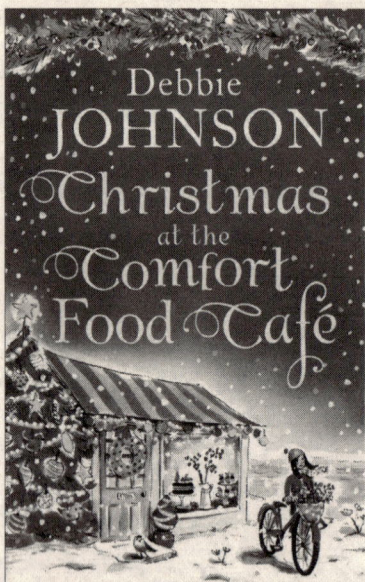

Debbie
JOHNSON
Christmas
at the
Comfort
Food Café

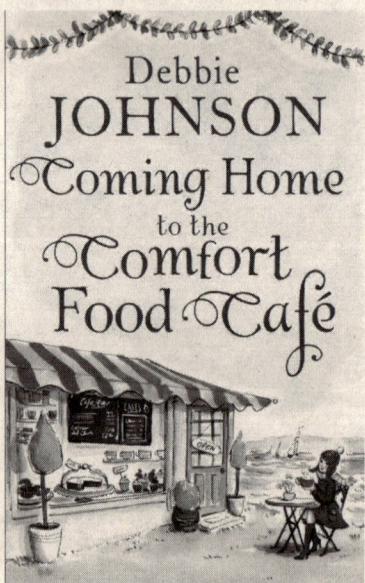

Debbie
JOHNSON
Coming Home
to the
Comfort
Food Café

Debbie
JOHNSON

Sunshine
at the
Comfort
Food Café

'As cosy as a
buttered crumpet'
MILLY JOHNSON

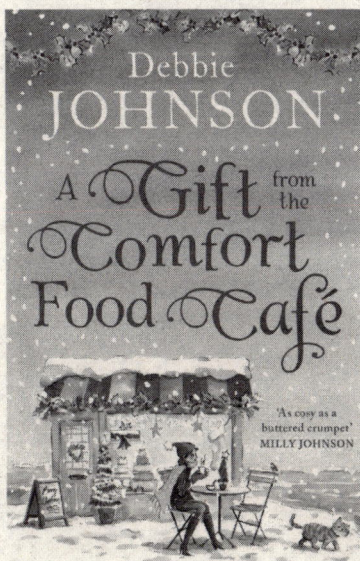

Debbie
JOHNSON

A Gift from the
Comfort
Food Café

'As cosy as a
buttered crumpet'
MILLY JOHNSON

Debbie
JOHNSON

A
Wedding
at the
Comfort
Food Café

Where a warm welcome is always
on the menu

Fern
Britton
Picks
Exclusively for
TESCO

EXCLUSIVE ADDITIONAL CONTENT

Includes an author Q&A and details
of how to get involved in *Fern's Picks*

Dear lovely readers,

I am absolutely thrilled to introduce our latest pick for Fern's Picks: *A Touch of Magic at the Comfort Food Café* by the wonderful Debbie Johnson. I'm delighted to let this enchanting tale whisk us back to the charming village of Budbury, where the air is crisp with autumn magic and the promise of cosy nights spent with a good book.

Meet Sarah, a reclusive author seeking solace from the world, only to find herself in a delightful predicament involving a fake boyfriend, the ruggedly handsome Aidan. Their unexpected partnership brings a sprinkle of romance and a dash of Halloween mischief that will warm your heart. Debbie's writing effortlessly captures the essence of friendship, love, and the joys of community, all wrapped up in the comforting embrace of good food.

I can't wait to hear how this story touches your hearts.

Happy reading!

With love

Fern x

Fern Britton Picks

Exclusively for

TESCO

Look out for more books, coming soon!

For more information on the book club,
exclusive Q&As with the authors and
reading group questions, visit Fern's website
www.fern-britton.com/ferns-picks

We'd love you to join in the conversation,
so don't forget to share your thoughts using
#FernsPicks

A Q&A with
Debbie Johnson

Warning: contains spoilers

Tell us a bit about yourself, and how you became an author?

I was one of those children who always loved writing stories. The first I remember is from when I was about five; it was called *The Lost Puppy*. Astonishingly, it was about a puppy who got lost! I always wanted to be a writer, but then as it does, life got busy. I was actually in my forties when I started trying seriously, which goes to show it's never too late. It was a very hectic time in my life – I was self-employed running my own small business, had three young children and like many women was also caring for an elderly parent. I have no idea why I decided that was the perfect time, just a feeling that if I didn't do it then I never would. Looking back it was insane, working all day, dealing with my family responsibilities, and then at night I'd go and write. There was no overnight success; it was hard work, and another five years until I was able to give up the 'day job' and become a full-time author.

And has being an author lived up to your expectations?

In some ways, yes, and in others no. On the whole it's a lot less glamorous than I thought it would be! There are occasional swish highlights – signing events, posh parties, getting taken out for fancy meals. But it's also sitting alone in your own home trying not to watch TV! It can be lonely, but I have great author friends too. My three children are now older and allegedly adults (until they need money or a lift), and I have two lovely dogs who are now my writing companions. As it is with the cycle of life, my parents are no longer around, the days of the school run and sports days are gone, and I should have a lot more time on my hands – but somehow I never do! I still absolutely love writing stories. It's such a joy when people get in touch and tell me about their lives, and how my books have helped them through difficult times. I love the fact that I can give women (mainly, I do have a few male readers) a few hours escapism from the challenges of daily life. While they read my stories, they can lose themselves for a while and give their poor tired brains a rest – and that is a real privilege.

The Comfort Food Café series has been really successful – where did you get the inspiration for it, and is it based on a real place?

The inspiration for the café and the village of Budbury came from family holidays in West Dorset. They were such happy times – loading up the car with kids, dogs, luggage, and taking off for an adventure. The first time we stayed in that area, I was blown away by how beautiful it was, how warm the people were, just everything about it. We all have places we visit and just feel at home in, don't we? Somewhere that just calls to us, where we feel instinctively calm and settled? For me, it's West Dorset. The lovely places like Lyme Regis, Charmouth, Burton Bradstock, Beaminster were full of delights for me, and the scenery is amazing. As a family we love a traipse around a stone circle or a long barrow (yes, we are VERY cool!), or a visit to a stately home, and Dorset has a lot of that too. The very first time we stayed, I found myself fantasising about never leaving – and when I started to imagine what an ideal life there would look like, *The Comfort Food Café* was born! So it's not based on one specific place, more of a blend of different ones.

This is the eighth book in the series, and each of the main characters is very different. How do you come up with your ideas for their stories?

I really enjoy writing each new book in the same lovely village setting. I think readers do as well, they always say it's like coming back to old friends – so in this one, we meet Sarah, but we also catch up with Cherie, Laura, and all of the previous *Comfort Food Café* ladies. It's always so nice seeing what they've been up to! In terms of ideas, I suppose I find life and people endlessly interesting. I am a very nosy person and love listening to a life story. My kids are used to it now, but they used to laugh at the way I'd meet somebody new, and within an hour I'd know everything about them! I am fascinated by ordinary women and their lives – women deal with so much, overcome so much, give so much. And on the whole, we have a good laugh while we're doing it all. So I suppose I have my curiosity to thank for the fact that I don't run out of ideas. I never base any of my characters on anybody real, that would just be rude – again, it's all snippets that I've stored away in my brain: nothing is wasted!

How much of yourself is in your characters?

There is a little bit of me in all my characters, some more than others. Sometimes when people who know me well read my books, they will say 'that thing she said, that sounded just like you!' But obviously I haven't been through all of the things they have been through – I'd have had a very dramatic life instead of the very boring one I have had! I think though that all my books are fun, there is a good sense of humour, and nobody takes themselves too seriously. I hope those are all traits I have a bit of too.

Friendship plays an important part in *The Comfort Food Café*. How important is that to you?

Friendship is everything to me, really. I come back to the theme of found family over and over again – the family that you choose being just as important, or sometimes even more so, than the one you were born into. I was an only child, and my mum was much older than average (I was very much a surprise baby in her 40s!) – so I did sometimes feel a little lonely as a kid. There were plus sides, and it definitely made me quite resilient and helped me develop my love of both reading and writing stories, but as I got older and formed wonderful adult friendships, I met the people who became my new family. I have a wide social circle, and some very close friends who I would literally tell anything. We have been there for each other through so much – births, deaths, marriages, divorces, illness, pandemics, job changes, menopause, child-rearing, dog-rearing, everything! For me, my friends keep me grounded and make me feel anchored in the real world. That's especially useful when my job involves losing touch with the real world! There is always romance in the café books, but at heart it is about friendship in all its many forms. Who wouldn't want a Cherie Bloom in their life?

There is usually a multi-generational cast of characters in your books. Why is that?

Yes, I have everything from newborn babies through to the almost 100-year-old Edie May in the mix! I've always enjoyed that. Like I said, I find people fascinating – young, old, in between, we all have our stories to share, don't we? I don't see any reason why generations shouldn't mix and get on. Yes, we have certain things in common with our contemporaries – maybe we have kids at a similar time or whatever – but that doesn't mean that people older or younger than us can't be in our lives and have their own value. I think whatever age you are, you tend to think you're wise, and actually none of us ever are – there's always more to learn, more to experience, and having an Edie or a Cherie around to talk to is a marvellous thing.

Plus both of those ladies are very young at heart – most of us probably feel younger on the inside than we look on the outside (I think I froze at about 21), and women like Cherie and Edie show the young ones how it's done when it comes to enjoying life!

There is always a lot of delicious food in the Comfort Food Café books – is cooking something you enjoy too?

I do enjoy cooking, and I'm a solid 'whip up dinner for the family' kind of person. Sadly, I've just never been much good at baking. I think Laura and Cherie are fulfilling some of my ambitions for me – I'd love to be able to make gorgeous cakes! Partly I think I maybe don't have the patience, but the idea of coming up with my own showstopper fills me with fear. I am, on the other hand, exceptionally talented at eating cakes – so that's something at least! I like to fill the café books with my favourite things, which means amazing food, friendship, beautiful views, nice men ('nice' is a very underrated quality when it comes to men!) and dogs. Lots and lots of dogs, especially in this one!

What's next for you?

At a guess I'd say writing, writing and then some more writing! I'm already beavering away on my next projects. Outside of working, I enjoy the simple pleasures of life really – family time, seeing friends, walking my dogs and going to the local pub quiz. I broke my ankle last year and ended up having two surgeries and being in the hospital for a month – so these days I never take any of these simple pleasures for granted!

Questions for your Book Club

Warning: contains spoilers

- How does Sarah's desire for solitude resonate with you? Did you find her reluctance to connect frustrating, or is her desire to seek refuge in a small town relatable?

- In what ways does her isolation impact her relationships, and how does Aidan help her break out of that solitude?

- We've visited Budbury several times now throughout this series. How does the village contribute to the atmosphere? And most importantly – would you want to spend a season there?

- The fake dating trope is a real classic. Do you enjoy its predictability? Were there any moments that took you by surprise or that were particularly moving?

- There is loads of delicious food in this book. Were there any recipes that made you feel nostalgic or comforted? If you opened a café, what kind of food would you want to serve?

- If you were in Sarah's position, how would you handle the pressures of family and personal expectations? What lessons can be drawn from her journey in navigating these challenges?

- Was there a particular moment that made you laugh out loud or brought a tear to your eye?

- Looking at the book as a whole – what was your biggest takeaway? Did it leave you feeling uplifted, and what message (if any) stayed with you after the last page?

An exclusive extract from Fern's new novel

A Cornish Legacy

CHAPTER ONE

North Cornwall, April, present day

Delia squinted through the windscreen, the sun ahead dazzling her. 'You'll see the turning on the right in a minute,' she said. 'Keep an eye out. I might miss it.'

Sammi tipped the last of the crisps into his mouth and sat up a little straighter. 'My eyes are peeled.' He pulled the sunglasses down from his head. 'Will there be some kind of landmark?'

'There's a big metal sign swinging on a post above the gates. Remember? You said it looked like a gibbet.'

Sammi chuckled. 'The gibbet! Yes, of course! Such a welcome.' He sat up straighter, alert. 'There!'

Delia saw the emerging gap amongst the tangled hedge of rhododendrons, with the rusted sign hanging from the post.

'Is that it?' asked Sammi. 'Can't read the name.'

Delia slowed, changing down through the gears. She wasn't smiling. 'Yep. This is it. Wilder Hoo.' The sight of the tatty sign that she had never wanted or expected to see again forced her stomach into a tight knot. Turning, she slowed the car and braked to a halt. 'I really don't want to be here.'

Sammi reached over for her knee and tapped it briskly. 'You're not on your own. I'm here, and those horrible people are gone. Come on.'

Delia put a hand to her chest and took a deep breath to control the old anxiety welling within. 'It's quite late. Let's go and find somewhere to stay tonight and come back tomorrow.'

'It's only half past four!'

'But it'll be getting dark soon.'

'Darling, it's April, not December.' Sammi's voice became soft and sympathetic. 'I know this is hard. But you can do it, and you will do it.'

'I don't want to do it.'

'The past is past. Dead and buried.'

Sighing heavily, Delia put the car in gear and slowly drove the winding tarmacked drive. 'Dead people can still haunt us.'

Stiff clumps of grass and dandelions had forced themselves between the cracked pitch, and in other places, huge potholes housed red, muddied puddles.

'It'll cost thousands just to repair the drive,' she said. 'Look at it.'

She knew that Sammi saw through different eyes. For him, this was an adventure. When Delia had first told him that the house had been gifted to her, he had been ready to celebrate, despite her horror of the whole thing. He seemed to feel only the thrill of an escapade.

Looking out of his side window at the ancient, rolling parkland with great oaks dotted across the scene he said,'Delia, this is utterly captivating. Please tell me there's a lake. I'm expecting Colin Firth to stride forth in his wet breeches and shirt.'

Delia was scornful. 'If only. No lake, I'm afraid. Just a beach and all these acres of parkland. Do you know, it takes four men with a tractor each an entire week to cut all that grass? When they get to the end, they have to start again. It's a bloody money pit.' Her eyes flicked to the avenue of ivy-clad beech trees ahead, the bare branches forming a tunnel over sodden leaves. 'That ivy needs cutting back too. Argh. Who can afford all this, I ask you!'

Sammi was not listening. 'How long is this drive again?'

'It's 1.2 miles.'

'Very specific.'

Delia sighed. 'My father-in-law preferred to tell everyone it was two kilometres because that sounded longer.'

'And all this land belongs to the house?'

'Yup.'

Sammi was grinning. 'I'd love to jump on a tractor and spend a whole summer mowing all this.'

'You really wouldn't. Back in the day, there were sheep and deer to crop it.'

'Sheep and deer! Delia.' Sammi laughed. 'And all this is actually yours!'

She shrugged. She was weary and wretched. 'Not for long, I hope.'

They rattled over a cattle grid and onto a sparsely gravelled drive.

'OK. Here we go.' Delia swallowed hard. 'Round this bend, you'll see the house.' She took a nervous breath and added, 'I couldn't do this without you.'

Sammi tutted, 'I wouldn't let you come on your own, would I?'

Delia steered the last curve – and there, suddenly, was Wilder Hoo.

Available now!

The No.1 Sunday Times bestselling author returns

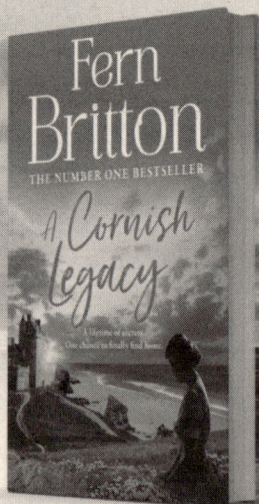

FERN BRITTON

THE NUMBER ONE BESTSELLER

A Cornish Legacy

Wilder Hoo house holds a lifetime of secrets.

When Cordelia Jago learns she's been left the crumbling manor house Wilder Hoo, perched high on the Cornish coast, she wonders if it's one last cruel joke from beyond the grave.

Having already lost her marriage, her best friend and her career, she's at rock-bottom. Now she's inherited a house she hates, full of unhappy memories.

But as she fights with its echoing rooms and whispering shadows, the house begins to exert a pull on her. The wild Cornish landscape, the stark beauty of seagrass and yellow gorse against the deep blue sea, begin to awaken a connection Cordelia thought she'd buried forever.

Could she turn around this monstrous wreck of a house – and, along the way, let go of the secrets of the past and heal her heart too?

AVAILABLE NOW!

YOUR NUMBER ONE STOP

ONE MORE CHAPTER

FOR PAGETURNING BOOKS

One More Chapter is an
award-winning global
division of HarperCollins.

Subscribe to our newsletter to get our
latest eBook deals and stay up to date
with all our new releases!

signup.harpercollins.co.uk/
join/signup-omc

Meet the team at
www.onemorechapter.com

Follow us!

@onemorechapterhc

Do you write unputdownable fiction?
We love to hear from new voices.
Find out how to submit your novel at
www.onemorechapter.com/submissions